MASTER SAWBONES

Jacqueline Lawrence

HUTCHINSON OF LONDON

Hutchinson & Co (Publishers) Ltd
3 Fitzroy Square, London W1P 6JD

London Melbourne Sydney Auckland
Wellington Johannesburg and agencies
throughout the world

First published 1978

Set in Intertype Garamond

Printed in Great Britain by The Anchor Press Ltd
and bound by Wm Brendon & Son Ltd
both of Tiptree, Essex

British Library CIP data

Lawrence, Jacqueline
Master Sawbones.
I. Title
823'. 9'1'F PR6062.A/

ISBN 0 09 133780 1

CONTENTS

Map 6
Chronology 7
1 MURDER IN MIDSUMMER 9
2 PLAYING POSTBOY 16
3 'SAVE A THIEF FROM THE GALLOWS' 26
4 RUNAWAY HILL 35
5 MOTTHAM 42
6 THE SCOUT-MASTER GENERAL 50
7 THE DEVIL WILL CARE FOR HIS OWN 60
8 A SURGEON AND PHYSICIAN 70
9 A VISIT TO BASING 82
10 CHADWICKE OF BROADOAK 97
11 AMBUSH 107
12 NOTHING SHORT OF A MIRACLE 116
13 THE WORKMEN OF NEHEMIAH 131
14 A COLD IN THE HEAD 141
15 A SOBER, SENSIBLE FELLOW 149
16 FRIENDS IN HIGH PLACES 158
17 THE HAND OF PROVIDENCE 166
18 THE GREAT ASSAULT 174
19 TREACHERY AT WORK 186
20 'AND HE WILL HANG YOU IF HE CAN' 198
21 'DARK, BUT NOT YET NIGHT' 208
22 DAVID AND JONATHAN 220
23 THE WINGS OF LUCIFER 232
24 A HAIR'S BREADTH FROM VICTORY 244
25 SHE LOVES ME NOT 250
26 A VERY GOOD REASON 259
27 'WALLER IS COMING!' 269
28 JOURNEY'S END 277

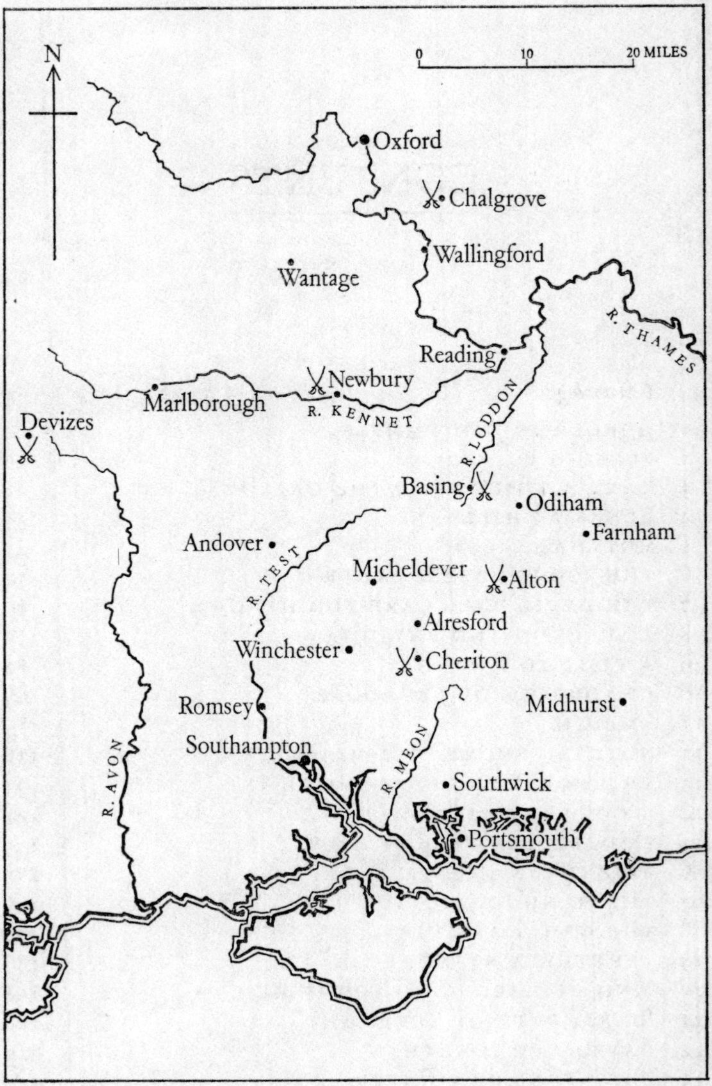

Southern England in the Civil War 1643

CHRONOLOGY

1642	August 22	King's standard raised at Nottingham
	December 5	Wilmot takes Marlborough
	December 13	Waller takes Winchester
1643	April 27	Essex takes Reading
	June 18	Battle of Chalgrove Field
	July 5	Battle of Lansdown Hill
	July 13	Battle of Roundway Down
	July 19–31	First siege of Basing House
	July 26	Rupert storms Bristol
	July 31	Bard relieves Basing House
	August 10–September 5	Siege of Gloucester
	September 20	First Battle of Newbury
	November 2	Bennet's men attacked at Alton
	November 12	'The Great Assault' on Basing House
	December 9	Hopton takes Arundel Castle
	December 12	Norton attacks Romsey
	December 13	Waller takes Alton
1644	January 6	Waller recaptures Arundel
	March 29	Battle of Cheriton

From a letter written by Sir William Waller to Sir Ralph Hopton, dated 16 June 1643

'. . . Certainly my affections to you are so unchangeable that hostility itself cannot violate my friendship to your person, but I must be true to the cause wherein I serve; the old limitation *usque ad aras* holds still and where my conscience is interested, all other obligations are swallowed up. I should most gladly wait on you according to your desire, but that I look upon you as you are engaged in that party, beyond a possibility of retreat. . . . That great God, which is the searcher of my heart, knows with what a sad sense I go upon this service, and with what a perfect hatred I detest this war without an enemy. . . . We are both upon the stage and must act those parts that are assigned to us in this tragedy; let us do it in a way of honour, and without personal animosities, whatsoever the issue be. . . .'

I

MURDER IN MIDSUMMER

Nicholas Howard finished the last wild strawberry within reach, wiped his juice-stained mouth with the back of a grimy hand, and sighed heavily. Sweat ran down inside his shirt and buff-coat, and he could feel it prickling his forehead beneath the flopping dark-brown hair. The narrow white ribbon of track down the centre of the valley remained obstinately peaceful: indeed, one might never suspect that there was a war at all. . . . Last October they had all thought the war would be over by Christmas; but now here was midsummer, and the end seemed further away than ever.

Nick brushed dust from his breeches and coat and stood up, shaking his black-plumed hat ferociously. It was up to them to put down this rebellion, and the sooner the better. He set the hat back on his head with care so that his eyes were shaded. A grasshopper landed with a small thump on his right boot, where it fiddled away quite unperturbed by the heat. Nick stared at it in boiling irritation, but it leaped off into the grass as the shadow of his hand descended upon it: clear away, as no doubt was the quarry for which they had all waited here so patiently since before dawn. He wondered for the hundredth time what had possessed him to become involved in such a hare-brained escapade.

These Hampshire downlands bristled with crop-eared rebels, and all the company he had brought was a half-dozen assorted rogues and his own extremely temperamental brother. At least the sharp-shooting poacher and the horse thief would be useful: but Robin was Prince Rupert's man, and belonged more to the hat-doffing chivalry of the honours of war, and Nick's war was far removed from that. His was waged with subterfuge, lies and surprise ambush, and sometimes sneaking murder in the dark, and Robin could neither appreciate nor approve it, and had spared no pains to tell him so. Nick cursed himself for a fool, glowering until his bushy black eyebrows met. Rob should long since have been back in Oxford. . . .

He stiffened, listening. The sound of cheery whistling came to him and he recognised the tune immediately, for it was a musical insult to the Roundhead commander-in-chief. It would bring every rebel for miles about their ears if by chance it should be heard; and it would certainly warn their intended victim a mile away. Nick stumbled hastily down the slope to deal with the offender, slipping and sliding clumsily on dry grass and powdery chalk. Robin lounged on one elbow at his ease, twiddling the one gold ear-ring which set off his long chestnut-coloured lovelocks.

'Captain Howard!' hissed Nick, his anger seething in the whisper which would at any other place and time have been a shout.

'Oh, hell! What have I done now?'

'Did you not hear me ask for complete silence?'

'Of course I did, I'm not deaf,' came the reasonable reply, and an innocent smile with it.

'Neither is the enemy!' Nick spluttered.

'I said nothing. It was you.' Robin smiled blandly. He enjoyed playing the fool, because he knew it drove Nicholas mad. Nick took off his hat and he would much have liked to belabour his elder brother with it. Instead he crushed the brim so fiercely that his knuckles were pale. Robin rose slowly and deliberately and stared down at him with mild brown eyes.

Nick's rage boiled over. 'Your foolishness appals me! Do you perhaps think it is less likely that your whistling will be heard by unwelcome listeners? Do you think that I will stand by and watch you hang us all?'

'No doubt you've a better idea for passing the time we are spending in this God-forsaken hell-hole? I'm weary of tarrying here on this fool's errand! I will relieve you of my company if you so desire. Only say the word, sir, and I will trouble you no longer.'

'May I remind you that you are here only because you asked to come, and that you gave your word to obey me, however difficult you found it? You shall stay until I say so, or I shall have you shot. I am not jesting.'

Robin studiously brushed the dust off his breeches and reflected. Nick tried hard to fathom the depths of the brown eyes, and wondered if his brother's conscience had begun to stir.

'You'd have me shot, eh? God's bones, that's a poor joke, brother. What would Aunt Nan have to say?'

'Are you going to be reasonable?'

'Never! You know the most infuriating thing about you is that you are always reasonable! You self-righteous pig! You'd have made a good crop-ear.'

Nick smiled. He had won the battle.

'My dear Nicholas, I still cannot understand why an honourable gentleman like you should be skulking about the countryside in the company of a crew of highway robbers. Why you do not leave the spying to the villains to whom it seems better suited, I shall never know.' For a moment there was silence: weary silence, for it was not the first time they had come to this point of contention, and, Nick suspected, it was unlikely to be the last.

'My dear Robin,' he countered, bowing gravely. 'I am afraid that an excess of honourable gentlemen such as you will be the ruin of His Majesty the King if he is not extremely fortunate.'

'Well, you cannot blame me for your turning spy instead of soldier and taking up with a band of horse thieves. Perhaps you'll regret it when they hang you.' Robin returned the bow with insolent grace, settled himself once more amid the ripening cowslip seed-spikes, and tilted his hat over his eyes.

Nick smoothed out the misshapen hat brim and retraced his steps through the hawthorns to his own vantage point, wondering how much more time they could afford to waste. The prize was tempting. The courier would be carrying details of pay and ammunition trains which Lord Essex was sending to local garrisons. With such details, the King's men could lay hands on extra money and supplies, and the Lord God knew how much they needed both. Surely the messenger had been warned, or perhaps gone by another way. They might just as well give up and crawl empty-handed back to Marlborough and confess failure to the scout-master general . . . who would be exceeding wrathful, because he had ridden all the way from Oxford specifically for the purpose.

A movement at the head of the valley caught Nick's eye. At last the dispatch-rider was coming. The heavy warm walnut of the pistol butt was firm in his hand, and his gloomy forebodings fled instantly before the anticipation of action. The rider came down the hill at an easy canter on the well-worn track, the hooves of the bay horse creating small puffs of dust. No doubt he was secure in the knowledge that the land hereabouts was all in the hands of his comrades-in-arms, and that it was well patrolled. He was in no hurry. It was too hot to hurry, and he would undoubtedly reach his journey's end before nightfall. Up in the clear sky a lark sang, and the young dispatch-rider raised his eyes to look for it. Journey's end was nearer than he supposed.

The sound of several shots tore through the song of the lark. The courier reeled in the saddle and then rolled straight backwards over the hindquarters of the bay, somersaulting once before he came to rest in a crumpled heap. The two mounted troopers at the foot of the valley retrieved the frightened horse with a jingling of harness, and the whole episode was over in a moment with the smooth speed of efficiency. The lark took up its song once more. Robin was already dragging the fallen man by the scruff of the neck towards Nick. The man kicked and struggled feebly in resistance, as trooper Perry, a well-practised pickpocket, extracted from the folds of his shirt a slightly bloody and bedraggled packet addressed to the colonel in command at Winchester.

At that moment the look-out began once more to wave

frantically. Another single rider appeared, this time from the opposite end of the valley, a solitary rebel officer, who hesitated for a full half-minute to allow his eyes to take in the scene before him, and then turned tail and fled in the direction from which he had come. Nick leaped for the riderless horse, spurring the beast mercilessly in the wake of the retreating enemy. The gap was, he thought, beginning to close quite noticeably. Nobody was going to spoil his carefully thought-out plan, not if he had anything to do with it.

The Roundhead had come a mile or so, and here was a copse of hazel, and then a little wood. He looked over his shoulder, and Nick could see the concern spreading on his face because his pursuer was so close behind. The man turned his mount off the road and plunged into the trees. Nick cursed. A clever enemy this one, and one who seemed to know his ground. The trees were thick, and Nick was forced to slow down, following a narrow track through the tangling undergrowth. It was dark here after the bright sunlight, for the leaves overhead almost shut out the sky. Where was his quarry now? It was dangerous to be half blind like this. Was that the sound of the enemy, or just the noise of his own mount's pursuit? Nick strained his ears to listen, but they were filled by the sound of his own galloping heart. Clutching branches caught at him as the horse ploughed on. He was long since hatless; his hair was in his eyes, and instinct was beginning to suggest to him that all was not well.

The whole world turned topsy turvy in a moment. A bullet sang past Nick's ear, followed swiftly by another which was so close it stung his cheek viciously. The horse in its terror slithered to a halt, but Nick went on travelling until the ground came up into his face with a resounding thump which left him numb and breathless. An age of silence passed. He lay on his face on the track trying to collect his scattered wits together, half expecting to see a whole troop of rebels emerge from the thicket. It was a while before the truth dawned, as the young Roundhead came forth, leering happily, from the trees – and still alone. Nick groaned aloud at his own foolishness. The clever enemy had turned the tables on his pursuer by setting a little ambush of his own. Nick's face began to hurt as the numbness wore off, and he found that his nose was bleeding profusely and that there seemed to be a huge jagged cut right across his left cheek from temple to mouth.

A tremendous blow caught him between the shoulder blades and sent every vestige of breath from him in an involuntary groan. The rebel officer's boot was kicking him unceremoniously, and Nick gasped and choked and wondered if he would ever get his breath back. The boot returned, the wide toe rolling him over on his back. Anger sparked Nick's mind once more into thinking clearly. The clever man seemed to have made a very stupid mistake, for he had sheathed his sword now, so sure was he that the fallen enemy with a bloody head was in his last agony. Nick put his hands over his battered face. It would not do for the man to look too closely. If he could feign death throes until he had enough breath to move. . . . He rolled and moaned and looked through parted fingers at his adversary and watched the smile die away, and a trace of pity replace it. The man went to his horse, took from the saddle bag a bottle, and came back.

Nick forced himself to his feet, drawing his sword in the same moment. The rebel staggered back, dropping the water-bottle, his face gaping in surprise. He half tripped over the trailing brambles as he fumbled for his own sword. But there was no fight, for before it was in his hand Nick's weapon found its way to the rebel's throat, and the horror-struck expression was fixed for ever on his face as he crashed, dead, at Nick's feet.

Nick Howard sank to his knees in the pool of blood beside his dead enemy, sobbing with relief. His shaking hands searched the man, and his eyes tried to avoid the hideous gaping grin. There were a few coins in his pocket, and a letter, that was all: a letter written in a childish hand, the ink very thick and black, and the prose well-considered and precise. A certain Judith was politely beseeching young Tom to come home to see his ailing father at Stoke Sutton. The epistle was addressed to one Captain Thomas Chadwicke at Southampton. Nick sighed. Stoke Sutton was but a few miles away, and yet poor young Tom would never again see either home or father. It was nothing short of horrible murder he had committed, and yet it had been unavoidable.

Nick replaced the letter and the coins, wiped his still bleeding nose with his hand, and found that hand shaking like a leaf. He took a last look at the messy scene of destruction and his stomach quaked. Nearby Thomas Chadwicke's white-socked chestnut still cropped contentedly at the leggy grass as if nothing had happened. Nick caught it by the bridle. He managed to lead it unsteadily to the edge of the trees before his heaving stomach forced him to kneel on the ground and be as sick as he could.

2

PLAYING POSTBOY

Half an hour later, still shaking, Nick found his way back to the small valley, which was once more peaceful as it had been. Their prisoner reclined awkwardly on the tussocky grass, nursing a roughly bandaged arm; his face was white, but otherwise he seemed little the worse for his mishap. The courier was no more than twenty, Nick guessed, and he looked as if he would be far more at home wielding ploughshares than weapons of war. He had a 'prentice's roundheaded haircut, and the sandy strands stood wispily on end on the top of his head like September stubble. His blunt, freckled nose was peeling where the fierce sun had burned it, and a pair of clear blue eyes stared at the leering captors all around him.

Robin was towering over the boy. 'I should hate to cause you pain, fellow,' he said, 'but I really must insist. . . .' In reply, the 'fellow' shook his head vehemently. Nick shuddered. He would not like to change places with Robin's victim, not for anything; Robin undoubtedly meant every word he was saying, even though his musical voice was full of sweetness.

'Tell us the sign, man! I have no wish to hurt you.'

'I do not remember any sign.'

Robin's face sneered viciously and his fist clenched on the hilt of his sword. 'Then my sword in your gut may be an aid to memory.'

'You think so?'

The sneer faded, and a kindly looking smile replaced it, but the hand on the sword-hilt did not move. 'Think of thy father, hodge. How would he feel to lose a son?'

'My father would be proud that I should have died so, in the service of God.'

His tormentor was momentarily checked, which was surprising. Robin was very seldom lost for words. 'So, thy mother, then?'

'My mother is dead.'

'Then I shall this day be kind enough to reunite you with her!' Robin was exasperated at the quiet defiance he had not expected to find. He struck the boy across the face with a blow so forceful that it must have hurt his hand, for he set to cursing. Then, out of the corner of his eye, he saw Nick standing a few feet away, and his anger drained away with the flush from his cheeks.

'My God!' he breathed. 'You look like a walking slaughterhouse. What happened?'

'I had . . . to kill him. The dispatches?'

'We have your dispatches ready copied. Perry said the seal was easily dealt with.' He handed the papers to Nick, who nodded as he looked at the careful copy they had made. Perry seemed to be an accomplished forger as well as a pickpocket. The letter was in cipher, and Nick could make neither head nor tail of it, but no doubt there were those in Marlborough who could. Perry's little leathery rat-face with its sharp-toothed smile peered out from behind the corporal's elbow to receive once more the dispatches.

'Now repair it. No one must know it has been tampered with, you understand?'

'Yes, sir. Half a minute'll do it, sir.'

'Good. Rob, send the copy off, will you?'

Nick watched Robin hand over the papers to the horse thief, who was splendidly mounted on the best horse he had been able to steal, a fine black Barb. With any luck he should be in Marlborough before dusk.

'This is fine sport, indeed, Nicholas.' Robin chuckled. 'I can see why it so appeals to you. What a joke, reading their orders before they do themselves! Now, this one. . . . We have not been able to discover anything. Not his name, nor the password, nothing. Not for love, money, nor fear. Shall I finish him now?'

Nick knew that tone of brisk determination, and that Rob liked to have a job quickly and neatly completed, and woe betide any who stood in his way.

'Let me try first, Rob. Let us not be too hasty.'

'We haven't got all day!' Robin protested, and then shrugged. 'But it's your responsibility, I suppose. . . .'

Nick faced the prisoner, who sat surveying him with obvious interest and considerable distaste, slowly licking the blood drips away from his upper lip where Robin's crashing fist had cut it.

'You met with an . . . accident?' the prisoner enquired coolly. And Nick saw clearly what had annoyed his brother. The gaze which met his was one of undisguised loathing, and there was a strange light in those blue eyes which he found vaguely disturbing. Nick's face was hurting damnably, and all at once he found that he, too, was very angry.

'Yes, indeed, I met with an accident, and I cut his meddling throat for him.'

Robin looked sharply sideways at his brother, and a wry face testified the truth of the assertion. He smiled his approval. The knave might well find his memory miraculously restored by such bitter physick.

'What is your name?' Nick sat down beside the man, not out of friendship, but because he knew that his legs would carry him no longer. The Roundhead looked at him for a moment with an expression of blank astonishment, and then replied, much to his surprise, 'My name is William Sloan.'

'That's better. Now, Master Sloan, I want the password you were given to get you through Winchester gates.'

'I'm sorry, you must invent one for yourself, malignant, for I have . . . forgotten it.'

The round freckled face was resolute once more. Nick sighed. He would have to take a chance. At least only his own life would depend on it. He rose cautiously to his feet and met Robin's eye. In it was unspoken eagerness to dispose of the young enemy, and Nick recoiled at the prospect. Less than an hour ago he had horribly killed Captain Thomas Chadwicke in broad daylight and cold blood, and this courier was a mere boy and very courageous. There was no point. . . .

'Take him with you. He may be of use. Let him be. He is already wounded.'

Robin gibbered noisily with speechless frustration, but Nick was rescued by the corporal, who proffered the repaired packet of letters for his inspection. Not even a smudge could be detected to give a clue to the interference it had suffered. Yet the corporal's face was not happy. He shuffled his feet and hovered, uncertain of his ground. He cleared his throat.

'Are you . . . well, sir? Are you sure you can . . . manage? Or would you like for me to deliver this?'

Nick smiled indulgently at the paternal concern. He felt far from well. He looked from the corporal to Sloan, and back again. There could be no question about it. It would be necessary for whoever delivered the message to wear the prisoner's uniform coat and sash, and the prisoner was short and slight. Nick began to laugh at the notion. The corporal's wide muscular shoulders bulged under his huge buff-coat, and his face looked faintly hurt.

'I'm only half dead, corporal. I've yet strength enough to play postboy. You find me a coat, and I'll wear it!'

William Sloan was not a willing party to the robbery. He kicked and struggled despite the obvious pain it caused him. He declined Nick's offer of his own coat in exchange, and stoically sat in his bloody shirt-sleeves, sullen and silent.

'I shall see you anon,' Robin said, 'at Sherfield Priors.'

'God with you, Rob.'

'And with you, Nicholas. Take care.'

Nick waved and coaxed the white-socked chestnut to a canter. It seemed an age since they had ambushed William Sloan, and yet the sun was still high in the sky. Though there was no time to spare if he was to meet the others tomorrow at Rob's house at Sherfield Priors, the house where they had grown up. It was good that Rob would have an opportunity now to see Frances and the boys, however briefly, and his own visit to them was long overdue. First, however, he had another and more exacting visit to pay, on the Roundhead garrison at Winchester, and he had to deliver to them a letter, which he prayed to God would be an easy enough task, provided that no one noticed that someone else had already read it. . . .

Nick felt the sun beating on his sore shoulders, and his head swam as if he had been carousing for a fortnight. He cursed feebly. This was hardly the best way to approach this particular venture. If something were to go wrong, he would need a clear head for sure, and probably a swift escape, or he was as good as dead.

He rode past a knot of countrymen hoeing a field of beans, and they looked up at him in idle curiosity, their heads nodding. People had been hoeing that field when he had ridden this way once before. . . . He could remember his feelings as if it had been yesterday, and the remembrance brought back with it the tide of bitterness he always felt when he thought of Elizabeth. He had been just eighteen when he had ridden by here to Winchester to meet for the first time the girl who was to become his wife. She was a good match for him, he had been told by his triumphant mother; the only daughter of a wealthy gentleman of Winchester, and her father had been only too anxious to match her with a Howard, albeit a younger son. It was no matter at all that on their first meeting Elizabeth had taken an instant dislike to Nick, and he to her. It was arranged and there was no escape for either of them, though dislike had only grown and deepened with marriage and time. Elizabeth had been the most exquisite creature he had ever seen, like a tiny marble statue, her red hair curling in tendrils about her face, and her green eyes always full of mockery at his every attempt to please her; until he had given up trying, and made her life as much of a misery as was his own. For two years of marriage the house had been full of hostility: and then, heavy with his child, she had hated him, she said, for making her ugly, though he had thought sadly that she was more beautiful than ever. It was almost as if she had known that giving birth to the child she would die, and that he would not weep a single tear for her. He had regained his freedom by the mercy of heaven and would not willingly relinquish it. Aunt Nan had stepped in firmly and taken charge of the care of motherless, squalling baby Lucy, and the rest of the family had stood back in total confusion. Nick squashed the thought of Lucy. If he did not keep his wits about him the child would likely be fatherless, and that did not bear contemplation.

His head ached lamentably, and the sweat poured down his face and soaked the flopping hair on his forehead until it stuck fast to his skin. Of late, Aunt Nan heartily disapproved of him: it was beyond her to see why Nick had taken to deception and subterfuge by becoming a spy, when he could so easily have taken the path of a gentleman, and raised a troop of horse.

Nick reined in at the top of St Giles' Hill and looked at the city of Winchester sprawled below in the meadows by the river, shimmering like some dream city in a vision. As if they had sprung from his thoughts, a troop of horse came on towards him through the heat-haze at a brisk trot, clinking and jingling, their orange-tawny scarves bright in the sunlight. For an instant panic swept over him. He must remember that he was their friend and not their enemy, and that his own sash was the same orange-tawny colour, and not the red of a Cavalier. His appearance was bound to excite curiosity, and he would be well advised to think of a convincing explanation before he was asked for one. Yet his head was whirling, and it was all he could do to stay upright in the saddle, let alone think straight. They were all round him now, one grasping the bridle of the horse and another holding a water-bottle to his lips. Their voices sounded far away at first, but the water choked the mist away and woke his stomach to the icy fear of discovery. Just suppose they were to ask him now for a password or sign, and he could not supply one? What would he do then? Die, that was certain.

The captain of the troop was addressing him, and asking him what had befallen. Nick took a deep shuddering breath and steeled himself to answer. His voice came out strangely, in an odd unworldly croak that would have been disowned by any self-respecting raven.

'I was . . . ambushed, sir, but managed to escape. I have urgent letters for the colonel. Could you direct me?'

'We'll do better than that, lad. My men will take you to him.' A pair of sympathetic eyes was regarding him. 'It is yet a mile and more to the headquarter. Can you ride that far?' he enquired.

Nick made no reply but nodded unhappily.

'At any rate, with my lads you'll not be held up at the gates. And they'll help you along if you need it.'

Nick smiled despite his fear. He was more than grateful for this stroke of good fortune which meant no awkward questions at the gate. He found himself riding between two young troopers towards the city, while the rest of the troop went clattering off down the hill, raising clouds of fine dust which hung in the idle air like the smoke from a stubble fire. There could be no going back now.

A few minutes later they pulled into the yard of the inn just below the castle walls. So here was the headquarter, convenient to the fortress yet, at the same time, considerably more comfortable. Nick took a deep breath as they clattered irrevocably through the wide arch of the gateway. Enquiring eyes were turning towards him, and he felt very much alone as he slid from the saddle. He would have gone on sliding on to the grey flags underfoot as his knees buckled under him, and the world spun round, save that an arm was thrust about him by the taller of the troopers. An officer took his arm, and so they led him across the court and into the building. Up a steep and seemingly endless flight of stairs they stumbled, and the hallway above was blissfully cool. The officer knocked at the second door on the left, and the door was opened from within by a guard. Nick was pushed gently over the threshold, sweating with a mixture of weakness and sheer terror, and his stomach was so knotted with fear that he was almost afraid to breathe.

The room was long, the ceiling low and heavy-beamed, walls panelled with dark oak which seemed to close in like a prison. In the centre of the room a wide table bore several finished letters, with ink, pens, and wax all methodically set out beside a half-empty wine bottle and a glass. There was a horse-pistol with ornate silver decoration sparkling as it caught the sun's rays streaming through the mullioned window. One of the windows was open wide, and through it Nick could hear the sounds from the street below. His nose smelled the familiar stench of rotting rubbish, and the knots in his stomach tightened almost unbearably.

The Roundhead commander sat at the table, a broad-shouldered man of middle age, bareheaded, clad in a buff-coat and half-armour; the quill in his hand scratched busily at the letter before him, and both the pistol and the wineglass were near to hand. At Nick's entrance he looked up, and his greying eyebrows met in a frown. He put the pen down, rose, pulled the window to, and came forward to inspect his mauled dispatch-rider with an expression of concern.

Nick fumbled hastily in his buff-coat for the package and found that his hands were once more trembling so violently that he cursed himself for a coward and a fool, and told himself that the colonel would never notice that the seal was damaged unless he drew attention to it by his nervousness. He steadied himself with an effort and handed the packet to the soldier, who set it on the table without even giving it a second glance. Clearly he would be leaving the reading of it until Nick had departed. Just now he was more interested in the ill-used appearance of the messenger, and Nick found that he was being minutely inspected by a pair of sharp grey-green eyes, and the Roundhead walked calmly round him as he stood swaying, dizzy and bewildered, before the table. 'Hmmm,' said the colonel noncommittally, and Nick wondered desperately what he was thinking. Then he crossed to the corner, took his helmet and gauntlets from the heavy chair which stood there, and dragged it to the centre of the room.

'Sit down, lad,' he said kindly. 'What happened?'

Nick gulped. He had been dreading this moment. In his confused mind the words of the spy-master general stood out firm and clear. 'Never vouchsafe more information than you must. For the more you say, then the more likely is your deception to be discovered.' This was the sort of contest the spy-master would have enjoyed, Nick reflected. And so might he have done if only he had felt in full command of his senses. He sat down heavily in the chair and put his hand to his head. He had felt just like this one night last year when he and Robin had been drinking in Oxford, and Rob had laid a wager that he could not cross the river by walking across the parapet of the bridge.

'Malignants were lying in wait, sir, I was . . . unhorsed, but I managed to escape.'

'How so?'

'I rolled into the bushes, sir. They lost me. It was . . . lucky.'

'Yes, indeed it was.' The eyes were curious, and two deep furrows between the colonel's brows deepened. 'Where did this happen?'

Nick stared back at the Roundhead officer as straight as he could, which was not very straight at all, because one eye was now close shut and swollen, and his nose felt like a burning coal. There was no harm in telling where they had ambushed the real messenger. Rob and the others would be well away by now . . . but they might find the body of the late Thomas Chadwicke. . . .

'I'm not sure. Not far this side of Alresford . . . perhaps a couple of miles.'

'What became of your assailants?'

'They made off directly, sir. I know not where. . . . I was so confused. And relieved, sir, you understand?'

Nick's stomach quailed. The excuses sounded hollow and unconvincing in his own ears; but the colonel's hand rested on his shoulder, and the voice was firm and encouraging.

'Yes, lad. I understand. You have done well. You may not know it, but it would have been ill for us if the enemy had laid hands on these.'

He touched the packet, and Nick understood for a moment a little of how Judas Iscariot must have felt.

'You have done great service, boy,' the colonel was reassuring him. 'I shall make sure that the Lord Essex hears of your courage. What is your name?'

'William Sloan, sir,' Nick replied softly. It was strange, but he found it far easier in some ways to be someone else. . . .

'You must stay here for the night, Sloan. I shall send you back to Reading tomorrow, if you are recovered. Unless you have any other orders?'

'I would . . . rather start straight back, sir. . . .' Nick interposed hastily. 'It was my order to return immediately.'

It was easy enough to fabricate: this colonel was very trusting. Nick wondered idly if somewhere a Roundhead spy was finding it as easy to deceive the King's men. Living by one's wits was not so difficult after all, if one was only clever enough: but he only wished that his heart would not rattle so loudly against his ribs, for he was sure that his enemy could hear it from the other side of the room. Suddenly, it was unbearably hot. The colonel was offering him a glass of wine, his voice echoing and re-echoing round Nick's head.

'Are you sure you are well enough?' the echoing voice said. 'You look dreadful.'

'Quite sure, sir . . . I just need . . . air,' he found himself replying in a distant, uncanny imitation of his own voice. He stood up, desperate now to be away while he could, but he was forced to lean on the table to stop himself from falling. Nick blinked at the colonel, and the sun flashed on the rebel's armour, blinding him. The man's grey-green eyes were regarding him again. Nick turned away, and clung to the back of the heavy oak chair for support. The leather of the colonel's sword-belt hung over the chair-back, and the sword in its tasselled leather sling swung and swayed: and sword and chair alike fell heavily to the floor with a tremendous din as Nick plunged headlong into the blackness.

3

'SAVE A THIEF FROM THE GALLOWS'

Nick awoke with surprise and a sinking heart. The bed was comfortable enough, it was true, but his only companion in the tiny room was a hard-faced infantryman who was engaged in looking out of the window and chewing tobacco. Nick closed his open eye and considered his position. It was several minutes before he could completely recall what had brought him to this place, wherever it was. He was bruised from head to foot, though he did not think he was irreparably damaged. Nevertheless, he would have been far happier if he had known whether they had discovered that he was an enemy. It was clearly a garret room he was in . . . not a cell in the bowels of the castle, and for that he was grateful.

'Ouch,' he said. The large infantryman turned, his attention caught by the sound.

'Well, William Sloan, you with us again now?' The grim face creased into a wide grin, revealing several broken teeth.

'My, my, you got an eye like a ripe damson there,' he observed. 'You had a nasty accident by all accounts.'

'Yes,' Nick sighed. That was true enough. He need not have worried for they had not yet unmasked him. The room was full of sunshine, and he was half asleep again until he remembered that he had to meet Rob and the others and began to wonder how long he had been here. As if it knew his doubts and would answer them, the cathedral clock chimed nine. Nick sat up suddenly, and it made him dizzy.

'Is it morning?'

'Lord, bless you, no. You only been here a couple of hours. Here, drink this.' Nick groaned.

'You had a miraculous escape from the malignants, boy,' said the soldier, scratching his ear in contemplation. Nick choked on the wine and water and nodded miserably, very much afraid now that in his present state he might unwittingly say something to betray himself.

The soldier stood up and stretched. 'Well,' he said, 'you'll feel better after a good night's sleep, that's for sure. . . . I'm for guard duty now, worse luck.'

He took up his helmet and left. Nick lay on his back in the fading light and listened to the footsteps retreating down the stairs. He was too tense to sleep, and his head throbbed unrelentingly. There would be no sweet dreams tonight. He was alone in an enemy city. Suppose he were to talk in his sleep and someone overheard him? Could he escape from the house while all was quiet? It would be too much of a risk trying to get clear of guarded gates without password or sign . . . and he would not get far without sleep. Sherfield was thirty miles or more. . . .

Soon Nick was in a deep and dreamless sleep which was uninterrupted until well after dawn, when the trooper came back through the door, looking spent.

'You look better, boy,' he observed. 'The colonel wants you to take a message back to Reading, if so be as you're recovered.'

Nick dragged himself out of bed, stiff, sore and woebegone from his curly crown to his feet. Yesterday's adventure had left behind a painful legacy, and at any other place and time he would cheerfully have admitted himself vanquished and crawled back to bed. As it was, he took an age to dress himself, and spent many minutes wrestling, stiff-fingered, with the unfamiliar buckles of William Sloan's swordbelt. He was contesting with the first large boot when the trooper spoke again.

'It's been a rough night,' he said. 'And I don't mean the weather.'

'What happened?'

'News came in 'bout midnight. That devil's spawn Rupert and his band of demons beat up the Lord Essex's quarters. It's bad, by all accounts. There's breakfast in the kitchen before you go.'

In the kitchen there was despondency as well as breakfast. The Cavaliers had struck at night through Essex's lines, scattering Parliament-men left, right and centre: the small force which had been mustered to block Rupert's path home had been smashed to pieces, and their leader John Hampden had been sorely wounded. The prince's men had been aiming at a pay-train, and now the whole army of Parliament was in consternation as to how the King's men kept finding out when the pay-trains were due, and by which route they would travel. Nick grabbed the mug of small-beer by his plate to wash down the piece of oatcake which seemed wedged in his throat and like to choke him, and studiously cultivated a rueful countenance which he hoped would conceal his inward glee.

Nick was given a packet to deliver to Reading with all speed, and a fresh horse from the line. In a very few minutes he was threading the alleyways to the Eastgate, wishing he dared to take advantage of the confusion to leave the city by the west, so that he might more quickly come to safety beyond the Wiltshire border. The scout-master general had, however, warned him more than once that such over-confidence was to be abhorred. Nick hummed a psalm-tune under his breath and rode out, unchallenged, past the doubled guard at the gate-house, his mouth twitching with the laughter he found hard to contain, and his mind whimsically tempting him to stop the horse and turn in the stirrups to shout taunts at his enemies, even as Robin might have done. But Nick's natural caution was too strong to be overcome, and he rode slowly and soberly home to Sherfield Priors.

Robin leaped from the front door and bounded down the steps, his enormous arms extended in a wide gesture of welcome.

'My dear Nicholas!' he boomed. 'I am relieved to see you! We had begun to wonder if you had not met with some mischance. Come in! Come in! I'll open a bottle of claret!'

He led the way into the hall, where Frances stood on the stairs, gravely waiting for them. She came down to meet her brother-in-law with all her usual grace, despite the size of her belly. It would not be long, Nick thought, before the fourth child would be born.

'Nicholas is dusty from the road, and no doubt anxious to rid himself of that . . . uniform,' she said, looking hard at Nick's disfigured face, and politely ignoring the black eye. Nick smiled awkwardly at her and thought balefully how villainous he must look.

He washed away the dust of the journey, inspected himself pensively in the mirror and was half frightened by what he saw. Out of the dark glass stared a satanic stranger with a dead white face, one eye closed under a hideously bloated purple lid, and the other looking mournfully out of a bruise-coloured hollow. From temple to mouth on the left-hand side ran an ugly gash. His nose was bruised all down one side, and it was, he noticed, slightly crooked. . . .

'My God,' Robin laughed from the doorway. 'What a foul visage!' He brandished in his hand a small phial from which he withdrew the stopper to sniff the contents, and wrinkled his own straight aristocratic nose in disgust. 'My dear wife sends this with her compliments and recommends it as a sovereign remedy for bruises: also cuts, black eyes, and other afflictions.' He waved a small piece of cloth with the other hand. 'Would you like me to anoint you, or shall you do it yourself?'

Nick seized the phial of evil-smelling liquid and dabbed gingerly. It hurt, and he cursed emphatically.

Robin threw up his hands in mock horror. 'Now, brother, no profanity, I beg you. You will upset our crop-eared guest!'

'Oh, Lord. I'd forgotten him. How is he?'

'Exceeding robust, unfortunately. But we can soon put a stop to that.'

'For God's sake, Rob! I've murder enough to account for.

And that's what it would be . . . wanton murder for its own sake, and nothing less.'

'Wanton bloody murder?' Do you know he nearly killed all of us crossing that river?'

'How could I know? Come on, tell me what happened.'

Nick once more attacked the bruised face, this time with vigour and tight-lipped silence, and Robin seethed visibly.

'Everywhere was thick with the swine, so we had perforce to wait till nightfall before we risked crossing the ford. He tried to creep away to warn the sentry, and when we brought him back he made so much noise that he damn near succeeded in rousing the whole rabble. Until the corporal thumped him quiet.'

'Did you . . . lose anybody?'

'No, but one of theirs got his arm broke and another ended up in the water and likely drowned. You should have seen that poxy villain's face! No . . . it was you we thought we'd lost when you didn't arrive by noon.' Robin's face was serious for once.

'I'm sorry. I came as quickly as I could.'

Robin turned towards the door. 'Come on, I'm starved. Let's have dinner.'

After dinner, when Frances had gone, there was silence in the darkening room. Robin sat nibbling a large piece of candied citron as delicately as a fastidious cat and washed his long fingers in the rosewater bowl by his side. With an air of aggression, he stood up. 'Are you going to deal with your psalm-singing friend?'

'I suppose so. Poor devil will be wondering what's to become of him.'

'And that, my dear brother, is a very good question. What is to become of him, indeed?'

It was clear that Robin had already been giving the question some thought, and Nick did not ask what conclusions he had come to. There was no need, for he already knew too well.

'Where is he?'

'Below stairs in the little parlour. Well guarded, you may be sure.'

Nick followed Robin down the dark stairway. Perry and another were playing cards in the parlour, and they were laughing uproariously. At Nick's entrance they sprang up, somewhat sheepishly. Nick looked wryly at the sizeable pile of coins on the table and motioned them outside.

The man Sloan sat in the far corner by the shuttered window with a rushlight at his elbow, his wounded arm in a tidy sling. He was reading a great book which rested on his knee. Nick recognised the volume as Robin's own Bible.

'Where did he get that?' Nick enquired.

'I lent it to him.' Robin smirked.

'What on earth for?'

'Hopefully, to keep him quiet for a while. He knows most of it by heart anyway, you listen.' Robin turned to the boy. 'Well, knave? How goes it?' he enquired, with polite hostility.

'In God I have put my trust. I will not be afraid what man can do unto me.' Sloan replied in a sing-song of zeal.

'Oh, Lord!' sighed Nick under his breath.

'Ye shall cry for sorrow of heart, and shall howl for vexation of spirit,' the man spat at him. 'For the Lord hath promised that he will smite the Amalekites.'

'Hold your peace, or this particular Amalekite shall smite thee most mightily!' Robin said, with feeling, rubbing his clubbed fist in the palm of the other hand. Nick knew that he must intervene now to prevent bloodshed.

'Well, William Sloan? I hear you tried to kill all my men. What are we to do with you?' he said briskly.

'That is for you to decide, Major Howard.' Sloan's earnest eyes stared at Nick in the same way they had done yesterday. Was it only yesterday? It seemed a long age ago, and he was very tired. He had killed a man yesterday. How many more would there be? The eyes kept staring, as if the enemy was determined to commit every detail of his scarred face to everlasting memory, and Nick found it unnerving.

'I ought to hang you.'

There was no response to that. Clearly, it was what he had

been expected to say. This Roundhead seemed insanely arrogant. But of course it was not to be forgotten that men like him were all so sure of a place in heaven that there was no room for doubt in their minds: God had to be on their side, whether he liked it or not . . . and this man was plainly looking for a martyr's death: he would not get it this time. Nick had made up his mind.

'But I'll not bother. You're not worth wasting good rope. Tomorrow I'll set you loose, and you may fend for yourself. Here. . . .' He threw the packet he had been given at Winchester, and it landed with a flat 'plop' on the floor in front of Sloan. 'See if you can find your way back to Reading with that. I've read it: it's an extollation of your courage in the face of adversity! You might have some good by it! Take this, too, in payment for the loan of your louse-ridden uniform.' A silver coin followed the packet. 'And give them Major Nicholas Howard's compliments!' Nick was pleased with himself. The look on Sloan's face was a picture. He was taken aback by such unlooked-for mercy. 'Go on, William. Pick them up.' Nick stood over the boy as he grovelled on the floor for the letter and the coin. To return to his regiment ignominiously and be forced to explain his misadventure would be to Sloan a fate far worse than death. He stumbled to his feet and shot Nick a look of such unspeakable venom that it was his turn to be taken aback.

'Remember that a mere malignant once had mercy on you,' Nick said.

'I shall not forget you, Major Howard, you may rest assured of that.'

'Oh, I almost forgot. There was a battle a few days since, at Chalgrove. . . . I hear that Hampden's men were beat, and Hampden is sore wounded.'

'May God damn you, Major Howard.'

Nick turned his back on a hail of biblical ravings which followed and beat a thankful retreat.

Robin stalked up the stairs one at a time, and with elaborate care, which was remarkable because he usually ascended by twos and threes, and with great noise. He turned back into the drawing room, which was lit now only by a few candles, and dimly shadowed in the half light. Now Nick was contented and very tired. He poured himself another glass of claret.

'The man's mad,' he said.

The explosion which followed this simple statement startled him so much that he dropped the crystal glass, and it shattered instantly into a thousand tiny slivers. Robin was furious, banging his giant fist on the table and shouting at the top of his voice so that Nick's ears buzzed.

'Not half as mad as you are! What do you suppose that madman would have done to you if you were in his position? You'd have no second bloody chance, you can wager your last silver penny on that! You fool, Nick. . . . You'll regret your mercy sooner or later, you mark my words!'

'Oh, for God's sake, Rob. Don't make such a song and dance! He's only one poor trooper. What could he do to you or me?'

Robin shrugged. 'What was it you preached to me a couple of days ago, before we set out? You were trying to explain to your foolish brother what difference there is between a spy and an honest soldier, do you remember?'

Nick did remember. This time he had disregarded the advice of the scout-master general. 'Never let an enemy escape unscathed once you have him at a disadvantage. In this undertaking it must be kill or die: and never wait for a man to turn round if you can strike him from behind.'

'All right, Rob.' Nick admitted grudgingly. '*Touché.* Now go to hell!'

Robin laughed heartily, his anger gone in the joy of victory. 'I shall most inevitably do just that! But I'll wager that you will be already there awaiting me! Why, even mother thought you were a devil's changeling. I can remember Aunt Nan saying when you were born that she wept because you were born at ten to midnight on the eve of All-Hallows. Mother swore she'd given birth to a little demon, and, by God, I'm beginning to wonder if she wasn't right after all!'

'I couldn't govern which day I was born.'

'No, of course you couldn't. But dying is another matter.

. . . What is it they say? *Nescitis horam?* You shall not know the hour?'

'Something like that. Your Latin seems to have considerably improved.'

'Nicholas, I am only trying to help you. Your hour may come sooner than you think, if you are not more careful.'

'Rob . . . I'm warning you. . . .'

'No, Nicholas, I am warning you! "Save a thief from the gallows, and he will hang you if he can." '

'Don't talk like an old woman, Rob. It doesn't suit you.'

'Old woman, eh? I'll get you for that, you little upstart!'

Robin slapped Nick on the back until his ears sang and his bruised shoulders protested, and then they were both speechless with laughter. He finished his glass of wine, with a broad smile and a toast.

'Confusion to William Sloan!' he said and pushed the glass away, yawning. 'I'm for bed, if it's to be an early start in the morning. Sleep well, Nicholas, you look as if you need to sleep for at least a week!'

Nick dragged himself up the stairs to his chamber, sat down on the bed, and stared at the floor. Now he was regretting his mercy, sooner rather than later, and it was already too late for second thoughts, for he could not now go back on his word, not even to a madman. '*Nescitis horam*,' he repeated aloud. It was truth, but he wished that Robin had not said it, because it seemed too much like tempting fate, and gave too much food for indigestible thoughts.

He undressed slowly and fell into bed, asleep almost as soon as his head touched the pillow. But he did not sleep well. His dreams were dogged by a pair of ice-blue eyes, full of unspeakable hatred, and by the acid voice of William Sloan whispering, 'May God damn you, Major Howard!'

4

RUNAWAY HILL

Two days later Nick sat under the apricot tree in Aunt Nan's garden in Marlborough with Lucy. Robin had departed that morning for Oxford and had seemingly taken the sunshine with him. The sky was overcast, but it was still oppressively warm. Even Lucy was too hot to gambol in her usual manner. She sat on the grass like a half-wilted flower, crooning to her favourite bartholomew-baby, Jezebel, since her beloved papa did not seem disposed to listen to her chatter but sat glowering at his own private thoughts.

There was a great deal to glower about. On their way back to Marlborough they had turned William Sloan loose, much to Robin's disgust. The rebel had been far from thankful for his liberty and had called damnation down upon them all at great length. He had declared that he had not asked for quarter, nor did he expect it. Nick had bidden Sloan go free and be grateful, and hang himself elsewhere if he had a mind to. The general had been far from happy at such indulgence, and yesterday he had rated Nick soundly for it. Robin, too, had spared no pains to tell him how singularly stupid he had been, and they had spent the rest of the day bickering over it, until Aunt Nan had lost her temper with them and declared that they were no better than the rest of their comrades, whose drunken rioting could be heard even from the town's end.

Today had begun just as badly. His Aunt Nan had insisted upon broaching the irritating subject of Nick's remarriage, until he told her in no uncertain terms that it was fine for her to talk, but she had never been married in her life. Now he was ashamed of himself for being so rude and wished that he could have started the day all over again.

'Soldier coming,' said Lucy, tapping his knee with patient insistence. 'Colonel John coming.'

Nick looked up. As usual, Lucy was right. Here was Aunt Nan trotting from the house followed at a respectful distance by her godson, Colonel John Bolle. Nick sighed, knowing that there would be no more peace, for John seldom had time these days for mere social visits. . . . Indeed, the last Nick had heard of him he had been with his regiment, garrisoning the small town of Wallingford for the King.

Lucy protested loudly and with violence at being dragged away to the care of her nursemaid: John Bolle waited stoically for the echoing howls to die away. 'I saw Robin yesterday, he told me you were here,' he said, stroking his beard. 'You look ill-used. How are you?'

Nick ignored the last remark. 'You appear to prosper, colonel? A regiment of your own, and a place in the councils of the mighty.'

John Bolle grinned somewhat wryly. 'Aye, things are well enough, I suppose. Except that I am short of money, and any regiment will melt like butter in the sun if there's no pay. As for the councils of the mighty, you are welcome to them, for all they do is quarrel amongst themselves, so that the enemy seems almost incidental. I hear you have been far from idle yourself. Robin was telling me of your latest escapade.'

Nick groaned inwardly. He dreaded to think what Robin had been saying, for he had an exasperating habit of embroidering any tale to his own satisfaction. 'All foul lies, I'll be bound. What brings you here, sir? I'll wager it's not just a visit to my aunt?'

'No . . . not exactly. I am off to the Western Army tomorrow with a pay-train, and to bring back guns. And you are to come with me to help guard the King's gold.'

'Oh,' said Nick, without enthusiasm.

'Don't sound so sad about it. The spy-master general thought I might keep your idle sword from mischief for a space. A spell of straightforward soldiering will do you no harm. Why, you might even learn something from it! Though they are doing nothing just now. Just looking at William Waller, and both sides'll wait until the last trump, I think, before they actually move . . . but it is not my place to speak. . . . I'll meet you at The Swan at dawn tomorrow and make an honest soldier of you yet! Pray give my compliments to Mistress Carteret and to your little maid.'

In a week Nick had found that soldiering, far from being straightforward, was miserable, disgusting, and extremely dangerous. Day after day they marched past countless fields of barley, beans, turnips and grass, scuttling coneys making for cover in warrens, hedges and green woods, trailing from one ramshackle barn to another to take shelter from the incessant rain which churned the ways to glutinous mud, and made his leaking boots squelchy and sticky on the inside.

Hopton came at last to fight because he could no longer avoid it. He found his way blocked by William Waller's army, dug in along the top of the ridge at Lansdown, not far from Bath. Nick did not see much of the battle. After the first charge the cavalry fled, and Nick fled with it until he came to a full stop in the churned mud and a six-foot pikeman trod on his hand. As far as he was concerned, that was the end of the affair, though he spent the rest of the day trying woefully to collect the scattered men together, ready for retreat.

William Waller retired calmly to Bath to collect reinforcements and supplies, and then drew forth to chase the King's men as far as Devizes before he attacked them once more, and they were forced to turn at bay and defend the little town as best they could, hastily building barricades across the main road as Waller drew his cannon up on Roundway Hill to batter them into ruin or submission.

John Bolle was shot in the shoulder as they retreated into the town, and Nick slung his body like a woolpack over the saddle of his horse to take him to the church, a grim little building they were using to house casualties. The very stones echoed to their howls. Nick emerged into the lantern-lit nave, staggering under the weight of John's limp body, and the scene that met his eyes was nothing short of a vision of hell: just like the old painting on the wall of the church at Sherfield Priors, the painting of souls in torment. Nick had spent hours as a child sitting through incomprehensible sermons in the family pew, looking over the restraining side gate with awestruck eyes at that painting until he had dreamed about it night after night, and now it had come alive before him in no dream. He left John in the care of some unknown butcher and staggered out to the churchyard, where he leaned on the wall, gulping sweet air to chase the salt-sticky smell of blood from his nostrils. There was no shortage of work for the surgeons in this war. They must all be doing splendid business; and what ghoulish business it was. . . . From nearby came a crash and the sound of falling masonry as Waller's cannon opened fire. . . .

Disconsolately, Nick searched for his horse. The King's Army of the West was about to cease to exist, and he for one was loth to die with it. The cavalry were all sitting draggle-tailed and dumb in the square, huddled unhappily against the first drops of rain, while there was a council of war to discuss their parlous position and their bleak prospects, as if talking would mend them. . . . More practically, the captain of ordnance was sending out parties of men to scour the town for bedcord to be beaten and boiled into slow-match, so that they might at least use what powder was left; and the harassed quartermaster was trying to calculate how long this little town might provide food for so many extra mouths. Now the rain began to pour down in a soaking deluge, postponing the inevitable end.

A stir went through the sodden crowd of men in the square. Out of Hopton's lodging came Prince Maurice. He stood before them in the dripping rain, and to Nick's immense surprise and relief told them that the cavalry were to break out of Devizes, under cover of storm and darkness, and ride to Oxford to fetch help.

As the clock of St John's struck midnight they set out through the blustering darkness, the prince himself at their head. They rode break-neck through the friendly muffling mud of the countryside. Horses bumped, blundered and jostled, breath shuddering and snorting, hooves splashing and thundering, their riders clinging silently and wearily, praying that they might not be followed.

They were in Marlborough, and so was a brigade under Wilmot, who had two days ago, on his way to reinforce Hopton, been caught and trounced. Maurice did not tarry but pushed on to Oxford with but a handful of men to follow him. Nick prayed that Essex was safely abed, even wishing him sweet dreams to keep him there.

It was noon when they rode into Oxford, to the great dismay and consternation of the populace, and there disappointment was waiting. Rupert and most of the cavalry were away to the north, escorting the person of Her Majesty the Queen through the dangerous Midlands. While Maurice combed the city for men to take back with him, his escort crawled away like slugs fleeing the bright light of morning, to sleep where they could find shelter.

Stiff-legged and saddle-sore, Nick tottered up the stairs to Robin's lodging. Rob's manservant was open-mouthed in amazement at his sudden materialisation, and even more so at his sorry appearance. Nick shaved, and ate, and felt better. He sent the man Harry, out with his ruined boots, and instructions to find a cobbler to repair them instantly, at whatever cost, otherwise he might drown. . . .

He sat down then, to write a few words of explanation, for Robin would no doubt be furious at his presumption if it were not apologised for in advance. Nick's mind was slow to sort out the jumble of words in his head, and the writing looked like the inky-footed traces of some drunken spider. He rubbed his sleep-swollen eyes and read the result, and concluded that it was so confused as to be almost unintelligible, but yet he had not the strength to write another. It was nearly five o'clock, and he had been awake for thirty-six hours, and far from idle. It was scarcely surprising that he was tired.

My dear Robin, I hope you will forgive my presumption on your generosity, but we are at a low ebb indeed. The foot is besieged in Devizes and we are desperate for all speed to be made, so that I have taken advantage of your bed and board, Harry will tell you. I shall trade my spent horse for yours here in the stable, and will make restitution when I am able. A clean shirt I have also taken, for mine is pickled. I shall be away in a few hours from now. Sorry I was not to see you here, but I trust you are well. John Bolle is sorely wounded and I know not how he fares, but I will find out when I go back. Forgive this evil scribble, but I am in need of sleep and so crave your indulgence. Meanwhile, I remain your affectionate brother, Nicholas.

He signed it, splattering ink-blots across the page. Robin would be very wroth about the horse, he knew, and the shirt also, but beggars could not be choosers, and he would make good the debt just as soon as he could. He managed to reach the bed before he fell asleep. Harry the manservant returned an hour later to find him flat on his back, snoring very loudly.

The next morning Maurice and two brigades of reinforcements left once more for the Wiltshire hills. By good fortune Essex made no attempt to stop them. In Marlborough they joined with Wilmot's men, who, although reluctant to meet again so soon with Waller, were better than nothing at all. At mid-afternoon on the Thursday they came back over Bishop's Cannings Down and found that Hopton was still in possession of the town, though he refused to come out, afraid that Wilmot's blithe message that succour was at hand was some trick of wily Sir William's, to trap them into making an ill-advised sortie from their refuge. It was, after all, far too soon for help to have come all the way from Oxford. . . .

The Parliament-men, also, were stupefied to find a new army at their back. Even the first charge met with little resistance. Waller's cavalry, convinced that the Lord must have deserted them, decided as one man to turn and depart. Like the gadarene swine they disappeared in a single horror-stricken body over the hill and down a precipitous slope. So steep was it that many of them broke their necks in their urgency. The infantry, thus abandoned, took to their heels or threw down their arms and cried piteously for quarter. It was victory; complete, incredible, triumphant victory.

A great deal of riotous rejoicing went on in Devizes that night. While the exhausted members of the garrison slept, their rescuers made merry. Nick toured the town in a dream-like state, searching for news of John Bolle. In one house he heard a drunken trooper imitating the canting sing-song of a puritan preacher. He stood on the table, berating the Lord for the fate of the Roundhead army. 'Where wert thou at Runaway Hill, O Lord?' he cried, 'and where art thou now?' Then he was overcome by emotion and sat down suddenly, taking extreme care not to spill the mug of small-beer in his hand. Even Nick could not resist a smile. In the morning they would all pay for their blasphemy ten times over, with thick heads.

Just after midnight he found John Bolle, sitting alone in a downstairs room of the house which had served Hopton for a headquarter. He looked old and very white about the face, and he carried his arm in a sling, but he welcomed Nick with his usual expansive smile. Nick sighed with relief: John, at least, would live to fight another day.

'Well, sir, I am glad to see you. How goes it?'

'Splendidly, by all accounts. I am glad to see you, Nicholas. I am told that I am indebted to you for my preservation?'

'Are you better already? I've written Rob that you are half dead!'

'Aye, I'm better. Yet I confess that I cannot remember anything, you will have to tell me what happened. I feared I might never learn if you perished. You look half dead yourself.'

'I'm tired,' Nick said briefly, staring hard into John's face, which was swimming before his eyes. 'But I can manage.'

'Of course. They'll not be able to call him "William the Conqueror" from now on, I fancy.' John Bolle smiled. There was no reply, and Nick had not heard a word of what he said, for he was sound asleep with his head on the table in front of him.

5

MOTTHAM

Great William the Con,
So fast did he run,
He left half his name behind him.

Cornet Mottham's voice echoed stridently across the room. That he was in fine high spirits was obvious, as also was the fact that he had already imbibed large quantities of sack. His half dozen companions lounged around the table in the same grand good fellowship, and the table was almost submerged in empty bottles and swimming with spilt liquor. Nick's irritation boiled up as he stood in the doorway surveying the squalor. Bath would be likely to remember the victorious Army of the West for some time to come, and it would not be with affection, but with revulsion at their disorder and their filth. Two steps inside the door and Nick ducked sharply to avoid being knocked on the head by an empty wineglass which hurtled through the air to smash against the whitewashed wall. He shuddered. Officers like these could do the King's cause no good; he would have been better off without them, and it was time somebody said so.

Nick detested Mottham. Though it was only a few days since he had met the man, there was something about this young officer which set his teeth on edge.

'The Earl of Crawford's men seem very well able to enjoy themselves!' he said sarcastically. 'It seems such a pity that they do not apply themselves to fighting the war with such enthusiasm.'

There was sudden awkward silence whilst the roisterers digested the insult which Nick was already beginning to regret. He half expected them to descend on him in force and wondered whether to flee, or try to cope with the whole half dozen at once, since they were very much the worse for drink. He only half regretted the insult, for he was sick and tired of pretended courtesy to them. The stupid fools had come galloping from Marlborough to relieve the garrison at Devizes, and Waller's men had inexplicably melted before them like sealing-wax before a flame. Now they took it for granted that the mere appearance of the Earl of Crawford's regiment of cavalry would put the fear of the Lord into the enemy. And that was not all. Mottham was a lick-arse, Nick thought bitterly. Since they had met, he had not ceased to fawn and flatter because he thought it might stand him in good stead for future advancement. If there was one thing that Nick hated, it was the honeyed viper-tongue of a flatterer. . . .

One of the long-haired gallants, his hat rakishly tilted over one ear, leaned his chair backwards at a perilous angle and squinted at the irate figure silhouetted in the doorway. 'Well, well,' he hiccuped. 'If it isn't Sir Ralph's very own pet Roundhead! Come lads, let us raise a greeting for our crop-eared friend!'

So the brawl was to be words after all and not blows yet awhile. Nick was casting about in his mind for a suitable retort when Mottham's smooth tongue came unexpectedly to his aid. He stood at the head of the table, his buff-coat unlaced, his left arm firmly encircling the neat waist of an ample-bosomed blonde girl with a snub nose.

'Now, Jack,' he said, 'I'll not hear a word against Major Howard.' He stumbled over the words, his voice thick with emotion and strong drink. 'For he is a good fellow, and hath dispatched many of the King's enemies.'

Jack was surprised by this unexpected censure from his friend, and so was Nick, until he thought about it for a minute or two, and concluded that it was only what he might have foreseen. Surprised Jack was, but not silent for long.

'And I say he's a snivelling Roundhead swine who won't drink with us!'

'Who won't drink with us? The man is only this minute come amongst us, and I've heard no one offering him a drink! God's teeth, I'll spit you for slandering my friend!'

Mottham waved expansively and went on to claim lifelong friendship in the maudlin tones of drunkenness until the others were almost weeping with the emotion of it all, and Nick stood by watching their play-acting in stupefied disgust. Now Cornet Mottham was waxing lyrical with a catalogue of Nick's imagined virtues, and was proposing a toast to his everlasting health and prosperity.

This was too much for Jack, who sat teetering on his chair with an expression of abstract unbelief all over his face. Mottham advanced towards him to reinforce the toast, whereupon Jack leaned the chair over a little too far and overbalanced it. He crashed backwards into the hearth, where he lay on his back, cursing feebly, his booted feet inextricably tangled in the chair legs. The others rushed to his aid, but found it a perplexing problem, for they were all finding difficulty enough keeping their own feet, let alone anyone else's. Nick elbowed them out of the way to untangle the unfortunate, and then went in search of more sober assistance. For a consideration, he obtained the services of a stout ostler and a wheelbarrow, and Jack was dispatched back to his quarters with his legs trailing and his hat over his face, still uttering muffled oaths.

The others disappeared in his wake, lurching arm in arm down the street, their boots slithering perilously on the filth in the gutters, philosophising loudly about friendship and loyalty. In a black fury Nick watched them go, and then turned back to the inn, his brand new boots stamping stridently down the two steps into the common-room. Cornet Mottham remained, sitting happily amongst the ruins, deep in the embrace of his ample-bosomed companion. He looked up peevishly as Nick stood over him in anger.

'Cornet Mottham. May I have your attention, or is that too much to ask?'

Mottham let the girl go abruptly, and she slid off his lap to the floor, where she sat, pink-faced with indignation, staring wide-eyed at the two men.

'The devil!' said Mottham, emphatically.

'May take you, as far as I am concerned. You are a good deal more use to him than to the King's Majesty. Have you forgotten that your company is outguard at the moment?'

'No, sir.'

'Then have you been out to make sure that they are, in fact, on guard at all?'

'Er . . . no. I was . . . just going out to inspect them, sir.'

'If I had been a bloody Roundhead, there would be precious few of them left to inspect! It is your duty to make sure that they know what they are about. And what do I find? A party of ungoverned idiots who challenge no one! William Waller and a troop of infantry could have walked through those gates with me tonight, and no one would have been any the wiser.'

Mottham's eyes bore a look of injured pride and damaged dignity. 'That is . . . hardly fair, sir. For is it not . . . unlikely that we shall be attacked here? They would not dare!'

'Unlikely, Mottham, not impossible. How do you know what they would dare to do? Waller has a score to settle, and Nat Fiennes and Bristol garrison are not far off. . . .'

'It's . . . it's . . . damnable poor of you, sir, to task me so,' stuttered Mottham in protest. 'After I saved you from a basting not five minutes since!'

Nick's face went white with rage, and the scar on his cheek glowed livid across it. Mottham gazed into the dark eyes and wished that he had said nothing. Nick looked him up and down as if he were some loathsome crawling creature to crush between finger and thumb.

'A basting, eh?' he said softly. 'What makes you think, my very dear friend, that I could not have defended myself more than adequately against you and all your comrades?'

To Nick's great satisfaction, Mottham quailed visibly.

' 'Pon my honour, sir,' he said.

'Oh, God above!' groaned Nick. 'Here's another with his

gizzard so stuffed with honour that there's not a scrap of room for sense!'

Mottham muttered a few half-audible words under his breath, and looked away from the stern gaze. He had enough sense to know that Major Howard was more than a match for him, and that he would rather not fight him in this mood, not even with a dozen sober comrades to back him up. He shut his mouth with a resounding snap, like a fish catching a mayfly.

'I ought to have you hanged as an example. And if you give any more trouble I shall not hesitate to do so. Do you understand me?'

'But my Lord Crawford says . . .'

'I care not what your Lord Crawford has to say. If he is foolish enough to employ you, then you and he deserve to hang together! I'll not warn you again. Now, out and be about your business before I put my boot behind you!'

Mottham sighed with an air of insolent defiance and shrugged his shoulders. He bowed stiffly and stalked unsteadily to the door, and Nick heard him shouting for his horse. The hooves drew off at a purposeful trot until he could hear them no more. Nick knew that he had made an enemy where he might have made a friend, and the thought of it annoyed him. . . .

In the cloudy sweat-soaked morning Nick was called to Hopton's headquarter. The reason for the call was unspecified, and Nick made his way thither with a sinking heart, suspecting that Mottham had already been crying injustice and shrieking calumnies to the sky, for Mottham had so many friends in high places. It was well known that the Earl of Crawford favoured him, and it seemed not unlikely that he might have Hopton's ear into the bargain. Nick spent an uncomfortable ten minutes in the ante-room to Hopton's office, trying to think what he should say about last night's unpleasantness; all of which proved to be unnecessary, for all that Hopton did was to order him to Oxford forthwith, to attend His Majesty's scout-master general.

Nick was surprised at the sudden summons and knew not if he should be glad or sorry. Certainly there seemed little prospect for him at Bristol. It would be an easy enough task for straightforward soldiers to take the place now. The defenders would be in poor spirits after Waller's defeat and Hampden's death and the news that Fairfax's army in the North had been routed three weeks since: now Rupert was on the march, and that would set Colonel Nathaniel Fiennes and his men to trembling for certain. Bristol would be easy prey. . . . Yet if he stayed, Nick might have seen Robin, and there, was, of course, a debt to pay. Nick had almost forgotten it, and the remembrance brought a curse to his lips: though there may be a way of settling his debt after all. As the clock of the church at the end of the narrow street struck eight, Nick went in search of Colonel John Bolle.

When Nick arrived he was arguing forcibly with the quartermaster about coats, shirts and snapsacks for the new men he had acquired from Hopton. The quartermaster's face lit up, for he was obviously more than anxious to escape the rough end of John's tongue, which did not lack strength, even while his arm still hung useless at his side.

'Nicholas, come in! I'll find you out later, William . . . and you see what you can do for me. . . .'

'I've come to ask a favour,' Nick said, wriggling uncomfortably. He hated to ask favours.

'Ask away, Nicholas. What can I do for you?'

'Rupert and his men are coming to join Hopton for the attack on Bristol.'

'So I heard. Robin will be coming.'

'Aye. That is really what I am here for. The general has this day ordered me to Oxford. . . . I should be away already, truth to tell. I owe Robin money for a shirt, a horse, and my board when I was at Oxford before the battle.'

'So you want me to lend you the money to pay him?'

'Oh . . . no. I've got the money here.' Nick counted out ten guineas into the palm of his hand and proffered them. 'It's just that I . . . do not know when I shall see him next, and I . . . do not like to leave it. Can I ask you to settle for me? Will you be here still, or are you off back to Wallingford directly?'

John Bolle laughed softly. 'I'm in no hurry. I shall be here. Oh, I might have known it. You'd not be in debt to anyone: not to the devil himself, I think. . . .' He looked at Nick's pained expression and coughed discreetly. 'Oh, God, Nicholas, forgive me. 'Tis such a very little favour, and I will be more than happy to oblige you. It's as good as done. Now, will you eat before you go? I've not breakfasted yet.'

'Thank you, sir, but no. It will be so late before I start out. Give Rob my greetings, will you?'

'With pleasure, Nicholas. But I insist that you eat before you go. Order you, in fact. You'll ride happier if you're fed. Good God, man, don't look at me like that! 'Tis not a sin to eat. You'll be no good to either King or Parliament if you starve to death.'

'If you insist, sir,' said Nick reluctantly, and before long he was facing a plate of cold, boiled mutton and bread. He had become accustomed to the short commons of an army on the march, besides which, his mind was already in Oxford, wondering why he was wanted. He ate moodily and stared at the plate, and John Bolle looked hard at him across the remains of the mutton.

'I hear,' he said, with his mouth full, 'that you've been making yourself unpopular.'

'Who told you that?'

'William. Crawford's men are in evil humour.'

'That quarrel was not of my asking. Well, not all of it. Ask Cornet Mottham who was in the wrong.' Nick pulled a wry face and studied his half-full plate, clutching the mug of small-beer so tightly with both hands that it looked as if he was trying to crush it. He took a mouthful and choked on it, and Colonel Bolle decided to change the subject.

'Come on, Nick. Eat. There will be nothing of you. What am I to tell your Aunt Nan?' John laughed, but Nick was in no mood to share the joke.

'Hang Aunt Nan!' he said, with feeling. 'Has she then set you to spy on me?'

'Oh, a plague on you, Nicholas Howard, you are sour today. Do not sulk on Mottham's account. He'll hang yet.'

'So shall I if I'm not on my way. You'll be sure to tell Robin that if he thinks I have cheated him, then I'm quite prepared to argue later? He's bound to want the horse back, but I cannot get another that suits me so well, so I've kept it. And I'm likely to need it more than he.'

Nick jingled the two guineas left in his pocket and hoped that His Majesty's scout-master general would remember that he had not been paid since last March. . . .

6

THE SCOUT-MASTER GENERAL

At dead of night Nick came to Oxford and narrowly escaped having his head blown apart by the ancient but highly lethal arquebus directed at him by Harry the manservant, who peered anxiously from the door of Robin's lodging in the confident expectation that it was a robber he had to deal with.

In the morning the sky was stacked with thunderclouds, and the air seemed heavy enough to crush the crowded buildings all together in one untidy heap of stony rubble. Nick crossed the quiet quadrangle and stopped before the iron-studded wooden door to take a deep breath before knocking. Inside, the sound of his knock bounced and resonated round the hall so loudly that he could clearly hear it, and as if in answer to the echoes, the first grumblings of thunder reverberated from the distant hills. Lightning flashed across the darkening sky as the grey door was opened by a tottery old man with a wrinkled face the colour of much-used parchment.

'Yes?' said the man's reedy voice, in tones of suspicion.

'I am Major Nicholas Howard.'

'Come in, young man,' quavered the voice. 'You are expected. Please to wait below stairs here while I tell my Lord that you have arrived.'

The man trotted upstairs with a speed and agility which belied his appearance of extreme age, and disappeared along a corridor full of shadows. The thunder was nearer now, and large splashes of rain spattered vehemently against the tiny window in the stone hall. Nick followed the dark little Methuselah along the murky gallery, and the long bony arm ushered him into a book-lined room with a gigantic table in the centre. The top of the table was buried in an assortment of maps, inkpots, quills, and untidy papers, and more were stacked underneath in drunken piles.

His Majesty's scout-master general stood at the tall mullioned window, obviously intent upon the lightning and the rain outside, his straight back turned to the doorway where Nick hesitated. He spoke without turning, as if he had eyes in the back of his head.

'Come in, Major Howard, and be seated, I pray you.' The accent was exquisite, tuneful, leisured and unemotional, the effect totally calculated and precise. His clothes were as splendid as Nick had ever seen, a wealth of elaborate gold-threaded embroidery set off with a froth of the finest mechlin lace at neck, wrist and boot-top. The general turned and looked down his long aquiline nose at Nick, inspecting him from the unruly crop of dark curls at his crown to the butterfly spur-leathers at his feet, and sniffed.

He was more like a dancing master than a spy, Nick thought, and his face reddened under the minute gaze.

'I have duties in mind for you, Major Howard.'

'My Lord?'

'I have fair reports of you. I think that you are the man I require. The commissions are . . . er . . . delicate, you understand?' The thin face smiled to reveal sharp pointed teeth like a weasel's, and the smile was not disapproving, Nick thought, but the weasel's eyes were cold and merciless, and made the back of his neck prickle with nervous perspiration.

'What are these duties, sir?'

'Do you know Hampshire at all?' The accent was clipped and purposeful now.

'A little, sir.'

'You shall know it better anon, no doubt. I have a map for your perusal.'

'I am to go to Hampshire, then?'

'Yes, major. To Stoke Sutton, to be exact. We have already one man there, but he is sorely pressed and in need of assistance, for reasons which I shall presently explain.'

'Stoke Sutton?' Nick's eyes clouded in puzzlement. He had seen that name before, but could not remember where. . . .

'Our man is a surgeon and physician, resident in that place. You will appreciate that he is busy, on account of the war. He is therefore in need of an apprentice. I am afraid that you will be required to make some acquaintance with the healing arts, in addition to the arts of war. It will be necessary to acquire some skill therein.'

'Me? A surgeon? Oh, no!' Nick muttered in consternation, his stomach already turning cartwheels at the prospect. If there was any job on earth which he would relish less, he would be hard put to find it. Raised eyebrows faced him.

'You do not like the idea?' He might look like a dancing master, but it was all sham. The general had no patience with squeamish fools who wasted his time.

'I was . . . taken by surprise, my Lord, I must admit. It . . . requires some imagination, that is all. What is the name of this surgeon?'

'Master Nathaniel Harrington. He is as stout and loyal as any you will find, but his years are advancing. That part of the country is a nest of rebellion.'

The spy master crossed to the table and extracted a folded paper from beneath one of the unruly piles, as if he had known precisely where it was. He continued. 'There are two very great rebels in the vicinity. The greatest is Colonel Norton of Southwick. But there is one other who will concern you mostly, and he is Colonel Thomas Chadwicke of Broadoak, which is not three miles from Stoke Sutton.'

Nick remembered instantly where he had heard the name Stoke Sutton before. A month since, not far from Winchester, when he read a letter from a dead man's pocket. Thomas Chadwicke's pocket. The aristocratic voice went on. 'This Chadwicke is on sick-leave, ostensibly. Yet he has two troops of soldiers quartered on his lands, and a veritable army of minions coming and going, to no honest purpose.'

'You mean he is a spy-master?'

'Exactly. And you are to watch him, amongst other things. . . . There is a great deal afoot in those parts just now, and I think it will keep you busy.' He cleared his throat and unfolded the paper on the table. 'You may be aware, Major Howard, that once we have Bristol and Gloucester in our hands, our purpose is to strike across the southern counties.' Here a long pointed finger adorned with a cluster of rubies prodded aggressively at the map. 'We shall need reliable guides who can discover for us the disposition of enemy forces, so we must have someone who will be accepted into his camp without question.'

Nick grinned broadly. 'And who more welcome and less suspect than a surgeon? I am beginning to understand.'

The sharp-faced general smiled benignly, and nodded. 'I had half a mind that you should go as a cleric, but somehow I did not see you in Geneva bands with that scar on your face. . . . However, there are other matters which I would charge to your hand, Major Howard. Some small tasks which may better appeal to your nature.' His sharp features became savagely enthusiastic as he warmed to his subject. The thunder, too, became enthusiastic, crashing overhead until every grey stone of the building seemed to vibrate.

'My Lord Winchester is preparing a fortification at his house of Basing. It will be garrisoned from here shortly, for I am informed that Colonel Norton is even now preparing to march against it. You will be most useful to my Lord, I think, to discover the enemy's intentions and works in the event of such an attack, and to contrive to inform him thereof.'

Nick's head spun with confusion. It sounded simple in the spy-master's smooth-spoken words, but it was his life at stake, and not the general's, after all. . . .

'We have the intention of . . . regulating the traffic along the wool road. My Lord Winchester is well placed at Basing to do so, and the Parliament-men can well do without their revenue from that source.' The weasel face sneered, and the thin tongue licked swiftly over the lips. He looked up from the map. 'They will need supplies at Basing in the event of hostilities. I have discussed the matter with the marquis, and we concluded that the Roundhead garrisons of Portsmouth and Southampton could perhaps do without any morsels that you might be able to . . . er . . . divert. He said that he was more than willing to lend you a few stout horse of his own to assist you in this.' One eyebrow rose in amusement and the pointed teeth glinted in a gentle smile. 'I told him that you were a master of the art of ambuscade.' He brushed an imaginary speck of dust from the embroidered garlands of his sleeve. 'Have you any questions to ask?'

Nick gaped dumbly, appealing with mute eyes to the hard staring face. He was confounded by the enormity of the task placed before him. The general laughed, softly mocking, and turned to another pile of papers. Nick spoke hesitantly. 'I am . . . not sure if I shall be equal to such a charge, my Lord. 'Tis a heavy burden you lay on me.'

'True. But do you suppose that I would be sending you if I thought that you would be inadequate? I have considered the matter at great length, you may be assured. I am pleased that I do not have to remind you of my maxim that over-confidence is to be abhorred.'

'When am I to start?'

'Master Harrington expects you a week from now. Meanwhile, may I suggest that you should . . . become used to the idea of being a surgeon's apprentice? It would be wise to purchase some sober garb which will not attract too much attention. Your hair seems quite suitable already.' He looked sideways at Nick's short, tangled mop and preened his own long greying lovelocks with visible pride. Then he took a small gilt key and opened a dark, heavy-lidded chest behind the door, rummaging about in its depths. He took out a handful of gold coins and put them on the table. 'This will help you to make any necessary arrangements.' Nick pocketed the gold pieces ruefully. It was just as well that he was not a poor man, for that small sum would scarcely break the royal exchequer: and he was owed a fortune in back pay; but then, so was everybody. . . . The map, once more folded, was being proffered, and he put it inside his hat. There was another packet of letters.

'Master Secretary Nicholas has given me these for you.

Your orders are here writ that you may study them at leisure. It is important . . . that is, I must insist . . . that they are then destroyed, and the sooner the better.'

Nick took the packet into his hand and looked at it; it was sealed with the royal seal. So it was that important. Nick pushed it into the folds of his shirt, and there he felt that it would burn a hole through the linen and the buff-leather, and show itself to the world.

'That will be all, Major Howard, if you have no more questions.'

'Sir.' Nick made for the door. His left hand was reaching for the handle when the exquisite voice called him back. 'Master Howard?' Nick smiled. Already he was being put to the test, it seemed. 'It would be interesting to hear how a surgeon's apprentice came by that scar on the cheek? It looks uncommon like a bullet graze to me.'

Nick put on a bland smile and opened his eyes wide in innocence. 'Why, so it was, sir, so it was. A mischance, sir, while I was attending to the wounded, for a musket knows not its enemy. I fear such injury is a hazard of my profession in these troubled times.'

The weasel face smiled widely, and one eye closed in a slow, deliberate wink. 'Good luck,' the embroidered general said. 'I think also that I must mention . . . that if you miscarry . . . should anything go awry. . . .' He hesitated for a moment, as if searching his mind for some subtlety which escaped him. The thunder rolled loudly above. 'I must make it clear that we shall not be in a position to help you in any way. It is unlikely, for example, that we should be able to arrange an exchange for you, as we might for an officer carrying out more normal duties. You are a spy, and spies are different, you understand? I am sorry, but you must fend for yourself.'

Nick gulped, though the words were no surprise. The silky smoothness of the voice appalled him. It was almost as if it were arranging a masque, not pronouncing a death sentence. Nick squared his shoulders. So he would be on his own completely. Well, that suited him perfectly, he thought, his chin jutting in a rush of obstinacy. If there was one thing he had learned by bitter experience in the last three months, it was that he could certainly rely on no one else.

'I am obliged to you, my Lord, for being so honest with me,' he said politely. 'I shall do my best to fulfil your trust.' His firm voice belied the sick fear within, and the general still smiled. 'I am sure that you will, Major Howard. Good day to you.'

Nick stepped briskly down the stairs, the coins jingling in merry chorus in his pocket, and the King's packet of orders rubbing insistently against his flesh. He peered out from the door. The thunder was moving away, but the rain still lashed down in a steady curtain of drops. By the time he had sprinted the short slithering distance through the little river-like alleyways to Robin's lodging, he was drenched.

Harry looked at him very oddly as he came in. At first Nick wondered what was so puzzling, and then followed Harry's enquiring eyes to his hand, which still held his hat. He had forgotten all about it and had neglected to put it on despite the rain. He shrugged and grinned at Harry's shaking head. 'I shall be leaving again tomorrow at dawn.'

'Yes, sir,' Harry nodded indulgently. 'I can't keep up with you, sir. Always coming and going. You in love, sir? You'll catch your death of cold so.'

Harry took the hat and discreetly extracted the folded paper, gave Nick a broad wink, and set it on the side-table. He obviously thought it was a love letter from some lady or other. Well, let him think what he would, it was no matter. 'I shall not be needing anything for a couple of hours, Harry. Go away and play, eh?' Harry winked again and withdrew with a grin so wide that it looked as if his face would split in two.

Nick stood at the tiny window high above the narrow street and considered. The air was sweet and cool now the storm had broken, and the lightning played like a devil's fork over the distant hills. The wet roofs sparkled, and over them the angular black shapes of the swifts screamed their high-pitched hunting cries as they feasted on the swarming clouds of tiny black flies left suspended in the air in the wake of the retreating storm. Nick sighed. It would be a challenge to live at close quarters with the enemy and be active against him, and the thought of it sent an odd thrill of excitement through him.

He made sure that the door was firmly locked before he took the packet of orders from his shirt and broke the seal, and stared unbelievingly at the heavy black signature which seemed to leap out at him from the foot of the page. 'Charles R.' he read. No wonder that the general had been so insistent that the letter should be destroyed as soon as maybe, for every word of it would make splendid capital for those rogues in the Commons. Nick studied every elegant phrase again and again until he knew the letter off by heart, then he tore it into tiny shreds. The fragments he piled with painstaking care into the hearth and set them ablaze, watching till the last red embers burned grey, and he crushed the remains into dust, brushing his sooty hands on his grimy coat. He had landed himself in the middle of a morass, he knew, and now he must pick his way out of it with all the prudence and circumspection he could muster. Perhaps with a week's grace the yoke would fit more readily. He must visit Marlborough to see Lucy. It might well be a long absence before he would see her again; if ever. A door closed down in the street with the sharp slam of finality, and he heard in his head the silk-smooth tones of the scout-master general: 'If you should miscarry . . . should anything go awry . . . you are a spy . . . you must fend for yourself.'

The map still reposed where Harry had left it on the side-table. Nick took it up and spread it wide, to reveal 'the County of Southampton, together with surrounding parts', carefully drawn and much-thumbed. He looked for Stoke Sutton, and his forefinger prodded triumphantly. Just a little village, it lay in a secluded valley between Alresford and Alton: ten miles or so from Basing; and not more than five-and-thirty from Marlborough.

Footsteps came up the stairs, slow and hesitating. Nick stiffened, and his right hand went to grasp his sword-hilt. It was too early for Harry to be coming, and those were not Harry's clumping feet on the stairs, nor was it Harry's energetic knock on the door of the outer chamber. He folded the map as quietly as he could and put it inside his shirt. It was uncomfortably obtrusive. He crossed the room cautiously and drew back the bolts, and the key turned softly to unlock the door. Outside was a red-faced portly individual whom he had never seen, and that portly person was puffing extravagantly from the exertion of stair climbing. He carried under one vast yellow-coated arm a huge parcel, and a book which looked very heavy, and he swept off his canary-plumed hat in an ornate gesture of salute.

'Have I the honour of addressing Major Nicholas Howard?'

'You have,' Nick said briefly and suspiciously, looking the fat man up and down and wondering what on earth could have brought him.

'Allow me, sir, to introduce myself. William Robinson, personal surgeon and physician to my Lord Marquis of Winchester. Your most humble servant, sir.'

Another courtly bow followed, and then Master William Robinson took out a handkerchief and mopped at his perspiring pink forehead. Nick could hardly stop himself from laughing, for he was such a comical-looking fellow, rather like a stout pig on the verge of an apoplexy, and he looked as if he might bow his fat head right off his shoulders. But Major Nicholas Howard bowed back formally and most politely, and spoke with even courtesy.

'Master Robinson, you are welcome, pray come within. But to what do I owe the pleasure of this visit?'

'Visit? Ah, yes.' At this he waved the large parcel a few inches from Nick's nose, his piggy eyes blinking busily, and Nick drew back in self-defence. 'I have here, sir, a number of items which I have been instructed to deliver.' He unwrapped the said items with a flourish, and Nick found himself confronted by a hideously cruel array of surgeon's tools, and the sharp steel twinkled like little stars reflecting the sunlight from the window. There was no escape. All was organised for him, and he was committed, body and, very likely, soul also. It was his turn to bow again, stiffly, more to hide his trepidation than anything else. 'I am indebted to you, Master Robinson.'

'And here also is a most excellent treatise on physick.'

'Thank you.'

'My Lord of Winchester desires me to inform you that he is looking forward . . . anxiously . . . to meeting you at his house of Basing, whither he is departing this very night. No doubt we shall be seeing you at Basing ere long?'

The enquirer sounded worried, and Nick wondered if my Lord of Winchester was half as anxious as this his servant.

'No doubt,' he replied, unwilling to vouchsafe any further details.

'I must . . . er . . . be on my way. There are preparations to be made for our departure.'

'Of course. I'll not keep you, Master Robinson.'

'Your most obedient servant, sir.' Another bow, which Nick returned sardonically.

'Yours, sir.'

The fat figure rolled off down the stairway, and Nick's shoulders began to shake with uncontrollable laughter. It was thus Harry found him a few minutes later, leaning against the doorpost with tears of helpless mirth pouring down his cheeks.

7

THE DEVIL WILL CARE FOR HIS OWN

A great deal of foaming grey water had rolled under the Kennet bridge since the last time Nicholas had ridden from Oxford to Marlborough, and last week seemed such a world away that he half expected to find the town changed beyond recognition. But it was the same, every stone of it, and still occupied by the trailing rearguard of Rupert's Bristol-bound hordes. Nick sighed. Rupert's ruffians would have made an everlasting impression on the wine-cellars of the town, on every willing woman within a five-mile radius, and no doubt on a good few of the unwilling ones as well. . . .

As he stepped over the threshold, little Lucy came hurtling down the stairs as fast as her stiff blue-figured damask dress would allow, and collided forcibly with his knees. Nick looked at the bright eager face raised to him, and felt a painful rush of love for the strange little creature who seemed so to worship him. He lifted her to his shoulder, and she squealed with laughter. She was remarkably heavy. 'Well, precious,' he said. 'I swear that you have grown to twice the size since I last saw you!'

Brisk steps above, and the rustle of satin heralded the arrival of Aunt Nan, who called sharply from the stair-head, 'What is it? Who is there?'

'Aunt Nan? It's only me.'

'Nicholas, my dear boy . . . thank God, for I thought it was – more soldiers.'

'Have you had trouble?'

'My dear child, you look so pale and thin. . . . Why are you here? You are not hurt?' Her eyes searched for signs of damage.

Nick laughed softly at her concern. 'Do you think that I would be carrying this plump pigeon if I were hurt?' He indicated the wriggling child on his shoulder. Lucy clung to his ears, and his pleading for mercy sent her into gales of laughter. 'I have business here for several days.'

Aunt Nan looked at him curiously but gave her question no voice.

'And then it will be a long while, I think, before I come again.'

Later he sat in Aunt Nan's parlour, drowsy in the warmth of the sun through the window. The war he had left behind him for a space, he hoped, as he sipped canary wine from one of Aunt Nan's best Venice-crystal goblets. Lucy sat at his feet, a small hand on the blue velvet of his breeches, adoring papa with her eyes, and even Jezebel lay forgotten on the floor. The house here was a warm, sun-kissed haven of peace and security, just like the old rambling house at Sherfield Priors. Which reminded him. . . .

'Have you heard from Frances?'

'Oh, good heavens, yes! It had almost slipped my mind. Frances was brought to bed of a girl-child on, ah . . . when was it?' She paused. 'The third day of July. They have christened her Ann. The babe is evidently another lusty child, and Frances takes these things in her stride. Your brother is very fortunate. If we could find such a wife for you, I think that it would suit you very well.'

Nick groaned and made a defensive gesture with his right hand. 'Oh, Aunt Nan, have mercy, please!' He smiled cynically and rather absently at Aunt Nan's precious chamber-clock on the mantelpiece. It was nearly seven o'clock. Lucy leaned heavily against him, her head drooped on his knee, sleeping soundly, her small mouth ajar, and Jezebel's tattered form cradled in one arm. Nick gathered child and bartholomew-baby in his long arms, and without a word carried them both up to their bed.

Aunt Nan was smiling fondly at him when he came back to the parlour. 'You used to look like that,' she said.

'Did I? Oh, God, was I ever that innocent?'

'Sometimes you look as if you are still innocent, though God knows what dark deeds you have wrought.' She sighed heavily. 'Robin was here yesterday, did you know?'

'No, I suppose he must have been. On his way to Bristol?'

'With the prince. He expected to see you there. I gather you owe him money.' She was frowning. It was not like the Nicholas she knew to owe anyone anything. This Nicholas was a stranger. . . .

The little housemaid announced dinner, with much blushing and many apologies for the lateness of the hour, but Master Nicholas was so unexpected. . . . Master Nicholas was also very hungry, and ate for some while in silence, so that Nan Carteret thought he had chosen to forget her comment about the money.

'I would've liked to pay Rob myself,' he said, putting his knife down. 'I was ordered away. But don't fret, he'll get his due. I left Colonel Bolle to settle for me. Poor John was horribly wounded at Devizes and gave us all a good deal of anxiety, but now he mends well enough, I think.'

There was something in the odd twisting of his mouth which told her that there was more to it than he was telling. But on his face now was the polite smile he had always used to keep the world at bay. She remembered little Nicholas after a beating, thin-lipped and silent, while Robin would howl and roar and thump his fists in his rage. Nick, bloody-nosed and badly cut from a fall from one of the apple trees, had only been furious with himself because his big brother had laughed at him. The tears, she remembered, had only come when too much laughing had brought Robin toppling from his perch in the same tree, and he lay beside Nick on the short grass of the orchard. In those days she had been the only one who could reach Nicholas. . . .

'Tell me about it, Nicholas,' she said gently. Nick shook his head and smiled sadly. Aunt Nan already had enough to worry her. She had sounded as if Robin's recent visit had been more of an ordeal than a pleasure, and he did not mean his own to be the same.

'How is Robin?'

'In the best of health and good spirits! So were his many comrades, but some of them lacked his good manners. I had to hit one over the head myself with a pewter plate, to save the housemaid from ravishment. Poor child! And she scarce fourteen! Really, it is not to be tolerated!'

Nick looked at Aunt Nan's fierce face with a new respect. She was a very resourceful lady, and someone would have an outsized headache as a consequence.

'There was a good deal of damage,' she continued calmly. 'Most of the crystal was smashed: all save the best, and that we fortunately managed to conceal from them. But no matter, we remain ourselves uninjured, and for that we must be grateful. But we are all so weary of this war, Nicholas. When will it all end?'

'When it is over, and not before,' he said, with what he hoped was an air of philosophy.

A cold draught cut across the room, and Aunt Nan drew her kerchief about her shoulders and frowned. 'You said that it would be a long time before you come back?'

'Yes.'

'Why? What lunacy are you engaged in?'

Nick kissed her hand and shook his head. 'Now, Aunt Nan. Ask no questions and you will hear no lies. Is that not what you used to say to us?' There was no point in enquiring further. The expression on his face was familiar, and she knew it to be nothing more than a bland face on obstinacy. She rose abruptly. 'I think I shall be retiring now. It becomes late, and really I am in need of rest after these last few days.'

'Wait, Aunt Nan.' There was something else he wanted to ask. 'Do you know if there is an army surgeon in the garrison here?'

'My God, Nicholas! You are hurt after all! Why did you not tell me the truth?' She flew back across the room at him, her arms and hands fluttering like the wings of an agitated skylark, and he had to hold her little body at arm's length. Though she was thin, her strength amazed him.

'No, Aunt Nan! For God's sweet sake do not fuss so! There is nothing whatsoever wrong with me. Not a scratch or even a bruise, you have my word on it! I have something to discuss, that's all.'

'They take wounded men to The Swan, I believe. Though what you have to discuss with a surgeon I cannot imagine.' She put on her most haughty face, as if she cared not a jot, though Nick knew she was about to die of curiosity. He chuckled. 'Good night to you, Aunt Nan.'

'But, Nicholas!' she pleaded plaintively, looking so like Lucy in her entreaty that he found her hard to resist. It was always the way of women, he thought, to feign helpless innocence to serve their own ends.

'When I need to employ a lady intelligencer, I shall bear you in mind for the post. Until then, I shall keep my own counsel. Sleep well, Aunt Nan.'

In the morning he started out briskly to The Swan. With every step his knees felt weaker, and his feet were reluctant to take another. As he drew nearer to his destination, his nostrils caught the acrid tang of rotting oak leaves and the smell of stinking hides from the pits of the tannery near the river, and his throat tightened and gulped with nausea. Never again would he be able to smell that smell without remembering. . . .

The garrison surgeon was indeed in residence, and the stench from the tannery seemed to bother him not at all. He was enjoying a respite from his duties, and he sat, dishevelled and bristling with unshaven beard, in the common-room, with a dilapidated ale-jack in his hand, and holding forth at great length to a company of worshipping small boys. The subject of his discourse seemed to be the means by which one could most damage one's enemy with the least possible effort. Nick listened, unobserved, for several minutes, and found the information interesting, if not entirely savoury. He coughed, and the blue-jowled surgeon looked up, his audience dispersing, shouting and hooting in the way that all small boys do. Nick's footsteps echoed in the empty room, and his voice came calling back to him from the grimy walls.

'Are you the surgeon?'

'I am. Who wants me?' He did not rise from the bench, but peered out from behind beetle-black bushes of eyebrows, and the hairs in his nostrils twitched as he snuffed the air like a suspicious hound.

'My name is Howard. Major Nicholas Howard. I have need of your assistance.'

'In what way may I assist you, major? You look most perfectly healthy to me. I am Surgeon-Captain Tomkins, sir,' he said, and his voice held more sarcasm than respect.

'Can you teach me a few basic principles of your – er – craft? In two or three days?'

Tomkins gaped, his warty face creased to reveal every rotten tooth in his head, and he burst into a cacophony of untuneful laughter, slapping his thigh and sending ale spilling in a torrent over the flag-stones. 'God's bones, sir, you've a strange taste in humour!'

'I am quite serious, I can assure you,' Nick replied drily.

Tomkins' grin slowly faded, and once more he looked faintly distrustful. Nick put his hand in his pocket and drew out a purse.

'I can pay,' he said. 'The King's gold. For your help: and more again for your silence.'

' 'Tis a strange request, major. But if there's money in it I shall ask no question. No doubt you have your reasons . . . and, besides, another pair of hands here will not come amiss.' He sighed wearily and scratched his head. 'There are still men here from the fighting. And the accidents! My God, soldiers are such fools!' He grinned again, a little uncomfortably, Nick thought. 'Present company excepted, I'm sure. . . . No offence meant.' He stood up and rubbed his hands together with apparent relish. 'So, sir, when you've a desire to learn, it will be my pleasure to instruct you.'

For the rest of that day, and for most of the next three, Nick followed Surgeon-Captain Tomkins closely. He learned the rough skills of the field surgeon which he hoped would be enough to see him safe in the uncertain future. He found it as ghoulish as he had expected, and more so. He learned how to set a broken bone; how to dig out a splinter or a bullet; how to stop a man from bleeding to death; and how to tell almost at a glance if it was worth trying or no. Most of all, Nick learned how to pray. He prayed that if he were to be hurt, then it would be a quick bullet between the eyes or through the heart, and then no more.

There was no shortage of work. Wounded men were brought in with depressing frequency, all too many of them marked to die: one stabbed in a brawl; one shot accidentally as a comrade with clumsy fingers cleaned a musket; and the charred victims of yet another exploded powder-keg, for as Tomkins always said, soldiers were such fools. . . .

As the wounded man under his hands shrieked and jerked, Nick frowned in concentration. He had done all he could. He rose, brushing the flopping hair out of his eyes with a forearm reddened like a butcher's. Tomkins stood hands on hips in the doorway, staring.

'You have nimble fingers,' he said. 'A gift for healing.'

There was a moment's silence broken only by the rasping croak of the senseless man between them. 'But I've heard that those hands are just as skilled at causing damage as they are at repairing it.'

'Who says so?'

'Just a friend of mine,' Tomkins said, winking knowingly. 'Man of Crawford's, riding through. . . . Happened to see you here. Interested to see that you'd turned surgeon.'

'Oh?' Nick shrugged.

'Oh, don't worry, I said nothing. Know nothing to say.'

'Good.' Nick smiled humourlessly, while his unsteady confidence seeped away.

'This friend,' said Tomkins, 'laughed. And said that Satan must be needing a surgeon-general, and that he would recommend you for the post.'

Tomkins turned on his heel, whistling nonchalantly. Nick wiped his blood-sticky hands on his dirty breeches and took himself to the common-room, where he sat for a good hour worrying quietly about the slackness of Tomkins' tongue, until the half-dead wreckage of another wretch was brought in, and he had something more immediate to occupy him.

Later on that last day in Marlborough he sat in the gallery beside Lucy on the window-seat, giving half an ear to her prattling as she stood tiptoe on her customary perch. The sunshine showed him the unmistakable red sheen on her brown curls as her little lace biggin slipped backwards from the crown of her head. The auburn tint reminded him of Elizabeth, and he did not want to remember at all. 'Poor little Lucy. It's not your fault,' he thought aloud, and caught just in time at the hanging sleeves of her gown to prevent her from losing her balance and falling head first.

'Papa?' She did not understand. 'Papa sing song.'

'Just one then, before you go back to Jennet. Must kiss me good-bye, for I shall be gone in the morning before you awake.' Lucy smiled dutifully. 'And it might be a long time before papa can see you again.'

'Want froggy song. Uncle Robin singed it.' She waited expectantly. He was for a moment mystified, and then he guessed the identity of the ditty she required. It had always been a favourite of his and Rob's.

> It was a frog, leaped into a pool
> Fol-deriddle, went souse in the middle.

He began, self-consciously, remembering the fat little tutor with the bulging eyes about whom he and Rob had really been singing.

> Scattered the tadpoles and set them agog
> Hey, nod noddy, all head and no body
> Oh, mammy, oh, nunky, here's cousin Jack Frog.

They had always called him 'Jack Frog' behind his back, and now Nick could not remember his real name at all. . . . Lucy clapped her hands in delight at the nonsense.

Aunt Nan came, her amber gown glowing in the sunshine, her lips pursed with disapproval of Lucy's favourite ditty. 'You are planning to leave early tomorrow, Nicholas?'

'Aye. I'll bid you farewell tonight, for I would like to be on my way by dawn.'

In fact he had every intention of sneaking away in the middle of the night, so that Aunt Nan would not see him go.

'Where exactly are you going, Nicholas?'

'I'm going a'hunting, Aunt Nan,' he laughed.

'But if we know not where you are how will we reach you, if we should need you?' she said limply.

It was a problem he had already pondered. 'I will find a way. Rest easy, dear aunt, and rely on the devil to care for his own.'

Nan Carteret drew herself up to her full height, so that she could almost look him straight in the eye. 'I am very much afraid that the devil will care for his own. That is why I cannot rest easy without news.' She curtsied with grace and turned on her heel.

His intentions to slip away unnoticed were completely confounded, for the whole town was roused at two o'clock in the morning by the frantic clanging of church bells, and by the rider who careered down the market street, shouting and hallooing at the top of his voice. Nick was already up and dressed in a sober grey kersey coat, breeches and wide collar of linen, and he would have looked the mirror of respectability if it had not been for the scarred face, his unruly mop of hair, and the long sword he was buckling by his side as he ran downstairs to catch the messenger. The white-faced drowsy vision of Aunt Nan watched him from the window, and rubbed its sleepy eyes in unbelief at her nephew's strange attire.

'Bristol is taken!' The rider shouted lustily. 'Bristol is ours!' He disappeared down the road, and from the square came the sound of cheering from the garrison.

'Bristol has fallen, it seems,' said Nicholas flatly, facing the stupefied Aunt Nan across the echoing hall.

'Nicholas, what on earth?'

'And my horse is saddled, and I must go. Lord knows I'm late enough already.' He blew her a kiss and made off. She watched him spurring Robin's liver-chestnut until it seemed almost to fly, and then he was out of sight. But she stood looking at the empty road for some time, clutching her cloak about her with both hands, and tasting the salt tears which came unasked. Upstairs she could hear Lucy's voice asking drowsily where papa had gone: so Nan Carteret dried her eyes very carefully and went upstairs to explain. It was all that was left for her to do.

8

A SURGEON AND PHYSICIAN

The gusty vigour of the wind surprised Nick as he reached the top of the ridge, for it had been very sheltered on the other side. His hair flopped infuriatingly into his eyes, blinding him until he pushed it aside impatiently. The green valley boasted several tracts of woodland, the huge trees handsome in their prime of summer foliage, and hazels coppiced between patches of cultivation and field, where cattle and sheep grazed peacefully.

To his left the spire of a church showed through trees, its tip gold where the sun caught it. There, then, was Stoke Sutton, about a mile away, he judged, and the rest of the village must be hidden from his view by the woodland. In the floor of the valley ran a sizeable stream, and he could easily trace its path even into the distance, for the banks were lined with pale grey-green willows dipping and distorted at the water's edge. Beside the stream was a small mill, the race foaming busily white and frothy even now as the mill-wheel turned slowly. A white chalk road ran along the water from Stoke Sutton village to the west. To Micheldever, he thought, holding the thumbed map in his mind's eye: and somewhere along that road to the right would be the road to Broadoak, home of Colonel Thomas Chadwicke. He knit his brows in puzzlement, trying to remember. To know the lay of the land as soon as possible would be vital if he was to be an assistance and not a liability dangerous to others as well as himself.

Basing was behind him, away over the hills, Alresford before him, and beyond Stoke Sutton the road led to Alton. . . . He sighed. At least he had now a vague idea of his whereabouts.

Along the chalk trackway a small party of cavalry rode two and two towards the village from the direction of Broadoak. The gusting wind brought to Nick's ears the clopping sound of the horses' hooves, and the psalm-singing voices of the men. The stallion snorted and whinnied a greeting to the mares in the valley. Nick patted its arched neck and chuckled. 'Steady, lad,' he said, 'we've enough to do without involving ourselves in that sort of trouble.' He led the restless creature back into the little knot of trees which crowned the hill. It was a time to look rather than to be looked at, he thought. And what he saw did not please him. The soldiers trotted tidily down the road, and even the unison of their voices gave an impression of well-ordered discipline; strange how one could tell these things, even at a distance. . . .

He heaved the horse's head up from the sweet turf from which it was reluctant to part, and climbed once more into the saddle, drawing his cloak close about his shoulders against the force of the wind. He set the chestnut to the steep sheep track down the hillside towards the road, his heart beating a racing gallop of excitement, and went to find the surgeon at Stoke Sutton. The dwelling of Master Harrington turned out to be on the very outskirts of the village, a half-timbered house in the old style, next to the churchyard and in amongst the trees which Nick had seen from the top of the hill. There was a flint wall around the house, with a wicket gate into the large and pleasant garden.

The gate clicked as Nick opened it, and a cacophony arose. The elms in the churchyard were populated by countless rooks, their nests black and spiky amongst the leaves, and one and all of them now took to the air and flapped about, squawking with gusto. Such a raucous chorus was clearly audible in the house, for a man appeared at the front door and came down the steps to see the cause of their concern. He was tall and spare, and it was hard to tell his age, for his darkly tanned face gave few clues to it. He was dressed in a suit of fine wool, and his wide white collar had a border of lace. He stood by the green clipped bay tree some two yards in front of the steps, his lean right hand lightly resting on the hilt of the long cruel rapier at his side, and Nick guessed that this must be the surgeon.

'Master Harrington?'

'Sir?' The grey eyes narrowed. There was an agreed form of introduction now, if this was the man. 'It is not often that we see strangers in this part of the world. Have you ridden far?' The man waited for the correct answer with a passionless stare.

'From Oxford. Safely, by the grace of God.'

The surgeon's face broke into a thin-lipped, one-sided smile. 'Master Howard, is it not? We were expecting you. Josh?'

A gangling, spotty youth came trotting round from the back of the building, touching his forelock to the two gentlemen.

'Take Master Howard's horse, and see it bestowed, lad.'

The boy grinned and took the bridle. 'I'll see to the bags for you, sir,' he said slowly. Then he turned to Harrington. 'Will I tell Matt that the gentleman has come?'

'Aye, and ask him to come by at seven if he can.'

'Will you come within doors, Master Howard, and be refreshed? I hope you will be comfortably lodged with us. My housekeeper is at this moment from home, but there will be dinner in an hour or so.'

The house was beautifully light and airy, and kept with methodical tidiness, for nothing seemed out of place: the fragrance of beeswax and lavender pervaded, and not a speck of dust could be seen. Harrington showed Nick to a spacious room with a dark oak bed in it. The bed-curtains and counterpane were of blue with white embroidered swans, and on the tiring-table already there was a jug of water and a bowl, to wash away the long journey's dust, and the saddle-bags reposed on the corner stool. On the windowsill a little rosemary tree grew in an earthenware pot to keep the air sweet in the old-fashioned way. The white walls shone in the sunshine, and Nick felt welcome in the house of Master Harrington.

He found his way downstairs into the large parlour where the surgeon awaited him, proffering a full glass. The windows were open to the sunlit garden and the Micheldever road, and green curtains stirred in the breeze. It was very quiet: so quiet that Nick could hear the bees busy on the verbena in the flower bed below until Harrington shut the casement, and pulled the parlour door to. Then the two men faced each other across the room, each wary, and anxious to come by the measure of the other. Nick wondered what the surgeon thought of him, as the grey eyes appraised him coolly.

'You have some good sentries there.' Nick smiled, as the rooks set up their unruly cackling again. The soldiers he had seen from the top of the hill were now retracing their steps past the flint-walled churchyard and the garden, leaving the village at a sober gathered trot, and they looked no less formidable from close to, Nick thought sadly.

'Aye. The rooks are our comrades. Several times they have been most useful: as you can imagine our need here is to be most secret.' Harrington's face carried a lip-curling sneer now. 'Chadwicke and his ilk are well thought of in these parts. Now, where to begin. . . . Here we have you, and I, and Rebecca, my housekeeper, who is a most resourceful creature, as well as a very good cook, I might add.' His face smiled now, and its relaxation made him look younger. Nick liked him instinctively. Here was a man after his own heart, he thought: no time lost, no wasted words, but taking up the task with both hands, and joyful to do so. 'We have also Joshua Jeffery, whom you have already met. He is a dependable lad. Lives over the stable here. His brother, Matthew, is the blacksmith in the village, and he also is with us. Both of them know the country around here extremely well, which will, I think, be a very present assistance to us while you are becoming acquainted with it. I was inclined, if you are agreeable, to take a stroll round the village while we have an hour to spare.'

'That sounds to me a most excellent idea. But there is one thing I should like to ask. Do you think it wiser for me to go by a different name? I wondered if you might think it expedient.'

'No, I think not. No point in complicating the issue. No one knows you here. And if they do, it will not matter a jot what you call yourself, for I think it will be your face will hang you. How did you come by that scar?'

'I met with an accident, in the shape of one Chadwicke.'

'Chadwicke?' Harrington blenched visibly. 'I was told that you had not crossed the colonel's path before.'

'Nor have I. This one was a captain, though his name was Thomas Chadwicke, also. It was Winchester, back in June. . . .'

'Oh, Christ!' Harrington sat down in the carved elbow-chair by the fireplace, suddenly, as if his legs were too weak to carry him. 'Was it your hand that killed Tom Chadwicke?'

'Yes. We had information, and he came upon us. . . .'

'I know all about the information. Was me that sent it,' Harrington said sharply, and looked him up and down again as if he could hardly believe what Nick had said.

'You must be a man to be reckoned with, friend. And a brave one if you stay here.' He sighed deeply and stretched his legs. 'If I were you,' he said with slow deliberation, 'I would get back to Oxford as fast as a horse could carry me: because if old Tom should by any mischance find you out, then he will tear you to pieces, personally, and with great joy. Young Tom was his only child.'

'I wish you had not told me that.' Nick smiled wanly at his host. 'I can hardly go back to Oxford, even if I wish to, can I? And surely it matters little. If I am caught, my Lord has already warned me that I shall die.'

Harrington's eyes narrowed, and his eyebrows twitched the merest fraction.

'There are ways . . . and ways, however,' he said drily, and rose once more from the chair. 'Will you come, then, to see Stoke Sutton, Master Howard?'

'My name is Nicholas.' He extended his hand. The warmth of friendship was already kindled between them.

'Well, Nicholas, my name is Nat.'

They spent an hour or more taking a gentle walk round the village. The row of cottages down one side of the green was white-washed, and the gardens had flowers and many bees. The green itself had several fine trees, and a large reedy pond which seemed to be fed from nowhere by a clear spring. It was alive with ducks and geese making contented noises as they foraged for tasty morsels, and chickens wandering among the tussocks, clucking and pecking.

On the opposite side of the grassy tract was another row of assorted dwellings, including a blacksmith's forge which stood somewhat apart from the rest, and from it came the clang of a working hammer.

'Matthew's very busy,' Harrington observed. 'It's blowing up for rain again.' He pointed a long arm up the street and towards the church. 'This way home, I think, and then you will have seen all.'

A small hostelry lay half way along the row of houses, and there was a coat-of-arms over the door, on a sign that creaked and protested in the freshening wind. Nick looked at it, puzzled because he did not recognise the blue and silver device on it. Harrington's eyes followed his and read the thoughts behind them. 'The Lovell arms,' he said briefly. 'The old squire here was Lovell. He used to own Broadoak . . . before. Judith, Chadwicke's wife, is his daughter. Phil was killed at Edgehill.' Nathaniel Harrington's face was oddly twisted.

The memory was clearly hurtful to him, and Nick felt like an intruder into the man's private grief. 'I'm sorry.'

'Don't be. Phil Lovell was a rebel, same as Chadwicke. But he was my . . . very dear friend, before the war. And my brother-in-law. Judy is my niece. Tom Chadwicke did very well out of that bargain. A lot better than he deserves.'

'I'd like to meet him.'

'You shall, soon enough.' Harrington marched off down the street, straight-backed, his long legs covering the ground at a brisk pace. Nat stopped in front of the church and waited for Nick to catch up.

'I should also warn you the parson here is another canting, snivelling, spying rebel rogue, and I do not trust him as far as the length of his own nose. That is the rectory, on the opposite side of the churchyard from us.'

'Thanks for the warning.' Nick looked at the ancient

twisted yew trees next to the rectory gate, and at the dark mystery of the rectory windows, and sighed heavily. There were so many things to remember. He must tread very carefully at first: just one mistake might well be too many.

Harrington's eyes regarded him sardonically, measuring him, he thought, against the difficulty of the task. 'You see?' he said softly. 'This enterprise needs extreme care, my young friend: but my Lord leads me to believe that you are the soul of discretion! Come, I think that it is well past dinner time. I will take you through the back way; with care, you will learn not to disturb our black-coated sentinels.'

He entered the yard at the back of the house through a tall side gate which opened noiselessly on well-oiled hinges. 'We keep this gate locked, for the most part, from the inside. But it is left open when there is occasion.'

Nick grinned. 'You have all well considered. I wonder that you need me at all.'

Nathaniel's smile faded. 'We need you. Make no mistake. There's a mighty parcel of rogues hereabouts. Come here, and I'll show you the stable.'

The chestnut whickered greeting from the first stall. Next to it there was a fine black, and an empty stall, and then two sturdy bay cobs, shining, smug and well fed. Josh emerged from the last stall, a bucket in his hand.

'Matt says he might be late. Had a hard day.'

The two men went into the house through the heavy back door. It opened into a large low-ceilinged kitchen, bright with scrubbed wooden table and benches, and a red-tiled floor which was spotless. The walls were hung with an array of heavy cooking pots and utensils, and the whole room was warm and steaming and full of appetising smells. Nick's stomach awoke with a lurch, reminding him forcibly that he had not eaten since yesterday and that he was ravenously hungry. A grey-clad woman bent near the fire, stirring at a pot of something boiling, and rose, pink-faced, to greet them. She was taller than Nick, only an inch, perhaps, shorter than the tall, lanky surgeon. She was handsome, and her hair under her cap was black as a rook's wing.

'This, Nicholas,' Harrington said, 'is my most excellent

housekeeper, Rebecca. 'Becca, this is Master Howard, from Oxford.'

'I am very glad to see you, sir,' she said, looking down at him, and then at the surgeon. 'I hope you haven't been flogging him too hard already, Nat Harrington.' She laughed a bubbling laugh, and Harrington looked somewhat abashed.

'You will have to get used to 'Becca,' he said, by way of explanation. 'She has a habit of speaking her mind most forthrightly.'

'And you, Master Howard, look in need of a good meal. Dinner has been ready this past half-hour, so I will be serving it if you two gentlemen are set, for I've no desire to see it spoil, and Matthew will be here directly.'

At dinner the conversation was all of codes and ciphers, until Nick's head swam with numbers and instructions.

Nathaniel sipped claret, and eyed Nick quizzically over the rim of the glass. 'Did William Robinson supply you as he was asked?'

'Yes. And gave me a little honest amusement, I'll confess.'

'An endearing sort of character, our Willy. A coward born and bred, and yet a fine surgeon and physician.'

'They will need one soon.'

'Surely. Norton has already made one brief essay with a couple of troops of horse. And no doubt there's more to come shortly. But I think that Matthew will be in a better way to tell you more of my Lord Marquis' affairs. What concerns me just now is how I shall make a surgeon of you overnight. It is a considerable problem.'

'The garrison surgeon at Marlborough has been at some pains to instruct me this past week. He assures me that I know enough to pass me off as a surgeon, except perhaps to another one. So I hope there is your problem solved already.'

'Oh, most excellent thoughtful! I think that you and I shall work well together my friend.' Harrington's one-sided smile lit up his narrow face and deepened the wrinkles at the outer corners of his eyes. The back door shut softly. 'That, if I mistake not, will be Matthew Jeffery.'

Rebecca's white-capped head appeared round the door of the parlour.

'Send him in, 'Becca. And you and Josh will watch for us?'

'Yes, Master Nat. . . . Just as soon as I've fetched a mutton pasty for Matthew. Will you go in, now, Master Jeffery?'

A stocky, somewhat older and more powerful version of Josh appeared, clad in an ancient leather jump-coat and venerable boots, looking spent. Nathaniel pushed a chair forward.

'Sit down, lad. You look finished.'

'Been pushed,' was the cryptic reply, as the brawny blacksmith flopped into the seat. 'Went to Basing last night to see Ned.'

'Becca came to place a jug of ale and a large pasty in front of Matthew, and was at once gone again.

'Who's he?' the smith asked without ceremony.

'This is Nicholas Howard, Matthew. One of His Majesty's intelligencers.'

Matt nodded cursorily and took a thirsty gulp from his mug.

'Norton and Harvey,' he said, 'are at Basing already.'

'They were there two weeks since.'

'Aye, with a rabble. But now they've two regiments, one dragoons, one foot, and they are taking the matter very serious, Captain Nat.'

Nick gaped. Nathaniel looked hard at Matthew.

'That is bad news, Matt. Has the garrison enough ammunition? How are they placed for supplies?'

'What garrison? My Lord hath no more than a dozen loyal gentlemen and their servants with him. Plenty of arms, they have, ammunition and food, but no men.'

'But my Lord said he would send a garrison from Oxford. . . . He wrote and told me!'

'Not arrived yet, Captain Nat,' Matthew said flatly. 'Long march from Oxford for foot-soldiers. Ned says they've already pushed them off once, but the rebels are all dug in round the park paling, and they're bound to make an assault in force before long.'

'So by the time our men get there it will be all over,' Nat sighed.

'Ned says they've a couple of drakes on the hall roof and

will take a few with them. They'll not let the bastards have it easy. But a couple of dozen cannot hold that place, surely to God?'

Nat Harrington cursed quietly and most emphatically, and for a moment he was silent. 'I told Judith that I would be over tomorrow morning. But I fear she'll have to wait. Josh shall take my excuse to the colonel, and we must be off to see what's to be done. Did Edward have anything else to say?'

'Most of it weren't repeatable in company,' Matthew growled grimly. 'But he said it'd help if they knew which side they was going to concentrate on. He was wondering if you could let them know somehow.' He munched stolidly at the pasty.

'He doesn't want much, does he?' Nat laughed bitterly at Matthew.

The latter inclined his head a fraction and looked at Nick with palpable hostility. 'So what does His Majesty's intelligencer have to say?' he asked, his mouth full. Nick gulped.

'That is a trifle hard on me, Master Jeffery. I am scarcely in a position to offer a great deal of constructive advice.' He racked his brains for something intelligent to say, and suddenly a dreadful thought dawned on him. 'Have the rebels got any great guns? Culverin, or demi-cannon, or anything? If they have then I think we must be lost. Who is this man Ned you keep talking about?'

'My brother, sir. The oldest of us Jefferys. One of my Lord Marquis' men at Basing House.'

'You saw him last night? Spoke to him?'

'Aye.'

'So you can actually get in to the house?'

'With difficulty, yes.' It was Nathaniel's voice which answered him. 'I can imagine it will be well-nigh impossible with Norton's men round the place in such numbers. I hope you can swim, Nicholas Howard?'

'Oh, Lord. Just about. Now, Matthew. Have they got cannon?'

'No . . . I think not, sir. But I couldn't get near enough to be absolutely sure. I was – afraid of being taken – sir.'

Matthew was subdued and half apologetic now, for Nick's tone did not invite mockery.

'You've done well, Matthew.'

'Will you be wanting me to go with you, sir, tomorrow?'

'I think it better not, perhaps. In broad daylight such an expedition is best undertaken by those who will arouse least suspicion. Your place is here, in your smithy, as usual. But we'll see what we can do to help your brother and his comrades, never fear!'

'Aye, that we will, Matt. Put your mind at rest. I'm thinking that Master Howard here will not be beaten so easily.'

'Will need a miracle,' Matt said, dolefully, and his eyes rose to Nick's face. 'You good at performing miracles, sir?'

Nick laughed, with a hearty joviality he did not feel. 'Make a habit of it,' he said. 'You'll see.'

Rebecca came. 'Looks like a funeral in here,' she pronounced. 'Has the corpse been decently interred? I take it all is not well?'

'Far from it, I fear. Colonel Norton's hell-hounds are even now braying at my Lord Winchester's throat. You were right about guns, Nicholas. . . . If they have guns, the castle will be lost.' Harrington rasped his blue jowl with his thumb and looked at the darkening sky.

Rebecca stood still for a full minute. 'I think I heard something today . . .' she said suddenly, much to Nick's surprise. 'Though I know nothing of military matters, you know that. But when I went to Broadoak today to take those things to . . . Mistress Chadwicke, the colonel had a letter brought. From Colonel Norton, it was. He was asking for some guns or other . . . cul . . . culverin?' her tongue stumbled over the unfamiliar word.

'Yes, yes?' Nat was saying impatiently. 'Culverin. . . . Go on.'

'He was talking to that captain – whatever his name is – you know the one?'

'Oh, God, 'Becca, tell us, do. It matters not which one of the rogues it was, but I'll wager it was Atkins.'

'Yes, that's him. Anyway, he's sent Captain Atkins to

Portsmouth, to bring them culverin. For breaking the walls at Basing, they are.'

'Oh, 'Becca, you are as clever as you are beautiful, and worth your weight in gold!'

Rebecca glowed almost visibly at his praise and smiled like a shy sixteen-year-old.

'You will be careful? You'll get short shrift from those wicked rogues!'

Nick saw that Rebecca held Nathaniel in something that was more than mere esteem: and it was also painfully clear that he was totally oblivious of it. Rebecca flushed guiltily as she saw Nick's eyes upon her. It was very sad, he thought. Why did people always make each other so unhappy?

'Don't fuss, 'Becca. We shall not be damaged. They'll be glad enough to see us, if the boys at the loopholes do their work. Now, will you be so good as to send Josh to me? I've a message for the colonel at Broadoak.'

She went without a word. Nathaniel turned to Nick once more.

'Well, what think you?'

'I think that we must stop those culverin, Nathaniel.'

'We do not even know when they are coming.'

'Then tomorrow we must find out.'

'More than one miracle, eh?' Nat laughed savagely. 'Oh, I wish that I had your confidence, Nicholas!' He raised his glass and winked slowly and with great dignity. 'A toast, Nicholas Howard. To your very good health, and mine. And to a miracle for Basing.'

9

A VISIT TO BASING

Next morning, Rebecca was already busy in the kitchen, and she greeted Nick genially as he came down the stairs. 'My, you are up betimes!' Master Nat is not abroad yet. He's not so good at waking in the mornings. Says it's old age!'

'Old age? Good God, he's hardly old enough to be in a decline!'

'Two and forty he is, you know! Though do not let on that I told you so! It's not a great age, though I suppose it must seem so to you, for you're scarce out of petticoats yourself.' Nick felt himself blushing, and glowered out from under the flopping hair on his forehead. She sighed. 'I only hope that you are old enough to deal with discretion in the matters you have taken up.'

'I'm old enough to die, if that's what you mean. And there will be someone to replace me, I've no doubt. Though I must say I hope I won't be called upon just yet!'

'God forbid, Master Nicholas, that either of you should!'

'There would be no replacement for him, I know that.'

'Please . . . let's not talk like that. Will you have bacon for breakfast? And I've some bread fresh from the oven.'

'I see,' he winked at the pink visage with its look of motherly benevolence, and smiled roguishly. 'So I shall be too full of wind to turn and run, eh? Have to stay and hang, that's all.' He settled himself on the bench by the table and she poured small-beer into the mug before him.

'It makes a change to have someone cheerful about the place in the morning. Master Nat is scarce human until ten of the clock, as a rule.'

'Is that a gentle warning? Thanks for it.'

'Bless you, no. . . . Well, I suppose in a way it is. Can be very testy at times, but don't you take no heed to it. You're a nice lad, Nicholas Howard.'

'Don't worry, Rebecca. I won't let anything happen to him, not if I can do something to prevent . . .'

'Lord love you, Master Nicholas. 'Tis not a question of letting anything happen. He's a grown man with a mind of his own, and a habit of doing foolhardy things. And I'd like to meet the one who's man enough to stop him.' She sighed philosophically, but her eyes shone with unhappiness, and her smile was awry.

'Or woman enough?' Nick said, and she was pinker than ever.

'I'm sorry. It's just that I . . . we all . . . think a lot of him.'

'I can see that.'

'What about you? I'll wager there's some lass somewhere eating her heart out over your absence.' She laughed. 'Pretty lad like you.'

'Not for me there isn't. Not that I know of.' It was Nick's turn to make a grimace and shrug his shoulders.

'Another carefree bachelor, is it? With many girls left sighing.'

'Not even that, I'm afraid. Just a sober, jaded old widower with a small daughter on my mind.' There was still the knotty problem of keeping in touch with Aunt Nan without writing directly to her. The less contact there was, then the better it might be if he should get caught: but he would find it hard to rest easy without news.

Rebecca's face was full of contrition, her hand stretched out to his, and her voice soft with pity. 'Oh, please forgive my unruly tongue. I've a habit of saying things hastily and ill-considered, and causing people pain. . . .'

'Pain? Oh, no, Rebecca, I'm not upset. In fact you have given me a very good idea. . . . Do you write letters, ever?'

By the time Nathaniel had stumbled sleepily down to the

kitchen, the problem was solved. Rebecca would write gossipy domestic letters to Aunt Nan, and if there was any news, then Aunt Nan could write back: it would be safer so, and a great weight was lifted from his mind.

Nathaniel stood in the doorway, yawning and scratching his head. 'Why the hell did someone not wake me up before now? We've a lot to do, and half the day is gone already! What's for breakfast? And what have you two been plotting? You look as close as a couple of poachers.' He sat down heavily on the edge of the bench, almost missing it. Rebecca and Nick exploded with laughter. 'It's all right for you,' growled Nat. 'There's the bags to be packed, and can you ask Josh to saddle the cobs?'

Rebecca wiped her streaming eyes on the corner of her apron and made for the door. 'The bags are packed, and the horses should be ready by now, I'll make sure. It's time that Josh fetched me some more water, anyway.'

' 'Becca, you're an angel,' said Nat to her back, with his mouth full of bread.

In less than an hour the two of them were on the road to Basing. Nat drew off the road into a hazel coppice on the top of a ridge looking down to the valley of the Loddon. Nick gasped. The house stood many-towered and turreted in a bend in the river, entwined in marshes and meres. A tall brick curtain-wall surrounded it, and to the north and west the lake and river were its protection.

'What do you think of my Lord Marquis' little place, eh?' Nat laughed softly.

'Incredible. I see why you were so anxious to know if I could swim. Though I do not see any doors?' Nick shook his head.

'You cannot see them from here. The main gate and the drawbridge are on the other side. There are two sally-ports into the meadow there, though the wall curves in such a way that we cannot see them. But I think there are those in the park there who can.' Nat indicated the flat tract of meadowland between the ridge where they stood, and the house. It was alive with orange-sashed soldiers. As if from out of the ground, an army began to appear before the house, the men swarming from the ditches they had dug, like ants from a half-excavated ant-hill; but unlike ants, they formed up immediately into orderly lines.

'Here's the attack, I fear,' said Nat, cursing passionately. 'The garrison now knows well enough from which direction it comes. There's naught we can do from here to aid them.'

Nick's heart sank like lead. 'Matthew said they had only a score or so of men to defend the place. They'll not do it.'

'They've drakes on the roof, don't forget. Perhaps we can go in later.'

'How do we get in, pray?'

'Across the lake. There is the culvert gate, if you know where to find it. Do not worry too much about swimming, it is shallow enough to wade: though there is less to be seen and shot at if you swim. Christ, look at those men there!' There were musketeers firing now, not raggedly, but in well-disciplined volleys, with the purpose of giving cover to their pikemen. 'And from the village also.'

Nick felt depressed and overwhelmed at this turn of events. Would they now be forced to stand by, helpless, and watch the house fall like a ripe plum into the lap of the enemy? Nat stiffened perceptibly, and there was warning in his eyes. His voice was suddenly very loud in the still coppice.

'Let us go down, then, and see what we can do to aid the wounded,' he said, and then hissed swiftly to Nick, 'Ride, we have company!'

Nat turned his horse back to the road. Nick stayed for a moment gaping, and then followed, but neither of them reached the track before a dozen horse-soldiers were up with them, and their way was blocked. Nat's eyes showed not a flicker of concern, but cast about for who should be their leader, and addressed him firmly. 'Corporal? I demand to know the meaning of this.'

'Meaning, sir? Why, I should say the meaning must be clear.'

The corporal spoke courteously, in a slow, countryman's voice, deep and good natured, as if he was explaining some basic truth to a small child. 'Why, we are taking you into charge, sir, for our captain gave us orders so to detain anyone we should find a-spying on us.'

'Your captain may hang,' said Nat, with feeling. 'I demand to see Colonel Norton.'

The corporal's face looked vaguely uneasy. 'Why, so you shall, sir, if my captain should say the word.'

'I can assure you that Colonel Norton and I are well acquainted. And he will be glad to see me, for I am a surgeon, and so is my friend here. You may look there in our bags if you doubt me.' He waved enthusiastically at the saddle-bags, packed lovingly by Rebecca that morning with all the tools of their horrid trade. Nick said nothing.

'Follow me,' said the corporal, doggedly, but not lacking a certain air of entreaty, as if he expected them to refuse. They followed dutifully in the wake of their captor and drew up on the edge of the green marshy tract before Basing House, where Norton's men were dug in. The attack seemed to be proceeding steadily, for the musketeers stood firm in three ranks, firing turn and turn about, while the pikemen advanced towards the impassive walls. Nathaniel and Nicholas stood side by side, watched from a respectful distance by four troopers with drawn swords.

'Did you say you were a friend of Norton's?' Nick whispered incredulously.

'I said I was acquainted with him, not a friend of his. There is a difference.'

'Is there anyone of note within a twenty-mile radius with whom you are not acquainted?'

'Probably not.' Nat smiled with bland modesty. 'Though I must confess,' he added balefully, 'that of late there seem to be more enemies than allies.'

The corporal came forward, together with the captain, and they conferred together with much head-nodding and hand-waving.

'Forward you two. To the trenchments there. Colonel Norton wishes to see you.'

Colonel Norton of Southwick stood in the foremost trench with several of his officers, watching the progress of his men towards the two sally-ports. The men carried picks and poll-axes and roughly hewn logs, as well as their pikes, and they were purposing to batter down the doors. The walls remained more or less silent, apart from the occasional musket-shot as the defenders tried to pick off as many of the officers as they could hit. But the drakes on the roof were telling, Nick was pleased to see. Someone up there had a sharp eye and a good aim and only fired when he was sure, so that they were falling a rank at a time. The guns themselves could hardly be seen from such a low viewpoint. They were nestling safely somewhere among the abundance of turrets and chimneys, and the high ramparts effectively blocked the view of anyone standing below. The colonel sported a plumed helmet which would have graced any field-marshal of the King's army. Harrington bowed and greeted the figure warily, like a cautious fencer saluting a wily opponent.

'My dear Colonel Norton, I would be obliged if you would call your yapping dogs away!'

'Master Harrington! I did not think to see you here! I do not know your friend.'

'Allow me, sir, to present to you a fellow healer, Master Howard. We have come in order to succour your wounded, for we were told that there was fighting.'

Nicholas bowed stiffly. Norton acknowledged him gravely and turned back to Nathaniel.

'I have here my own regimental surgeon, Master Harrington. I am surprised to hear that you are so solicitous for the welfare of my men, for I should have thought your sympathies were elsewhere?'

Nick bit his tongue sharply. So Norton knew Harrington for a Royalist. They were finished before they had begun. But Nat was more than equal to the occasion.

'My sympathies are certainly elsewhere, I do not deny it. But I am a surgeon: and I think that politics matter little to a man who has a bullet in his belly. Perhaps one day I may remind you of that? And Nicholas is my assistant, who has come to help. Any man from Stoke Sutton will tell you that.'

Norton looked him up and down and smiled. Harrington's chin jutted aggressively, and he looked as if he would willingly have struck the smiling face, but he said nothing. It was Richard Norton who broke the uneasy silence.

'All the men of Stoke Sutton seem willing to aid us this day, Master Harrington. For here also we have the rector of St Peter's. Master Preston has even now been inspiring us with his fine preaching.'

The preacher half stood, half crouched in the trench a few feet away, a sorry figure in muddy gown and very rumpled Geneva bands, striving to keep his balding head as low as possible so that he would not make a target for the Basing marksmen. So this was the long-nosed parson Nat had warned him of. Nick stared curiously at the wispy little man with the watery eyes, and found it hard to restrain his laughter, for a bright pink pointed nose was indeed the most prominent feature of Master Preston, and it made him look very much like a white mouse.

There was an undecided wavering of the men before the house as the officer who had been leading them reeled and fell, clutching at a blood-soaked leg. Another shot from one of the drakes ploughed half a dozen of them to the ground. A few men broke from the line and fled, and the others followed, leaping back into the ditch to lie panting and cowering under the cover of the earthworks.

The colonel sighed heavily. 'Very well, Master Harrington. There is a number of wounded at St Mary's.' He glanced at the fire-spitting church in Basing village. 'But your friend I would rather have here under my eye, for I know him not. My own surgeon is here, and will need help, no doubt. Master Preston? I think perhaps a little more encouragement is needed . . . ?'

The parson rose full on his feet and began to call upon the Lord for assistance at the top of his voice, shaking his bony fists at the battlements. Isaiah, Nick thought, as he rolled up his shirtsleeves. The sing-song voice rose to the sky, which was a sullen grey now, as if it, too, disliked Basing House. 'And I will camp against thee round about and will lay siege against thee with a mount, and I will raise forts against thee. And thou shalt be brought down to speak out of the ground . . . and thy speech shall be low out of the dust.'

A bullet from a sharp-shooting defender deprived Colonel Norton's splendid helmet of its proud plume. Harrington winked gleefully at Nick. 'I shall be away to St Mary's,' he said. 'It grows warm here.'

Nick shuddered as another bullet sang past. If there was one thing worse than being shot at, it was being shot at by your own side. He took the tools the corporal fetched for him and began to work on the nearest casualty with obstinate determination. The men were once more moving forward out of the trench, and Colonel Norton was giving orders for petards to be brought up to the doors, to blow them in. Nick tried harder than ever to concentrate on what he was doing. He could feel Norton's suspicious eyes boring into his back, and it made him nervous.

The rector of Stoke Sutton droned on mercilessly, raving at the deaf walls of Basing House. 'Thou shalt be visited of the Lord of Hosts with thunder and with earthquake and great noise, with storm and tempest and the flame of devouring fire . . . !'

Great noise was right, thought Nick. The preacher ranted, the man before him cried in pain, and through it all the steady, slow voice of the sergeant of musketeers chanted its clockwork litany. 'Bring up your muskets . . . take your aim . . . front rank . . . fire!' Another crash echoed as the volley went thumping harmlessly into the brickwork, for surely they could scarcely hope to aim successfully at the men behind the loopholes? The acrid smoke billowed chokingly in the sultry air of afternoon, and the first petard went up with a roar as the man who fixed it sprinted for his life away from the gate.

Nick went on to the next man, willing himself not to look, and praying that they had not made a breach. Norton watched him still, as if he would search his soul for its contents. He had to look. There was no breach, thank God; and the others were pulling back because they could not make the petard fast to the other door. The returning rebels brought back with them as many of their wounded as they could drag, but a few were left lying in the park, and the rebel surgeon dodged the bullets as he worked.

Norton was at Nick's shoulder. 'Are you not going out there to aid those others?'

'I've plenty to do here, thank you, colonel. I'm afraid heroism is not my particular gift. And he's due *6s 8d* a day army pay for doing it. I'm not.'

'But you're a surgeon.'

'Not an army surgeon. I'm not risking my neck out there for King, Parliament, or Lord of Hosts. I'm sorry, colonel.' To his surprise, Norton began to laugh. 'Do you know, Master Howard, I had half a mind that you were a malignant? But I do believe you may be honest after all.' Nick grinned mirthlessly, and Norton turned away.

'St Barbe, go to Colonel Harvey at The Falcon, bid him to draw off. I think that we'd best bide our time. On Sunday we should have the culverin to aid us. Then we shall see about my Lord Marquis' papistical fortress!'

Nick's hand shook as he probed for the bullet for which he was searching, and two brawny pikemen held his writhing victim steady. Sunday, then, the guns were to arrive. Today was Friday, so there was no time to stop them, except tomorrow. It had to be tomorrow. . . . Nick swatted the horsefly that was busy biting his left arm and rose to his feet, sweating in the hot, smelly stuffiness of the ditch.

'By your leave, Colonel Norton?'

'Yes, Master Howard?'

'I should like to take these poor men back to Basing and see if Harrington needs any help.'

'That sounds reasonable to me. But I doubt you will find Harrington over-burdened. There was little to do on that side. Though they have some good marksmen in there,' he added balefully.

'Evidently,' Nick said, trying to keep his gaze and his voice steady, despite his growing fear of Colonel Norton's perception. 'I wonder, sir, if your own surgeon is able to manage now? I think that we would as soon be back in Stoke Sutton before darkness.'

'You are very subtle, Master Howard. I have no authority to detain you. Go take your malignant friend out of my way, and keep him from mischief.'

Norton's face still bore its mildly amused smile, and Nick's hand itched to wipe it from his face for ever: but he bowed slightly, and smiled the old lying smile of innocence and friendship, and turned on his heel to supervise the loading of the carts. The preacher sat in exhausted dejection on a heap of earth, wiping his perspiring brow with an extremely discoloured kerchief; but Norton was at the cart-tail, giving cheery words of comfort and hope to the men in pain, and Nick could not help admiring him, for the men clearly worshipped him. Nick trudged back to the horse lines to find the bay cob, and rode back, depressed, through the small stand of trees to Basing village.

Nat was propping up the front door of The Falcon and swilling ale with several of his Roundhead acquaintances, and he hailed Nick loudly and ostentatiously. 'Nicholas! I see you have been well occupied?'

Nick dismounted wearily. 'There has been a good deal of slaughter, yes,' he said and felt light-headed suddenly, wanting to laugh now and shout with glee that Norton's men had been stopped in their tracks. 'Those drakes on the roof,' he continued, 'have wrought damage and to spare.'

Nat drew him aside. 'Did you manage, lad?'

'Norton said we can go. They are going to wait for culverin before they attack again. Sunday he said they would be here.'

'Well done, Nick. I knew Norton would be eating out of your hand! Now we must get to the house before dark.'

'Before dark? Oh, God, you mean we go now, in broad daylight, with Norton's men watching?'

'I'm afraid we must. Matthew can do it in the dark, but I would not risk it on my own, let alone with . . .' He stopped suddenly, embarrassed, and shrugged apologetically. 'I'm sorry, I did not mean . . .'

'Don't apologise. A hindrance like me, I know. Truth it is, and I'm sorry, too.'

'You must follow closely my instructions. First, we must make off as if for home, and be sure that there is no one following. . . .'

The thought that Norton might send someone to follow them made Nick very uneasy indeed, and he was still uneasy when, having crept past the gloom-absorbed sentries, he found himself with Nat at the water's edge an hour and a half later. The air was still and sultry, and clouds of small flies hovered over the surface of the open water. It was deathly quiet there, and every small sound seemed to shatter the silence. Even the fish breaking the surface to catch flies made resounding plopping noises, and scattered ripples on the dark grey water. Nick stood amid the bracken and twisted trees on the lake edge, his heart thumping in his throat as if it would emerge at any moment. He looked at Nat, and wondered if behind that lean, weather-beaten face, Nat was afraid, too. The water seemed miles wide.

Nathaniel went down deliberately into the rotting reeds of the margin and beckoned Nick to follow, crouching low among the mottled green-brown stems and the untidy flower-heads of the rushes. The stirred water became muddy, and the disturbed waterfowl made off in squawking, noisy panic. Nathaniel and Nicholas cowered in the water while the two sentries on the bank walked past, peering into the bent grey alders at the lake-brim. They met, conferred briefly, concluded that a hungry fox must be prowling . . . and returned to their posts, two hundred paces apart.

Nat launched forward for the edge of the reed-patch with exaggerated care. Nick's knees trembled already with the effort of preventing himself from being bogged in the soft ooze of the lake-bed. To his unspeakable horror, he found that the murky water was full of looping, fat horse-leeches.

'Now. If you can, safer to swim.'

The muddy water swirled horribly about Nick's face as he struck out into the open water, his mouth tightly shut so he would not swallow any of it. He aimed for the sedge-covered margin of bank under the walls and tried hard not to splash. His ears strained to hear the sounds of alarm which he expected at any moment, and his body waited tensely for the bullet from the shore, or worse still, perhaps, one from the wall. . . . But they both reached the land and crawled out, much bedraggled.

'The gate is a few yards along. Keep flat. Not a word until we are inside.'

Nick nodded in silent misery as, shivering with cold and every limb aching with cramp, he wriggled behind Nat at the very base of the tall defences, and knew why God had condemned the serpent to crawl for ever on his belly. They came to a grille let into the wall at its foot, and a small pit in the ground concealed a stone that was not just a stone, but a door. Nat edged close to the grille and spoke in a whisper so loud that Nick glanced over his shoulder to the distant trenchments.

'Hey, within!' said Nat. 'Is that you, Ned? Open up for mercy's sake!'

'Who is it?'

'Nat Harrington. And a friend to see my Lord.'

'God's mercy! In broad daylight? Don't budge till I've the gate open.'

The stone ground aside smoothly, and Nat disappeared head first through the yard-square opening. Nick slithered after him at great speed and breathed a sigh of relief to be safe as the stone once more slid shut after him. Nat was shaking himself like a half-drowned water-spaniel, his teeth chattering.

'I did not think to see you, Captain Nat.' It was Edward Jeffery, Nick could see, for the likeness between the three brothers was unmistakable. And Edward stared at him with curiosity. 'This friend for my Lord?'

'From the King. My Lord is expecting him, I think. We've been out there all day. . . . You are doing great works, here.'

Ned Jeffery laughed. 'My Lord is on the bowling green, taking his exercise. He'll not change his custom for Beelzebub himself.'

Nick gaped in astonishment. There were not more than a dozen men standing to arms around the walls: and here was the Marquis of Winchester and several other exquisitely dressed gentlemen, playing at bowls on the neat green. Nick felt a rush of admiration for these people who could keep up such a brave show of ease and gallantry when at any moment they might be destroyed . . . and all of it after holding at bay a small army for the best part of a day. . . .

'Good,' said Nat. 'The whole family of Paulets is here for the sacrifice, it would seem: and we are a couple of crawling beasts out of the morass.' They went down the stone steps leading to the bowling green, sticky with lake ooze, and even the grinning gargoyles on the pillars snarled silently at them as they passed. But Lord Winchester politely ignored their appearance, extending his gracious hand in its musk-perfumed glove to greet them.

'Major Howard, I am honoured to make your acquaintance. And much indebted to you, for I think you have taken a grave risk to be here tonight. My brother, Lord Edward, and my cousins, Sir John and Colonel Augustus.'

The gentlemen bowed as one and smiled carefree smiles. And Nick knew that they were all scared half out of their wits.

'Not waste your time with manners!' Nat whispered urgently.

'Have you lost many men, my Lord?'

'One dead, I fear, and two wounded, though not mortally, I am told.'

'How many left?'

'Er . . . forty-one, I believe?' He glanced at Lord Edward, who assented with the slightest of nods. 'And of course William the surgeon, and the women.'

The marquis might have been discussing the weather, for his voice was sweet and calm.

'Norton says he intends to wait until Sunday before he attacks again. Though I would not take that on trust.'

'It's a damnable bore,' observed Lord Edward Paulet. 'But I suppose it will be nice to rest until Sunday.'

'It seems likely that they will have culverin, from Portsmouth, arriving on Sunday.'

Colonel Augustus whistled, but the marquis remained impassive.

'They will find the walls thick enough,' he said.

'Do you think your precious walls can stand up to that sort of hammering?' Colonel Augustus looked white behind his abundance of sandy beard.

'We are hoping,' said Nick, with several pairs of anxious eyes upon him, 'to postpone their arrival somewhat . . . preferably until you have a garrison here, so that if they breach the walls, you will have men to defend.'

'And how, may I ask, are you proposing to do that?' asked Lord Edward, wrinkling his nose as if there was a bad smell before it.

Nick sighed. There quite probably was a bad smell before it, because the mud was messy and green, but he did not like Edward Paulet, for some reason.

'You have, perhaps, an army of your own?' laughed Colonel Augustus, in good-natured mockery.

'We have four men. It will do. That is not your problem,' said Nick, and Lord Edward raised his ginger eyebrows.

'We have plenty of others,' he observed.

'Was that you shooting plumes off Norton's helmet, earlier on?' Nat grinned at Lord Edward, and he smiled like a schoolboy. 'Plumes? Yes! It was Norton, was it? I thought it might be. Great sport! Pity that brown-bill throws a bit high, or I might have solved all our problems at one stroke!' So Edward Paulet would finish the war single-handed, and be a hero. Nick made a wry face and hoped suddenly that Edward Paulet would get his foolish head shot off in the process. . . .

'Must go. Before it's dark,' Nat said, glancing at the gathering shadows, and the last glimmer of the sinking sun between the clouds. Nick bit off an angry retort to Lord Edward and continued.

'I know not when your reinforcements are coming.'

'Neither do I,' the marquis said drily. 'The Lord God only knoweth. However, we would be much comforted if we thought that someone could get to Colonel Peake and tell him to make all speed.' Lord Winchester sounded vaguely irritated.

'Colonel Peake? Your garrison-to-be?'

'Yes, Major Howard.'

'I'll see it done. Rest assured we shall do all that we can to aid you.'

'I do not doubt it. I bid you both God-speed.'

Nat was already there at the wall with his long, raking

stride, and Nick was forced to sprint after him. For his part, he decided, he was glad he did not have to sit and wait as they did at Basing House. He must make for them a miracle. He followed Nat through the culvert gate to cross once more the yawning void of festering water, under the cover of approaching twilight. As he launched himself into the water he smiled, for through his mind there ran the lilting tune of Lucy's 'froggy song'. 'It was a frog leaped into a pool. . . .'

10

CHADWICKE OF BROADOAK

'Oh, Lord,' said Nat, in tones of mild exasperation. 'I must be a half-wit to play the fool with all these midnight foul-deeds at an age when I ought to know better.'

'We're nearly home. What ails you?' Nick laughed at his groaning companion.

'I'm wet, I'm cold, I'm dog-tired, my bones are aching all over, and I've no one to blame save myself,' was the weary rejoinder. 'Thank God 'tis only a couple of miles: I thought I would never get out of that rancid slime!'

'I can assure you that you've no monopoly of aching bones or weariness, Nat. I shall be glad to rest.'

'Rest? You'll not be resting! You said that you would send a message to Colonel Peake, and I'm not going, I can tell you! Christ, it's cold!'

'I'm not going to Peake, either. I was going to send Josh. He wanted to help this morning, he was sadly disappointed that we would not let him come: and he'd be better able to find the way.'

'Send a lad like that? Boy's only eighteen. It's a heavy burden for such young shoulders. Supposing he was caught? I would rather he was sadly disappointed than sadly dead.'

Josh was in the yard before the gate clicked shut behind them, rubbing his sleepy eyes in the light of the hazy quarter moon. Rebecca, too, was still awake, and Nick saw her peering white at them through the kitchen window.

'Will you write to Peake?' Nick said to Nathaniel. 'And I will help to unsaddle the beasts.'

'I can manage, Master Nicholas!' Josh protested.

'It's quicker with both of us, Josh. Then I want you to saddle up the chestnut, for I've an important errand for you.'

'For me?'

'Aye. There's a letter I'd like delivered.'

Nick felt guilty. Josh's face lit up with a shining smile of surprise and delight. He would offer his life gladly now, before he knew what dying was all about. It was so easy for the young to be heroic. . . .

When they went in, the letter was ready and waiting in the kitchen with Nathaniel. Josh stood in the rushlight's flickering glow, wide awake now, his eyes glittering with excited anticipation.

'I want you to take the road to Oxford,' Nick said. 'Somewhere north of Basing there will be troops on the road: Colonel Peake and his men, bound for the house. Give him this. For the love of God, make haste to it, and straight back. Stop for nothing, and be secret. If the rebels find that letter on you, it will be a hempen halter for certain.'

'Yes, sir. I'll do my best for you,' Josh said, resolutely. Nick looked at the determined face and felt remorse.

'It's not for me, Josh: but for the King, and the marquis, and all the brave men in Basing House. Now, off with you.'

Morning was sunny and warm like July should be, and they set off for Broadoak after breaking their fast, though both of them were still weary after yesterday: Nat ashen-faced, and Nick still gummy-eyed and sleepy with the sun on his back, as they rode out along the green valley into which Nick had gazed only two days before from the top of the down. Already he seemed to have been here for a lifetime. So many places he had seen lately, he thought, and belonged to none of them. He had become an outsider, a wandering mischief-maker who shattered the peace wherever he went, and took the war with him on his saddle-bow. But the valley here was as yet undisturbed: the clear, spring-fed stream sped along over its smooth, stony bed, foaming where the mill-wheel churned. The water here was quite deep, the legacy of the recent ample rains washing and gurgling around the knotted green-grey roots of the willow trees entwined on the bank.

Nick watched the water, fascinated, for a moment, and then drew up suddenly. He had an idea.

Nat was still peevish from being dragged too early from his bed and impatient up ahead; he was making restless noises and looking beseechingly at the sky. He restrained himself for a few moments, but before long his patience ran out.

'What are you mooning over? I should have thought you had seen enough water yesterday?'

'Do you know anything about guns?'

'A little. Why?'

'Just supposing Colonel Norton's culverin should have an unfortunate accident, and fall into the water?'

'Be a hell of a job to get them out again. Take several days, and then they'd have to dry them. A brilliant idea, Nicholas. There is, however, just one small point. How do they get there?'

'I'm thinking of that. . . . Give me time, and I shall think of a way.'

'But you haven't any time. They will be through here tonight if they are to reach the house tomorrow.'

'Through here . . . down by the water. . . . I wonder how Josh is faring?'

'I wish I knew. But for your own sake, forget about him now, keep your wits about you. Chadwicke is no fool, more's the pity. He can smell an honest man a mile away, and we are nearly there.'

They turned off the road into a hollow way running to the south along the side of a hanger of magnificent beech trees. The lane was bounded on the other side by a field with a thick hedge of bird-filled hawthorn, and it climbed steadily for nearly half a mile before the land levelled out. They came out of the trees a furlong or so from a large house and its outbuildings, in a hollow on the sunny side of the hill. Broadoak was a long, low, winged house of warm red bricks and black beams, with a flight of steps up to the front door and tall brick walls on either side. A gateway gave into a flint-cobbled yard with stables, and Nick could see sentries at the portal and soldiers and horses within. Opposite the front of the house a flint wall enclosed an orchard of robust-looking fruit-trees.

They were greeted by a small stout serving-woman who looked at Nathaniel with some distaste.

'Master Harrington? Please to come in. The colonel is busy at the moment. I will tell him that you are here.' She left them without ceremony. Nathaniel winked, unabashed, and followed unbidden in her wake.

'Come, Nicholas,' he said. 'Let us follow Lilith, and we shall see what makes the colonel so busy, I'm sure.'

Nat stopped and stood nonchalantly in the outside doorway. Nick looked at the scene with interest. It all seemed so unreal, that he should be here in a Roundhead's house for a social visit, and that all these enemies were blissfully ignorant of his real purpose: at least, he hoped that they were. . . . In the yard an officer on horseback was remonstrating with a big, brawny grey-haired man in a buff-coat and orange sash, whom Nick recognised as Colonel Chadwicke. How odd it was to recognise a man he had never seen, from the image of another who had been his only son, grinning dead in the brambles of a glade not far away. . . . The voices of both men were raised in heated argument.

'My dear Colonel Harvey, you must tell Dick Norton that I cannot perform miracles. It is a slow job to move culverin all the way to Basing.'

'But you said Sunday!'

'I'm sorry. It has proved even slower than I anticipated. They will not be here until late tomorrow at the earliest, and even if I send them through the night to you, as you desire, it will be well into Monday before they can arrive.'

Nick willed himself not to look at Nathaniel. Another day's grace: circumstances were playing right into their hands, and what a stroke of good luck that they should overhear the vital news just by chance, without having to arouse suspicion by asking a single question. Both of them strained to hear the angry voices across the yard, and both of them tried hard to pretend that they were not listening at all.

'So I have to tell Dick that you will send them through the night, but that they cannot come before. I think he will be far from happy.'

'I shall send them with all the speed I can muster, you have my word on it. I could do with my men back here, especially my second in command! But even so, I am convinced that it is not wise to move in the dark so near to Basing. . . . However, if you wish it, and Colonel Norton wishes it, I am in your hands.'

'I am sorry, Colonel Chadwicke.'

'So am I, Colonel Harvey, so am I. I can accommodate you no further. Believe me, he is lucky to have them, for they are sorely needed to defend Portsmouth. Tell him so, I beseech you, and offer him my respects, but say the culverin are not to be expected before Monday noon. Good day to you.'

Colonel Chadwicke turned on his heel to come back to the house. He walked slowly and with obvious difficulty. Nathaniel drew back into the house, and Nick after him, and they both watched Thomas Chadwicke limping towards them along the passageway. Nick felt a pang of guilt and pity for this enemy with the hobbling gait whose only son he had killed, and was shocked. Whatever emotion he had expected to feel on first meeting the colonel, pity was certainly the last which would have occurred to him. The lined face creased reluctantly into a half smile, as Chadwicke bowed to greet them.

'Harrington, I am glad to see you. Judith was quite out of countenance when you could not come yesterday. But I hear from Colonel Harvey that you had more pressing duties elsewhere.'

'Yes, indeed. This is Master Nicholas Howard, the . . . er . . . son of an old friend, and the new assistant of whom I spoke last time I was here.'

'You are welcome, Master Howard. Colonel Harvey has already commended you to me. . . . You must both stay to dine with us tonight. Let us find that wife of mine; she will be overjoyed to see you both. . . . She was about somewhere not long since, I think in the still-room.' He winced as the weight went back on his injured leg, and the twist of his mouth did not escape notice.

'How's the leg?' said Nat coolly: how he hated Chadwicke. Nick could feel the air full of ill-will. And Chadwicke must be aware of it, though seemingly he was choosing to ignore it.

'No worse than usual,' he said, cheerfully enough.

Nick's pity must have shown on his face, for when the colonel disappeared in search of Mistress Chadwicke, Nat fetched him a sharp dig in the ribs with his elbow and whispered, 'Do not get sorry for him! Save your sympathy for deserving cases. He'd shoot you between the eyes and sing a psalm at the same time. For Christ's sake, use your sense! Here they come.'

Chadwicke rolled back into view, and behind him came a young woman in a sombre dress of black boratto, with the house-keys jingling from the girdle about her tiny waist. Her square collar, sleeves and apron were of spotless white linen, and she was neat and slim and serious, the picture of propriety. So this was Nat's niece: and she looked admirably suitable for the wife of a sober, godly Roundhead colonel, Nick thought, except that the colonel was old enough to be her father, and that seemed rather a pity. . . .

'Uncle Nat! What a pleasure it is to see you! I thought that you had forsaken us. You will stay to dine? I've already asked Lilith for a gooseberry tansy!'

'Then how can I refuse? Judith, this is Master Nicholas Howard.'

'Master Howard, you are welcome to Broadoak.'

Nick found himself looking into a pair of grey eyes, very wide apart, set in an oval face that was the colour of honey because it had seen much sunlight. Her nose, he thought, was a little too big, but her hair was a very fetching corn-colour where it showed under her cap.

'I know Uncle Nat will not say no to a cup of canary. I will have it brought to the garden, it is such a lovely day.' Then her smile died a little and she hesitated. 'That is . . . if you should wish it, Thomas? Will you come also, or are you too busy?'

'Perhaps I will join you in a while, my dear. Gentlemen, if you will excuse me, I have work to do.'

Chadwicke trudged laboriously into one of the inner rooms, and Nicholas and Nathaniel followed Mistress Chadwicke into a high-walled garden that was full of sunshine, and of lavender and camomile in bloom, in tiny beds edged with hyssop and box. In the angle of the wall a brick dovecote was full of birds, fluffed and sleepily cooing in the July warmth.

'I'm surprised to find you here, Judy. Day like this, and you cooped up in the house? I thought you'd be off riding somewhere.'

Nat sipped the golden wine and viewed her with one raised eyebrow. Judith Chadwicke blushed, obviously much put out.

'Thomas would rather I stayed here.'

'Of course, I forgot.'

'Uncle Nat, you know he does not like me to ride out of the estate. It is not seemly.'

'Is that what he told you? I can remember a time not so long ago when seemliness did not bother you over-much.'

'I am loth to offend him, Uncle Nat. It seems such a little thing. He has been so patient with me, and even after all his trouble. . . . The pain from his leg has been dreadful. . . .' Mistress Chadwicke turned her wide eyes on Nat, and they were full of entreaty. Nat grunted, and smiled unwillingly: it was clear that she could bend him like a pliant willow to her will.

'If the leg is bad, then I will look at it for him. If you can persuade him to let me see it.'

'Oh, I will, Uncle Nat. It has been such a long time. . . .' she said, almost to herself, then turned to Nick, and offered explanation. 'It was April, when Reading fell. . . . I know not what Master Howard must think of our bickering.'

Nick thought that she knew not, and probably cared not, either, for her smile was polite but decidedly cool.

'Hmmm,' said Nat, and sniffed, for the arched side-gate from the yard was opening, and Thomas Chadwicke came into the garden and shut it behind him with a firm thump which woke the white doves and sent them fluttering in anxiety. Judith Chadwicke also fluttered her white chemise-sleeves like wings, wiping her hands nervously on her apron. 'Uncle Nat, please do not make me laugh at dinner like you did the last time you came. Thomas was angry with me for my wanton behaviour.'

Nick looked at the cool eyes and the tidy figure of Mistress Chadwicke, and decided that whatever her faults might be, wantonness was hardly likely to be among them. She was the model of stiff righteousness, he thought, and he was not really sure that he liked her. But Nat was about to make another rude remark, he knew, and it was time someone employed a little diplomacy.

'You have a beautiful garden here, Mistress Chadwicke.'

'I am glad you like it. It is my favourite place.' She smiled again, this time with a hint of gratitude in her grey eyes. 'But I seldom have time these days to sit here. We are very busy, having so many people at the house.'

'I can imagine,' he said, drily, with one eye watching Thomas Chadwicke drawing closer.

'What has brought you to Stoke Sutton, Master Howard?'

'Nathaniel has more work than he can cope with these days, so he asked me to come and help.'

Nat cast off his ill-humour and became jovial, although he looked very tired and drawn, and Nick found himself yawning in sympathy. It was extremely tiring, he found, making polite but guarded conversation to a Roundhead colonel.

The comparative peace did not last long. At dinner Chadwicke and several of his officers began to discuss the battle at Devizes, and bewailed Waller's bad luck. Nat, having drunk numerous glasses of wine, rediscovered his animosity and began to dispute hotly, when he would have been better employed keeping his mouth firmly shut. Nick ground his teeth and waited for the inevitable to happen.

'And what, Master Harrington, do you know about soldiering, may I ask?' One of Chadwicke's lieutenants was waving a sticky, stubby finger at Nat. 'You are a sawbones, and it is none of your business.'

Nathaniel looked down his nose. 'I've seen more battles, young man, than you have had hot dinners. The late Colonel

Lovell and I were in the Low Countries for nearly two years . . . so I am not totally unaware of the basic principles.'

The young man, thus demolished, lapsed into sulky silence. Colonel Chadwicke was holding forth. 'Captain Atkins says, and I must say that I am inclined to agree with him . . .'

Nick felt irritated by these idiots who were pontificating about something they did not understand. Judith Chadwicke's eyes were staring fixedly at him across the table. He wondered how much of the annoyance had been showing in his face, and made a deliberate effort to relax, unclasping his tightly clenched fist. The young lieutenant was casting about for another opponent. 'And what does the other sawbones think?' he asked with a perceptible sneer. Resentment boiled up in Nick's mind and indigestion in his stomach.

'If you want my opinion,' he said, 'I can assure you that you are all misled. It did not happen as you imagine. Your men just broke and ran because they wanted to. There was no more to it than that.'

Nat's eyes were flashing warnings across the table, but Nick took no heed. He was past caring, for the white-hot anger burned all before it.

'I suppose you know all about it! Were you there, then?'

'Yes, as it happens, I was.'

There was stunned silence in the dark-panelled room as Nick's words echoed in his own ears. Nat looked sick, his face as white as death: and the colonel's face showed great interest.

'I did not know that you had done any fighting, Master Howard?'

'Hardly fighting,' Nick said calmly. He was committed to cross swords now, and it was no lie: hardly fighting, more just staying awake. . . . 'My home is at Marlborough, not far from Devizes. So I went to help, because I am a sawbones. I've no desire to tell you your business. I hope I have not offended, but I wish only to deal honestly with you.' He smiled innocently and hoped that God would forgive him. Nat's eyes rolled to heaven and he smiled, too. Even the colonel's stern face lit up in appreciation.

'Then we none of us can argue with you. Honesty is a rare

commodity these days. . . . I wish that more men valued it so.'

'If you will excuse me,' said Judith Chadwicke in a soft voice, 'I will leave you, gentlemen.'

Nick saw no more of her until she came to bid them farewell with demure courtesy. She spoke a few words low to Nat, and he began to laugh. He was still chuckling as they rode back down the hollow lane towards the Micheldever road.

'A good day, eh?' he said with a smile. ' 'Tis all on a plate for us. They come this way in the dark tomorrow night, and we shall have for them a small surprise! It is a stroke of luck that Atkins will be in command.'

'How so?'

'Because he is a very stout man, is Atkins. Provided, of course, that all he is asked to do is sing psalms, and there is no enemy in evidence. You've a long face?'

'I'm tired.'

'Do not feel too sorry for friend Chadwicke. He'd spare no mercy for you.'

'He seems a nice enough fellow.'

'Aren't they all? God in his mouth and the very devil in his heart! God's blood, you gave me a fright! I thought you were bent on killing the both of us with your pratings at dinner.'

'It was you who started the argument, remember? All day long you've been arguing!'

'True enough, I admit it. But you finished it good and proper, my very righteous friend! Masterly it was, lad, but a little too dangerous for every day! Our Judith says that I'm to thank you most heartily for keeping the peace. . . .'

It was too much for Nat, who began once more to chuckle with relish. 'May God forgive you, man of Belial! Does that not cheer you, Nick? She likes you, does Judy. We'll see you cuckold Chadwicke yet!'

'Nat, for God's sake hold your peace! You should be ashamed to say it! You've said more than enough for one day already!'

'All right, all right. I'm sorry. I won't say another word. . . . I wonder if Josh is back in one piece?'

11

AMBUSH

On Sunday evening the mist came up from the stream as the daylight faded, wreathing over the road and through the trees. Matthew, Nathaniel and Nick gathered in the beech trees at the end of the lane from Broadoak, all clad in black. Now it was just a question of patience. They had planned it down to the last eventuality; young Josh had all day been watching the slow progress of the guns, and even now was in the orchard before the house while Chadwicke's men rested and dined, waiting for them to leave on the last stage of their journey. Nat was uneasy, shifting in the creaking saddle of the black gelding as it sidled and snuffed the air with flaring nostrils, chafing to be gone.

'I hope young Josh knows his business.'

Matthew smiled his rare slow smile, and nodded confidence in his younger brother. 'He'll keep his head down, Captain Nat, never fear. Is a sensible lad, our Josh.'

'He certainly did superbly well yesterday,' Nick agreed. 'He should have plenty of time to get down here to warn us. It will take an age to get them on the road.'

'Aye, I suppose so. I'll wager it will take them a good half-hour to come this far from the house. I wonder they thought that dinner with the colonel was worth the trouble of getting there.' Nat sniffed, shivering.

'I've a suspicion that it's more than dinner they're after. They may be collecting more men: that's partly why I sent

Josh up there to watch. If there are too many, then we shall have to think again.'

'That's a joke,' said Nat. 'Four of us against two dozen is too many already, to my way of thinking, but perhaps you do not agree?'

'If you've any better ideas? It's up to you to say so.'

'No, of course not. But it is ridiculous.'

'Hush, someone coming.' Matt's keen hearing detected footsteps before either of the other two was aware of them. One set of feet were running swiftly as if the hounds of hell were after them, and then came a low, breathless whistle. 'Here, Josh,' said Matt, and the hazy moonbeams between the branches showed the shadowy figure of the boy climbing over the bank and running towards them, panting from his rush down from the house.

'Setting out now. Same number as before.'

'Splendid! The colonel obviously wants to hold on to the rest of his men just in case. Thanks, Josh. Now, let's go through it again, just to make sure. . . . That's two culverin, two powder wagons, and how many men with them?'

'Two gun crews, six men each, some of them driving, a dozen dragooners for escort, and Captain Atkins.'

'You're a good man, Joshua Jeffery. Whatever the outcome here, you've done more than worthy service this past two days.'

Josh glowed with pleasure at the praise. His nose wrinkled in delight and his teeth shone a white smile in his dirty face.

'Now, Josh, down to the water with you. You should have enough time to get your breath back. Remember, not a sound until we attack, and then as much noise as you can make. I want them to think we have at least fifty men here! Have you got your musket?'

'Yes, sir.' Josh dashed off enthusiastically into the patchy mist and was swallowed by darkness beyond the rustling willow trees.

'Now. Is all well? Best separate now. Do not fire until the last wain is well round the corner. Make sure of your marks, for we cannot afford to waste our bullets.'

Nat chuckled. 'I can't wait to see Atkins' face. I'll take an oath he'll fill his breeches as soon as the fun starts. Yes, all is well.'

'You, Matthew?'

'Aye.'

They separated. Nat remained a few yards away from Nick amongst the beech trees, and Matthew was behind the hawthorns on the other side of the lane, mounted on the sturdy pony from the forge. One of the cobs was firmly tethered away beyond the stream ready for Josh to make his escape. Nick prayed for Josh's sake that the beast would not break loose when the sudden noise startled it. Nat sat, grimly fastening the black silk mask over his face, his eyes gleaming devilishly through the eye-slits in the moonlight. Nick made sure that his own mask was secure: recognition was something they could not risk.

The water of the stream gurgled merrily below, and the mist was cold. Nick was already beginning to contemplate what might go wrong, in his usual agony of nervous anxiety before action. It would be all right soon. . . . Nat was right, though. It was ridiculous to ambush twenty-five men with only four. They would have to count on the confusion of darkness and mist, and the demoralisation of sudden onslaught, and trust that Atkins' men would think themselves outnumbered.

It was a forlorn hope indeed, but there was no other way to save Basing House. Oh, God, how much longer would they be? They had to gain three or four days at least, for Josh had found Peake's men, with Lieutenant-Colonel Sir Henry Bard, still at Wallingford, waiting for their colonel to arrive. And it was a long, long march from Wallingford to Basing: though Bard had sent an enthusiastic letter saying that they would set out immediately and not wait for Colonel Peake, but march with all speed. . . .

Distant rumblings of gun wheels, cartwheels, sounded down the lane. They were so near to Broadoak. The gunfire would bring the whole legion down on them, so it would have to be done quickly. If a spark were to get to the powder. then it would be very quick for all of them, for they would be blown to pieces: but the mist was damp, too damp for that to happen, Nick hoped. He could see them now, slow-moving guns in the seething moonlight, in front of the trundling wagons with their axles groaning under the weight of their loads on the uneven ground. The escort trailed beside the wagons, drooping drowsily in their saddles.

Nick cocked the flintlock pistol in his hand with a click as the last wagon turned the corner, and fired it at the driver of the leading gun. Then the three of them spurred forward into the mass of stupefied humanity before them, uttering blood-curdling yells that would have done credit to the armies of Lucifer. Three or four of the escort were making off at great speed towards Micheldever, wide awake now, and in a desperate hurry to save their skins. One of the powder wagons was already on its side in the water, for the horses deprived suddenly of the guidance of a driver had plunged off the road and down the bank in their fear, and were splashing and floundering in the stream. Josh was down there leaping about between the flailing hooves, cutting the traces and making sure that all the powder and shot was soaked. Nick seized the bridle of the team-leader of the second culverin, and wrenched the horse's head round so that the gun turned towards the stream, and then its own weight began to carry it, and the horses with it, into the churning foam.

The moonlight reflected off the half-solid strands of mist, so that they looked like clutching hands in the darkness, and gave the scene an air of unreality, like some devil-dogged nightmare full of wild riders and confusion. Josh was laying the musket about him like a club, swinging it by the muzzle-end, and whooping with diabolic gusto. Matthew was busy throttling the driver of the other gun, and at least two of the other artillerymen were staggering in dazed circles, wounded. One Roundhead clung doggedly to Nick's leg, trying to drag him down. Nick found the empty pistol was still in his left hand, brought it down heavily on the man's monmouth-capped head, and the grip slackened abruptly as the man slid from view. Nat was in dire trouble, hemmed in by Captain Atkins and three others who were doing their best to defend the other ammunition wagon. A horrible rending noise echoed along the valley as the second gun, driven by

Matthew, rolled down into the stream, taking half a willow tree with it. Matthew and the pony were in the water, and then he and Josh were away on the other side.

Nat decided that it was high time to give up the unequal struggle, and he broke clear, hotly pursued by Atkins and his troopers. One of the dragoons was levelling a musket at Nick; he saw it out of the corner of his eye and ducked instinctively, and the bullet came screaming over his head, hitting the driver of the ammunition wagon. The man doubled over, clutching at his belly, and fell forward with his head over the side of the wagon. Nick wheeled the chestnut to follow in Nat's wake, just in time to see the black stumble and fall with a sickening crash, and Nat with it, the pair of them rolling over and over on the white road in a patch of moonlight where the mist was thin.

Atkins' sword was raised to run Nat through as he struggled to rise, hanging on obstinately to the bridle of the frightened gelding. Nick's arm went numb for a moment as it caught the full force of the descending blow. He found himself shouting and raving nameless curses at Atkins, whose startled eyes revealed an extremity of terror. . . . Nick laughed triumphantly as his sword ran through Atkins' shoulder until the hilt was stopped short and could go no further. The captain gibbered with fear and pain, and his men looked on in stunned horror as Atkins' blood spattered them, while Nick made off to Nat's assistance. He found Nat already back in the saddle but swaying dreadfully, his face the colour of uncooked pastry in the lurid moonlight. They met the others down by the mill.

'Nat, are you all right?'

'No, I'm bloody well not all right! I've put my shoulder out, I think. Oh, damnation!' He lurched forward ominously and would have fallen, but that Matthew's sinewy arm went round him.

'Hell fire!' said Nick, and took a look behind. There were soldiers pouring from Broadoak lane, and the colonel himself rode at their head. 'Josh, get him home. 'Becca will take care of him till I come back. If they want him for Broadoak, tell her to say he has an ague or something. Matt, take the spent horses and hide them somewhere, and see to that black, he's dead lame. . . . And get these clothes changed, all of you.'

'Where are you going?' said Matt, his deep voice charged with suspicion.

'Lead these lads away,' said Nick. 'Got a fast horse could do with a good run. See you later, I hope. Now get him home, for the love of God. . . .'

Nick turned the stallion back towards the pursuers and stood full in the glare of the moon, to make certain they would see him. He charged back towards them like a madman, as fast as his horse would go. It was the last thing they had expected, and before they had realised what he was at, he was through them, scattering them in all directions like the running feet of children scattered the clucking hens on Stoke Sutton green. The safest place to lead them would be back to Broadoak, for at least he could be sure that all the soldiers from the house would be occupied already, and he knew the way.

They were after him now, shouting and sword-waving: very brave fellows when there was no opposition, as Nat had said, and the thought of it made Nick laugh out loud. It was superbly funny to ride up to the house like this, and to spit in the face of the enemy. His laughter echoed in thundering silence now, for already they were far behind him. The army horses were no match for the chestnut's speed, and he could feel that the horse, too, was enjoying the run, its hooves pounding out of the trees like some devil's tattoo, and its ears pricked willingly amid the tossing mane. Before the house he turned, and the stallion leaped the wall like a bird in flight. They were off down the hill through the alleyways between the laden apple trees, as the pursuers came out of the beeches at the head of the hollow way.

Nick crossed the stream in the mist, unseen by the sorry remnants of Atkins' small force, who lay licking their wounds in a state of disbelief and numbed horror. He left the horse with Matthew and hurried back to the house through the churchyard shadows, with sickening fear creeping back into his heart. Surely they would soon be coming to fetch Nat.

They would need the surgeon's help tonight: and the surgeon was in no shape to help anyone, not just now. . . .

He found Nat half walking, half crawling up the stairs, clearly in great pain, but pushing Josh off, and swearing that he needed no help. Rebecca was pale and very quiet, wringing her apron in her hands, and trembling from head to foot. Nick gripped her by the hand. 'He's got enough strength to curse. . . . I think he'll do very well in a little while. Get him to bed, now, and hide those clothes. I'll be with you when I've changed myself. Josh, go to bed now. Go on, man, now, not next week! They'll be here soon, if I'm not much mistaken.'

As he washed away the blood and dirt, and donned once more the grey kersey coat and breeches, he could hear Nat's feeble protests from across the hall. Rebecca was dealing with him firmly, it seemed. All was quiet outside, and there was only darkness in the room above the stables. It was just as well that only one of them would be going to Broadoak, for there remained only the one horse. . . .

'Come on, Nat, let's get you put to rights. I'm sorry it's only me, but if it's good enough for Norton's men, then I'm sure you'll not complain. 'Becca, I want you to hold him still while I heave his arm. I'm afraid this is going to hurt like hell.'

Nat gritted his teeth in determined silence whilst Nick pulled at the arm, and the sweat poured down both their faces. It did not take long, and the joint ground obligingly back into place. Nat lay back on the pillow and fainted clean away.

'My God, he's dead!' said Rebecca, and burst into tears.

'Nothing of the sort. He'll do very well, now. Keep him still. Better that he should sleep if possible. If they come, make sure he keeps his mouth shut, for he may be mazy for a while. I beseech you, do not cry, or you will betray us all. You must stay with him now, every minute . . . and if they come, remember he has an ague. . . .'

'I'm sorry, oh, I'm sorry, I thought he was dead . . . so white he looked. . . .'

'I know, dry your eyes, please dry your eyes. Better?'

Rebecca blew her nose resolutely. 'I'm all right,' she said firmly. 'It was just a shock.'

'I'm off downstairs. Remember, it's an ague he's got. And we've been in all evening.'

'Is it true? Josh said you saved him. . . . We thought that they would kill you for certain.'

'Hush, Rebecca . . . and do not worry. Just keep calm, for everybody's sake.'

Nick left them and went down to the parlour. It was chilly in the dark. Five minutes later, when a corporal-of-horse came from Broadoak to fetch the surgeon, he found a subdued, anxious household, for Master Harrington was in bed, sick, being tended by his capable housekeeper, and Master Howard's slight shoulders were hunched as he pored over a weighty discourse on anatomy, his dark eyes peering out of his pale scholar's face like those of a surprised barn-owl in the candlelight.

'At this time of night? I do not understand. Is there some sort of trouble?'

'Trouble?' said the unmusical voice of the corporal. 'I should say so! Captain Atkins and his men been attacked by a troop of Cavaliers.'

'I'm sorry, Master Harrington has a high fever. He is far too ill to be out. The cold air would kill him.'

'But there's so many wounded. Captain Atkins nigh bled to death, and the colonel's reopened his old wound There are two troopers dead.'

'I will come as soon as I can. 'Becca, where are my boots? We are at such sixes and sevens. . . . I must saddle up myself, I will not wake the boy at this time of night. . . . A troop of Cavaliers, you say? I did not think there were any malignants hereabouts, except up at Basing. Where on earth did they come from?'

'Where on earth? Aye, sir, you may well ask that. The Lord only knows! But Captain Atkins says there was a good two-three score of them, and only twenty of our men . . . and John Willet swears they was some of them fiends from hell. . . . Do you know, sir, one of them led the colonel and his men a merry chase, and then he disappeared in a puff of smoke and they haven't seen him since. Fire and brimstone there was, Willet says. The horse's hooves never touched the ground, sir. . . . It flew, breathing fire and brimstone, and he was laughing. And he disappeared, just like that!'

'Ugh!' said Nick. 'Sounds very nasty. Quite, quite horrible!'

'Legions of Lucifer, sir,' said the corporal, coughing and wheezing in the cold air of the yard, and as if he knew a great deal on the subject.

'I hope they do not reappear too soon, at any rate. May God protect us! I'm ready when you are, corporal. After you. . . . I'm not sure of my way, you see.'

12

NOTHING SHORT OF A MIRACLE

Half way up the hollow lane, the remaining powder wagon was blocking the road, an axle broken in its too-hasty retreat towards the house. The corporal groaned aloud, like a bull-calf tormented by gad-flies, and the sheer effort made him cough. 'Oh, God, another affliction!' he spluttered. 'It's the devil's own work tonight, and no mistake!'

At Broadoak soldiers and servants ran hither and thither, beset by the same creeping horror of the demon visitation. The young lieutenant who had been all aggression at dinner on Saturday was sitting on the third stair from the bottom with his head in his hands. Judith Chadwicke came sweeping down the stairs, barefooted, and in a nightgown that was splashed with someone's blood. Her hair flew loose about her face as she shouted orders for more water and linen to those below, and bid them briskly not to stand there gaping. The poor confused lieutenant got cold comfort. 'And what, may I ask, are you doing here?' she said sharply, coming on him at the foot of the stairs. 'Nothing, by the look of things! What are you doing, I said!' She shook the man by the buff-coated shoulders, holding him at arms' length as if he were some malodorous crawling creature that she would really rather not have touched.

'I don't know,' he said pathetically. 'I don't know what to do.'

Mistress Chadwicke leaned on the large dog-legged banister 'God give me strength!' she cried in exasperation. 'And where will we be if the Cavaliers should come back, and we are all unprepared? There should be men on guard. . . . Has the other wagon come back yet?'

'Can't get it, axle's broken.'

'Oh, dear God! Then they must bring the powder up here. . . . We cannot let it all go. Put it in the small barn or somewhere, but not too near the house.'

'Has the captain come to himself yet, madam? Or the colonel?' the lieutenant was sadly beseeching.

'No! The colonel is certainly not yet awake, and he and poor Captain Atkins are both of them far too ill to be bothered. It is your command, lieutenant, your responsibility! Have you sent to Colonel Norton yet to tell him what has happened? And to ask him if he can spare men to help defend us?'

'Oh, I hadn't thought of that.'

'Well, think of it now! What about the corporal, here? Send him.'

'Yes, madam,' the lieutenant said, somewhat woefully, and addressed the corporal without getting up. 'Corporal, go to Basing and explain to Colonel Norton, and tell him that we need help.'

'Yes, sir. Surgeon's here, sir.'

Judith looked up from the seated lieutenant, and her face fell, for the one she was expecting did not come forth from the shadows.

'Where is Uncle Nat? Is he not with you?'

'I am afraid that he is very ill. Got an ague, and in a high fever. I could not bring him: it would kill him to be out in this mist.'

'Then thank God that you are here, Master Howard. I must not waste your time. There are men sorely hurt.'

'How is the colonel? Let me see him first.'

'He looks dreadful. He should not have ridden out. Uncle Nat told him that he should rest, or he would never be well. And then this.'

'The corporal was telling me that supernatural agencies had been at work.'

'What rubbish!' she said emphatically, much to his surprise. 'They will make any excuse for their ineptitude!'

'Hard words?'

'Oh, I wish that I could lay hands on one or two of those supernatural agencies. They would soon be proved human enough!'

'Then I am glad, madam, that I am not your enemy, for I should be most apprehensive.' He smiled at her, but her eyes flamed savagely at him.

Mistress Chadwicke was in no mood to trifle, and he should have known better. . . . 'You mock me, sir?'

'No . . . I . . . It is just . . . not the reaction I would have expected, that is all . . . not very . . . gentle,' he said sheepishly, angry at his own idiocy.

'But the carnage wrought here! These Cavaliers are monstrous!'

'I wonder if you would have been quite so angry if they were King's men here hurt?'

'But . . . that would be . . . different!'

'Would it? Why so?'

She pouted at him like a petulant child. 'You are a malignant, Master Howard! My husband's men are true . . . steadfast . . . honest.'

'Madam, I did not suggest that they were not. Has it not occurred to you that Cavaliers may be sincere, and as steadfast in defending that which they believe to be right, though you may not: that they feel pain, also, as keenly as any Parliament-man! I'm not anything,' he lied, staring her so straight in the eye that she turned away. 'I'm just the one who goes behind, trying to repair the dreadful damage they do to one another.' He had already convinced himself of his own good sense. What a great pity that not a word of it was true. . . .

'Thomas is in here.' She opened the dark door wide. Colonel Chadwicke lay under the coverlet in the big bed, his breath rasping painfully, and he looked much less formidable than when galloping through the darkness an hour or two since.

'I think I shall need two of those stout steadfast men to

hold him, please,' said Nick, shifting the huge Bible from the bedside to the other side of the room.

'There's water and bandages here. And the fire is hot to heat – the knife,' Judith Chadwicke said, shivering. 'Is there enough light? And is there anything else you will be needing? Lilith will fetch anything. Will two men be enough?'

'Yes, two should be enough: and no, there is nothing more I shall need. I will call you . . . if . . .'

'I am not going anywhere. Oh, do not worry, I shall not faint or be ill or anything. I am a soldier's daughter, remember.' She swept out. Presently he heard her voice calling, and she returned with two very tired-looking dragoons, whose boots made thunderous noises on the floorboards. Nick turned to employ his deft fingers to make repair of Chadwicke's horribly torn leg. It would be a long, long time before the colonel would ride out again: if ever. He looked an old man, lying there. And his young wife stood by, straight-backed, her face set into an impassive stare, until Nick wondered just what, if anything, she was feeling behind those cool, grey eyes, and how she would have dealt with the enemy who had laid her husband here, if she had known he was so close. . . .

Now her concern was all for others, and this time it was Nick who was receiving her orders. 'Master Howard, I think that you should see Captain Atkins straight away. It is a clean enough wound, but he is run right through the shoulder, and I had much ado to staunch the blood.'

'I'm with you, madam. Come on, lads, you too.'

Captain Atkins was buttressed by several pillows, his eyes staring blankly into space, the base of his neck swathed thickly with much-bloodied linen, to cover the gaping wound where the sword of a devil had bitten.

'Captain Atkins?' said Nick softly, bending towards him. Atkins started in terror and tried suddenly to rise, his whole arm flailing wildly in the air. Nick caught the wrist before it hit him in the eye, and a hideous suspicion began to crawl through his mind. 'Hey, be still, will you? I'm the surgeon!'

'Oh, God,' moaned Atkins, and subsided, limp, to his

propping pillows. 'For a moment I thought . . . it . . . was . . . him. . . .'

'Who?' asked Nick kindly, though he already knew. 'Never mind. Poor fellow, this is a nasty wound, but I think I'd best leave it be. I can do no better than you have, madam. And, my dear captain, we can do without all the leaping about: otherwise it will be a shroud you need, not merely a bandage!'

'Am I . . . going to die?' the captain whispered plaintively, his eyes brimful of horror, and the sweat on his face coursing like rain-drops on a window.

'Not if you do as you are told. Mistress Chadwicke seems to have dealt with you efficiently and promptly. Well done, madam, you are a good surgeon!'

'I've seen you somewhere before,' said the voice from the bed, very clearly. 'I know I have.'

'Very likely,' said Nick, his heart thudding sickeningly. 'But do not worry your head about it just now. It's rest you are needing. The worst is over now, and no demon is going to come and murder you in your bed.'

The cheery words brought a weak grin to the captain's face, and the captain's cold, clammy hand gripped Nick's in silent thanks for the reassurance. He did not know that, behind the mask of smiles, the surgeon was grimly considering whether it might be better for the captain to bleed to death after all, just in case he might remember. . . .

'There are several broken heads,' Mistress Chadwicke was saying, 'and several bullet wounds. I cannot do a great deal to aid them, I have not your skill in such things.'

'Skill? Oh, yes. . . .' Nick cringed inwardly. He hoped fervently that such unskilled hands as his would never be let loose on him. His head ached abominably as they moved from man to man in the shivering night, while the mist swirled thickly outside, its dead hands fingering softly at the window latches. The candles burned low now, but otherwise Nick had no idea of the time. Shadows danced on the wall of the great parlour as the nearest candle guttered and went out with a splutter, and Nick watched another man choke his last breath away as Judith Chadwicke cradled him in her arms.

She had a long smear of blood on her forehead, and her brown hands trembled a little: but she said nothing at all, not even with her eyes.

'Mistress Chadwicke, will you not rest? I am indebted to you for your help, but I think you need respite.'

'Please, let me help you . . . until I know . . . if Thomas will recover. . . . Please, do not make me sit and wait!' Now she was on the edge of tears. Nick looked at her bewildered child's face and felt pity, because she was afraid that the colonel might die. 'Your husband will live, provided he is cared for properly . . . I promise you. Though it might be a long time.'

'How long?' she asked anxiously: a little too anxiously, Nick thought, puzzled.

'I cannot say exactly. But he must be sensible.'

'He isn't! Oh, Master Howard, I begged and prayed he would not go out tonight. Now it will be months before he can go back to the army! Why, Master Howard, did he not listen?'

' 'Tis no use to ask me, Mistress Chadwicke. But I gather the matter was of some little . . . importance.'

'Importance? I think that this is a disaster!' she shrugged hopelessly. 'And I am so helpless.'

'You seem far from helpless to me,' he said, in frank admiration, and it brought the ghost of a smile to her eyes. Then Lilith was standing in the doorway, grotesque and stumpy in the flickering light, her hard face set like the stone gargoyles at Basing . . . watching them, Nick thought.

'He is stirring, madam.'

Judith Chadwicke whirled round. 'I will come straight away. That is, if you can manage, Master Howard?'

'I can manage, I'll be up to see him again when I've finished here. Try to keep him quiet.'

More than an hour later Nick straightened his aching back, knee deep in the gory aftermath of his own handiwork, where he had been trying to extract a musket-ball. His own handiwork twice over, for that musket-ball had been meant for him, except that he had seen the gun levelled and ducked just in time. . . . He exchanged grim glances with the rheumy-eyed troopers who still held his victim in their steady unflinching grip and sighed, and his regret was genuine. 'Three dead. And that one, I fear, will make a fourth by morning.' He rose, wiping the arms and hands that were sticky with blood from fingertip to shoulder. 'All right, boys. Go now and take your breath. My thanks for your help.'

Nick took a deep breath himself and reeled upstairs to search the unfamiliar maze of rooms for the chamber where lay Thomas Chadwicke. He found Judith sitting on the bed with Thomas' hands in hers, and now there were tears on her face. 'Thomas?' she said softly. 'The surgeon is here.'

The colonel's eyes opened, and he smiled. 'Master Howard. Is that you?'

'Yes. How goes it, sir?'

'Painfully, I fear.' He twisted his face into an agonised grimace, his teeth clenched hard together. Judith flinched. Nick saw that her hands were black with bruises: it was that, then, that brought the tears to her eyes, and not pity at all. . . . There was nothing but steel behind those eyes, and those hands must be very cold. . . .

'I think you are indestructible, colonel. I wish that I were half as strong as you seem to be.'

'Where is . . . Harrington?'

'Sicker than you are. At home, in bed, in a fever. I've left him in Rebecca's care. It is time you slept, and no more talking. I'm afraid that you must be bidden until you are a little stronger.'

Chadwicke spluttered with hoarse laughter and choked on it. 'I shall need to be . . . stronger. Norton will see me shot for this . . . shambles.'

'Please, Thomas. It is not your fault! You did tell Colonel Harvey that it was unwise.' Judith's voice was acid with indignation.

'My dearest. We shall come through, never fear.'

'Hush now, Thomas, please.'

'Goodnight . . . er . . . morning, Colonel Chadwicke.' Nick tiptoed from the room and went downstairs. Dawn had come and gone, and every gauze-wreath of mist was melted, but the last wounded artilleryman clung tenaciously to the half-severed threads of his life, like a spider will cling to its mutilated web.

Nick left him snoring in a drugged sleep on his pallet in the panelled chamber, went to the garden, and sat desolate on the dewy grass, feeling the hesitant caress of the little breeze which had already carried the mist away. He should have been happy, he told himself, for they had been successful beyond all likelihood and expectation. Only the recurring thought of Captain Atkins made him feel decidedly insecure, so that once again he debated whether to take just one more life: though with the broad daylight, he decided, the brave captain might be encouraged to put all down to imagination. . . . But it had been a poor night for Nat, who lay hurt at home . . . and might so unwittingly betray them all.

The first fat bees of the day buzzed greetings to the costmary and comfrey in the garden-beds, and a tall, dark shadow fell on the damp grass by his side. Judith Chadwicke stood there, pale and hollow-eyed from lacking sleep, and he noticed that although she had a cloak upon her shoulders, her feet were bare, like any gypsy's.

'They told me you were out here,' she said, as he scrambled to his feet, and pushed the hair out of his eyes. He would have liked to curse at the disturbance, and his retreating headache came back and hit him viciously between the eyes. He decided, irritated, that Nat's niece was a self-opinionated, perverse, insensitive nuisance.

'I hope you do not mind, madam, I just need peace and quiet – and fresh air, to wake me up a little.'

'You must be very tired: and hungry, too. I know not what we should have done without you, Master Howard.'

'Thank you, but I am certainly not hungry. I think that without me you could have managed perfectly well. You were very brave, madam,' he said with stiff politeness, and bowed. 'And I salute you for it.'

'I was very . . . angry, you see,' she said simply. 'It is easy to be brave when you are angry. But now I am . . . afraid. Suppose they should come back?'

'I think that it is unlikely,' he said with conviction. 'They would not be so foolish, surely, as to rely on surprise a second time?'

'I am sure you are right. I owe you an apology, sir.'

'Apology? Good heavens, what for?' He laughed nervously. He had the uncomfortable feeling that he had perhaps been too unkind, too hasty in his judgement of her. At any rate, he was by now certain that there was more to Mistress Chadwicke than the obvious.

'For calling you a malignant. I know now that I was wrong.'

Nick stared into the grey eyes. They were very bright and innocent and earnest, and self-dislike made him squirm.

'You made me think about a great many things that I had never considered,' she continued, while he wished that he had never considered them, either. 'But, of course, even Uncle Nat has some sympathy with the King. So they cannot all be wicked. . . . I had not really thought about it before.'

'I'm sure the colonel would rather you did not think about anything.'

Nick muttered under his breath, in a sudden rush of resentment. It was not his own fault he was here; it was Thomas Chadwicke and those like him who had put Nick in this dreadful position where he was neither fish, nor flesh, nor yet good red herring.

'I'm sorry? I did not quite hear you.'

Everyone had to be right or wrong to people like the colonel, and if you were not for them then you were against them. Nat was right: it was a villain, but a subtle one, with God in his mouth and the very devil in his heart. . . .

'Colonel Chadwicke is fortunate to have such a loyal, courageous lady,' he said aloud. To his surprise the colonel's lady burst into tears, half laughing, half weeping, like a creature demented, tears flooding through her fingers. 'God!' she wailed. 'If only you knew!'

Nick was utterly confounded. He put out a hand to touch Mistress Chadwicke's and then changed his mind abruptly and drew it back again. He must rely on words, and words alone, and that was difficult because he had no idea what was making her cry, and he had never been skilful with words. . . .

'I think, madam, that you are very tired, and overwrought. It has been very hard for you, this – er – misfortune. The world will look better when you are rested.'

'It won't, it won't,' she sobbed. 'He was nearly better. He could have gone back to the army! And now it's to be done all over again!'

She had an odd way of putting it, Nick thought. 'He will not die, madam. Fret yourself no further, all will be well,' he pleaded with her, and the pleading sounded weak and ineffective. But she was drying her eyes already, the storm of weeping spent as quickly as it had come. She sighed. 'You do not understand,' she said calmly. 'Would you believe that only yesterday I wished him dead? Have I shocked you? Do you think that I am very wicked?'

Nick looked at her troubled face and began to laugh helplessly. 'Good Lord, no! It's easy to wish somebody dead if you are irritated with them. I'll wager that the good colonel can be very irritating, when he's a mind to?'

The breeze caught at her hair, and lifted it behind her like a corn-coloured curtain in the sun. Nick gulped. 'You have very beautiful hair,' he said, impulsively, and then suddenly self-conscious, wished that he had not, for he must be careful what he said to the colonel's wife. . . . Her face blushed pink, and she curtsied, obviously much embarrassed.

'You are very kind, sir, but I must go put my cap on. I had quite forgotten it. Thomas would be angry that I should so sinfully flaunt before the eyes of men.'

'Excepting himself, of course,' Nick said bitterly. 'For fear that anyone should covet his worldly goods.'

Judith gaped at him, as if she could not believe what he said. 'It is vanity,' she said severely. 'Thomas says that we should mortify the flesh.'

Of course, that was just the sort of thing Thomas would say, for Thomas had his own salvation very much at heart, and that of his pretty wife. . . .

'Do you always do what Thomas says?'

'Is it not my duty?'

'To let someone else think for you? Makes life easy, I suppose.'

'You are very . . . forthright, sir.'

'Blunt,' he said, annoyed. 'It is in my nature. I have little skill at flattery. I am tired. Please forgive me.'

'Forgive you an honest opinion, sincerely expressed? Aye, sir, I'll do that. Thomas always says . . . honesty should be admired. . . .'

'Like that hair! "If a woman have long hair, then it is a glory to her." Is that not Isaiah? Tell that to Thomas! No vanity, but glory to God.'

She blushed scarlet now, and he knew that he had gone too far, and that he must change the subject, or there would be trouble.

'Is Thomas asleep?'

'Yes, I left Lilith to keep an eye on him.'

'I think, then, that you yourself ought to try to sleep while you can. I shall stay for a few hours, so that you will not need to worry. Then I really must go back to Stoke Sutton, to make sure that Nat is all right.'

'Oh, poor Uncle Nat! I'd almost forgotten him. Is he very sick? He has been very busy lately. I thought that he looked pale on Saturday, not at all himself.'

'He is very low presently. And I think that he will be so for a good while.'

'I ought to go to see him.' Her forehead wrinkled in concern, and Nick was riven with anxiety. Certainly it would not do for her to see Uncle Nat while he was afflicted with a most peculiar ague which necessitated the carrying of one arm in a sling. . . .

'I think that it would not be wise at present. He needs complete quiet. Perhaps in a week or so we shall see,' he said hastily. 'And you are, I think, for the moment most needed here. Nat will understand.'

'Then will you give him my good wishes, and explain?'

'That I will do most happily, madam. And now, inside with you, or you will take a chill, and that is a calamity which we can do without!'

It was two o'clock before Nick rode back into Harrington's yard. Rebecca was humming a tune to herself as she worked in the kitchen. There was no need to ask, Nat must be much better. 'He's in high old spirits,' Rebecca said. 'Though he complains his shoulder aches. It's only an hour since he woke from sleeping. Matthew is up there with him.' As if testifying to the truth of her statement, Nick heard echoing laughter from upstairs. Nat's voice was raised in tones of protest, and then Matthew's deep-throated chuckle sent them both off again. Seemingly, it was a great joke. Nick's head throbbed with the noise.

'Here he is,' said Nat, his whole body shaking with mirth. 'I'm damned if I can see his horns, can you? Oh, Lord, Matt, you'll be the death of me! It hurts abominably when I laugh!' He lay there weakly, cursing horrendously, and nursing his injured arm.

'I wonder,' Matt rolled about on his chair. 'Take your boots off, Master Howard, and show us your cloven hooves!'

'For pity's sake, you two. What has got into you?'

'I've had one John Willet in the forge half the morning. From Broadoak, with some horses to shoe.' Matthew snorted again with the laughter he could not contain.

'How lovely for you,' Nick sighed, wearily.

'He regaled me with some cock-and-bull story about how he saw the devil last night. It's all round the village.'

'Surely it's not that amusing?'

'Oh, I don't know,' said Nat, unrepentant. 'You didn't tell me your middle name was Lucifer.' He stretched his good arm. 'How is my very good friend, Colonel Chadwicke?'

'He'll live. But some of them didn't.'

'How sad! What's ailing you, you mumpish oaf? You should be laughing yourself silly! A glimpse of success you've given us! Come on, man, smile!'

'I'm too bloody tired to do anything, Nat. I'm sorry.'

'Poor old Nick. Are you feeling sorry for those canting bastards again? Or is it yourself you are sorry for?'

'I don't know, Nat. I don't know anything any more. Truth to tell, I've almost forgotten which side I'm supposed to be fighting for.'

'Did you have a hard time?'

'Not really, Judith Chadwicke was incredible. She was the only one in the place who had any sense. Heroic, she was.'

'You don't surprise me. She would be.' Nat nodded in approbation. 'You don't know her like I do. Fights like a wild thing when roused. A very strong-minded girl, our Judith.'

'That is why she does everything that Thomas Chadwicke tells her to, I suppose?'

'You're a hard man to please, Nicholas Howard.'

'Anyway, Mistress Chadwicke sends you her greetings, and hopes that you will soon have a remission of your . . . ague. It's about time you had a quiet rest.'

'All right! I'll do as I'm told. And, Nick, I am most heartily grateful to you for what you did. I would be dead meat if it were not for your courage.'

'Go to sleep, Nat! Come, Matthew.'

'And you got your miracle! I'll wager that Lord Winchester will be grateful, too.'

'Go to hell, Nat!'

'Should that not be "come", Nicholas? Here's 'Becca! 'Becca, rescue me. . . . Fetch the demon away!' Nat chuckled wickedly.

'Downstairs, Master Howard,' 'Becca said, firmly, and took him by the arm. 'Your meal is waiting. Come, now, or it will be cold.' She piloted him, unresisting, to the kitchen where she stood over him purposefully while he forced the food down. It stuck obstinately in his throat, and he felt certain that he was going to be sick: but he was not. He pushed the empty plate aside and sat drooping over the table, too tired now even to move. Rebecca touched his hand gently.

'How are things at Broadoak?'

'Confused.'

'But Judy is well in command, is she?'

'Seemingly. She surprised me.'

'Yes, of course, it would be a surprise to you. You never knew her like she . . . used to be.' Rebecca took the plate and stood there holding it, shaking her head regretfully.

'Used to be?'

'Never afraid of anything. And wild . . . always wild and headstrong, and giving orders. . . . Phil used to say that she would have been better a boy.'

'Good lord. I see. . . . She's changed?'

'Since she married Tom Chadwicke. All the old spirit seems to have gone . . . and yet perhaps it's just hidden out of sight. She's quiet, and obedient, but I suspect she may find it far from easy. . . . Never did like being bidden at all, and it must take a deal of determination to keep the peace with that old curmudgeon. I don't know why she bothers, I'm sure.' Rebecca sniffed disdainfully.

Nick did not know, either. 'Love?' he suggested. 'It does strange things to people. She wants him to be happy . . . and he seems contented if she does as she's told.'

'No doubt of that. And he adores her, it's true, the old hypocrite,' she said, with hearty dislike in her voice. 'But what she feels . . . it's anybody's guess.'

'She seemed worried over him last night. I thought it might be all up with him, but he's as strong as a horse. I'm going to bed, now. Thanks, Rebecca.'

'Good night, Master Nick. You deserve your rest.'

However deserving he might have been, he slept far from well. At first it was the persistent pattering of rain that woke him, and then it was nightmares. Only when they all declared a truce did he sink into the deep sleep of exhaustion, to be vigorously shaken back into reality again by an anxious Rebecca.

'God's mercy!' she said, 'I thought you would never wake! There's a visitor below stairs . . . very anxious to be away, because it's nearly dawn. I had to disturb you, I'm sorry.'

'What? Who . . . is it?' He was puzzled and still half asleep, his tongue reluctant. 'Who . . . the hell?'

'Ned Jeffery.'

'Oh, no!' Basing. It was Basing. It was all over, all for nothing. Nick was out of bed and fumbling for his clothes in an instant, and blundered downstairs like a drunken man, his shirt-tail still hanging behind him. It was very cold and the rain lashed down with bouncing glee into the yard outside, rattling like a thousand muskets on the oak-shingled roof of the stable. Ned Jeffery sat in the kitchen, damp, bedraggled and begrimed, stretching out his cold feet and swollen hands towards the fire. He rose and bowed stiffly.

'From my Lord,' he said briefly, giving a letter into Nick's shivering hand.

'What happened?' Nick forced out the awful question, unable to wait to read the answer in Lord Winchester's elegant script. But he need not have worried. Ned's hard soldier's face lit up behind its two or three days' growth of beard, into a broad boyish grin of sheer pleasure.

'Sir Henry Bard arrived, ten o'clock last evening, sir. With musketeers and dragoons to relieve Basing.'

Nick's mouth dropped open. 'My God, that was quickly done!'

'Thanks to you. Forced march all the way from Wallingford,' he said, 'with the musketeers riding *en croup*. Oh, Master Howard, you should have seen those rebels run! We thought we were finished, and then comes a miracle!'

'Not my doing. Josh went to fetch them. It is to him that my Lord's thanks are due.'

Ned shrugged, his grin wider than ever. 'You're too modest, sir,' he said. 'I've spoken to Matt. He was telling me a fine story about some guns, and of how the colonel at Broadoak had a visitation from hell! Will give them all a hearty laugh at Basing! Oh, how I'd like to have seen Norton's face when he heard of it!'

'Thanks for coming, Edward. I must admit that when 'Becca told me you were here, I . . .'

'Thought we were beat, yes, I know, sir. It was all over your face. I must be going back, if you'll forgive me. Will I tell my Lord that you will come?'

'Yes, Edward. Soon, but I cannot say when.'

Edward muffled himself once more in his steaming, still sodden cloak, disposed his droop-brimmed hat on his drenched hair and, whistling, rode away through the pouring rain.

'Lord be praised!' said Rebecca, shutting the back door on both Edward and the storm. 'Lord be praised. It's nothing short of a miracle.'

13

THE WORKMEN OF NEHEMIAH

The first part of August was cold and wet, but between almost daily visits to Broadoak, and calls upon Lord Winchester at Basing, Nick had little time even for the luxury of contemplating the vileness of the weather. 'Norton and Harvey are fled to Portsmouth, I hear?' observed Sir Henry Bard, with the energetic enthusiasm and glee which was his most noticeable feature.

Even Lord Edward allowed himself a supercilious grin of amusement. 'To drown their sorrows, and, I hope, themselves also,' he said, sniffing at Nick in obvious distaste, and leaving him in no doubt that he would have liked to see him follow them.

The castle was buzzing with activity. Money, plate and other valuables poured into the marquis' treasury; and wheat, oats, hay, peas, pigs and poultry appeared daily to stock the storehouses. 'Preparing for a siege,' said Lord Winchester, watching the carts roll in, his jaw firmly set with aristocratic obstinacy.

'Colonel Augustus is out and about?' Nick enquired. 'I have not seen him.'

'He and his troop of robbers are out terrorising every town for miles,' said Henry Bard in reply, ignoring the marquis' staring disapproval.

'They are merely . . . exacting contribution,' Lord Winchester observed, cuttingly. 'Especially from Basingstoke. He will essay Winchester, also, now that the garrison there is so much reduced. The county is rotten with rebellion and shall be made to pay for it. If Norton returns then I do not doubt that it will be a long contention, and we have many mouths to feed. I should not like to see the women and children starve.'

'Women and children, my Lord?' Nick asked, in a voice that was full of the misgivings from his heart. Women and children, useless in terms of war, were merely a liability, and a hungry one at that.

'Many loyal gentlemen have sent their dependants here, as well as their valuables. And I shall do my best to see them safely housed.'

'Oh, I see,' said Nick limply, and the marquis, sensing that a challenge was imminent, bowed and took his leave with unhurried steps across the bowling-green.

'He's cool,' said Henry Bard, grinning hugely, and in obvious admiration. 'Hath a great sense of honour.'

'True,' Nick agreed. 'Yet it disturbs me that he has no idea of . . . expediency.'

'Lord Edward's the one for that. He'd sell his soul, I think, for the sake of expediency. Odd fellow. You don't like him, do you?'

'No, I do not.'

'Honest, you are, Howard. I would have thought a little too honest to win the game that you are playing.'

'Is that a compliment, sir? Or a warning?'

Bard laughed uncomfortably. 'Must it be either? You take things too seriously. You're as bad as Colonel Augustus.'

Nick did not smile. 'As far as I can see, sir, with the exception of your good self, Colonel Augustus is Basing's brightest hope.'

'Now, who's paying compliments? Not "sir" me. My name is Harry! Now, cheer up. Come and see the fortifications. I'm rather proud of them.'

They went out in the pouring rain beneath the wall with the deep ditch at its foot, and a brave show of purple toad-flaxes and yellow hawkweeds growing out between its bricks, and came on Edward Jeffery, with a large party of infantry, digging earthworks in the waterlogged meadow. Edward's spirits seemed also to be dampened to the point of drowning. 'Hell fire!' he said, hitting his foot with the shovel by mistake.

'Oh, come now, Ned, you haven't dug that deep yet!'

'If we had, Master Howard, this poxy rain would have put the fires out soon enough, I'll swear it.'

'You are doing great works there. A legion of moles couldn't do better.'

Edward sighed balefully. 'When I took up arms, I thought I'd be fighting with sword and musket, not pick and shovel.' He splashed his feet in the two-inch-deep puddle which had collected at the bottom of the ditch.

'Like the workmen of Nehemiah,' Nick said, smiling, and thankful that for the most part his own work was under a stout roof and not out in the torrential rain, under the grey sky.

'Who? You've already been too long with the psalm-singers, sir.'

'The workmen of Nehemiah,' Nick repeated patiently.

'Worked, I believe, with tools in one hand and weapons in the other,' added Henry Bard helpfully. But Edward seemed unimpressed.

'Aye, sir. But they were building walls, as I remember, not hedging and bloody ditching.' Ned wiped his face on his sleeve, for he was sweating, despite the cold.

'True enough, Ned. Cheer up, life is not so bad.'

'Oh, I agree, Master Howard. That is why I'm not so keen to die yet awhile. And to my mind, this is a sight too much like digging your own grave.'

'Lord, Lord!' groaned Henry Bard. 'This one's another merry cricket, right enough! Not your grave, man. Keep on digging, and we'll have enough for the whole army of Parliament, every last man of it!'

The men at Basing were not the only ones who were digging. Aunt Nan wrote that Robin was with Prince Rupert at Gloucester, digging mines and tunnels to hasten the end of the matter, which, thanks to Colonel Edward Massey, looked like being a long task, and nothing doing on either side of the wall except the exchanging of very rude messages.

'Young puppy!' Nat vowed. 'Boy ought to show more respect for his elders and betters!'

'Respect? Youth? Ned Massey's same age as Rupert – and me. I was at school with Ned, and it seems only yesterday. . . . He's a good man. 'Tis a pity that he's not ours. The common soldiers worship him! And he's as obstinate as the devil!'

'Insolent young scoundrel! May he rot in hell!' Nat said, with real bitterness.

'Something upsetting you, Nat?'

'Colonel Augustus is dead. Went to Winchester. Nat Fiennes came at them out of 'Hampton and cut them to pieces.'

'God rest his soul,' Nick said sadly, his heart heavy for the sharp-eyed, sandy-headed colonel who had been Basing's brightest hope. . . .

'And God damn Parliament!' Nat glanced up at Nick, and his face had an odd worn look about the eyes. He was far from well, Nick thought with alarm. His shoulder was slow to mend, and Nat's face stayed pale and his temper short, though on enquiry he maintained that he was perfectly well, and he always knew when rain was on the way, so that it provided a useful function.

Though Harrington was still ailing, he was not long idle. He spent his days making war by letter, writing to his hundreds of acquaintances and friends, and keeping several loyal letter-carriers well occupied, including the stout widow Jeffery: the redoubtable mother of Ned, Matt, and Josh took Nat's missives across-country, sewn firmly in her bodice, and handed them on to the next messenger. There were letters to Kent, where a secret rising of Royalists was planned; to Sussex, whose loyal gentry were preparing to welcome Hopton, just as soon as Gloucester had fallen, and he could once more gather together the scattered members of his army; and letters-of-news for the spymaster at Oxford written in invisible ink made of powder-of-gall washed over with calcined copper. Joshua Jeffery came and went through the night, on the perilous Oxford road he now knew very well.

Nat marvelled at his courage, just as Nick had done: he sat among his pens and ink, and swore that he would trust Josh with anyone's life, even his own, if it should come to it. . . .

Nick left all the ciphering to Nat, who seemed so greatly to enjoy it, and devoted his time to collecting his share of news. There was news in abundance, most of it from Broadoak, for Colonel Chadwicke was not long idle, either. Messages buzzed to and from the quiet house in the down-hollow like bees from the busy summer hives in the great orchard. Judith Chadwicke would sit for hours in the colonel's room, writing, as the colonel dictated, letters to his friends and orders for his spies. Dispatch riders galloped in and out of the yard with much clattering and jingling, and even the pigeons in the dove-cote were employed in the service of the match, Southampton was threatened. . . .

Captain Atkins, in his innocence, became a mine of information. Nick spent hours talking with him as he sat in bed, and the captain thought that he had found a firm friend: a friend who had saved his life and now beguiled his enforced idleness. Nick was warned, in confidence, that he should have a care for his safety, for there were rumours that malignant spies were abroad. As they chatted over their chess game, Nick was kept fully informed of the state of the war: Crawford was at Lymington, Maurice at Poole, Dorchester, then Weymouth, then Exeter: Portsmouth was short of match, Southampton was threatened. . . .

Frequent dining with the colonel and his officers, as well as putting meat on Nick's bones, served also to remind him what he was fighting for. He kept his own counsel as far as he could and offered no opinion unless he was asked directly. To his surprise, it was often easier to tell the truth than to fabricate, which was a relief as the fewer lies he told, the less likely was he to be confused into discovery. While the officers were busy tearing each other's arguments to shreds, they found little time to contend with the quiet, shy, scholarly surgeon who seemed half the time to be staring absent-mindedly out of the window.

Judith Chadwicke came and went about her duties of running the house like a cold shadow and treated everyone with the same distant courtesy. Nick found her intriguing because of it. He found it hard to believe that this worthy puritan wife was the one Rebecca and Nat had described to him as a wild, ungovernable girl. At least, he disbelieved until a fine spell of weather came towards the end of August. He had paid his usual visit to the colonel and was asked if he would request that Mistress Chadwicke might now go up to write some letters. Nick searched the house for some time before he found her, with Lilith. She was chewing the end of a pen and impatiently trying to set down a list of what should be consigned to the laundress.

'Three dozen pairs of falling-bands,' she said, pink with effort, 'and a dozen shirts . . . no, a dozen and a half . . . and . . .'

'Only seventeen shirts, ma'am. There's only seventeen here.'

'There are eighteen, I know. I've counted them twice already. I'm sure there are. Where is the other one?'

'Not here, ma'am.'

'Oh, no! Not again! It's so many people here. I'll never get it finished. I cannot do it all, it's not fair! And I wanted to walk in the garden!'

'Good morning, Mistress Chadwicke.'

'Good morning, sir,' she said shortly, hardly lifting her head, her brown brows furrowed with puzzlement at the mysterious disappearance of the eighteenth shirt.

'The colonel says he would like to have some letters written.'

'Would he indeed? Well, he can write his own for once, because I am busy, and you will kindly tell him so!' she exploded, throwing the pen away and making a wide gesture to indicate the piles of linen on the floor. So wide was the gesture that her elbow caught the ink-bottle and sent it flying, and ink splashed in all directions for several feet.

'Oh, it's not to be borne!' she wailed in fury, stamping her foot on the floor. 'That was your fault, Master Howard! And you shall help to clear it all up! Oh, Lilith, what shall I do? Half of it is spoiled anyway, and as it is I know not what we shall do for bed-linen . . . especially if there is any more fighting! We must buy more, whatever Thomas says! It was my money, all of it, so I shall have some say in the spending of it!' She ranted and raved and Nick tried manfully to keep a straight face, but she reminded him so much of little Lucy in one of her towering rages that he could hardly help himself. Besides which, there was an ink-smudge on the end of her long, straight, righteous nose. 'Lilith, fetch water quickly to mop up this mess! And there's no need for you to stand there looking so smug, surgeon!' She turned on him with all the force of her fury. 'It's awful! Thomas will be furious. Look at what you've done! It's dreadful!'

'It was your doing, lady, and none of mine,' he said and began to laugh. 'And it's beautiful . . . even the smudge of ink on your nose.'

'You, sir, are extremely impertinent!' she spluttered, raising both fists so that he expected her to strike him, and that made him laugh even harder.

'I'm sorry!' he hiccuped, trying desperately to control himself before it was too late. 'I'm sorry, but, oh, you look so . . . absurd. If only you could see yourself!'

To his astonishment, she wrinkled up her nose and giggled deliciously. For the first time, he realised, he had seen her smile a real smile, and not that polite apology which she put to everyday use to keep the safe barrier between herself and others. He cursed himself because he should have seen it before. He had nothing to lose, he decided. He winked at her as boldly as he dared, half-expecting a shocked rebuff.

'That,' he said, 'is a beautiful smile. Pity you don't use it more often.'

'It's no good, Master Sawbones, trying to make your peace with me by paying compliments. I shall not forgive you that easily!' She tossed her head, her eyes sparkling at him in amusement. He had made a friend, he thought. 'I must clean the ink from my face. And then I must go to see Thomas.' The light in her eyes went out abruptly.

Nick looked after her as she dashed from the room, her skirts held high and not a thought for her vanished dignity, and nearly collided with Lilith and her bucket of water at the door. Nick bade the serving-woman good-day with bland good-humour: then he took his leave of Broadoak and rode home to Stoke Sutton with a smile of enlightenment all over his face, feeling strangely contented.

That evening he told Rebecca about it, while Nat sat poring over another lengthy missive for my Lord at Oxford. 'You were right about Judith Chadwicke,' he said, stretching his arms to the kitchen fire, thankful for an hour's peace.

'In what way?' Rebecca cocked a wary eyebrow at him.

'It does not come so easily, being what Chadwicke wants.'

'Did I not tell you so? After all, it was she that told me so herself.'

'I see,' Nick said, rubbing the narrow scar on his face, and looking hard at Rebecca's turned back, which gave him few clues.

'Imagine what it must be like,' she said, 'living with that overbearing old kill-joy. Poor child!'

'Then why did she marry him in the first place? Was it . . . arranged?' He thought balefully of his own marriage, and of how trapped he had felt.

'Lord, no. She did it of her own free will. But I can see why. Her father was dead, and she was alone. There was no one else in a position to offer her marriage . . . nor likely to be, with this war. And she's getting old now. Poor Judy was afraid she would be alone for ever.'

'Old? Damn ridiculous! How old?'

'Three and twenty.'

'My age. And not so long since you were telling me I was a babe in arms.'

'Ah!' she said wisely. 'It's different for a woman, Master Nicholas. . . . Nat and I told her to think again: to put it off until she got over the shock of Phil's death. But she wouldn't. And now she repents at her leisure, as they say.' Rebecca leaned over the table, lowering her voice to a conspiratorial whisper.

'She says it's like being married to her father. She was counting on him being away at the war, you see. For she can bear it with patience, provided he doesn't . . . well . . . touch her, if you see what I mean. But he's been home since April. . . . First this leg, and then all these spyings and affairs.

Then young Tom was killed, and the old reprobate wants another son, so she's had precious little respite. Won't leave her alone for five minutes together.' Nick now knew why the girl never smiled. No one knew better than he what it was like to be married to someone you hated. That was why she had asked, on the night of the ambush, not if Tom would live, but how long it would be before Tom could go back to the army. What a legacy of misery he had unknowingly left that hot June afternoon. . . .

'I beseech you, do not tell anyone. I was not supposed to say anything, not even to Nat. She would rather die than let anyone know. Die of shame if she knew I'd told you! But you understand now, don't you?'

A movement in the doorway caught her eye, and Nick's. Nat had been standing there for several minutes, listening intently, and neither of them had noticed. Rebecca blushed, and Nick met his gaze uncomfortably.

'Hmmm,' Nat said, 'May I give you a word of advice, young fellow? You must not entangle yourself too far in other people's affairs, however pretty those people may be. Or you might find yourself cornered, and maybe even – confounded. Matthew is coming round the back. 'Becca, can you let him in, please?'

Matthew stumbled in through the door, panting and soaked to the skin, his ancient leather apron running with rain.

'Quick!' he gasped. 'Colonel Sir Humphrey Bennet's at Andover!'

'Humphrey Bennet?' Nick said, curiously. 'Well, well, what of it?'

'You know him, sir?'

'He is an old friend of my aunt's, yes.'

'Maybe "was" by now. Norton's rebels are going to attack Andover. Imminently.'

'Get Josh to saddle up, while I write a warning. Is it raining again?'

'Aye, like the second deluge was on its way, sir.'

It was indeed raining as if the second deluge was on its way. It rained through the end of August, and on into September. The harvest was ruined, the grain beaten flat in the fields. And young Colonel Edward Massey held Gloucester for the Parliament until Lord Essex arrived on the fifth day of September to relieve the city. Rupert's damp, dejected Royalists withdrew from their flooded works and marched back towards Oxford, half starved and in heavy-hearted despondency. Things had begun to go wrong for the King.

14

A COLD IN THE HEAD

The evil weather, and too much burning of the candle at both ends, succeeded where both Waller's army and Captain Atkins' men had failed and laid Nick low. He had caught a cold in the head and crawled about as miserable as sin. He sniffed his way over to Broadoak in the torrential rain to see the colonel, and tottered up to Chadwicke's paper-strewn room still shaking the raindrops from his hair, feeling thoroughly unpleasant. He found Tom Chadwicke and his wife staring at each other across the table in stony silence and immediately regretted that he had come, for by the atmosphere in the room, he gathered that he had interrupted a tooth-and-nail conflict. Almost before he had exchanged the usual stiff formalities with them someone else arrived, and that someone was in no good humour, either.

'Colonel Richard Norton to see you, sir,' wheezed the corporal hesitantly, unsure of whether the moment was entirely opportune. The words had no sooner left his lips than the whole house began to vibrate with the approach of Colonel Norton who came storming in, still in his dripping cloak, ducking his head only just in time to avoid the door-lintel. He threw his wet hat and gloves on the table in front of Chadwicke and came straight to the point. 'I've a carcass of bones to pick with you, Tom,' he said, 'and I'll not be kept waiting. I've work to do.'

'Excuse me,' said Nick hastily, and made for the door, but Norton laughed.

'Don't mind me, sawbones, I'll not keep the colonel long. Good day to you, Mistress Chadwicke.'

Nick followed Mistress Chadwicke from the room and shut the door behind them, but, despite the door's stoutness, they could not help but hear, because Colonel Norton was shouting fit to lift the house-roof.

'I've been made a laughing-stock, and I do not like it!' he said.

'I am . . . sorry you think that, Dick. Am I in some way responsible?'

'That business at Andover,' said Norton. 'Bennet was warned, you know. Somebody got to him and told him we were coming. And that makes me look very foolish, does it not?'

'Knew you were coming? It was a secret. I do not understand.'

Nick understood, even if the colonel did not. Humphrey Bennet had sent a reply full of the warmest gratitude for the warning letter, after he had beaten Norton off. . . .

'I have a . . . friend, in Crawford's regiment,' Norton continued. Nick stiffened. One of Lord Crawford's men was a spy for Parliament. He wondered if it was anyone he knew. 'He says that Bennet was definitely warned. And those culverin you promised me at Basing. They never arrived. We said Sunday, did we not? If they had come when you said they would, the place might be ours now.'

'Might be ours? I fail to see how I could have stopped that ambush. I warned Harvey . . . and I nearly lost my life over those guns. Really, it is too bad to lay the blame at my door!'

'Let me finish, Tom. Whoever it was must have known that the culverin were delayed, for the ambush was not until the Sunday night, as I remember.'

'All right, Dick. But the King's men would still have arrived the next day. And I suppose you'll blame me for that?' Chadwicke's voice was even despite the provocation, but the tones held more of weariness than patience, Nick thought.

'We might still have held it. That place is as secure as the Tower if you are inside it. You've treachery here, Tom, and I think you had better find it out before we are all lost.'

'Now look here, Dick,' said Chadwicke, beginning to get angry. 'You are being ridiculous. What has unmanned you, that you must jib at shadows? My men are hand-picked, like yours. There are no spies here. I'll stake my life on it.'

'You have, Thomas. You already have. Someone is passing information to the King, and you had better watch your step! If I didn't know you so well, I'd swear it was you!' Norton's hand turned the door-handle, and the door opened a crack. 'And I tell you another thing!'

'What?'

'That Bennet. I'll have him – for breakfast, if it's the last thing I do! And I warn you, Tom . . .'

'Warn? That's an odd word to use to an old friend. I am sorry, Dick. I can assure you of my continuing loyalty . . . and that of my men, also. Will you stay to refresh yourself?'

'No, thanks, Tom. I'm sorry. I lost my temper. I've a good deal to worry over, just now. Yet things may soon resolve themselves. This offer of assistance I've had from one of Crawford's officers seems to be genuine enough. I'd like to make the most of it, if that meets with your approval?'

'If you wish, then by all means. I rely on your judgement, as ever. What is his name, this friend of yours?'

The door shut again, and the voices were murmuring no louder than a whisper. Nick ground his teeth in fury. Now Norton was really being less than helpful.

'Give you good-day, Tom, Master Howard. Your servant, madam.' Norton was gone, his wet cloak dripping behind him, leaving an embarrassed silence. 'I'm sorry about that,' Chadwicke said, shrugging helplessly.

'I . . . understand,' Nick replied, shifting uncomfortably, and not quite knowing what he should say. 'They tell me you are not so well today, sir. Might I suggest that you should rest for a while?' Nick sneezed.

'Rest? I suppose so. Though I ought . . .'

'Please, Thomas. Master Howard knows best. Though I

think that he himself is not in the best of health today.'

The colonel went to bed, without further protest. 'Oh, God,' he lamented. 'What a day! I try to keep faith, but the Lord God seems to make it so difficult. I'm only human.'

Nick wiped his nose; it was sore, and streaming. 'You try to do too much, sir. That leg needs rest, or it will never heal.'

'It would have been better for me to die.'

'Oh, come, sir. It's not like you to be so miserable. Why do you say that?'

'He took my son. Why did he not take me instead? What had Tom done? He was a fine boy. Strong in the Lord.'

'No doubt,' said Nick, desolately. 'But it is not for us to guess what the Almighty has in mind for us, is it? Now, things will look better if you rest. I shall be off home. I envy you. You are in the best place, today.' He sneezed forcibly.

'Thank you, Master Howard,' said Judith. 'I wonder if you would wait below in the parlour for me. I should like a word with you, if I may?'

Nick sat downstairs in the parlour, shivering and miserable before the fire, staring into its crackling depths in contemplation. There was a traitor in Crawford's regiment. Nick's head throbbed in sympathy with the squalling rain which hurtled, crashing, against the window-panes. The sentries in the yard would be cowering in the doorways. It would be foul for Robin, marching his men back from Gloucester towards Oxford, racing against time and Essex for the possession of the homeward road. 'Atishoo!' Nick sneezed.

Judith Chadwicke appeared. 'You, Master Howard, should not have come out on a day like this. You'll catch your death,' she said.

'I think I have caught my death already,' he said lugubriously, staring into the steam which wreathed up mysteriously from the mug she put into his hand.

'Come, physician, heal thyself,' she laughed, and Nick sniffed.

'What is this?'

'A blackcurrant posset. My grandmother's recipe. Can you not smell it?'

'I cannot smell anything today,' he said, thickly. 'Looks like ink. What does it taste like?'

'You are like a child! Drink it!'

He took a cautious sip, and gave a yelp. 'Oh, God! It's hot! And it tastes like ink, too. Must I?'

'It is not polite to refuse, you know. Besides, it is good for you. Lord knows you need something! Drink it while it's still hot. Go on, just to please me!'

'As long as you understand that I would not drink poison for anyone else,' he laughed, and drank most of it down as fast as he could, until he choked and spluttered. He put the cup down again. 'Ugh! You are very kind, madam, I'm sure. I must go back home now,' he sighed, looking at the grey view from the window, and shivered at the prospect of another drenching.

'Poor Master Howard. Are you cold?' She looked at him in concern and shook her head.

'Freezing,' he said, and felt dreadful. Judith crossed to his chair, and laid a smooth hand on his forehead. It was bliss, and he wished that it could remain there for ever.

'You have a fever on you!' she said sternly. 'You must stay here by the fire, and then you will feel better, I expect, tomorrow morning. I do not know what possessed you to come in the first place. Men are all the same, obstinate and intractable.'

'If you say so,' he nodded in misery. 'Oh, Lord, I'm miserable!' He blew his nose, and she laughed again.

'Poor old thing! Come, there is some left, you did not drink it all. I will be back in a moment. I am going to see if my poor Tom is feeling any better.'

When she had gone, he stretched his shivering hands out to the fire, and thought of little Lucy. It would be her birthday soon: three years since Elizabeth died, and it seemed more like thirty. Nick wondered if Lucy stood on tiptoe on her window-seat and looked at the rain. Maybe by now she could see without standing on tiptoe; she must have grown since he had last seen her. . . .

'He's asleep.' Judith Chadwicke came back. 'He's having a very bad day today, what with the weather, and all these arguments.'

'You mean Norton? I am sorry I overheard, but I could not help . . .'

'Oh, that is not really what upset him. He and I had a quarrel this morning, too. I lost my temper, and said a lot of things.'

'For which you are now sorry, I know.'

'No, I am not! I meant them. It is high time I told him some home truths!'

'That sounds a little forbidding?'

'Would you not agree, then, Master Howard, that it is always better to tell the truth?'

'I . . . I am not convinced. Sometimes the truth hurts too many people too much.'

She sighed. 'I suppose you are right. . . . I am sorry for what I said. At least you are honest with me, and do not tell me only what you think I might like to hear. I like you, Master Howard. It is not often these days that one meets someone who can be trusted.' A wave of desolation swept over him. Here was the colonel's wife telling him how honest he was, when all the time he was the spy in their midst, lying and cheating, and deceiving. . . .

'Oh, Mistress Chadwicke,' he said, and sneezed again. 'Let me give you a word of advice. Never trust anyone. Except yourself.'

'I trust myself least of all, Master Howard.' She stared out of the window. 'I find it so difficult to be patient. I do not make enough – allowance – for him. It must have been a terrible shock, to lose his son like that. It is difficult to appreciate what grief it is to lose a child. . . .'

'Impossible, unless you have one of your own. I think it would break me to lose my . . .' he had said it before he realised, because the thought of Lucy had been fresh in his mind. Judith Chadwicke's eyes were drawn wide with shocked surprised; but it was too late to unsay anything. The truth must be told now.

'You have children, Master Howard?'

'Only one. A little girl. She will be three years old next week.'

'In Marlborough?'

'Yes. At home in Marlborough.'

Her voice was suddenly very small. 'And – your wife, too? You must miss her, Master Howard?'

'My wife died when the child was born.'

'I'm . . . so sorry.'

'Do not be sorry. I wasn't. She and I . . . did not see eye to eye about anything. And never would have. It was a mercy, really.' He shrugged, his smile bitter and his voice sharp and unnatural. He was conscious that the grey eyes were now staring at him very hard. 'I've shocked you. But you could not understand.'

'Oh, yes, I can. Perhaps better than you think. It's very sad.'

'What is?'

'That there should be no one to weep . . . for someone's dying.'

'Not sad. I'm glad there is no one to weep over me.'

'You will feel a lot better tomorrow. Now, please can we change the subject? I do not want to talk of death. It frightens me to think that one day I must die, too. Are you ever afraid, Master Howard?'

'All the time,' he said, with conviction and perfect honesty. 'And I wish that you would stop calling me "Master Howard" every second word. I was christened Nicholas.'

'Oh,' she gulped. 'Indeed I would like to call you Nicholas, because you are my friend, I think. But I must not. Thomas would not like it. He would consider it not quite . . . polite.' She was blushing furiously and turned back to stare from the window. The back of her neck was very pink against the starched white of her stiff collar, and a few wisps of hair strayed from her coif like threads of twisted gold silk. He would have liked very much to kiss her, he thought suddenly.

'My dear lady, you may tell Thomas that I'm not unduly bothered whether or not you are polite to me. I am glad that you count me as a friend: very glad. And if you were ever to need . . . a friend, I should like to feel that you would think of me first of all.' He bowed at her, mockingly, but it was himself he was mocking. And she curtsied gravely and smiled her lovely smile.

'I must go tell Lilith you will be staying,' she said. 'And then I'll peep in at Thomas. If you will excuse me, Master Howard?'

Nick sat alone and cursed himself. He was not only a dishonest knave, he thought, but also a stupid fool, because he had begun to covet that which he could never have. The aching within him was nothing to do with a cold in the head; it was an ache of love for his enemy's comely wife.

A long time passed before there was another letter from Aunt Nan. She had written on the last day of September, and one look at Rebecca's stricken face and the odd jaggedness of the writing told Nick that something terrible had happened. The two armies had met, not far from Newbury, and a battle had been fought for passage. Robin was dead: like thousands of others, in a bitter fight which had cost both sides dear, and gained nothing for either.

15

A SOBER, SENSIBLE FELLOW

Now Nick redoubled his efforts to bring down the rebels, throwing himself with added eagerness into the completion of the task before him. He had two very good reasons for doing so. The first was undoubtedly revenge, for he meant them all to pay dearly for the death of his brother. The other reason was more complicated, and at first he would not admit it to himself: if his days and nights were filled with work, then his heart and mind might be distracted from the colonel's pretty wife.

To avoid Broadoak completely was impossible, he found, for the colonel was a lot closer with his papers when Nat was about, and there was information they must have. The marquis' men waited eagerly to sweep down on any unwary supply-train, and there was the small matter of a traitor in Crawford's regiment, whose name neither of them could discover, despite every effort. There was great alarm in the House of Commons. Rumours were rife that Royalist spies were active in Hampshire, Surrey, and Sussex, because the King's new baron, Hopton of Stratton, was planning to strike across the south-east counties. Sir William Waller was given orders to raise a new army to replace that which, at Roundway, he had so sadly lost.

Nat came back from Broadoak looking anxious. Nick met him in the yard and watched the weariness of his dismounting, and it made him worried. These days he looked perpetually tired, and so much of his natural ebullience seemed to be lacking.

'Panic,' Nat said. 'They say Royalist spies are everywhere.' He smiled wryly.

'Very likely, Nathaniel, very likely.' Nick winked at him. 'Any signs of Waller yet?'

'Not yet. Don't need Waller. You, my lad, are in enough trouble already.'

'I'm shaking in my shoes. What's afoot?'

'Serious trouble.' Nat was not joking, his face was like thunder.

Nick's heart sank to his feet, as he racked his brains, wondering how he had transgressed. 'What have I done?' he asked, although he did not really want to know.

'For a start,' Nat said, 'Judith is complaining loudly that you have been trying to avoid her, and she is furious.'

Nick went cold but could feel that his face was turning a brilliant red. 'Is that all? What rubbish!' he said aggressively. 'Anyway, does it matter?'

'By the look of you, I should say that you think it does. What on earth are you up to? Come on, let's have it! I'm no fool, and neither is she. It is obvious that you have been making great efforts to keep away. When we were there last week, you rushed off as soon as she put in an appearance.'

'Mind your own business, Nat.' Nick clenched his fists. He was going to lose his temper, and that very soon.

'Look here! The way you are proceeding, it will hang me also. So it is my business! Is there something between you two? I will not be put off! You will answer me here and now!'

'No,' Nick said, very quietly. 'There is nothing whatsoever between Mistress Chadwicke and myself. And that is the truth.' He turned away to go into the house, but Nat's long arm shot out, and Nat's hand caught him by the shoulder and spun him round.

'But you wish there was,' he hissed. 'You stupid, bloody fool, Nick! No, you come back here and listen to me. Answer me just one question. Are you in love with Judith?'

Nick could not look at him and lie, because Nat already

knew the answer. 'Yes, I suppose I am. I know I'm stupid, so there is no need to take me to task. You can be as angry as you like, I deserve it. But it cannot alter anything.'

'Poor Nick! Poor Nick! A pair of bright eyes . . . and something we none of us bargained for. I should have seen it coming.' Nat's eyes were no longer flaming with anger, but full of pity. He sighed. 'But I fear that I may not be the only one who has guessed. There is a message for you, from the colonel. He would like to see you as soon as may be, in order to discuss something. A matter of great importance he says.'

Nick felt very sick. 'It might not be that,' he said, lamely.

'Whatever it is, it could be nasty. So take care, friend, I beg you. I do not want to have to explain away your sudden death to my Lord at Oxford.'

'I'll go now. Get it over. Oh, God, I wonder what he wants from me?'

'Anxious to get it over? Always impatient, you are, Nicholas! But be cautious, please. You may kill yourself if you will, but spare a thought for the rest of us.'

It was Judith who met Nick in the hall, neat and tidy as ever, her golden-brown face smiling politely above the square white collar, as if there was nothing wrong at all. 'Good afternoon to you, Master Howard. My husband is at the moment from home, but he will be back in an hour or so, he said, he has not gone far. He said you might be coming. So come up, I pray you, and wait.' She hesitated, and then a trace of sarcasm stole into her voice. 'That is, if you do not mind my company for a while?'

'It would be a pleasure, madam,' Nick lied, thinking of the utter misery it meant to him.

'I'm sure,' she said, as he shut the door of the parlour and turned to face her. 'Then why, Master Howard, have you been avoiding me of late? For weeks I have hardly seen you to speak to.'

'Avoiding you? That is absurd. It is not so cold today.'

'Absurd. Yes.' Her voice was scathing, and the weather she

wished to ignore. Lilith brought canary-wine, which Judith poured. Then there was uncomfortable silence in the parlour, except for Nick's tuneless whistling under his breath. Judith took up her sewing and sat by the window, stitching away furiously at the piece of linen, and Nick watched her, and heartily wished that he had never been born.

'Why are you staring at me?' Judith said, angrily, sucking a bleeding finger where the tiny needle had stabbed it.

'Staring? Am I? I did not mean to. I was just . . . thinking.'

'You, Master Howard, do a deal too much thinking, to my mind! Is there something wrong?'

'Why? Should there be?' He smiled defiantly, his tone that of a hostile child which knows itself to be wrong.

She threw the sewing on the floor, and made a small gesture of hopelessness. 'It will never be right! I shall never be any good at needlework. Anyway, I cannot concentrate.' Judith got up and crossed the room towards him, and he watched her small feet approaching across the waxed floorboards, and did not dare to look at her face. 'Something is worrying you. Please tell me about it,' she asked softly. 'You said that we were friends.'

'I cannot. Please do not ask me to tell.' It was his turn to plead, but he knew he was losing the fight, and that, anyway, he had never really wanted to win it. Tom Chadwicke was not at home. Judith was standing so close that he might have reached out and touched her: and that, above all else, was what he wanted to do.

'I've done something to give offence. I know it,' she continued.

'No, far from it. You have been blameless, absolutely blameless.'

'Then what is it?' Her face was all innocence. He stared into those wide grey eyes again, and knew that he was lost.

'Oh, God! The woman doesn't know! You said once . . . do you remember . . . that you liked to be told the truth. And I said that sometimes it is better left untold.'

'Of course I remember.'

'If you want the truth, then you shall have it, for what it's worth. Madam, of late I have become . . . fond of you. I . . . love you. I've tried not to, God knows. But I cannot help it. There, now you know, and it does no good. I'm sorry if I cause you any embarrassment. I'm sorry.'

'Sorry? Oh – Nicholas.'

'I'll go. Will you tell the colonel I'll come tomorrow?'

'No, do not go. Why? If it's the truth that you love me . . . then I want you to stay.' She caught at his arm, and he did not try to free himself. What could he do but kiss her? He had dreamed so many times of kissing her, only this time it was real. Her arms went close about his neck, and her body was warm against his. He was left in no doubt that her feelings for him were far more than friendship. He knew that what he did was wrong, and he could not have cared less: nothing else in all the world could matter. But then she pushed him away, her cheeks flaming, and his arms were emptier than ever. 'Oh, God, what have I done? What would Thomas think of me?'

'All right, I am a rogue. It was my fault. And I was the one who told you to trust nobody. It is best . . . to forget . . . all about it.' His heartbeat pounded in his ears, and it was an effort to make himself think.

Judith sat once more on the window-seat and put her hands to her burning cheeks. 'Oh, you are right. It would be best forgotten. It is easy enough to see it, and to say it. But after . . . that, nothing can ever be quite the same.' She spoke to herself rather than to him. He looked at the ceiling's strapwork decoration and smiled a smile of agreement, though he wanted to weep like a child. 'Nicholas Howard,' she said. 'I love you. You cannot ask me to forget that.'

'You must. For your own sake. There are many very good reasons; not the least of which is the fact that you are married to Thomas Chadwicke.'

'Yes, married. And what have I just done? Played the harlot, and nothing less!'

'You have done nothing wrong. Just kissed me, that is all. A kiss. It means . . . absolutely nothing. . . .'

'Oh, God, Tom is coming. I can hear him.'

'Good old Tom!' said Nick, bitterly. 'Good old Tom. I

wish that I was rogue enough not to care that you belong to someone else. But it can bring nothing but pain to all of us.'

'Belong? I am not anyone's property! My heart and soul are . . . my own, and you know it!'

'Oh, Judith, I love you so. I always shall.'

Her eyes met his with such yearning that he had to turn away before all his resolutions crumbled. It was all very well to steal another man's wife, if only he had been the respectable surgeon she thought him to be. It was another thing, however, to be a malignant spy . . . a deceiver. If she found that out, then surely she would hate him for it.

'I'd like you to remember, Judith. Whatever happens, I love you. Whatever happens.' He repeated it, hoping that it might never be needful for her to remember.

'Oh, hush, here's Tom up the stairs. Where's the needle gone?' She picked up her sewing in a rush of fumbling haste. When Thomas came in, the mask of polite formality was once more in place, and the warm lips that Nick had been kissing just a few short minutes before were now enquiring coolly if the colonel had a successful expedition.

'Most successful, thank you, my dear, most successful. I wonder if you would come to my office, Master Howard? It is kind of you to attend me so promptly. We have seen little of you lately. I trust you are in good health?'

'Thriving, I thank you. You seem to be mending so well, sir, that there is happily little occasion for you to have need of my services.'

Nick cast his sharp eyes over the untidy table in the office. Papers were everywhere, and some of them packets, already addressed. How very careless of the colonel. . . . The top packet had a familiar name on it, a name which leaped out at him. There was no mistaking it: so it was someone he knew. 'To Lieutenant Mottham, in privacy and haste, these.' Mottham must have bribed and fawned his way to promotion, but of course that would not be enough for him, so he had done exactly what one might have expected, and tried to set a foot in the other camp, also. No real surprise . . . and yet Crawford must be told as soon as possible.

'You must be wondering why I asked you to come.'

'I must admit, sir, that I was intrigued. I hope I have not given cause for complaint?'

'No, indeed, Master Howard. It is merely a . . . proposition I wished to put to you. General Waller is raising an army – you are no doubt aware?'

'Yes, sir, Captain Atkins did mention it.'

'It had occurred to me . . . that is . . . I wondered if you had ever thought of – taking up arms yourself? You are a sober, sensible fellow. Just the sort we really need. What do you say?'

Nick was astonished. Was the colonel really that stupid? Had he been so completely taken in? Or was he using a very clever ruse to scare a malignant spy out into the open? Tom Chadwicke's face was impassive, telling him nothing. Such a question needed a careful response, or else all would be ruined.

'I do not know what to say, sir.'

'I'll give you a commission. Surgeon-Captain Howard. How does that sound?'

Nick's brain turned cartwheels. His knees were weak. Now he knew how Hercules must have felt, trying to take the sky from Atlas without bringing it all crashing about his ears.

'I'm flattered, sir, I really am. But no . . . I could not do it.'

'Why ever not?'

'I am too much of a coward, for a start.'

'That I cannot believe.'

'My heart would not be in it.'

'Then you are a – Royalist, Master Howard?'

'I did not say that.'

Nick stared the colonel straight in the eye and talked for his life. No, he thought, I didn't say it. But I shall not deny it, either. He had no doubts that if he gave the wrong answer then the colonel would have him quietly destroyed. An enemy without mercy lurked behind those eyes; but also, he thought, a potential friend.

'I am a peace-loving soul. I do not like the thought of . . . killing. I cannot explain to you if you do not understand.' He shrugged. The colonel could believe it or not, but it was true anyway . . . every word of it. He did not like to kill. Yet that did not mean that he would not do it.

'That is odd,' said the colonel with a smile. 'Judith told me you would say that, and that you would refuse. A man of conscience is worthy of respect, Master Surgeon.'

Nick breathed a silent prayer of thanks to his guardian angel and loved Judith even more; for, without knowing what she was at, she had gone a fair way to saving his life, he was sure.

'I suppose arguing with you will not change your mind. No, you'd not be the man I think you are if it would. But if you should reconsider, please tell me. The offer shall stand. A captain's commission. Think about it, Master Howard.'

Nick wished that Judith had not spoken up for him. If ever she was to find out, she would never forgive him, and it would be better to die now than to have her hate him.

'I am honoured, sir, by your offer. But I think it – unlikely – that I shall change my mind.'

'So be it. You are an honest man, Master Howard. Very much like my son. You would have liked Thomas. . . . Colonel Norton will be as disappointed as I am that you have decided not to join us, for he he said that he had been considering making an approach to you himself. Will you stay and dine with us today?'

'I regret, sir, I must be going. I promised Rebecca that I would be back. As it is I shall be late, and she will be wroth with me.'

Nick reeled out into the cool evening, his stomach heaving dreadfully.

He needed fresh air, and time to think: time to stop himself from shaking. Should he run now? He could not run. If he did, then Nat and the others would be in danger. He had no choice but to stay. At least Judith loved him, if only for the moment. He would stay and snatch what happiness he could, before the noose tightened around his neck: the noose he had put over his own head.

He told Nat about the colonel's offer, and Nat laughed savagely. 'My God, Nicholas. I take my hat off to you! Poor Tom! You know, I almost feel sorry for him?' Nat chuckled, full of cruel glee. 'So poor old Tom trusts you like his own son. His son you murdered, and not content with that, you'll have his wife as well! Don't leave him anything, will you? You've not a streak of mercy, have you?'

Nick ignored Nathaniel's delight. A hard knot of unhappiness gathered between his eyebrows. 'Do you not think that Norton is suspicious?'

'No, not he. If Norton was suspicious then you would be in gaol in Portsmouth, and a few of his sturdy Hambledon boys with you to persuade you to admit your guilt. Norton's a soldier, Nicholas. Straight. Like they think you are! You are bloody convincing. Do you know, when you first came I had my doubts whether you would be vicious enough? But you make the rest of us look like stained-glass saints!'

'Vicious? Nat, I do only what I'm forced to do,' Nick protested.

'Oh, yes? John Willet was more than a fraction right, I'm thinking. But devil or not, I admire you. Mind you, you must be grossly insulted to be offered a captaincy for Parliament, when you've already a higher rank in the King's army. Hold out for a lieutenant-colonel's commission at least. That would be a lot more tempting.' Nat's cynical face leered at him, and he wanted to hit it on the nose.

'Nat, there are times when I could cheerfully kill you.'

'I shall die laughing before ever you come to draw your sword. It's years since I heard anything so funny! Poor old Chadwicke's met his match! And Norton, too. You'll be a general – if you don't hang first, that is. I wonder which it will be, a general or a corpse?' And Nat was still laughing out in the yard as Nick slammed the back door behind him.

16

FRIENDS IN HIGH PLACES

The Earl of Crawford thought it preposterous that one of his officers should be accused of treachery. The accusation was too ridiculous even to mention to the lieutenant. He knew that in the past there had been some personal argument between them, and only spite could be to blame for such outrageous assertions. Nat read the crisp missive with silent dismay and looked to Nick for an explanation. His reply was a miserable nod, as Nick haltingly described the unpleasantness at Bath, watching Harrington's face creasing slowly into its most ill-humoured frown.

'I hope that my Lord Crawford will in fact do as he says, and not mention you to the lieutenant, my friend.' Nat helped himself to a measure of sack so generous that it spilled in glistening drips over the brim of the glass, and spoiled the polished table. 'Or you are a dead man.'

'I'd not thought of that,' said Nick woefully, thinking of it now. If Mottham knew where he was, then it was all up. He kicked viciously at the sullen smouldering logs in the fireplace, and the pile collapsed with a crackling shower of sparks, so that he had to draw his foot back hastily.

'Do not lose hope, however, Nicholas. It is not yet a lost cause.'

'Merely mightily distressed!'

Nat ignored the bitter comment and continued, 'There are several courses of action still open to us.'

'Well? Crawford will not believe me. Not ever. So now you tell me what to do.'

'We could perhaps find Lieutenant Mottham, and remove him: but I think that might be rather, er, hazardous. We'll leave that possibility until we have tried other means.'

'What other means? And I would defy anyone to kill Mottham quietly, certainly.'

'Another possibility is that you should rapidly take up your friend Tom Chadwicke's kind offer.'

'Nat, be serious. This will be the death of us all.'

'I was never more serious in my life. It is the only way to be sure of saving your skin. I think I would, if I were you. Why do you not have a drink? And stop pacing up and down, you make me dizzy.'

'That's too bad. I cannot think sitting down.'

'You cannot think at all these days. I wish you would stop mooning over Judith and get some sense into your head before you kill us all.'

'Nathaniel, you are insufferable! I've more on my mind than Mistress Chadwicke just now.'

'Indeed I'm relieved to hear it. Would the Lord Hopton listen to you? Could you not go straight to him?'

'I could. But he would take the matter back to Crawford. Hopton knows there is no love lost between Mottham and myself, and he has a poor opinion of any of his officers who wrangle amongst themselves.'

'Surely if you were to put it – er – delicately?'

'I'll not fawn and flatter and creep, if that is what you mean. Even if it means I am risking my neck. But do not disturb yourself, Master Harrington, I shall not risk yours if I can help it!'

'Oh, Christ! There are times when you gall me beyond endurance, Nicholas Howard! You may go hang yourself! Or join the rebels and have done, it's no odds to me!'

'Nat, let us not fall out over it, I need your help. I'm sorry.'

'Sorry! There are lives at stake beside your own, and maybe the whole war, and you are sorry? Is there not someone who will intercede for us? Do you know anyone who has Hopton's ear? It is an ally we need.'

'I have few friends in high places. I've not been out of my way to cultivate any!' said Nick, with disgust.

'Give me patience! What about Sir Humphrey Bennet of Pythouse, Lord High Sheriff of the County of Southampton? He is a family friend, you said. And he most definitely owes you a sizeable favour, does he not?'

'Nat, you are brilliant! He is a friend of Ralph Hopton's, I know. Why did I not think of that?'

'Hmmm. . . . I'm not brilliant, merely desperate. Sir Humphrey is at Alton presently. I think that it may be expedient for you to pay him a visit.'

Nick set out the following day for Alton, and Josh with him. The day was full of bright October sunshine, and the hedges festooned with the silver filigree of sparkling, gossamer, spider webs. 'Cheer up, sir,' said Josh. 'Beautiful day.'

'Yes, Josh. Real autumn.' Nick looked round at the trees and the bracken turned to shades of gold, and watched the cloud-shadows chasing each other across the green grass, and the dappling shadows of the trees, their leaves spinning through the air. One could hardly be despondent when the world was so bright and fresh, and Josh always reminded him that there was still laughter, despite everything. Tears of mirth rolled down Nick's face as he listened to Josh's cheerful account of how a Roundhead sergeant had threatened him with the fate of King Egon of Moab when they had come face to face in the dark below Winchester castle walls. Josh's imitation of a stout Anabaptist was so true to life that Nick thought he might burst with laughing.

'And I couldn't remember what had happened to King Egon, sir. So I asked him. He was at great pains to tell me!'

'I can imagine. Was it not painful and extremely messy?'

'Aye, it was, sir. Horrible!' Josh rolled his eyes.

'You should have been a player, Josh. You have mistaken your calling.'

Josh sighed. 'I was sorry I had to smash him on the head with my musket. I suppose I should have shot him to make sure he was dead, but I couldn't somehow. Do you understand?'

'Of course I understand. . . . Makes you feel sick, does it not?'

'Yes. Do you know, I thought it was just me, sir? That I'm a coward, and you're . . . well . . . so brave. Do you really worry sometimes?'

'Oh, Josh. You, of all people, are never a coward. Of course I worry. Everyone does.'

'That's good to know, sir,' said Josh, introspectively. 'My, this wind's got an edge to it. I'm not sorry we're nearly there.'

Colonel Sir Humphrey Bennet seemed surprised to see his visitor, but he welcomed him with a friendly hand and a call for refreshment, and readily dismissed the two officers with him, so that they might talk privately.

'Well, Nicholas? It is good to see you. But to what do I owe the pleasure of this visit? Is it a social call?'

'Not entirely, sir, no.'

'How is your Aunt Nan? And the babe?'

'They are well, I think, sir, thank you.'

'I was . . . grieved . . . to hear of . . . your brother's death. You must bitterly regret his loss.'

'Yes, I do. Most bitterly.' Nick went quiet, wishing that Humphrey Bennet had not raised the subject. The wound was too new, too raw to be touched without pain.

'Colonel Bolle was most afflicted. I saw him the day after. They were good friends, I believe?'

'They were very close, yes. How is John? I have not seen him for months.'

'He is in very good health, though seldom in good temper. I think he has a difficult time with those men of his, bickering and fighting between themselves. He was telling me that he himself had a narrow escape. At Devizes, was it not? And that you were responsible for his deliverance. I myself owe you much, for we should have been cut to pieces at Andover if it were not for your timely intervention.'

Sir Humphrey puffed at his pipe of tobacco, emitting wreaths of smoke that made Nick's nose itch, and leaned back in his elbow-chair, surveying Nick's black-clad figure with curiosity, and making him feel very ill at ease. 'I must admit,' he said at length, 'that you are looking a little . . . strange. I'd have taken you for a rebel, if I did not know better. However,' he coughed, 'there is something I can do for you? I should be glad to repay my debt.'

'I should not like you to feel under any obligation to me for that, sir. It is my duty to render what service I can,' Nick said stiffly. He had rehearsed his speech many times in his head, yet still it seemed difficult to explain the complicated series of events which had led up to his visit. The words he had weighed so carefully last night eluded him this morning. He limped to his conclusion, his eyes intent on his boots, which were very dirty. 'I am not trying to cause trouble, sir, please believe me. I am convinced that it could be of extreme importance. I know how difficult it may be for you to take a hand in the matter. Lord Crawford is a hard man to cross.'

'It seems not so hard for me to risk a few bitter words, when you will lay down your very life. Is it not – likely – that you will be discovered to them?'

'I am beginning to fear that it is inevitable. But what am I to do? Turn tail, and leave the others to take the consequences?'

'I will do what I can to aid you. A man like that in a regiment is like a canker in an apple: treachery will spread to all it touches, I've seen it before. I've not much sympathy with Crawford. He is puffed up with pride and fed on flattery. That's how your traitor has come so far. If it is not checked it will be disaster, you're right on that score.'

'I am indebted to you for your sympathy and for your indulgence, sir.'

'I cannot promise you that I shall be much help, but I will try. Though Waller will be making a move soon, I think. And 'tis John Bolle's men at Wallingford, or else my own here, must delay him until my Lord Hopton is within striking distance. Which of us it is depends on the direction he takes.'

'He is bound for Basing, I hear, sir.'

'I was afraid of that,' Humphrey Bennet sighed heavily. 'I've seven hundred men all told. But I can count on half of them to run at the first sight of an orange-tawny sash and a pike or two. And last I heard, Sir William has seven thousand. In a standing fight we have no chance. No chance at all.'

'I fear they are intent on destroying you, sir. I heard Colonel Norton say so. It went hard with his pride at Andover, and he is anxious to taste blood.'

'As long as it is his own blood, I've no objection,' Bennet said drily, heaving himself out of the chair and crossing the room to stare out of the window at the busy market-square and the church with its tapering spire and flint-walled yard. 'Look at this town,' he said. 'It is a pighole full of rogues and rebels. Will be impossible to defend, you mark my words. Too open.'

'I wish that I could do more to help you, sir. Thank you for your hospitality, but I think I must take my leave, now.'

'Already? Take care, my Roundhead friend.'

'I'm not a suicide, sir.'

When they reached home Nick was silent and doleful, and he made off to the quiet haven of the parlour to sit brooding by the window, cursing Mottham roundly for causing all the trouble. He pondered Nat's suggestion to kill the man before he did any more damage and discarded it as impracticable. What on earth had possessed him to embark on this venture?

Nat's laughter set the whole house echoing, and grated on Nick's nerves like a nail scraping on a window-pane. It was all so futile, he thought. The world would go on when he was gone, and the vast majority of people in it would never even know that he had ever existed.

Nick wondered what Judith was doing at that moment. The colonel's house was run to the time of the clock, and no doubt she was even now dining with the colonel, and Captain Atkins and the others, and looking as cool and as tidy and self-assured as ever. Did she ever think of him with the same fierce longing? What would happen when she found out the truth about the man who said he loved her, the man who was her trusted friend? Would she think that his love, too, was a lie?

The rooks circled the church tower and cawed in the elm trees as the golden afternoon turned to deep blue with the approach of evening. The discoloured elm leaves were falling fast, torn roughly from their branches by the whirling wind, dancing an erratic funeral dance in the air before coming to rest in the churchyard in the dark between the gravestones. He could not tell Judith the truth, it would be too cruel; more cruel than to continue in falsehood. If she really loved him it would be a hard choice for her between Nick, and her duty to her wedded husband and to the cause her father had fought and died for. He was so afraid she might choose duty. . . .

'Do not tell me what you are thinking about.' Nat's mocking laughter came from close behind. 'Let me guess.'

'What do you mean, Nat?'

Nat bent to coax the sullen fire to burn more cheerfully and then rose, brushing the dust from his dark green breeches. 'Bright eyes,' he said. 'Why do you not tell the woman you are besotted, and so give us all some peace of mind? It is no good to think about it.'

'She knows,' Nick said briefly. 'I've already told her.'

'Then why all the despondency and grief? Why do you not get on with it. You are both lunatic!'

'Get on with it? What can I do? There's no way. . . .'

'Oh, go to! Do you need me to tell you? Woman's only waiting to be bedded. You're no reluctant virgins, either of you. She's as hungry as you are, and you know it!'

'Nat! In the name of honour and decency!'

'Honour? Decency? You make me laugh! I should have thought you forfeited any claim to either a long time since. You have committed most of the other sins, so I fail to see why you should jib at this one. As well be hanged for a sheep as a lamb.'

'Seemingly you are good at giving people advice, Nat Harrington! 'Tis a pity you do not take some of your own physick and leave others to mind their own affairs!'

'It's not you I am bothered about! Life's hard enough for Judith. Will you make it harder, you stubborn fool? If you break her heart, I shall tear you into tiny pieces!'

'You two fallen out again?' said Rebecca, with masterly understatement and diplomacy, bustling in with a taper to fire the rushlights, although it was a little early.

'Look at that great nincompoop, 'Becca. He'll take a dozen men single-handed, but when it comes to a woman, he's scared to death!'

'That's not what I'd heard,' sniffed 'Becca, sceptically, looking down her nose at Nick, and pulling the curtains to shut out the twilight. 'Jenny Weston at the alehouse doesn't seem to have found you shy, Nicholas Howard? She told me she'd be quite willing to oblige you if you've a mind.'

Nick blushed up to the roots of his hair. It was true he had kissed the innkeeper's daughter, several times. But it had all been a joke, one night when he and Josh had been drinking rather too much wine. . . . Nat was laughing, and Nick wanted to smash his fist into the middle of that cynical smile. He pulled the curtains aside again to look out of the window. The rooks were alarmed by something. There were dragoons from Broadoak at the front gate, and up the path towards the house limped the ungainly figure of Colonel Thomas Chadwicke, closely followed by two helmeted troopers: though it was no time of day for paying neighbourly visits.

17

THE HAND OF PROVIDENCE

'Good evening, Colonel Chadwicke. This is a surprise.'

'I am sorry to bother you without warning. I hope you will pardon the intrusion?'

'No intrusion, sir. Please come in! Nat is in the parlour.' Nick steadied his trembling hands with effort.

'You are welcome, sir. 'Becca, bring some canary for the colonel. Would you like to sit down?'

'Thank you, no. I will not be staying. I am summoned to headquarter, and am on my way thence.' The colonel turned to the careful adjustment of his orange sash. 'You'll not . . . come with us, Howard?' he muttered.

Nick felt sick, and Nat's one-sided smile of satisfaction and triumph shone across the room. No, sir. But I wish you a safe journey.' Safe, but not successful, he prayed: and then he had second thoughts even about the safety, for if the colonel should be killed. . . . Nick pulled himself up short, appalled at his thoughts. What had he become to wish a man dead like that? Though that man was his enemy, and husband to Judith.

'I'm sure the general would be only too glad,' Chadwicke tried again. 'A captain's commission?'

'I am a surgeon, sir, remember?'

Chadwicke sighed. 'And I think it likely that your professional services will be needed here before too long.'

'Fighting, here?' said Nat gleefully, his interest firmly captured.

'In a very short time, I fear so. That is why I am here. I shall be away for a s'ennight at least. Probably longer.' He wrestled with his buff-coat and brought forth two packets. 'In the event of hostilities in this area, it will be difficult, if not impossible, for anyone save the soldiery to move about freely. My wife suggested I give you these.' He handed one packet each to Nick and Nathaniel. 'You will find that they are safe-conducts, signed by myself. You will need army passes in order to carry out your usual business. I have left Captain Atkins in charge at Broadoak, but you can never tell. These will make your passage easier.'

'Or more difficult, if the soldiers are not of your party,' said Nat cuttingly.

'I give you the papers. It is up to you to use them or not, as you please. I offer help at my wife's insistence, though why she should hold you in such esteem, Master Harrington, has always been a complete mystery to me. Left to myself, I confess, I should not worry over-much concerning your safety.' Nick sighed. It was a tangled spider's nest of lying and unhappiness that they had woven for themselves. But now he had been presented with a golden opportunity. The colonel would be away for at least a week; and there was one here who must take advantage of it, to grasp at love and see if he could hold it fast in the midst of all the hatred.

Nick and Nathaniel stood side by side on the doorstep to watch Colonel Chadwicke and his escort ride off into the noisy wind-blown darkness. When the last trooper was out of sight, Nat turned to his companion, his eyes full of questions.

'Well? If that is not Providence smiling on you, I do not know what is.'

'All right, Nat. Eat, drink, and be merry.'

'For tomorrow? Do not say that, lad. You tempt fate too far. But you would be a fine fool not to enjoy your opportunity.'

Nick lay awake for half the night, trying still to make up his mind whether to tell the truth to Judith. In the grey light of morning, which brought with it another rainstorm, he was no nearer a solution. He was grateful to the storm for giving him an excuse not to set out for Broadoak straight away. Nat said naught, but stared at the blinding sheets of rain cascading across the green and hiding even the church from their view, and shrugged, turning back to his knife-sharpening as if the matter no longer interested him. Providence, however, seemed determined to deal another blow. Out of the stinging storm splashed the asthmatic corporal with a message from Captain Atkins. A group of his men had run into a party of the marquis' men from Basing House, and there were casualties. Could the surgeon come now and see to them?

'Come along, Nicholas,' said Nat, gathering up his tools. 'While the rain holds off a bit.'

'Providence again?'

'Undoubtedly. Do not spit in its face, man.'

Judith met them at the door and the wind caught her prim cap and whipped it away, so that her hair tumbled around her shoulders.

'Uncle Nat, Master Howard,' she said. 'It was good of you to come. I hope it is not a fool's errand we have brought you out on, in this dreadful weather. The captain thought it better that you should come. There are four men hurt, but I think that none is mortally wounded.'

'I will have a look at them, said Nat hastily, elbowing Nick out of the way. 'There is no need for you to bother, Nicholas. Be so good as to hand me my bag, would you? Now, Judith, lead the way. There is a small matter I would like to discuss with you.'

Nick fumed inwardly and stamped into the house. He had a feeling that Nathaniel was hatching some vile scheme known only to himself, and, try as he might, Nick could not guess at it. He made his way to the warm, welcoming kitchen with its huge oak dresser and the rows of plates on it shone at him like eyes. Lilith stood at the wide scrubbed table attacking a pile of linen with smoothing irons.

'You look sour, Master Howard?'

'Indigestion, Lilith. And foul weather.'

'Oh, yes?' she replied, sounding somewhat unconvinced.

He sat on the bench in the huge fireplace, and Lilith stared at him. He felt hostility in her glance.

'I'll get you a drink, sir?'

'No, thanks,' he said, absent-mindedly stroking the tabby cat with which he shared the bench. The cat, awakened from its repose, stretched, and its claws gripped at his sleeve. 'Ouch!' he said. 'Do not mind me, Lilith. I'll just sit here.'

'As you wish, young master,' she sniffed. A righteous sniff, he thought. Even the tabby cat sprang from the bench and stalked away in high dudgeon.

Lilith went on purposefully with her ironing, and peace descended on the kitchen, while Nick sat hunched and dejected, wondering what he might say to Judith. Presently the corporal came in from the yard, shaking the wet off his cloak, and stood shivering before the fire.

'Ugh! If this is autumn, I am in dread of what winter holds,' he wheezed.

Nat was a long time, for it was nearly dinner-time when he came in, very jovial. 'Been looking for you everywhere, Nicholas; I've been talking with your friend Captain Atkins. He won't have a word said against you, since you saved his life. . . . A most excellent fellow! Is delighted we shall be staying to dine. Oh, I told Judith we would. Hey, Nicholas, are you asleep in the corner there?'

'Nat, you are drunk!'

'Been drinking, yes . . . with my very good friend Captain Atkins.' Nat grinned a trifle vacantly. Nick was puzzled. It was most unlike Nat. As a rule, Nat liked to make sure his wits were close about him.

At dinner Nick toyed with his food and listened miserably to Nat, Captain Atkins, and the lieutenant arguing about gunpowder. Nat was well away, and Judith was ignoring Nick completely, though he tried hard to catch her eye. Nick sat still and taciturn and drank much more than he should have done on an empty stomach. Nat was waxing lyrical about cutting someone's arm off, and the others were discussing some particularly gruesome accident which had befallen a friend of theirs. Nick was jolted out of his wine-soaked contemplation with a hideous rush. They were asking him how he came by the scar on his face.

'Was it an accident, or a fight? I've always wondered,' Captain Atkins enquired innocently.

The lieutenant laughed. 'A fight? Surely not! Master sawbones will not argue with anyone, let alone fight. Peaceable soul. 'Tis a pity we are not all like him! But how was it?'

'Someone . . . tried to kill me,' said Nick's tongue, before his brain could stop it. He was making an effort now to regain control of his mind. It was being faintly disobedient, and he cursed his stupidity to be so befuddled.

'So what did you do, Master Howard?'

Their faces were eager with interest, when all he wanted was to be left alone. Only Nat lolled back sleepily in his chair, very drunk.

'Defended myself.' Just like he was doing now. 'Would you not have done the same?'

'Indeed I would have. And what happened?'

'I killed him.' Nick said simply. 'And I would prefer not to talk about it.'

The lieutenant whistled. 'Good Lord!' Atkins' voice was very soft. 'I'd never have believed that you would kill anyone.'

'That, Captain Atkins, only goes to prove how little you know about me. I regret it, but it is no use to regret, is it?' His tongue was clumsy and his brain working tortuously slow, but he knew that he had already said too much, and he must try to think of a way out. . . .

The lieutenant shook his head, still disbelieving. 'Who was it?' he asked.

Nat emitted a loud hiccup. It was so well timed that it might have been a warning.

'An army officer,' said Nick, and then looked at Nat, whose eyes were blazing with fury. The hiccup had indeed been a warning, and Nat was far more in command of his senses than Nick was himself.

'One of theirs? Or one of ours?'

'I said I would rather not discuss it, I'm sorry. Come on, Nat. It is time we went home.'

'Hell fire!' Nat's speech was slurred. 'I'm not going home in this rain. I'll catch me another ague. . . .'

'Come on, Nat. It's not raining now.'

'Judy won't turn us out, will you, Judy? You'll find us a corner?'

'Of course, Uncle Nat. I would not dream of turning you out. You must both stay here.'

'There is no need, Mistress Chadwicke, to trouble yourself. I can get him home. The rain is not so bad, and the fresh air will wake him up a bit.' Nick began to heave Nathaniel out of the chair, but Nat was being less than helpful and had gone very heavy.

' 'Tis no trouble at all,' said Judith firmly, looking Nick straight in the eyes. 'Uncle Nat shall have Thomas' room, and the green chamber is all ready, for I thought that since the weather was so bad. . . . Listen to that awful wind!'

'But – '

'Hold your tongue, you fool,' whispered Nat. 'Will you spoil all, you drunken idiot?'

The light dawned very slowly on Nick. The whole thing was a conspiracy, and Nat was responsible for it. He was stone-cold sober, but he played drunk with tremendous gusto until Nick and the lieutenant carted him up to his room between them and tucked him up snugly in the colonel's bed. Nick pulled the curtains round it, and Nat was smiling all over his face. 'Good night, Nicholas,' he said, and began to feign thunderous snores.

Nick sat on his own bed in the green chamber, his dizzy head in his hands, bewildered and extremely angry, mostly with himself. The wind rattled the windows and roared menace to the clustered chimney-pots of the old house. He walked slowly to the unshuttered window, leaned on the sill, and looked out at the blustering night. The orchard lay below, tossing branches naked in the dark, and he remembered the night of the ambush. There was the wall he had jumped to evade his pursuers. There had been confusion in the swirling mist: a frightened lieutenant, and a bleeding captain – and Judith. A noise of rustling sounded in the corridor outside, loud in the stillness of the sleeping house. The door opened smoothly, and Mistress Chadwicke came through it, without knocking.

'May I come in?' she said.

'Judith?'

'Now do not tell me you were not . . . expecting me to come. Nat said you wanted to talk to me.'

'Nat said that? I'll kill him!'

'So you do not wish to talk to me?' She crossed the room to stand before him.

'Not . . . talk. No.'

Talking was the last thing he wanted to do just then. His arms were about her, and her kiss offered him all the world he wanted. Beneath her dark grey cloak she wore only her night-shift, and all his high ideas of honour and decency were scattered to the four winds of heaven: for was it not the hand of Providence?

It was not quite so easy to kill a conscience. As he lay beside her afterwards, his conscience began to gnaw at him with the insistence of a maggot, and even while he caressed her corn-coloured hair, his mind was thinking of Lilith's hard suspicious face that afternoon. Judith's eyes were closed.

'You are angry with me?' she asked.

'You? No, never. I thought you were sleeping. I am angry with myself.'

'Why?'

'I am a rogue. But I love you dearly. Please believe me.'

'Why should I not believe you?'

'Because I have . . . lied before. I am a rogue because I should have confessed it all before . . . taking advantage of you.'

'I love you, Nicholas.'

'You may change your mind when you find out. Judith, I must tell you. . . .'

She sat up, holding the sheet to her. 'No you must not,' she said.

'I do not want to know how or why you have lied. You have your reason, and that is good enough for me. If you really love me, that is all I ask.'

'Oh, Judy . . . I wish . . .'

'Wishing's no good. I love you, though I can offer you nothing. But I'll not ask for yesterday, or tomorrow. I know nothing about you. None of us does; it was true what you said to Captain Atkins. I've thought about it ever since.'

'Then you must let me tell . . .'

'No. I have decided. I would rather not know. I cannot help loving you. I am a wanton. But I do not care.'

'You will care, when Tom comes back. And one day you will hate me,' Nick said bitterly.

She smiled. 'Maybe one day. But not tonight.' She stroked the hair that curled behind his ears.

'If Tom should find out. . . .'

'You are afraid that Tom will find out? I shall not tell him, if you don't! Are you such a coward? Oh, I am a fool, I do not need telling so. . . .'

'Tom may go to hell as far as I am concerned! And if you think I am afraid of him, then I can tell you . . .'

'Fighting talk, eh?' She giggled, and lay back on the pillow. 'Do you know, at first I wondered if you were not . . . too good to be true? What are you laughing at?'

Nick laughed helplessly until the tears rolled down his cheeks. 'Too good to be true? My darling, you may be nearer the truth than you know.'

'Did you really kill an army officer? You must have been very angry?'

'Yes, I killed. . . . But not in anger. I cannot claim that excuse.'

'Was it – Tom Chadwicke?' Her grey eyes were wide, and he could not look at them.

'Yes,' he said, gaping, amazed that she had guessed. He lay on his back beside her and looked at the green bed-curtains with their decorative nosegays delicately and painstakingly worked in thread of silver, and he was afraid of what she would say next.

'Poor, tormented Nicholas! I knew it somehow, tonight, when you said it. My Tom would kill you for it. Did you know that?' There was a gust of wind, and the draught blew the curtains so that the nosegays seemed to dance. Judith shivered and stretched out her arms to him. 'Nicholas, I'm so cold. Kiss me warm again.'

18

THE GREAT ASSAULT

Winter returned on All Hallows' Eve, and so did Thomas Chadwicke. Thick frost-ferns embellished the kitchen windows as Nick sat at the wide table polishing probes and sharpening lancets, and all the while wishing fervently that he could plunge the sharpest of them into Colonel Chadwicke's too sturdy heart. It was Nick's four-and-twentieth birthday. Judith had laughed when he told her, and declared that he was an ancient, for was he not two whole days older that she was herself? He had watched her turn home for Broadoak and felt sick with misery and fear, wishing not for the first time that he had been strong-minded enough not to give way to his passion for her.

They had found a ready ally in the stout shape of Widow Jeffery. Her cottage was not far off the colonel's land and well hidden in the trees, and Mistress Jeffery herself was a redoubtable lady who was not one whit daunted by any rebel rogue. Many times in the past she had carried Nat's letters-of-news, and now she fearlessly carried messages between Nick and Judith, and willingly volunteered her home as a haven for them to meet.

However, matters could not long continue as they were. Four-and-twenty, and old age was creeping up on him; Nat shook his own greying head and said that Nick should have a care, or else he would never get to twenty-five, and Nick knew that he was right. So in the dark evening he went out with Josh to drown his sorrows in quarts of Jacob Weston's small-beer, served by Jacob's pretty flirting daughter. When he was drunk enough, he took Jenny into the hayloft, where she giggled and offered him solace with no resistance at all. But all he gained from the experience was a thumping headache in the morning, not to mention a profusion of regrets and guilt to add to the onerous burden which weighed already upon his shoulders.

On the second day of November, Sir William Waller struck Humphrey Bennet's men at Alton with full force and little warning. The news that Bennet had been drubbed was brought to Broadoak by a gloating Colonel Norton, who met Chadwicke in the great hall just outside the firelit room where Nick sat playing chess with Captain Atkins. Their voices came drifting to him through the half-open door.

'Yesterday. We captured ten heavy guns and six cases of drakes which they were husbanding. A splendid haul! Will be useful when we come to the walls of Winchester and of Basing. One of them was a half-cannon.'

'Then you have your revenge, Dick?'

'I was not there, more's the pity. And Bennet's away to Romsey with a good few men left still. But I can wait. I shall personally settle with him when the opportunity presents itself.'

'No doubt.' Tom Chadwicke sounded unenthusiastic. He looked round the door and then rolled in, leaning up against the wainscoting.

Chadwicke approached the table slowly. It was obvious that his leg was paining him. There was no doubt that Tom Chadwicke was no stranger to suffering, nor was he one to quail readily under its burden.

Nick looked up at the stoic resolution of Colonel Chadwicke's face, and at the tall, arrogant form of Colonel Norton, and sighed. Richard Norton leaned on the windowsill and looked out to the garden where Judith walked, the heavy stuff of her cloak hanging limp in the moist air, her breath in misty clouds about her head.

'That wife of yours is a restless creature, Chadwicke?'

'She always walks in the garden. Every day, whatever the

weather. And has taken once more to riding out of the estate. Insists on going alone. I must confess it worries me.'

'Would worry me, too. Too many rogues and vagabonds about, let alone the soldiers. It seems very dangerous.'

Chadwicke sighed, and shrugged with the air of a sad child trying to find an explanation for something which it does not quite understand.

'It does not please me, and she is well aware of that. Yet she says she does not like always to be trapped in the house and persecuted by the continual company of too many people.'

'Trapped? Persecuted? 'Tis an odd way to put it.' Norton shook his head. 'But women are ever prone to strange fancies, are they not, Master Howard?'

Nick ostentatiously studied the chessboard and felt irritation. 'I am not really qualified to judge that, sir. I am scarcely an expert on women.'

'*Touché!* That puts me in my place, does it not? Neither can I pretend to be a master in such matters. You are quick-witted when you've a mind, sawbones.'

'You are too kind, Colonel Norton. Check, Captain Atkins.'

Norton and Chadwicke crossed to the door, discussing the invasion Waller's men had made of the cattle-market at Alresford, which had made the general unpopular with even the most fanatical local Parliamentarians.

'Ran off all the cattle. Every one, to feed the army. People are furious.'

'The army must be fed, if we are to conquer Winchester and Basing.'

'Aye. But Hopton is on the road from Salisbury: and Crawford will be joining him, I hear.'

Nick clenched his fists. Oh, yes, Norton would no doubt have heard every detail of Crawford's movements and intentions, and Nick would have laid a ready wager who had told him. If he could only lay hands on Mottham, he would snap him in two like a dried twig.

Waller marched his new army to Basing. He found the marquis' men firmly ensconced and expecting the visit, the mighty doors and the gate-house closed against the rebels. So they camped about the house in the swirling mist, and shivered and coughed in the damp air that came up, full of agues, from the marshes, and the sentries started at every will-o'-the-wisp that shone its cold, wicked, deceiving fire across the steaming water. The mist gave Lord Winchester's men concealment as they made a sortie in the night to fire any building which might give cover to the enemy in the event of an assault. The grange was burned, and some of the outhouses, even though they contained valuable supplies: the supplies would be better used to feed flames than Waller's rebel host. A good part of that host fled for some distance when they felt the heat of the licking flames which were no will-o'-the-wisps, but more than warm enough to consume them all; so Waller drew back on Basingstoke and ordered petards, shells, and scaling ladders to be brought with haste from Windsor. It would need all their resources to crack Basing walls.

Nick and Nat were amused to hear of Waller's temporary discomfiture, and they knew that the Paulets were most probably laughing, too. They would go on doing so until the Roundheads attacked the curving curtain wall and the turrets and gargoyles of Lord Winchester's beautiful home with the heavy guns they had taken from Humphrey Bennet at Alton. Bennet was in disgrace, having to bear the brunt of both the marquis' anger and Hopton's disappointment, as well as Crawford's displeasure, and none of it was his fault. He seemed resigned to their censure, worried only that he was having little success in pursuing the matter Nick had asked him to take up.

Waller sent a trumpeter to treat with Lord Winchester, who kept him waiting for hours, perishing with cold in the draughty courtyard while he composed a lengthy and elaborate epistle in reply to Waller's terse note demanding his surrender, drawing up his own terms to offer to the Roundhead general. Waller was to enlist himself and his whole army with the King, or to lay down his arms, admit his treason, and throw himself upon the mercy of His Majesty.

Waller fumed and drew up his troops and guns before the house, and the news was soon abroad in Stoke Sutton. Indeed, it was the main topic of conversation as the villagers clustered in small excited groups to gossip on the green after the service in St Peter's on the Sunday morning. At noon Nick and Nat reached the house and found a sorry desolation of slaughter in the park, and work and to spare waiting for them. Nick's heart was cold when he thought of the carnage that must already have been wrought inside the walls. Fat Willie Robinson would be more than occupied, puffing and blowing and purple-faced, and he was single-handed.

The great guns boomed from the shelter of the trees which still stood between the village and the house, and Nick sighed. He and Lord Edward Paulet had fought an acrimonious contest over those trees, and Lord Edward had won. Nick had known they would have been better felled, and here he was proved right, and it was too late. He hoped that Lord Edward was satisfied. Nat trotted off to Waller's headquarter in Basingstoke town, and Nick stayed in the village. St Mary's and The Falcon were already bursting at the seams, and there was, as usual, a notable dearth of surgeons. It was a nightmare of shrieking, dying men, and frightened women, and precious little news of how the battle was going, though the occasional hint came through the ever-open door with the ceaseless stream of mangled, mutilated rebels.

Not all of them were rebels. Some of the marquis' own men were brought in, to Nick's immense disquiet. He looked at each face and feared that it might be Ned Jeffery, or someone else that he knew. He heard the tale from one of them, a pale, skinny musketeer of extremely tender years, whose fear and pain made him only too anxious to babble his story to any man who would listen. Colonel Peake had led a sortie into the meadow, and there was bitter fighting hand-to-hand. Nick shuddered. It sounded to him like indescribable folly to leave the sanctuary of those stout walls in order to be annihilated on the open ground by the superior numbers of the enemy. Peake would have done better to stand by the works, to defend any breaches made by the demi-cannon. Nick would have credited him with more sense. . . . But Colonel Peake was not quite out of his mind. Soon he fell back on the house, and the rebels were thus encouraged far enough to be lured from the shelter of the trees and the earthworks, encumbered by their scaling ladders and battering-rams, to be shot to pieces by the drakes on the roof, and by the musketeers who waited with Sir Henry Bard along the wall-top. The survivors, such as they were, fled so rapidly that they left even their colours behind them. The petards failed, too.

Everyone in the church shivered with the black cold that bit deep as any steel, despite the braziers they had brought in to warm the air. Man after man died miserably under Nick's hands until he lost count of the numbers. One suffering face after another was before him, and knotted hands clutched and tore at him from all sides. Even the puritan chaplain was for once silent, his capacious sleeves blood-soaked though they were rolled up well beyond his elbows. He was busy tending men's hurts and praying for their souls, instead of sermonising their bodies to greater efforts of arms. The floor under Nick's feet was slippery with blood, the columns splashed, and the two chancel steps dripping with it: the sweet rancid smell of death floated amongst the stout roof-beams with the wisped smoke from the braziers, until it seemed that even the stone cherubs must be stifled.

Another storming party had been repelled, caught in the inward curve of the wall when my Lord's Dutch engineer had craftily blown a breach in my Lord's own fortifications, so that the garrison could bring an unexpected hail of retribution to bear on the marauders. Now numbers of pikemen were brought in: red-coated men of the Westminster Regiment, their coats stained darker by their own blood, shed by their own men. More than seventy of them had been fired on, by mistake, by the musketeers who were supposed to protect them, and the Red Band's Westminster banner, with its silver stars besmirched with gore and shame, lay low in the meadow, with only the dead for company.

Nick heard St Mary's clock chime three, the bell singing clear above the deep throaty roar of the half-cannon a furlong away in the trees. His stomach quailed within him, and, retching, he crept outside to clear it of staleness and disgust. The cold air made him splutter and cough more than ever, and there was no respite, for every breath brought with it the familiar odours of gunpowder and smoke which made his sore eyes water. Wind struck sharp on his sweat-beaded forehead and the angry throbbing scar across his cheek, and blew his dishevelled hair into deep tangles. Inside he could hear some poor devil wailing for a surgeon, and he was appalled that his inadequate aid was all there was to offer. He would have been much happier fighting, he thought. It was far easier to cause pain than to alleviate it.

Suddenly a flurry of rain came down, stinging him to retreat again within the church door, and before long the rain was beating on the tall windows as savagely as the guns had been beating on the towers and ramparts of Basing House a few minutes ago. With the rain, the dampened guns fell silent, and Waller gave the order to draw off, to wait for the storm to cease. The attack was over. Basing had survived the great assault, but Nick worked through the night to do his pitiful best for the victims.

Willie Robinson, too, must have worked through the night in the gracefully painted, panelled rooms of Lord Winchester's palace. Nick wondered how many men would be left in any condition to fight. They would all need rest, but many would be forced to stand yet to their arms, to watch for the renewal of the attack, while Waller's men could sleep, untroubled by any such fear.

When Nick arrived in Basingstoke, he found that it, too, was full of wounded. Nat, unshaven and white, was still at work. Nick rubbed his own bristling chin and felt sharp pain from the scarred cheek that complained bitterly of the cold. Nathaniel smiled as he described how even the marquis' women had fought. Some of the rebels had come near enough to see them on the roof, and many of them had broken heads as a consequence, for the ladies had been flinging flints and tiles at them. Nick marvelled at the courage of the womenfolk. He could imagine that his own beloved Judith would fight like a fiend if the occasion should ever arise. He smiled, wondering what Judith would have thought to see him now, dirty and bearded like the most disreputable of villains. Then it occurred to him that she was not his Judith at all, but

Thomas Chadwicke's, and that he himself was nothing but a malignant, and to Judith all malignants were villains of the most iniquitous sort. . . . He sighed, and followed after Nat in search of much overdue refreshment, before both of them should fall asleep where they stood.

An hour or so later they sat nodding in the warm common-room of the smaller of the two inns in the market-square, and watched the sleet settling damp and slithery on the cobble-stones. In the distance, trumpets brayed and yelped, and sent a stir through the metal-clanking warriors clustered round the fire. Someone dropped a lobster-pot helmet with an oath. It seemed that Lord Hopton's men had driven in the rebel pickets to the West, and now his trumpeters blew the loudest levitts of their lives, to let Lord Winchester know that once more he had been timely delivered from impending destruction. Consternation sped like winged Mercury through the ranks of Parliament, and the busy drums beat muster as the army of Waller prepared to depart.

Nick could hear Nat's deep voice humming happily as they stood in the low doorway of the inn, watching the disappointed faces of the Parliament-men marching out to nowhere through the driving sleet, bedraggled and not a little saddened by the wasting of their efforts.

Nick was anxious to be away. It would not do, he thought, to be recognised by any of his erstwhile comrades. He dashed to the inn-yard to retrieve the chestnut before some Cavalier thief stole it, and in his hurry under the echoing archway he collided with the bulky figure of Lord Hopton. The King's general stood blinking for a moment, in obvious puzzlement, while Nick hastened to apologise profusely for his clumsiness. Then recognition dawned in Hopton's eyes as a smile lit up his ruddy, good-natured face, and he winked gravely.

'Well,' he said, 'I am glad to see that you are thriving.'

'My Lord.'

They had gathered a small crowd of curious spectators, and the knot of officers who had been following behind Hopton looked hard at the stranger. Nick was in mortal fear that the general would be his undoing; but the smiling blue eyes twinkled in jovial conspiracy.

'Thank you for your service, Master . . . Sawbones,' he said, bowed, and with a jingle of spurs was gone.

Two days later, Ned Jeffery brought a letter from him. He was on the march for Odiham, and desired his intelligencers to keep him informed of the state of the enemy in that country. Waller was at Farnham now, his men encamped more contentedly in pleasant rolling parkland, much comforted by the fact that they were under the shadow and protection of the great castle and its mighty guns. Ceaseless skirmishing filled the next two weeks, and the two surgeons in Stoke Sutton were hard put to keep up with the rush of plaintive demands for their services. Nick blessed my Lord at Oxford, for he found that a surgeon's guise was admirable defence and concealment of his true function. And several times he had cause also to bless the generosity of Colonel Chadwicke, whose safe-conduct was the instrument of Nick's salvation when his own explanations were simply not good enough. . . .

The men at Broadoak stood, somewhat uneasily, to arms, as did the men of sundry assorted small garrisons in large houses and small hamlets all over the county. Nick made sure that Lord Hopton was kept well informed where everyone was. Yet it was a great pity, he thought, that Waller, also, would be as well served by his intelligence, and no doubt Lieutenant Mottham was most willingly playing his part in that. Daily Nick prayed that the traitor would be confounded, since prayer seemed now to be the only way left open to him. . . .

One cold afternoon in late November Nick went to the forge with one of the cobs, which had chosen to go lame just as Josh was departing on his way to deliver one of Nat's letters. Matthew was already busy, cursing and swearing at a sidling, kicking animal with a loose near hind shoe.

'Sorry,' he said, neatly avoiding the vicious hoof aimed at his face. 'Stranger in a hurry. Leave it here, and I'll bring it back later.'

'Stranger?' Nick felt a twinge of alarm.

'Bad mannered one, too. Full of oaths. Went to the alehouse. Odd-looking fellow, all muffled up in a cloak. Almost as if he didn't want to be recognised.'

Nick wandered back towards the church with Matthew's words sending strident alarums through his head. He was nearly half way up the street when an unfamiliar figure emerged from The Lovell Arms, and Nick stiffened in sudden realisation. The man's face was hidden, his black hat pulled well down over his eyes, and he was well wrapped up in his cloak. Yet Nick would have known that swagger anywhere, however carefully it was disguised.

Mottham glanced anxiously about him before making off up the street towards the forge to collect his mount. Nick drew back hastily into the alley between two houses. It was a pity that he had not thought to tell Matt to delay the man, just in case, but it was too late now, and he was forced to watch impotently as Mottham disappeared into the forge yard. He ran as fast as his legs would carry him back to the house, leaped up the stairs three at a time for pistols and sword, and clattered out to saddle the chestnut in fumbling haste. By the time he had come once more to the smithy, Mottham had gone. Matt looked up from the anvil and wiped the sweat out of his eyes, a mystified frown on his face.

'Matt, where did he go?'

'What on earth? Oh, he asked direction to Broadoak. Hey, what do you want him for?'

Matt called after the empty road, and watched Nick kicking the stallion in the ribs, already half way across the green, with hens scolding, and honking geese scattering to all sides. He kicked the horse all the way to Broadoak lane after Mottham's retreating figure, but knew that it was useless, and that the traitor was too far ahead to touch, so he set himself to wait in the trees, quaking and freezing, his face stiff and sore with the merciless cold.

It was nearly dark when his quarry reappeared, and, to Nick's dismay, Mottham had now an escort, a half-dozen dragoons riding all about him. But this might be the only chance he might have to rid them all of a dangerous enemy. Nick allowed them to come as near as he dared before firing the first pistol, squinting with the effort to see his target. The bullet went whizzing harmlessly over the heads of the riders. Nick cursed and tried harder for the second one, especially since Captain Atkins had moved between Mottham and the pistol, and he was loth to shoot a friend. . . . The second bullet smashed home. Nick heard a cry of pain, and peered blindly through the gathering shadows to see the confusion and consternation he had caused. It was not Mottham who had fallen, nor yet Atkins. The trooper behind them had caught the bullet, and slumped to the ground with two comrades bending over him. Nick turned and fled before he should be seen and pursued, cursing and raging in thwarted disappointment.

'Where the hell have you been?' demanded Nat testily as Nick stormed into the parlour, furious and fretting, his hands and feet tormenting now with the return of warmth.

'Pig-hunting. And I missed the damn pig!' He threw himself into the chair and cursed once more.

'What pig?' Nat enquired, more calmly.

'Mottham. He was here, today, and I missed the bastard! If only . . .'

'If only? My dear Nicholas, the pan is scat, the milk spilt. . . . No good lamenting. I wonder what our traitor is up to now?'

'We shall find out!' Nick frowned into the fire and rubbed his smarting cheek.

'No doubt. Did you hear that Major Van Druske and his horde of rabble attacked Hopton's headquarter last night? Nearly very nasty, by all accounts. My Lord was very put out.'

It was not long before they found out what Mottham had been up to. Three nights later, when Hopton's Cavaliers made an attempt to return Major Van Druske's compliment, they found that Waller had been warned, and there was a warm welcome waiting. Nick wrote a disconsolate letter to Humphrey Bennet to explain what had transpired. Humphrey Bennet's reply was even sadder, for he had to confess total failure in persuading either Hopton or Crawford to listen to his warnings. Nick threw the letter across the room in frustration. Not only had Humphrey Bennet failed, but Mottham had been saved from what seemed like certain self-destruction. He had been tried at Odiham and found guilty of murdering some local man who had made an effort to protect his daughter from Lieutenant Mottham's unwelcome attentions. The one who had intervened to save him from the gallows was none other than the Earl of Crawford himself.

19

TREACHERY AT WORK

Till the end of November the petty strife and scrapping continued unabated, and the Lord Hopton grew even more put out, because, for the most part, his men were coming off worse. Even the unquenchable Nat was somewhat crestfallen at this state of affairs. They sat round the scrubbed kitchen table devouring plates full of Rebecca's rabbit stew, and even that did not cheer them.

'They say that Norton's Hambledon boys are doing great things for Waller,' said Josh sadly. 'Can I have some more, please, Rebecca?'

'I've heard that there is a regiment of Kentishmen come to join him,' Nick added, wiping his plate clean with a chunk of bread, and sighing in anticipation of the indigestion that was bound to ensue.

'Two regiments,' Nat corrected him. 'Not one.'

Rebecca sniffed disapprovingly at them all. 'You men are all too easy daunted. You are forgetting, all of you, that those brave London trained-bands will soon be griping to go back to their homes. Why else do you think that Waller has not yet marched out to smash your Lord Hopton? Because he is afraid that they'll set up the cry of "home" like they've done before.'

'At least we have Petersfield and Petworth,' said Nat, grudgingly. All we need is Midhurst, and the road is open. All Hopton has to do is march. God, 'Becca, I cannot eat all this! And it's hot as hell!' He took a mouthful of his second helping and choked on it.

'All he has to do is march,' said Nick, thinking aloud. 'I don't know why he is waiting.'

'He is waiting for reinforcements. Crawford is set at Alton to watch Waller, and I hear there is a regiment come from Wallingford to help him.' Nat wiped his mouth and laid his knife down.

'Wallingford?' Nicked leaped up. That was where John Bolle's men had been. 'Did you say Wallingford?'

'I did. Are you deaf, then?'

'You don't know who, by any chance?'

'General Sir Jacob Astley's foot. Commanded by Colonel . . . Bull, or something. I cannot remember exactly.'

'Colonel John Bolle.' Nick filled in the name and grinned.

'Yes, that's it! How did you know?'

'He is a very good friend of mine. If he is at Alton, then I must go to see him. Perhaps I shall get another shot at Mottham if Crawford's men are there, too.'

Nat groaned. 'As you will, Nicholas. But be discreet, I beg of you. He is not worth getting killed for.' He sat back and pushed the plate away, shaking his head emphatically, and then rose and walked out.

In the event Nick found that it was not so easy to pay a visit to John Bolle. On the outskirts of Alton he was seized by pickets and detained in some worthy citizen's outhouse. It was early evening, and they refused to let him go despite all his protests, for they had found in his pocket the pass from Colonel Chadwicke. In a way Nick was pleased. Alton was too near Farnham and Waller to be entirely safe for the little Royalist force, and it was encouraging to see that John's men were on the alert for any possibility of attack.

He should have left the pass at home: and he was likely to be spending the night in the stinking little dungeon, for they would not disturb the colonel at this time of day, they declared firmly. At length he managed to find a young lieutenant who would dare to brave his commanding officer with a message from the captive.

Colonel Bolle was sitting in the room at the inn which served him for an office, drowsing before the fire with his feet on the table, enjoying a well-deserved respite between arguments with Lord Crawford. He was not pleased to see the young officer.

'What the hell? Did I not give orders that I was not to be disturbed?'

'Sorry, sir. But we've caught a rebel.'

'My congratulations. Lock him up till morning.'

'He wants to see you, sir.'

'If he has anything to say, let him tell it to you or to your captain.'

'He's well . . . odd, sir. And I'm not really sure if he is a rebel or not, to tell you the truth.'

'God's blood, man! You cannot tell the difference?'

'He has a Roundhead pass in his pocket. But he says he isn't. He says he is an old friend of yours and . . . he sounds as if he has some sort of authority. . . . It's difficult.'

'Wouldn't you deny it? And say you were an old friend of mine? But you certainly intrigue me. What does he look like?'

'A rebel, sir. With a mighty scar across his face. He said I was to tell you his name was Howard, and that you would know.'

'Good Lord! Why did you not say so before? Send him up, lieutenant, straight away, and give back anything you've taken from him. . . .'

Nick was more than somewhat relieved to be released from the dark little prison, for it smelt powerfully of rats, and the burly bewhiskered Welsh pikemen at the door of it had been discussing with relish what painful steps they would take in order to make him divulge the secrets they were certain he possessed.

'My dear Nicholas! I do not believe it! Come in and welcome! Where have you sprung from?' John wrung Nick by the hand, and ushered him towards the fire.

'Stoke Sutton. It's over Alresford way. I'm supposed to be a respectable surgeon.'

'Surgeon? Ugh! How unpleasant. But respectable? You?

Never!' Colonel Bolle roared with laughter. 'Have a drink, friend, and warm yourself. We are a bit low on supplies, but I've a bottle or two of decent canary to hand. Are you all right?'

Nick rubbed his arm ruefully. 'Your sentries are bloody rough! But I am glad they know their business. Ouch, my elbow! It is a difficult place to hold, this town.'

'Aye, Colonel Bennet found that out, right enough.'

'He knew he could not hope to defend it as it was. He told me so.'

John shrugged. 'Now the same task falls to Crawford and myself. And Waller's too close for me to rest easy. But with any luck we should be in Midhurst soon. Crawford will take it in two days, we hope, and my regiment will be moving there to hold it.'

'Then the way is open into Sussex?'

'They are already on the march towards Arundel. The frost makes the going easy. No mud.'

Nick gave a low whistle. Hopton was not so backward after all. 'So Alton is an important outpost?'

'Aye, we are between Waller and Hopton's path of retreat, if it should be needed.'

'I wish you joy, John. I only hope you will take care not to be . . . surprised: like poor Humphrey Bennet was.'

'Surprised? No, not I! Too open. I can see them coming for miles down that road. And my scouts watch all the roads, day and night. I've good scouts. But that exquisite buffoon Crawford has forbidden us to dig trenchments except up on the hill round St Lawrence's. Says that trenchments and earthworks are all very well for my infantry, but they are likely to be an impediment to the movement of his horse: so he will not hear of it.'

'I can imagine. He is a difficult character to deal with.'

'Difficult? Damn nigh impossible!' John sounded bitter and disillusioned, his voice cracking with discouragement. Nick drained his cup and put it down gloomily. John was not going to like what he had to say.

'John?'

'Yes?'

'There's treachery at work, in Crawford's regiment. A spy for Waller.'

'A . . . spy?' John's eyes narrowed suspiciously. 'Are you sure of this? You do not know who, I suppose.'

'Lieutenant Mottham. He needs watching, John.'

'Oh, Nick, really!' John began to laugh, holding his sides and rolling helplessly in his chair. It was several minutes before he regained his breath. Nick flushed hotly and remained silent. This was not quite the reaction he had expected. 'Your pardon, Nick, but it's too funny. That idiot? He is too much of a fool to be a spy. I know he was nearly hanged at Odiham over some doxy or other, but that is scarcely treachery. He does not take life seriously enough for that. He's amusing. Harmless, he is. Can be unpleasant, but harmless.'

'Not harmless, John. Believe me.'

Bolle looked at Nick's earnest face and shrugged apologetically. 'You still remember that episode at Bath, don't you? Neither of us likes the man, Nicholas. But that does not mean that he is a traitor.'

'I've seen him, John; visiting the rebel garrison near Stoke Sutton.'

'No doubt he has had reason to do so. Why, only this morning Lord Crawford sent him to see Sir William Waller at his headquarter.'

'He what? What folly is this?'

'Calm down! You know Crawford. I told you we were short of drink, did I not? So Crawford sent Mottham to get two or three barrels of sack from Sir William, so that he does not go short. Promised Waller beef in return.'

'Oh, God, I do not believe it! How can you all be so foolish?' Nick could have wept. He cradled his head in his hands, shaking it in disbelief and horror.

'It must have been you who put all this moonshine into Humphrey Bennet's head? Crawford was raving about it yesterday. They fell out over it. Nearly came to blows.'

'Yes, it was me. And I honestly thought that you, of all people, would have more sense. I implore you, John, just watch him. That is all I ask.'

'Let us talk of something else. I am loth to quarrel; it has been so long since I've seen you. Come, tell me what you are up to.'

Nick took his leave reluctantly. John walked with him to the edge of the town and stood in the pool of lantern-light between the sentries to wave him farewell before turning to make his rounds of the picket-line, his brisk soldier's step echoing hollow through the frosty streets of Alton, keeping time with 'Prince Rupert's March', as one of the sentries whistled it to keep himself company in the dark. It was nearly dawn when Nick reached Stoke Sutton. He went to bed for a couple of hours, rubbing his bruised arm and cursing Welsh pikemen.

Matt came in the afternoon to find him, looking disturbed and anxious. 'I saw that stranger again,' he said. 'The one you wanted to shoot.'

'Where, Matt? When?'

'Just after dawn. Down by the mill.'

'What on earth were you doing at that time of day? Poaching again?'

'Sam Langrish said he would let me have a couple of rabbits, so I went to collect them.'

'Hmmm. And what was our friend at, down by the mill?'

'He met Colonel Norton, and Colonel Chadwicke, so I was curious, and tried to get close enough to hear what they were saying.'

'Well?'

' 'Twas mighty difficult. They had troopers there and were on the look-out.'

'Yes, Matt?' Nick had a momentary vision of the still deeps of the brown mill-pond, and of the matted rushes pale and sickly spotted by the great elmwood water-wheel, and wondered how Matthew dared to contemplate coming close, risking death as he was, in the open.

'So I went inside, didn't I, and lay along one of the roof-beams, though the race made too much noise for me to hear everything.'

'But you heard something?'

'Good bit, yes. Norton was talking about getting even with Sir Humphrey Bennet.'

'So they are intending to strike at Romsey. Anything else?'

'He said something about going to Cowdray. . . . I think I heard right.'

'Cowdray. Is that not by Midhurst?'

'Aye, sir, that it is.'

'Then you heard right, certainly. Oh, Lord. Crawford must be half way there by now. But I'll wager he finds the rebels there before him! Oh, damn Mottham! Damn the man!'

'There was something else, sir.' Matthew cautiously broke in on Nick's imprecations, his broad-bridged nose wrinkled in puzzlement, and he scratched his square chin. 'Something I didn't really understand, but you might. They were talking about . . . leather guns, or some such.'

'Leather guns?' said Nathaniel from the back doorway. 'Who has leather guns?'

'Waller will have, when they arrive from London, Captain Nat.'

'My God,' hissed Nat. 'Then Waller is certainly up to some design which requires a nimble execution.'

'Leather guns? What on earth?' Nick enquired, as puzzled as Matthew, for he had never heard of anything of the sort.

'I saw them once, in the Low Countries. Easy to move. Light. If you should want to go across country at speed. But they've the same power as an iron or brass field gun. Ideal for a surprise attack on a town.'

'Poor Bennet,' Nick sighed. 'They mean to destroy him, it seems.'

Nick took pen and paper forthwith, and wrote a letter to Humphrey Bennet of Pythouse, to warn him of Norton's design. The next morning they heard that Lord Crawford had come to Midhurst to find the Roundheads already firmly established, almost as if they had known he was coming. . . . Nick wondered if John would connect Mottham with the setback, and hoped that perhaps the traitor would in future be more closely watched.

The ground was still hard with frost on the twelfth day of

December, and the cold showed no signs of relenting. Hopton's men were in possession of Arundel, town and castle, with little opposition. Waller stayed still where he was, seemingly frozen to the spot, and all his army with him: and Humphrey Bennet remained altogether unmolested at Romsey.

Nick rode through the grey afternoon to the Widow Jeffery's tiny white-washed cottage in the trees to meet Judith, and found that she was already waiting anxiously at the window for his arrival.

'You are early.'

'I must be early back to Broadoak,' she explained apologetically. 'The place is an unbelievable muddle.'

'Muddle? How so?'

'Tom is gathering all the men together, ready to ride away somewhere tonight. You can imagine what it is like. He ordered dinner early, so that they can be prompt to depart before dark.'

'Surely there is enough moon for them tonight?' said Nick, his soldier's brain at work. Judith looked at him oddly, and he wished that he had not said it.

'Is there? I wouldn't know; I am not conversant with the moon. They are going to attack someone, I expect.' She laughed, and stroked the tuft of hair that curled behind his ear: but he was still thinking, hard.

'Where on earth are they off to, then?' he asked, making tremendous efforts to keep his enquiring voice casual and nonchalant.

Judith laughed, and shrugged. 'How should I know? Nobody knows except Tom, and he will not tell. It is supposed to be a great secret, evidently. Are you here with me, or five miles away?' She shook her golden hair peevishly.

Romsey, he thought grimly, was more than five miles: Norton's personal revenge was on its way. . . .

'Sorry I was . . . thinking.'

'Well, stop it. Do not be sad. I love you, Nicholas.' She kissed him, and for the moment he forgot all about Humphrey Bennet. It was not as if he could do anything to help, not just now. And Judith could make him forget everything except that he was a man, and desperately in love.

Judith sat watching him dress, and smiled with studied wickedness in her grey eyes. 'Nicholas, you are getting rather fat.'

'Too contented, that is the trouble.' He grinned balefully. She was beautiful. It was a pity that she did not really belong to him.

'And you need a new shirt. You look very out-at-elbows.'

He stood beside her and bowed in mock obeisance. 'Yes, madam. Is there anything else?'

'A hair-cut? Otherwise you will begin to look like some . . . Cavalier.'

Nick forced a humourless smile, but Judith did not laugh this time. Her eyes were wide and sombre, and in them lurked the shadow of tears.

'Are you, Nicholas? Are you?'

Nick looked at the oak-beamed ceiling of the tiny bedroom, and at the latticed windows, and then at the dark, boarded floor: anywhere but at Judith.

'Am I what? Out-at-elbows? If you say so.'

'A . . . Royalist?'

'My politics, sweetheart, are my own concern. And there is no need to bother your head over them.'

'Is there not? Then tell me the truth. I have been very foolish in some things, but I am not an idiot. Colonel Norton said there was a spy at Broadoak; so I thought about it. It seems very odd that things began to go wrong for Thomas very soon after you arrived in Stoke Sutton. You have already admitted that it was you who killed young Tom. . . . There must have been a reason for it. Are all these things coincidence? Am I merely . . . imagining?'

Nick sat heavily on the bed. 'You said, that first night, you did not want to know, love,' he said, though he knew that the time for truth-telling was upon him at last.

'I want to know now. I cannot rest so. It worries me. Uncle Nat is a malignant. I know that. It is no secret.'

'And he would hardly welcome . . . a rebel into his household. So I am a nasty, wicked Cavalier, love.' Nick's smile was bitter. 'Oh, yes. You are right. Of course you are . . . and you must have known all along. But what are you intending to do about it?'

Judith was weeping silently, her face in her hands, her hair tumbling round her. Nick stretched out his achingly empty arms to her, but he did not dare to touch her, because he was afraid that now she would push him away.

'Oh, what can I do? What can I do? I have no choice. I go on loving you . . . because I cannot stop.'

'Judith, I love you so much. I am still the same man. Only the politics are different. . . . Can you forgive me? I wanted so much to be honest, but I was afraid. I thought that truth might hurt you more than the deception.'

'Hurt me?' She sobbed. 'There is nothing to forgive. You tried to warn me, did you not?'

'Warn you? Oh, damnation! What a predicament I've landed myself in!'

'You said you loved me . . . whatever happened. And you told me to remember it. Is that what you meant? Is that what you were trying to say?'

'Yes, love. And I always shall love you, come what may. Though I could not blame you if you hated me for what I've done to you.'

'Never could I hate you, Nicholas. Not for any reason. But I wish that I knew what to do. . . . Oh, God! I really must go home now. Do I look as if I have been crying? I will come again, just as soon as I can.'

Nick leaned on the front wall of Widow Jeffery's garden and watched Judith ride home towards Broadoak. Behind her the grey clouds opened into a gold-pink cloud-palace of brittle brightness that held a hint of heaven. Nick sighed, loving Judith from the grey hood of her kersey cloak to the neat soles of her little boots. It was comforting in a way that he no longer had to lie to her; but it was also an impossible situation, and he knew not what to do, except to go on loving her. . . .

He dawdled back to the village through the doleful winter lanes, unwilling to let reality take hold of him. The bracken on the road banks had been golden a short while ago, and before that it had been alive, green sprouting and vigorous.

Now it was white and stiff with hoar-frost, and stark dead like young Tom Chadwicke. The trees were bare now, and the wind cut across the downs like a sharp sword. A sword of vengeance, he thought, with sudden foreboding.

There was no one at home save Rebecca, and that suited Nick very well, for she left him to sit in the parlour alone and did not interfere with his unhappy thoughts. Josh was away up to Odiham to deliver a letter for Nat, and Nathaniel himself was visiting an old friend in Winchester. Rebecca sang as she worked in the kitchen, and in the end Nick gave way to his hungry stomach's complaints and joined her there. It was bitterly cold in the parlour, anyway, since he had let the fire burn out. A clear night, and the moon shone down like a yellow eye from the star-freckled sky. It would be a fine night for the attack on Romsey. . . .

Nick was still sitting in the kitchen when Nathaniel came back, though it was after midnight. Nat stamped in, puffing and blowing and cursing the cold.

'It's been a bloody day,' he said. 'I've news.'

'So have I,' said Nick.

'You first.' Nat shed his cloak and sat down by the fire to take his boots off. 'And I certainly hope yours is better than mine.'

'I hear Chadwicke and his company are off somewhere for a secret destination to attack somebody. Poor Humphrey Bennet is in for it.'

'Eh? Poor Humphrey Bennet's had it! Norton smashed his men into tiny pieces this morning. And I saw the remains crawl into Winchester. But evidently they did not have any leather guns, Norton's men.'

'Didn't have any? That's odd. Very odd. Poor Bennet. Is he hurt?'

'Winged, I think, but seemed well enough, and went straight to see the Lord Hopton. I fancy that he has the same creeping suspicion as myself.'

'What?' Nick was puzzled. He did not like the look on Nat's face.

'That those guns were never intended for an attack on Romsey at all . . . but . . .'

Josh came crashing through the door, and the other two sprang up in alarm.

'Here!' he gasped, breathless. 'What are Chadwicke and Atkins and that crowd of villains doing up at Swainshill copse? They were hanging about there as if they were waiting for someone to meet them. I came straight home as fast as I could. I wondered if you might know anything about it?'

Swainshill copse was well to the north-east of Stoke Sutton. Horrible realisation suddenly came to Nick, and he cried out. 'Oh, my God! They are going to Alton, Nat! Waller's going to take those guns across country to take Alton! And John will not be expecting them from the north-west. He's watching the roads, he said, and not the hills. Oh, God, I've been such a fool. I thought they were for Romsey!'

He leaped up the stairs three at a time for pistols and sword. John was watching the roads, not the hills: and Humphrey Bennet had said the town was too open to defend. There were no trenchments for shelter. With the leather guns Waller would sweep down and circle the town, and they would be suspecting nothing. It was up to him to warn John, for he should have seen it coming. Josh was already in the stable, with the horses saddled.

'Where are you going, Josh?'

'With you, sir. To warn your friend.'

'Are you sure? It will be dangerous, and John would not expect . . .'

'You'll find you way easier with me, sir. God send that we are not too late!'

'Amen, Josh! Amen.'

20

'AND HE WILL HANG YOU IF HE CAN'

At eleven o'clock a courier came galloping into Alton with a letter for Lord Crawford from the Lord Hopton, to advise him that Sir Humphrey Bennet thought there was a possibility of an attack, and to give him orders to evacuate the town if there was any danger of a standing fight. General Crawford sent out scouts in all directions to look at the roads, especially the road from Farnham, just as Nick had feared he would. The roads were clear, every one, not so much as a rabbit stirring, let alone a body of hostile troops approaching: for Sir William's men were marching well to the north of the town, over the rough heathland and through the woods, guided by Thomas Chadwicke's men. General Crawford concluded that the alarm was false, and went to bed in a fit of spleen with Humphrey Bennet for the needless disturbance, pausing only to take a good-night drink from one of the barrels of sack which Sir William Waller's men had so kindly delivered to him that very morning.

Josh and Nicholas raced at full pelt through the bitter cold across the frozen fields and through the wild places towards Alton. It seemed that the thudding hoofbeats and the clinking harness would surely wake every sleeper for miles around. The moonlight was bright as noon, showing the very blades of grass in sharp detail. The two riders could see for miles: but if they themselves were seen, only disaster could ensue.

Nick prayed for clouds to appear from nowhere to shade the moon's yellow face with its smug, leering smile, yet the god he called on must still have been sleeping despite the ear-splitting din of their progress, for the prayer remained unanswered.

If Alton was lost, it would all be his fault. Alton was important. He should have known that Waller would not go to the trouble of procuring leather guns from London just for a little place like Romsey, however close it might be to Southampton. He should have foreseen it, but he had been blinded, with too many things on his mind. Now Mottham would be waiting to welcome his Roundhead friends with open arms. Two regiments only, to defend Humphrey Bennet's pighole, and likely half Waller's army would be ranged against them, with the advantage of surprise, and the leather guns that were, Nat said, as powerful as any brass or iron field gun. . . .

Now they were less than two miles from Alton, but they could go no further. Anywhere there was passage for a horse to the edge of the trees, there were also watchers. The woods were running alive with rebels, hundreds strong, and the two Royalists spent a breathless hour and more trying to find a way through, but without success. The town was completely encircled. For a good mile or so round it, there was nothing but open fields, and even on foot a man would be seen and caught long before he could come near enough to warn anyone.

'There is no hope of going through, sir,' Josh concluded. 'There is no cover anywhere for aught that is larger than a rabbit, not once you are clear of these trees. I doubt we could crawl as far as Alton. Not with this moon.'

'There is but one way,' said Nick, pushing the brown curly tangle off his forehead, his face pale in the moonlight, and the scar stood out clear across his cheek, like a new-made gash.

'What's that, sir?'

'You go home, now, Josh, and leave me to it. I will play surgeon and see if I can ride in openly without being arrested.'

'Oh, Lord . . . no, sir. 'Tis a foolhardy thing, to ride into their hands, so. Do not send me back, sir. I cannot go back. They'll have you, for sure.'

'If they do, then it is unlikely they will harm me. I have safe-conduct from Chadwicke.'

'Sir, please let me come with you. You never know, you may need . . . help.'

'There is no reason for you to come. No sense in both of us risking our necks. I order you to go back.'

Josh's wild eyes were full of hurt. 'Please, sir. Do not order me. Let us both try. If you are discovered, then the rest of us will run risk anyway.'

'It may not work. We may indeed both be taken.'

'Likely, sir.'

'Are you not afraid?' Nick said, looking at Josh's dogged face. Perhaps there might be a chance for one of them, even if the other should fail. . . .

'No more afraid than you are, sir,' said Josh, grinning.

'Come then, friend. May God be with us.' Nick took a deep breath and urged the lathered chestnut forward out of the holt and down the short grassy slope to the white open road. Under his shirt he could feel the pass that Colonel Chadwicke had given him. It might once more serve to ward away any trouble. Briskly they trotted down the road, and round the bend, and a hundred yards further on were Roundhead dragoons coming out of the trees to block their way. Their uniforms seemed oddly familiar, Nick thought: perhaps they had been at Basing. . . .

They were given the sharp command to stand. Nick's stomach was in a state of turmoil, but he forced back the nausea and the sweat of fear, and smiled politely at them as if he could neither understand nor imagine why he had not been allowed to proceed. 'I beg your pardon, soldier?' his bland voice said, as he blinked like an absent-minded scholar. Josh smiled. It was a beautiful impression of a rather vague man of peace: too bad it did not have any great effect on the rebel who came forward to address Nick in tones of confident command.

'Who are you?' he demanded.

'Nicholas Howard, surgeon. At your service.' Nick bowed cheerfully, doing his best to forget the suspicious eyes.

'Where from?'

'Stoke Sutton, sir.'

'Where are you going?'

'Alton.'

'Then I am afraid that you must turn around, surgeon, and go home. No one passes through to Alton tonight.'

The man was not a local, Nick thought. It was a countryman's voice, but not of these parts, and he was sure that somewhere he had heard an accent like it. . . .

'But I must insist. I have business there. I must be allowed to pass.'

'What is your business?'

'I told you. I am a surgeon. I am required at Alton. It may mean a man's life.'

'Then it will be yours, Master Surgeon. I cannot let you go. No one goes to Alton tonight. I have orders.'

'I demand that you should stand aside. You may search my bags if you wish, you will find my instruments there. I demand passage in the name of humanity!'

'You demand? No, sir. You must go back. And the man with you. Who is he?'

'My servant.'

'I am sorry. But I can allow no exceptions. 'Tis more than my life is worth. But I think your arrival may be Providence. You can stay here, if you keep peace, though I shall have to put you under guard. We may need you later.'

'You have no right to put me under guard! I am a man of peace!'

'Man of peace, eh? So you say. And I've naught but your word, you see. . . .'

The sergeant was almost apologetic, but the look on his face showed that he remained unconvinced.

'No, not my word only. I have a safe-conduct here, signed by your own Colonel Chadwicke. He would vouch for me.'

The helmet shaded the face. Nick hoped that the flicker in the eye was not his imagination, but the rebel's growing uncertainty. Josh sat behind Nick, looking beyond him, between the troopers, at the glaring chalk road in the moonlight, and pondered whether to make a break for it. If he was shot, at least there was a chance that the sentries might hear the noise, and be warned of the presence of the enemy. He looked at Nick and knew that he was studying the same road, and making the same decision. The sharp-faced sergeant read his mind.

'Chadwicke's not here,' he said and turned to the man behind him. 'Search their bags. And bring them off the road before we are seen by those malignant scouts.'

'Pistols, sir,' said the trooper rifling their baggage. 'Pair each. All loaded.'

'And what, may I ask, is a man of peace doing carrying these?' the Roundhead enquired, fondling Nick's expensive horse-pistols with a covetous leer.

'We both carry pistols as well as swords, simply because even men of peace need to protect themselves against highway robbers and . . . unruly soldiers,' Nick replied virtuously. It was perfectly feasible, after all. . . .

'Where is the safe-conduct you spoke of?'

'Allow me to present it to you, sir.' Nick's cold hands fumbled in his shirt for the vital document and offered it to the rebel for inspection. 'You will see Colonel Chadwicke's signature at the bottom, there. What a good thing that the moon is so bright.'

He was more optimistic now. With just a little luck, he thought, he would have talked his way out of custody and into Alton. The dragoon squinted uncertainly at the crowded script, holding it but a couple of inches from the end of his nose: then he deliberated for a minute and looked up.

'I don't know,' he faltered. 'It seems to be in order. . . .'

Nick's heart thumped. His mouth was dry and his lips were cracked with smiling false smiles in the cold, his hands clenched tightly on the reins, ready to go the instant it was safe. At least they had not been forced to dismount; that in itself was a good sign.

'Fetch Colonel Chadwicke. And hurry,' the sergeant said suddenly to the nearest mounted trooper, who turned and was across the clearing into the trees almost before Nick could draw a shaking breath.

Nick looked uneasily round the glade. Large trees and a tangle of brambles surrounded it, and the floor of it was a carpet of old leaves and knotted tree-roots, and the remains of last summer's bracken fronds, beaten flat by the trampling of many booted feet. The moon shone still, so that there was little shade, and it too smiled a false smile. There was nowhere to hide away. There were infantrymen in double rank between Josh and Nick and the fringe of trees skirting the open fields round the town: the yellow regiment from the Tower Hamlets, which had been at Basing. Chadwicke was coming, and he was no fool. . . .

'Do not disturb the colonel on our account,' Nick said decisively. 'We will go home, if you wish it.'

'Not now, you won't,' replied the sergeant with conviction. 'I haven't sent for the colonel for nothing. You'll be useful when it comes to the fight, anyway. And my officer is coming, so it's not up to me.'

An officer on a heavy bay lumbered into the clearing between the trees. Too late Nick remembered where he had heard an accent similar to the sergeant's, and where he had seen the uniform before: not at Basing. He had worn it himself, to Winchester, way back in the heat of summer. The young officer had been a mere trooper then, but there was no mistaking the sandy-haired, freckle-faced man with cold blue-grey eyes which had haunted Nick's dreams: the malevolent eyes of William Sloan.

'What is this?' Sloan said, as he set eyes on Josh and Nick.

'Two . . . er . . . prisoners, sir. Trying to get to Alton. One of them says he's a surgeon.'

'Does he indeed? Well, well, what a pleasant surprise it is to see you!'

'You . . . know him, sir?' the sergeant gasped, reddening. 'I'm sorry if I have made a mistake, sir. He insisted he knew Colonel Chadwicke, so I've . . . asked him to come.'

'Oh, excellent, sergeant. There is no mistake, believe me! The colonel also will be very glad to see this man: for is he not the one who killed the colonel's son? That is where he came by that great scar on the face. Is it not so, malignant?'

Nick wondered how on earth he had ever thought that this man would be more at home with a peaceful plough-furrow than on a blood-soaked battlefield. There had been a mistake, and it was Nick who had made it, though Robin had tried so hard to warn him. 'Save a thief from the gallows,' Robin had said, 'and he will hang you if he can.'

Josh began to edge away towards the trees. If he sat tight, Nick thought, Josh might yet escape in one piece. It was the only chance left now, in this horrible situation when all his nightmares had come true at one moment. Three yards away, Tom Chadwicke sat his grey mare and stared, incredulous. He had heard Will Sloan's every word.

'Are you . . . sure, Sloan?' he said, with a clear effort at calmness.

'Aye, sir. Certain. I was there. The man's name is Nicholas Howard.'

'That's true,' the sergeant volunteered helpfully. 'He said so himself, just now, Colonel Chadwicke.' The colonel nodded, speechlessly.

'Major Nicholas Howard,' continued Sloan, with relish, 'an intelligencer to the King.'

His look cut through Nick like the wind had that afternoon. Like a vengeful sword it had been. But it was not the cold that was making Nick shiver now.

'My God!' said Chadwicke, under his breath. 'What a fool I've been.' Then his voice, too, grew sharp and loud. 'Howard, is this true?'

Nick nodded assent, and shrugged. There was no point in denying anything now. The lying was all over, all finished, and life with it. The colonel still stared at him.

'Major Howard?'

'Yes, Colonel Chadwicke?' Nick smiled a slow, sardonic smile. It was an effort, but he would not let them know how much he was afraid.

'I must ask you to surrender your sword.'

'I regret infinitely, but if you want it, you must come and . . . fetch it.' Nick bowed, in what he hoped was a suitably contemptuous manner. As Nat always said, it was as well to be hanged for a sheep as for a lamb. Josh was Alton's only hope, now.

The colonel's face was a mask of twisting hatred for the man who had killed his only son. 'Cut him down, boys,' he ordered crisply. 'Ten guineas for the man who lays him low for me.'

If it had not been so tragic, Nick thought, it would have been funny. Every penny of Chadwicke's money had come to him by way of Judith: and here was Chadwicke offering ten guineas of his wife's money to the man who would kill her lover, and he did not even know it.

A rebel still held the bridle of the stallion. Nick kicked him in the face with sudden force, and the man reeled back with a bleeding nose. Then they were all round him, and falling on at once. Nick drew his sword. If he could keep their attention for a while, perhaps Josh could make a run for it, for he was not far now from the edge of the trees.

The rebels were trying to drag Nick from the saddle, but he hung on with all the strength he possessed. He cut one down, and then another. The horse reared as he struck out at the nearest man. One of the Roundheads was behind him, tugging fiercely at his cloak in an attempt to throttle him. He freed the strings which fastened the cloak round his throat, but in doing so he lost control of the frightened, plunging horse. He was so hopelessly off balance now that he was forced to jump from the saddle before he should fall out of it. Nick dodged the kicking hooves, and made for the trees in the confusion. He had completely lost sight of Josh. There was only the deep velvet-blue of the sky with its freckling of shiny stars, and the moon, lower now, still smiling through the bare-twigged oak branches above his head. The pikemen were still with him. He turned with his back to the nearest tree trunk and faced them, and prayed God that it would be quickly over.

Josh watched the small, hard-pressed figure of his dear friend fighting for his life, and thought of Alton. He decided that General Crawford and Colonel Bolle could fend for themselves, for they had plenty of help. Nick had no one except Josh, and Josh would not see him die alone.

Nick's arm was upraised to strike at the lunging attacker before him, as with the other arm he fought to keep his balance amongst the tangling roots and bracken-fronds. There was a long, hideous moment when time seemed to stand still. He could see the pike's gleam in the merciless moonlight as it sped towards him, and he knew that it was sharp. He had ample time to know the sickening dread of what was to come, but not enough time to avoid it. He watched the pike come down, and felt the steel tearing through his coat, and the threadbare shirt, and then rip his arm from wrist to shoulder: then it bit deep into his side. There was searing pain as his body tore itself away, and he was bleeding and gasping for breath. Josh had Chadwicke by the throat and was shouting abuse at him and shaking him like a terrier shakes a rat, but one of the pikemen turned and began to belabour Josh across the back with his pike-staff, and he was on the ground, bent double and vomiting.

Nick slid to the ground at the foot of the oak, his back hard up against it, crying with pain. His sword fell from his useless hand. Through the haze of semi-consciousness he could see Chadwicke rubbing his bruised throat and kicking savagely at Josh, who lay helpless still. There was an awful cruel smile on the colonel's face, and the colonel's voice echoed in Nick's ears, along with the agonised beating of his own heart. 'Sloan,' Tom said, 'you have done well. Have this one taken to Farnham, to the castle. I am sure Sir William will be overjoyed to talk to him.' He indicated Josh, who was struggling to his feet, still choking.

'Sir.' Sloan came to precise attention, glowing with the word of praise, and with the great joy of his vengeance. Nick fought the pain for breath, for sight of his enemy, and for knowledge of the fate of Josh who was hurt and in peril. . . . Captain Atkins knelt on the ground at Nick's side, fumbling with kind but clumsy hands at the torn shirt and coat to come at the wound beneath, trying desperately to bind it with his scarf. Others were dragging Josh away. He was on his feet now, unsteady, but still fighting. Nick saw him double up one of the rebels with a well-aimed kick, but then they bound Josh's arms so that they could have greater purchase over him, and led him away out of sight.

It was too much of an effort to keep his eyes open, Nick found. So he closed them wearily and thought that he would faint. Everything in the world was caught up in a dizzy vortex, and now all he wanted was to die, but still he heard the voices of his captors round him. Colonel Chadwicke was near, very near.

'This one,' he said, 'is mine. Is he dead?' The voice was passionless. The captain's hands shook.

'No, sir. Not yet. The bleeding seems to be stopping for the moment.' He answered, and his voice was shaking, too.

'Oh, I am glad to hear that. What splendid good fortune.' Chadwicke's voice was bitter and mocking, and there was no trace of charity in it. Nick knew that he must be smiling still.

'Sir?'

'We do not want him to die, do we? Take him back to Broadoak, carefully.'

'I doubt if . . .' Atkins was cut short, as the colonel ignored his doubt.

'Take half a dozen men. Get Harrington, the surgeon. Persuade him to accept my hospitality at the house. If he . . . declines, then you may have to lock him up until I return. You understand?'

'Yes, sir. You mean you want me to arrest him?'

'You could call it that, yes. But tell Harrington that I implore him to save his friend's life. I should be extremely grieved to see Nicholas Howard die of his wounds. He has played Judas Iscariot, and like Judas, he shall hang for it! I shall make sure of that. For it is a spectacle I would not miss for all the world. . . . Now, lads, I think I am in debt to one of you?'

The sound of clinking coins rang across the clearing, loud in the great stillness after the fighting. A stillness like that of death itself.

'Oh, God,' moaned Nick. 'Oh, God. Somebody help me, please.'

21

'DARK, BUT NOT YET NIGHT'

The rebels took Nick up from where he lay on the frozen ground, wrapped him once more in his cloak, lifted him gently on to a horse, and one of them mounted behind him to make sure that he would not fall. He felt dizzy and sick, and kept his eyes tightly shut so that he would not see the menacing world lurching about him. The hands of his enemies were not unkind, but still he felt a welling resentment towards them, because he would far rather have been left still to die where he had been, under the tree, in peace.

It was a long, slow, tormented journey back to Broadoak, and misery and despair were his close companions. It was the corporal riding behind him: Nick recognised the man's odd voice, and remembered that he had once compared it to a bull-calf with a sore throat, and Nat and Josh had fallen about, laughing. The voice was still of wheezing, grating harshness, and the corporal seemed more like an ox than ever. Nick was grateful now for those brawny solid limbs which kept him in the saddle.

The odd voice spoke again. 'Well, John Willet, I fancy we have here your devil?'

There was no reply, only sullen silence. It was the captain who broke the silence, absently, almost as if he was talking to himself. 'No devil here. . . . 'Tis human enough. Oh, God, I knew I'd seen him before, that night. I even said so . . . and he just . . . smiled.'

' 'Tis human enough, aye, sir. And most courageous.' The corporal's voice had in it a trace of regret. 'To face us all, alone like that. And then to come to Broadoak, cold as ice, and face us all again. Though any one of us might have known him.'

'I knew I'd seen him. . . . I wonder why he did not just . . . finish me, quietly?' said Atkins, ruminating on the chilly thought of what might-have-been. 'He could have done. . . . No one would have known.'

'Pardon me, sir,' John Willet said. 'But what you are both forgetting is that 'tis a nasty evil malignant that's killed a good many of my comrades and yours. It is written, sir, "He made a pit and digged it, and is fallen into the ditch which he made. His mischief shall return upon his own head, and his violent dealing shall come down upon his own pate." ' There were 'Amens' from two of his comrades. Nick thought bitterly how appropriate were the words of the psalmist, and those words rolled round and round his head, until the horse stumbled, and wrenched his side dreadfully, and he could hear his own voice moaning with pain.

Captain Atkins sighed heavily. 'Hold your peace, Willet. This devil knows what hell is like. Parker and Killigrew, go with Willet to fetch the surgeon. Try not . . . to waste time.'

Nick heard the horses trotting away. He felt an odd sense of distance, a detachment of mind which made it seem as if this was all happening to someone else. He hoped against hope that Harrington would realise what had happened, and contrive somehow to escape. But he knew in his heart that Nat was bound to guess at the truth, but that even if he did, it would make no difference. He would stay and be doomed just as Josh had stayed: for doomed they must all be. My Lord at Oxford had made it abundantly clear that there could be no help for a captive spy: no way out for Nat, either, except at the end of a hempen rope dangling from a gallows, and then hung on a gibbet, to be an example to others. . . . The corporal's strength was hard put to it to keep the pair of them on the horse's back.

'Easy, lad,' he was saying in Nick's ear. 'Hang on just a little while, we are nearly home.'

'Nearly home,' Nick echoed, his voice a hoarse whisper. His mind turned to little Lucy, and he wondered if he would ever see her again. Home. 'Where your heart is, there shall your home be.' That was what Aunt Nan always used to say. So where was home? He had none, and several, for his heart was well divided: some of it was with Lucy and Nan Carteret; some of it lay dead in a nameless grave with Robin's body; but a great part of it was definitely here. He opened his eyes on light grey, frosty morning, and they were riding out of the shelter of the beech trees, the house of Broadoak before them.

He was terribly weary. 'All right, friend,' the corporal was saying. 'It's all right. We'll get you to bed, and Mistress Chadwicke will tend you till the surgeon comes.'

Nick's mind came leaping back to his torn body with sudden dreadful anxiety, as he thought of Judith. 'No!' he whispered, striving to make himself heard, fighting the choking in his throat, his eyes wide open. 'Please . . . not let her see me . . . like this. . . . Oh, please!'

The corporal listened, and nodded understanding. 'I've an idea she will be very distressed about this, sir,' he said, to the captain.

Atkins looked at the gruesome bloodstained figure of his young enemy. 'Aren't we all?' he said. 'Excepting for the colonel, and John Willet.'

Nick choked uncontrollably as the horse lurched again, tired under the weight of its double burden. Once more his side began to bleed, and he could feel the sticky warmth of blood running down. The corporal turned the horse into the yard, and before he had dismounted there was already a little dark red pool splashed on the flagstones.

'Hurry!' said the captain. 'Get him indoors, and I will find Mistress Chadwicke.'

Judith was coming down the stairs, hunched in her grey cloak, for her morning walk, though this morning she had been in two minds about it, so severe was the cold. But she was too restless to stay indoors. She shivered and longed for spring again, and the warmth of sunshine. Even the garden was feeling the cold, sad with untidy, spiky stalks, and withered leaves, and the all-pervading smell of death and decay. The sound of horses broke in on her thoughts. It was early for Thomas to be returning. . . . She turned towards the door, and through it came the corporal, carrying his bedraggled burden. Her stomach had been feeling vaguely peculiar all morning, and now she was afraid that she would be sick at once. She looked again, hoping and praying that her eyes were playing her false. The burden was Nick, his face the colour of unbleached linen, and his dark hair stuck in clumps to his sweating forehead. His lip was bleeding where he had bitten it. Judith clung tightly to the banister at the foot of the stair, trying hard to ward away the wave of panic and faintness that was sweeping over her.

'Oh, no!' she whispered, over and over. 'Oh, no!'

'We have here a prisoner, ma'am. Hurt badly.'

'A prisoner?' she echoed, her mouth dry, her mind refusing still to accept the evidence of her eyes. 'There is some mistake, surely?'

'No mistake, madam, I regret to say,' said the captain, gravely, stabbed by the hurt grey eyes. 'Madam, are you ailing? Where may we put him?' Atkins regarded her blanched face with concern. He had his arms outstretched, because he was afraid that she might fall. 'Please, madam,' he said, insistently. 'He needs attention without delay, or he will die.'

'I do not understand.' Her voice was even, with only the slightest quavering. 'Why is it that you bring Master Howard here a prisoner?'

'Major Howard, madam. He is a Royalist officer. A spy. One of Sir William's men had come across him before, unluckily for him.'

'Such a nice fellow,' the corporal's gruff voice muttered. 'Seems difficult to believe, don't it?'

'How was this . . . discovered?'

'He was trying to warn the garrison at Alton that there was an attack coming, and our men stopped him. He nearly got away then . . . talked his way out of it. But one of the general's men had seen him before. It turns out that he is the man who killed Captain Chadwicke.'

'Oh, God,' said Judith. So Tom knew everything: almost

everything, and his anger would be unbounded. . . .'Put him in here. I've linen ready here.'

'Nearly killed you, too, didn't he, sir?' said the corporal briskly, carefully depositing his groaning load on the bed.

'That's true,' Atkins said without rancour. 'And yet I cannot help . . . admiring him for his courage. Are you well, madam?'

'I am quite well, thank you, Captain Atkins.'

Nick opened his eyes, and remembered. On this bed he had lain once before, on an October night, with Judith's warm body beside him. The bed-curtains were pretty, with their carefully embroidered silver nosegays; but the pain was blinding him so that he could hardly see them, as Judith's hands, unexpectedly steady and assured, cut away the stained coat and shirt. She must be half-blind, too, for there was such a multitude of tears in her eyes. As fast as she wiped them, they returned, despite all her efforts to hold them back. He wanted to comfort her, to tell her not to cry, but it was hard to find the words, let alone the breath to give them utterance. She was bending low over him, but he was parched and breathless and his tongue was heavy, and all that he could think of were the words she had said to him in jest, the afternoon before.

'Good thing,' he whispered, 'I never got . . . a new shirt.'

He tried to smile, but never knew if he succeeded or not. The black vortex came up to engulf him, and there was no one with him there, not even Judith. He was alone with the pain, and spent the day in confusion and despair: but his despair would have been deeper if he had known the grim passage of events in Alton.

Dawn had seen the garrison waking to find the rebel host gathered in the open fields surrounding the town. Five thousand Roundheads, under the command of Colonel John Birch, had materialised as if from the bowels of the earth, by some means nothing short of devilish. Rather than risk the loss of so many valuable men, and mindful of his orders, General the Earl of Crawford gave command of the indefensible pig-hole into the hands of Colonel Bolle's foot, gathered his horse together, and beat a hell-for-leather retreat towards Winchester.

John Bolle, however, was not prepared to give Alton up so easily, and his undying optimism told him that somehow reinforcements might yet be sent to save them. He gathered his seven hundred men into the churchyard of St Lawrence, and made ready to defend it. The little band held stubbornly to the churchyard and then fell back into the church itself, where they made themselves a barricade of dead horses, and fought on for several hours. In the cold grey afternoon, John Bolle died, clubbed to death under the chancel-arch, vowing that he would himself run through any of his men who cried for quarter. It was only then that the pitiful survivors threw themselves on the mercy of the enemy, and Alton was lost.

Nick's world was full of voices, and shadowy glimpses of people that he knew. He found it hard to sort out the real people from the ghosts, for they were all around his bed, and some of them talked to him. But when he tried to answer them, he found that it was impossible to make them hear. It took all his strength to go on drawing breath after painful breath, and he longed now only to stop and rest.

Elizabeth was with him, giggling and gay, clad in the green velvet dress she loved to wear, with its expensive white lace and jewelled buttons. While he watched, her laughing face turned into a grinning death's head which made him weep in terror: but Aunt Nan's voice was soothing in his ear to comfort him, and he remembered that he had fallen out of an apple tree in the orchard, and hurt himself. . . . A long time ago, it had been: so long, that if he went back to the orchard, he would see his own little daughter waiting for him beneath the trees, but his way back was blocked by a pike that glinted at him in the moonlight. . . . Robin was beside the bed. Robin held out both hands to Nick, and he would willingly have grasped them, but someone was mopping his clammy face and cracked lips with cold water, and that someone would not let him go. Though Nick cried out to see him again, the shadow faded from view. It was then that he remembered. 'Alton,' Nick found himself gasping, 'must go to Alton,' and found that he was being held down by iron bands. But it was his own weakness holding him back. There were no hands, no restraining hands. There was no one there, no one at all.

'Uncle Nat! Uncle Nat, he is waking, I am sure of it.' Judith's voice was quavering.

Nick heard footsteps and felt hands, hands he knew must belong to Nathaniel, capable and firm. Nat's voice told him to rest. 'Lie still, Nicholas. You'll not be going anywhere today.'

Nick clasped at the hands. 'Is that . . . you, Nat?'

'Yes, of course it's me! Who were you expecting, the Archangel Gabriel? Though I fear that you and I will both be making his acquaintance before long, if I know Tom Chadwicke.'

Nick blinked the mist away and peered up at the faces. 'Nat, I'm . . . sorry.' He choked. Judith was wiping his face again.

'Lie still, lad. And be quiet. You did all you could. More than most of us could have managed. It's not your fault.'

'Hurts. Help me, Nat.' Nick bit his lip, and it began once more to bleed.

Judith mopped at it distractedly, and she was sobbing, her eyes already red and swollen with weeping. Nick sank once more into half-sleep, listening hard to the voices, although it was difficult to hear them, because there was such a ringing and a roaring in his ears.

'Uncle Nat, can you not do anything for him? For God's sake!' she pleaded.

'Judith,' came Nat's reply. 'I've done all. . . . He will not last until Tom comes back, which I think is probably fortunate. He's as strong as a horse and as obstinate as sin, or he would never have got back here at all!'

'Don't let him die. Please don't let him die.'

'Judy, please believe me, the kindest thing I could do for him now would be to take my pistol and shoot him. He is in such pain, Judy. Let him go.'

'But if he dies, then I shall die, too!' she wailed despairingly.

'Nonsense!' was the emphatic reply. 'Your life will go on, just the same.'

'Just the same? No, never the same. . . . Not now. Only Tom, and no one else. . . . I cannot live like that. And I shall tell Thomas so, when he returns.'

'Now, do not be stupid, child. You must be strong and sensible, for Nick's sake as well as your own. Do you think he could die in peace, knowing that Tom will make you suffer for ever because you were unfaithful to him? He will, if he finds out, as sure as night follows day. You ignored my advice once before. But not this time, Judith, I entreat you, not this time!'

Nat's voice was hard and insistent, and Nick knew that he would take care of Judith. It was odd, somehow, knowing that they were expecting him to die soon. Dying happened to other people. . . . If only the pain would go away, just for a few minutes, so that he could think. . . .

'Now, you go to your room, Judith, and bathe your eyes, and take a few minutes to think. You'll not have a morsel of sense in your head as long as you stay here. Go on, or Tom will be back.'

'But . . .'

'Do as you are told. If there is any change, then I will tell you, child. I promise.'

There was a pause, and then the door closed, and Nick knew that Judith had done what she was told. Nat's voice was speaking in Nick's ear now, very close, very persuasive and urgent.

'Nicholas? I pray you may hear me, friend. If you keep on fighting, you will win, only do not give up. I know it hurts, but it shall not be your master. We'll get out of this, both of us. But only if you do not give up. It is dark, but not yet night. Just keep on fighting! Nicholas, can you hear me?'

Nicholas heard and clenched his teeth, and determined that he would not die yet. He would see Thomas Chadwicke to hell first. . . .

Tom Chadwicke came to look at his beaten, dying enemy, and

found that enemy asleep. He went away to see his wife, instead, and found that she had locked her door against him. Judith sent Lilith with a polite but cool message to say how much upset she had been by the day's events, and that she would not see him. Chadwicke shrugged and went to his own bed, to sleep alone. He had become accustomed of late to sleeping alone, ever since he had been away in October. He frowned. That was not the way to get sons. He would have a sharp talk with his lady wife in the morning, if she was sufficiently recovered, to remind her of her duties. . . . Then his face softened. On the other hand, it must have been a shock to her, finding that her uncle and her friend were nothing but malignant spies. 'Treachery,' Colonel Chadwicke sighed, and took up the ponderous Bible he kept beside the bed, turning the softly rustling pages until he came to the Psalms. 'When shall he die, and his name perish? Mine own familiar friend, in whom I trusted, which did eat of my bread, hath lifted up his heel against me. . . . By this I know that thou favourest me, because mine enemy doth not triumph over me.' He read it again, aloud: so hard to believe. . . . Such a sober, sensible fellow, whom he had loved almost like a son. He shut the book with a thump, and it was a long time before he went to sleep.

Nick wakened again at one o'clock, the night so still that he could hear the distant clock of St Peter's in Stoke Sutton chiming the hour. He turned his head laboriously to look around the room. The bed-curtains were drawn only to one side, so his view was unimpeded: even so, it took him a long time to remember where he was, and why. Across from the foot of the bed sat Trooper John Willet, his head on the tiring-table, cradled on his arms. Beside him was his steel helmet, and his sword hung from the chair-back. He was clearly on guard, but his slow, steady, stertorous breathing testified to his confidence that the prisoner was not about to make off, at least, not in the immediate future.

Nick was excruciatingly uncomfortable. He tried moving to find an easier position, but there wasn't one. His arm and side were a concentration of agony, and he was in a torment of thirst. The pain of his thoughts was even worse than the aching of his wounds. He had failed miserably, and now he could not even die when he so ardently desired to do so.

Sleep eluded Judith. She paced up and down in her room, wild with worry: for Nicholas, dying in agony just a few yards away; for Uncle Nat, who was a prisoner, and Tom would have him hanged; and for herself, and the future. She shivered in the cold. It was stupid to pace the floor in a night-shift, in the cold and darkness, for what good would it do? Judith forced herself to lie down under the bed-covers and close her eyes. She lay on her back and thought of praying. She had prayed hard that night her father had gone away to the army, and not two weeks later he had been struck down at Edgehill, and died under some ragged Oxfordshire hedge. She had been alone. So alone that when Thomas Chadwicke had come with an offer of marriage, she had not hesitated to accept. This time she would be more alone: there would not even be Uncle Nat to help her, but only Thomas . . . and life could never be the same.

Judith gave up the pretence of trying to sleep, went to the clothes-press, and took out her cloak. The smell of orris-root came to her nostrils, as it had that other night back in October. That night there had been no trooper on guard outside the door of the green chamber. . . . But the trooper, although obviously somewhat astonished, stood aside to let the barefooted wife of his colonel pass. Softly she closed the door behind her, and the rhythmic snorting of John Willet was hardly interrupted at all. Judith looked down at the still figure with its tightly closed eyes and unshaven, blood-smeared chin, and felt sweeping desolation.

'Oh, Nicholas,' she sobbed softly. 'Oh, Nicholas, my love.'

'Hello,' he said, opening his eyes and peering up at her. 'What?'

'I could not rest. So I came to see how you are.'

'Still here.'

She bent and kissed his forehead. Her hands were soft, and immeasurably kind, and she gave him a drink to ease his thirst. 'I . . . love you,' he said. 'Stay, Hold hand.' He gasped with pain, and his hand twisted hers until the tears came to her eyes.

'I'll stay,' she promised. 'For as long as you need me.'

'Always,' he sighed. He was dizzy and tired and in pain, and now he could give up and die with her beside him.

She was stricken with sudden fear, knowing what was in his mind. She could almost see him slipping away from her. 'Please, do not give up, my darling, please!'

His head moved restlessly on the pillow, and he did not want to listen, she knew. Yet still she must try to talk away the Angel of Death, even though she might so be crossing the will of Almighty God.

'Oh, God,' he moaned. 'Hurts.'

'If not for me, then for your little girl. She will miss you. A child must have a father. . . .'

'Lucy?' he said. 'Lucy?'

'That is a pretty name, Nicholas. Is she pretty, your little Lucy?'

'Very.' His eyes stared distractedly up at her, and he was suddenly wide awake. 'Ask 'Becca to write.'

'Write? To whom?'

'To tell . . . Aunt Nan. She knows.'

'All right. I'll ask her. Rest, love.'

But he was not now disposed to rest. There were other questions he had to ask. He must have the answers, and then he might think of resting. 'Alton?' he said.

Judith looked at him sadly. It was best to tell the truth, because he would already suspect it, and he would surely know if she lied. 'They captured Alton today. Lord Crawford made his escape with the cavalry, but the infantry were trapped. In the church. They were very brave, but most of them . . . were killed.'

'What about their colonel?' Nick whispered, anxiously.

Her face told him the answer before she uttered a word. 'He . . . died. I'm sorry. Was he . . . a friend?'

'Oh, John, not you, too. . . .' Nick was silent and wanted very much to cry.

Judith wanted to cry, too, but she would be strong, for both of them. 'But Joshua Jeffery escaped. On the way to

Farnham. He pretended to be very ill, and his escort stopped out of pity. He was away into the woods, they said, and they could not find him again.'

Nick smiled widely. It was not all bad, then, even in this dark hour. He had always said that Josh should have been a player. If Josh had any sense at all, he would be safe now, behind the stout walls of Basing, with brother Ned. 'Good old Josh,' he breathed. 'Thanks, Judith. . . . Good night.'

'I love you, Nicholas. I wish that I could help you.'

'You have. Long night . . . made shorter.' He was asleep almost instantly

Judith heard the distant clock chime the hour of two. She sat, watching him, for some time, her own head nodding with weariness until she could hold it up no longer. She put her head on the pillow beside his and went to sleep there.

When Captain Atkins came, at six, he found the three of them still sleeping. John Willet with his head on the tiring-table, snoring and snuffling with gusto: and the colonel's wife and the colonel's enemy hand in hand like a couple of children, sharing the same pillow. Many small things had of late been puzzling the captain, but now at once he saw all with understanding, and the certainty that his odd, nagging suspicion had been right. He touched Judith lightly on the shoulder. 'Madam,' he said, softly, 'I think the colonel will be here soon. Perhaps it is time that you were going?'

22

DAVID AND JONATHAN

Everyone at Broadoak was miserable for the next two weeks, and Nick was the most miserable of all. Lilith fed him gruel and mutton broth, and bullied him unmercifully, calling up the twin spectres of repentance and retribution until he was sorely tempted to spit the broth back at her even as a babe might have done. Certainly he was no better than a babe, for he lay just as helpless and irksomely dependent, sad in his isolation and listening to all the sounds from the busy household of which he was now no part. Voices talked about him, and he could hear only occasional snippets of what they said; the busy footsteps for the most part passed his door; and from the yard, the horses' clopping hooves sounded as Colonel Chadwicke's rebel minions came and went, and he could do nothing against them.

It was a cold, snowy Christmas morning before Nick felt even half-human again, and he lay propped on a mountain of pillows and wondered where Judith was. Once or twice she had come to see him, but he knew that she dared not come too often, lest anyone should suspect that there had been more than mere friendship between them. Christmas at Broadoak, and it was as grim and gloomy as any other day, for, of course, Tom Chadwicke and his ilk did not believe in celebrating half-pagan festivals with riotous rejoicing, and that, Nick thought, was their trouble. . . .

Three days later he was not merely half-human, but bored

to distraction, so he lay and stared at the old tapestry which hung on the wall near the door, because he could not think of anything better to do. He shut Judith firmly from his mind, because lately he had been pondering for too long on what might have been, and had all the while been telling himself that no amount of pondering would do any good at all. Resolutely he stared at the tapestry, and its faded green-gold patterns of twisted foliage and strangely dressed huntsmen, their stiff hounds about to rend to death a rather alarmed-looking hare. No wonder the hare looked alarmed. Those sharp-toothed monsters had been poised to tear it up for the last twenty years at least, and it must have been in an agony of anticipation for all that time. Nick smiled at his own whimsical thought, until it occurred to him that he himself had nothing better to anticipate. When the pain kept him awake at night, he wondered what it would be like as the rope tightened swiftly and irrevocably about his neck, and worse if dying was not the end, then what exactly happened afterwards, and if repentance now might yet change it. . . .

Always at least one soldier kept watch in the room, and one outside the door, and he had been told that there was always another guard below the window, despite the fact that it must be a thirty-foot drop. No one could escape, whole or not, from a house full of Roundheads. Tom Chadwicke was taking no chances.

The colonel had no heart now even to face Nicholas, though Nat was plagued by his frequent visits and cheered by the fact that not all seemed to be going Chadwicke's way. He had been turning out volumes of angry correspondence to Sir William Waller, demanding permission to execute the two Royalist spies at once, but Waller steadfastly refused for some reason best known to himself. Then Tom begged at least to send one of them to Southampton for safe-keeping by Colonel Norton, but this, too, had been refused. Still Tom did not come to see Nick at all, but sent instead his second in command. Atkins came every day to inspect the prisoner, and stayed sometimes to play chess, or to talk self-consciously of how a timid tailor's son from Reading had come to find himself a reluctant soldier.

Nat came, too, to dress the wound, and he seemed pleased. 'You are making a very speedy recovery, my friend,' he said. ' 'Tis no doubt due to the most excellent solicitous care you have been receiving.' He smiled wickedly at the corporal, who stood, hand on sword, warming his back at the fireside. 'For whatever reason that care may be given,' he added, darkly.

The corporal coughed, somewhat uncomfortably, and turned away to spit into the fire. Nick swore. Nat was hurting him dreadfully.

'The colonel must be happy to know that I shall live to meet justice,' he said, defiantly, though the thought of imminent execution sent cold shivers down his back.

'Do not recover too soon, though, will you? For myself I've no desire to meet with justice yet awhile,' Nat said, unsmiling, the same cold fingers playing along his spine.

'It cannot be soon enough, for me. I cannot stand much more preaching from Lilith. Oh, God, that hurts! Remember, Nat, that I am your only ally in this cockatrices' den!'

Nat licked his lips in concentration, leaning further forward. 'Not quite the only one, I think. If you will not hold still it is bound to hurt. I shall have to ask the corporal to hold you.'

'No, you won't. Just get on with it. How is . . . Mistress Chadwicke?'

'Judith is a little white about the gills just now, and has been feeling unwell, I gather,' Nat said.

'It would make a change to have someone different to talk to. I've nothing to do. Though Captain Atkins has been kind enough to call in every day. I think I shall die of boredom before they ever come to hang me. Oh, Nat, for pity's sake!'

'If you are chafing for visitors and conversation I think you will be overjoyed. I nearly forgot to tell you. We are to have an important visitor, you and I.'

'A visitor. Who?'

'A gentleman called Riley. The colonel tells me that he is very anxious to talk to us.'

'Who is Riley?' asked Nick, with misgiving. 'Do I know him? Hell fire, that hurts!'

'The new spy-master general for the Parliament, I believe. Poor Tom is so impatient to hang you and have done, but it seems they are all bent on thwarting him. Master Riley desires information, so poor Tom will be forced to give us house-room a while longer.'

The panic rose in Nick's throat and swept over him until the very room spun round. 'Can I have water, please?' he said. 'I do not feel well.'

There would be no lack of conversation when Riley arrived. There would be endless questions, which must be answered, or else. . . . Nat was afraid, and Nat was not one to be afraid without reason.

'I thought you would be pleased,' he said breezily. 'Give you something else to look forward to, eh? There, that is done. You'll be as good as new in three or four weeks. Barring misadventure, that is. Now. A drink, you wanted?'

Nat went away and Nick lay exhausted, pondering the awful news. He was tempted to save himself at all costs, for he knew that now there would be a way offered to him. Riley was bound to ask, and if he answered right, the prison doors would open wide, and he would have freedom and life: as a spy for Parliament. Freedom and life were worth serious consideration, and Nick considered them for a full half-hour before recoiling in self-disgust. Anyway, he told himself, Tom Chadwicke would still want his head, but for other reasons which had little to do with politics, and Tom would pursue him still, whichever side he was on.

Judith found herself constantly on the edge of tears, of self-pity, rage and frustration. She was helpless to comfort Nick when he needed her; and always there was the fear in her mind that the captain might tell Tom what he had seen, for surely now he must know the truth. She wept private storms in her room, but went about her normal household duties with the well-practised mask of cold efficiency, determined that no one should guess the turmoil within her. Now she did not even know if it would be kinder to pray for a quick death for her lover after all, when before she had prayed so hard that he should live. 'In times of trouble,' her father had said, 'always turn to the word of God for comfort.' Judith smiled. He had given her a beautiful Bible when she was just a child. In it she had kept small secret treasures to remind her of things, and of people: flowers from summer . . . and letters. . . . Nick should have that book, and she would make sure that there was comfort in it for him. It would be quite easy to conceal a small scrap of paper between those stiff, yellowed pages. Uncle Nat had said that Nick had been complaining of boredom, so there was her excuse to ask Thomas. Not even Thomas could deny Holy Scriptures to a man already condemned to die. No one would suspect the colonel's wife, except perhaps Captain Atkins. The risk was worth taking. Time was coming when Thomas would have to be told the truth. She was sure of it now, but still she was determined to conceal it from him as long as possible, for as Nick himself had said, sometimes the truth could hurt people so much more than falsehood. . . .

Nick's nagging anxiety about Judith's health was put to rest later in the day when she arrived to see him, unruffled and tidy as ever in the black dress with its wide white collar. Her face was a shade paler than usual, and there were dark circles under her eyes, but the eyes loved and laughed at him in the same old way as she smiled politely, offering the book to him.

'Master Harrington says that you are at a loss for an occupation. My husband and I agreed that it might profit your soul to read this.'

'Thank you, madam,' he mocked. 'My soul will undoubtedly be much easier for your kind consideration.'

'I should be happy to think so, sir.' She set the heavy volume down beside him, and touched his hand. He could feel the warmth of her love, and longed to throw caution to the winds and draw her down to him, to kiss those polite-smiling lips. It was an age, he thought, since she had been in his arms. Almost as if he knew, the corporal's keen glance surveyed them with something sharper than mere interest. She straightened her back, looking every inch a prim, puritan wife. Her eyes held a severe expression, as if she would command him to something. 'I must entreat you to read it carefully,' she said. 'And you will find comfort therein.'

She smiled and was gone, taking her warmth with her, and leaving him only the sepulchral reality of his solitude. Nick shivered. It was hardly just sorrow leaving him cold. The weather outside was freezing. The corporal stooped over the fire, feeding the rapacious flames which flickered more with appetite than with the generous giving of heat. The square of sky Nick could see through the window was steely grey. Today there would be more snow. Large, fluffy flakes of it kissed the lattice with their soft, whispering mouths, and went on tumbling, unprotesting, to the ground beneath. Outside the window it would be a chilly task for some poor trooper to guard the precious prisoner. With a sudden surge of vengeful spite, Nick hoped that it was John Willet's gaunt figure out there in the snow, and that he was very cold indeed.

The big Bible sat on the coverlet and silently admonished him for his reluctance to open its chased-leather cover.

'It's too dark to read,' he said aloud to it, excusing himself for his hesitation, and then wondered whether, after all, his sanity should be called into question, that he should talk to a book.

'Sir?' said the corporal, anxiously. 'Something you wanted?'

'Nothing, corporal. Nothing, thank you. Just talking to myself.'

'Shut this cold out, shall I?' The corporal crossed to the window and drew the shutters, leaving the room flickering in the dimness of fireglow while he fumbled to light the candles.

'This'll stop your Hopton?' said the corporal, wheezing loudly. 'Slush and mud and snow like this would stop anybody.'

'Lord Hopton? Stop him from doing what?'

'Oh, I forgot you didn't know. Stop him from relieving the castle at Arundel. He marched out of Winchester day before yesterday.'

'Arundel? Oh, yes. It's funny, I'd almost forgotten the war. It's so peaceful here.'

'Peaceful? Oh, God, aye, sir. Though not from my point of view. We've been stood to arms this past week for fear of attack. We're isolated here, you see. King's men at Basing, and Winchester only a step or two away, and our nearest friends are Colonel Norton's men at Southampton.'

'Yes, of course. I'd not thought of it like that, I must confess. Very uncomfortable.'

'Why do you think the colonel's so keen to have you quickly dispatched, sir? Before he runs the risk of losing you. Though it seems to me a little hard, sir, to hang a man when he cannot yet stand on his own two feet.'

'I thank you for your sympathy, corporal. But I daresay the colonel has his reasons,' Nick smiled wryly.

'That's as may be. I'm sure the colonel knows best.' The corporal coughed asthmatically and, like a true diplomat, changed the subject. 'This winter weather's a bastard. I'll wager you are feeling it, sir. Shoulder ache?'

'Yes, damnably. You said Hopton is on the march?'

Shuffling noises came from outside the door, and Trooper Killigrew was holding it open for Captain Atkins, who came in with a steaming pewter mug in either hand. He wore a wide smile, though of late he had been feeling anything but cheerful, because he had been wrestling with his conscience. The captive spy had been his very good friend not so long ago, and friendship did not stop just because a man's politics were not what they had seemed: especially when, like Atkins, a man is shy and slow to liking, so that any friendship was an effort. It was a pity that duty should now forbid it. There was also that delicate matter of the colonel's wife. . . . The corporal came smartly to attention.

'All right, corporal. You go down to the kitchen for a pipe of tobacco. I will keep an eye on Major Howard. Come up again in half an hour.'

'Yes, sir,' said the corporal, amazed at the opportunity, and disappeared speedily before the captain should change his mind. Atkins handed one of the mugs to Nick, and sat down.

'I've brought something to warm you. Much to Lilith's disgust.'

'Rot Lilith,' said Nick bitterly. 'May she drown in her own broth!'

'I'll drink to that,' Atkins laughed. 'How do you feel, apart from uncharitable?'

'Awful. Dying of melancholy.'

'Harrington said you were beginning to complain that idleness was wearisome. You must be mending, I think.'

'Do not worry, my friend. The colonel will soon put that to rights.' Nick grinned at Atkins' square visage, and for a moment imagined that there was a shadow of pity on it.

' 'Tis a poor choice, friend. Melancholy or the rope.'

The captain looked back over the rim of his mug, and now there was no mistaking the expression of regret.

'Both my own fault. I took the risk, knowing what was like to happen. Now I pay the penalty of mine own lack of judgement. But it is good to hear you say "friend". Or was it merely a slip of the tongue?'

'Damn you, malignant.' Atkins laughed uneasily, and shook his fist in mock anger. 'You twist words nimbly. I . . . am a friend, I suppose. Though my conscience would have it otherwise.'

Nick sipped the warm wine, and thanked God that Atkins, at least, was childishly honest, even if he was also a little slow-witted and, at times, nothing short of boring. 'You are a Christian soul, captain. To forgive so readily my attempt to kill you.'

'Was a pretty half-hearted attempt, when you came to save my life afterwards. Though I knew . . . almost knew . . . who you were, and you might wisely have killed me for it.'

It was Nick's turn to feel uneasy, when he thought of how nearly he had come, that night of the ambush, to finishing the job. 'I did not save your life. It was not my doing. Mistress Chadwicke saved you.'

'Then she, too, is my friend.' Atkins hesitated for a moment, his face betraying brow-twisting perplexity. 'And also a friend of yours, I think?' He reddened, his quiet voice laden with meaning, and, in reply, Nick blushed guiltily.

'Aye,' he admitted reluctantly, wondering by what means the captain came to know. 'A most dear friend. But I would be grateful if you would not . . .'

'Don't fret,' the captain added hastily. 'I've known a while.

But no one else seems to, though I think that one or two might suspect. . . . I'll not tell.'

'A friend indeed. The colonel would not like that.'

'I'm not the first.' Atkins laughed. 'David and Jonathan were on different sides, remember?'

'And this is certainly a good enough substitute for the wilderness of Ziph!'

'Outside it is, at any rate. White wilderness, and cold as the grave.'

'Don't say that. It makes me feel peculiar.' Nick shuddered. He had no wish to be reminded.

Atkins' good-natured eyes lit up like lamps with their misery. 'Sorry,' he said, gruffly, and squared his chin. He had made up his mind.

'Can you move these pillows for me? God, I wish I could get up.'

Atkins prodded the pillows ineffectually. 'Harrington says very soon you can try.'

'But what good will it do? I shall be cooped up in here, just the same. This room seems to get smaller by the hour.'

'Well, there is no need to get gloomy over that. I have already suggested to the colonel that he might be generous enough to allow you to walk in the garden once you are able. Harrington is to be given a half-hour's liberty every day from tomorrow. Colonel Chadwicke considers it safe enough, within those walls.'

'Never fear. It will be a long time before I can climb walls.'

Atkins' eyes were wide and earnest. He took a deep breath and spoke, soft, cool, and deliberate, and Nick could hardly believe what he was saying. 'There is a gate. Perhaps I might forget to lock it?'

'Do I understand you?'

'I hope so. It must be soon. I will give an opportunity, but I dare not do more. The rest must be up to you. . . .' His face was bright red, and he ignored Nick's incredulous eyes, turning to the shuttered window, as if he could see out of it. 'Hopton is on the march. Did you know?'

'Yes, I heard. Colonel Norton is trying to stop him?'

'He has been charged with that task, yes. And is come galloping out of 'Hampton to fall upon Hopton's rear. 'Tis a fool thing to do.'

'He is no fool, whatever else he may be. And he has the devil's own luck.'

'Like you. And he will need it. Though the weather is for Parliament.'

'Damn Norton, and damn the weather! Damn them both!' said Nick.

'One thing,' said Atkins. 'When my debt is paid there is no more . . . obligation between us. And can be no more friendship either. It is a matter of honour, you see?'

'Honour? Oh, yes, I see.'

The sound of heavy boots and a sepulchral cough came up the stairs. 'That is my corporal coming back. I'd know that cough anywhere.'

'Like a bull-calf with a sore throat,' Nick said.

The corporal came into find the captain crying with laughter, and even the prisoner smiling, and he looked amazed.

'Give you good night, Major Howard.'

'Good night to you, Captain Atkins.'

A little man inside Nick's head hit him with a hammer between the eyes, repeatedly and painfully. The thoughts galloped through his mind with all the speed and confusion of Waller's fleeing cavalry at Roundway. He must trust the captain. He had no choice, though the sickening thought occurred to him that a bungled escape attempt would give the colonel a grand excuse to kill the prisoner. But if he let this chance go, it was certain that there would never be another. Lilith came in with Nick's dinner, and to her immense surprise he ate every scrap of it without one single word of protest, and listened uncomplaining to the sermon that accompanied it.

After he had eaten, he turned to Judith's Bible, still puzzled at the way she had told him to read it carefully, as if there was something more to it than met the eye. Nick opened it, and stared at the fly-leaf. It was inscribed in ornate script, as forceful as Judith's own. 'Judith Lovell, her book. From her loving father, Philip Lovell, November, 1629.'

Nick counted. She had been ten then. He tried to imagine Judith, ten years old, with the tall, grave, fair-haired man whose portrait hung in the parlour over the mantel: the rebel who had been Nat's good friend. Nick wondered what Philip Lovell would have thought now of his daughter with her Cavalier lover, and sighed. He had no heart to read scriptures, because his conscience was riddled with worms of guilt.

He turned the pages over idly. Here was a bunch of sweet herbs, pressed and dried: a small piece of linen embroidered with the Lord's prayer in such uneven stitches that he knew it must be Judith's work, and here was a single half-leaf of note-paper, with Judith's round childish scrawl on it. 'Nicholas, I love you always,' it said. The words swam before his eyes, and he looked hastily to make sure that he was not being watched. The corporal sat by the fire, slumped in his chair, his chin forward on his armour breastplate, looking incredibly uncomfortable, but he was undoubtedly sound asleep. Nick smiled. Judith had found a way to say what she wanted to say, though she must know the dangers of committing such sentiments to paper. She was not afraid of anything, his Judith. . . . Tomorrow, he was determined, he would get out of bed, and walk.

Walking took a lot more effort than he had anticipated. Nat was dubious about the whole venture. 'You must not rush your fences,' he warned, and leaned forward to make pretended adjustments to the sling about Nick's arm. 'Nor yet your gates,' he added in a whisper. 'But you must get out before Riley comes.'

'What about you? I cannot go without you.'

'You can. You must. You are weak, Nicholas. You would not stand a chance. I can contrive better with you out of my way. Is that more comfortable?' he enquired, loudly.

'No, it's bloody painful!'

'Please, Nicholas. You have no choice.'

'I suppose so.'

Nick found that his legs were disobedient. A good deal of pain went by before he made his first shaky circuit of the garden, and then it was for the most part the firm grip of the corporal's arm which supported him. The cold was a shock. He had forgotten how the wind could bite, even through eight-foot walls, and every step he took jarred his side and sent little fire-arrows of pain twinkling down his injured arm until he was ready to faint. The corporal half carried him back up the two flights of stairs to his bed, and Nick could have wept with discouragement.

The corporal smiled and shook his head. 'I think that John Willet was maybe right about you. Your obstinacy, if not the rest of you, must be gotten of the devil.'

Nick lay back, exhausted. 'Oh, Lord. I wish I was not mortal. Yet soon enough the hangman will finally prove John Willet wrong.'

'I should say you've a week or so, sir. Riley's got to come from London.'

'So I've time to make my peace with the Almighty, then. Will you give me the Bible? I think that I shall read a little.'

Colonel Norton succeeded in delaying Hopton's army, though he lost a good number of his men in the process, and ended up being besieged in Warblington House by a sizeable force of the King's men. And the weather was for Parliament. The King's army was snowed up for several days. It was the fifth day of January when the thaw set in, and Hopton marched on, but too late. On January the fifth, the beleaguered men in Arundel castle had already begun to treat, and the next day they surrendered.

Nick watched the icicles on the eaves dripping and melting to soggy nothingness in the winter sunshine, and with them, he thought, melted the days of his life. Riley was due any day now, and it was an ordeal he looked forward to with dismay. Only his daily half-hour's liberty in the garden relieved his gloom. Time was running out. Where would he be, a week from now? Cold in his grave, that was sure, and anyone's guess whether his spirit would walk in heaven or in hell. And Judith would still be here, warm and beautifully human, and, worst of all, the exclusive property of Colonel Thomas Chadwicke.

23

THE WINGS OF LUCIFER

In the garden, Judith walked. The wooden pattens under her shoes slipped and slithered on the damp stones and the last of the grey slush. These days she felt trapped, even here. The cold wind whipped pink colour back into her white cheeks, and wrested coils of hair from under the cover of her hood and coif, and Captain Atkins, sheltering in the arbour from the gaze of prying eyes, found that it was not hard to see why the young Cavalier had lost his heart. He might himself so easily have trodden the same dangerous path that the spy had taken. . . . 'Madam?' he called. 'Might I have a word with you?'

Judith stiffened. The captain came smiling towards her, his boots crunching on the gravel walk, fighting the tossing wind for possession of his cloak. 'Captain Atkins! You took me by surprise!'

'I am sorry. It is good to see colour in your cheeks, madam. You have been so pale of late.'

'I have been troubled,' she said, and there was fear in her eyes.

'It is understandable, of course, that you should be troubled. But I shall not tell anyone about . . . you and Nicholas Howard. You have no need to worry.' He looked her straight in the eye, and hoped that she would believe him. She was shaking, he noticed.

'No need to worry? When the man . . . I love . . . will die on the gallows?' She was past caring now. The tears in her eyes spilled over and ran down either side of her nose. Atkins was embarrassed and upset. He must have said the wrong thing.

'I . . . er . . . hope that Major Howard enjoys his walks in the garden?'

'I think that he is very grateful for them, Captain Atkins. But they watch him almost as if they expect him to leap over the wall! Which is scarce likely, though John Willet would have him endowed with supernatural powers.' She turned on him, angry now, because he was one of the captors who watched. She was certainly resolute enough for anything, Atkins thought.

They had come half the length of the path, almost to the corner of the west wing of the house. There stood a magnificent holly bush, green, shining, and resplendent, like a sentinel amongst the dead things.

'This is a fine holly bush,' said Atkins pointedly. 'Have you noticed that from here, madam, it hides the gate? No guard could watch him from here.' Her hand flew to her mouth in surprise as the captain calmly continued. 'I had the latch and hinges oiled last week. It opens easily when unlocked. And I have here the key.'

'Are you suggesting . . .?'

'Yes. Tomorrow.'

'If you could lend me the key, then, I think I might ride, tomorrow.'

'What a splendid idea, madam.'

'At what hour?'

'I will bring him out at ten o'clock by the colonel's chamber-clock. But it must be quick.'

'I shall have a horse waiting.'

'I shall be just here, a minute or two after ten. I will call the guard . . . to tell him to check, you understand, that the gate is fastened. I should not like the colonel to think that I had failed in my duty.'

'Of course,' Mistress Chadwicke said quickly. 'I shall take all the blame myself.' The pride was back in her face, he thought. She would risk anything to let this man go free.

'If I dismiss the guard tonight to talk with him, there will be suspicion on me tomorrow if he escapes. I cannot talk with him easily without being overheard.'

'Then do not try. I have a means of telling him secretly.'

'My dear lady, you are very resourceful,' Atkins said, bowing like any courtier, out of sheer admiration for this woman who was not afraid of anything. 'And very brave.'

'And you, sir, are very kind.' She curtsied. 'And I shall do my best to see that you do not suffer for it.'

'I am only paying my debts . . . to you both,' Atkins said, anxiously. 'A life for a life . . . and no more than that.' He bowed again and turned abruptly on his heel.

Judith stared after him for a minute, and then turned back to the house, drifting unseeing, like a sleep-walker, not even feeling the warmth within doors, for she could not stop shivering. She fled up the stairs, and sat on the bed in her chamber. Waves of nausea and faintness swept over her, and she held tightly to the sturdy dark oaken bedpost, as if in some strange way its solid form could hold together the familiar friendly world which was dissolving all round her. A quarter of an hour passed before she felt well enough to move.

Now she had an ally, it should be easy . . . but Tom would be furious. She knew that his anger would have to be faced, sooner or later, but still she was afraid: though over and over she told herself that Tom was kind, that Tom loved her, and would not harm her, surely? All that mattered was that Nick should escape, and she prayed God to give him strength to flee from Tom's vengeance, out of Tom's reach for ever, and away from them all. Only when she thought of that did the torrent of tears overtake her, because she knew that to her, Nicholas Howard might just as well die tomorrow, for she would never see him again. Had she not said to him that she did not even want the future? Then, the words had come so easily to her. Now her heart must accept parting, one way or the other. . . .

Judith walked up and down, weeping. A sight of her

reflection in the mirror brought her up short, and she contemplated the unfamiliar dishevelled image in alarm. The old dress of black boratto was beginning now to be strained at the seams and was uncomfortably tight to wear. It had to be tomorrow. Judith washed the tears away with icy cold water from the great crock on the tiring-table, and took up her hairbrush. Better that he should go now, before he had to know. There was no need to say anything, then there would be no guilty obligation to hold him. He must go: she must stay to face Thomas alone. She was strong enough. Strong enough for anything, her father had always said. And today of all days, the colonel's wife must look calm and serene, or she would betray herself, and others.

The door was locked, and the key lay before her on the little writing-desk by the window in her sitting-room as she wrote the note. She must try to keep her promise to Captain Atkins, and to make sure that there was as little as possible to throw suspicion in his direction. 'Tomorrow,' she wrote, 'the gate will be left unlocked. When the guard is called away, make haste. By the back-yard gate I shall have a horse waiting.' She read it, and then added, 'God speed, love.' When it was dry she folded it, and tucked it neatly into the waist-band of her apron, where she had unpicked a few stitches. She smiled. Uncle Nat would be proud of her, she thought; she would have made a splendid spy. . . .

The mistress of Broadoak unlocked the door and called a servant to attend to the fire while she was gone, then she walked with precise feet the few yards down the gallery. The young trooper stepped aside and opened the door for her, blushing as she smiled her gracious thanks. Nick sat in the chair by the fire, arguing hotly with Trooper Willet. He was strong enough to be very angry by the look of things. Though his face was still white, and the arm hung limply in its sling, today there was some of the old fight, and the same obstinate gathering of those bushy eyebrows she loved so much.

'Such strife,' she muttered gently. 'I hope that you two will not come to blows.'

'If I had two hands to fight with,' Nick replied darkly,

'then your advice, madam, would have come far too late.' He stood up and bowed politely at her, his face still bearing its frown.

'I trust your arm is mending well, Major Howard?'

'Well enough, thank you, madam. And Willet here would mend my soul, also.'

The door of Tom's room must be open, she thought, for she could hear the chiming chamber-clock striking five. As punctually as she had hoped, the new guard came in: it was Parker, wiping the remains of dinner from his chin.

'Oh, mercy!' lied Judith, 'I had not realised it was so late! Do not wait on me, Willet, I am sure you must be hungry. Parker, draw the shutters. We do not want Major Howard to take cold, do we?' Her hand held the note as she brushed past Nick. On the way she pushed the little square-folded paper into his hand. He raised one eyebrow in enquiry, and she knew that he was surprised, but Parker's turned back did not see it, and by the time the trooper was back from the window the precious message was safely hidden inside Nick's arm-sling, and Judith was discussing a new remedy for chills, her words tumbling over one another like last week's snowflakes.

When Judith had gone, Nick sighed. This morning he would willingly have dispensed with the steadying scarf, which seemed too much like the bonds of a captive, but now he was grateful for it for more than one reason. It offered splendid concealment for the little missive, until such time as he could read it, but also his arm was aching so, now that it was tired.

Young Parker was in a sociable mood, full of gossip as they sat by the fire until late. Nat had been fleecing the soldiers, playing at card games and dice, until Tom Chadwicke had found about it, and there was trouble brewing, and likely punishment for some of them. Nick listened, smiling absently. Eventually even Parker got bored and drowsy, and Nick pleaded exhaustion and went to his bed, to lie there with eyes closed in feigned sleep until he heard his companion snoring. Only then did he unfold the note and read it, and the contents made him tremble. Tomorrow or never. There would be no second chance, and the penalty for failure was death.

Nick crept out of bed to put the paper on the fire before the glow died. It was a cold night. With a shadow of fear he recalled that night of day-bright moonlight when he had ridden out to Alton: over a month since, but already it seemed to be sunk in the far-distant past. On his way to bed, Captain Atkins peered inquisitively round the door, like an unshaven thief, and winked.

'Is all well, Major Howard?'

'Yes. Very well,' Nick replied, with a cheer that he did not feel, and then settled himself to try to rest, his stomach churning in the old anticipation of danger.

Judith also lay awake, and then went to look at the moonlight gilding the twisted branches in the orchard so that they glowed with an uncanny brightness that made her eyes and her head ache. Or was it the unshed tears that made them hurt so? Tomorrow there would be no light at Broadoak. The rest of her life stretched interminably before her, the light gone out for ever. For four hours she slept, and rose to the promise of a fine day, to fight the hideous sickness that gripped her this morning worse than ever and refused to be quelled.

With dawn came a dispatch-rider on a lathered horse, cantering, splashing through the slush into the yard. One of Colonel Norton's men panted in, steel helmet glinting in the pallid sunlight, and went stamping off to see Thomas. He was there for some while, so that prayers were late, and Judith paced the floor in an agony of impatience until the household was gathered, listening to Thomas' strong vibrant voice saying the morning prayers with his usual enthusiasm. Judith looked at the solid, square, bareheaded soldier who was her husband, and sighed. Here was a good and righteous man who had given her nothing but kindness and love, and in return she had wronged him terribly, because she loved another man. . . .

Tom read from the Ecclesiastes, and Judith wept inwardly. 'To everything there is a season, and a time for every purpose under the heavens,' said the voice. The time had come for Nick to be gone, and now she was desperate to have it accomplished. 'A time to be born, a time to die . . . a time to kill and a time to heal . . . a time to weep and a time to laugh.' The atmosphere in the great parlour was stifling her, and she thought that surely she would swoon. Suppose that someone should shoot him before he was clear? Suppose the arm would not stand up to the strain of being used so soon?

'A time to embrace and a time to refrain from embracing.' Judith clenched her fists in her apron and choked soundlessly on the sobs that rose in her throat. 'A time to get and a time to lose.' Tom's righteousness was relentless. The time for losing had come, and she could stand it no longer. There was no comfort in those words. Then, mercifully, the praying was over, and the servants and soldiers dispersed hastily to their duties. Judith stood mute by the window, holding to the sill for support. Tom's arm wrapped itself around her shaking shoulders.

'How are you, my dear? You do look pale.'

'I am quite well, thank you, Thomas,' she said stiffly, recoiling from his patient tenderness, and avoiding his too-kindly eyes. 'I lack fresh air, that is all. The weather is so much better this morning. I think perhaps I shall ride for half an hour.'

'Do you think that it is advisable? It is very cold.'

'Do not fuss so, Thomas. I shall be much better for it, I can assure you. Shall I . . . take a trooper with me?'

'I think that it might be wise. Take the corporal, by all means. I will tell him to wait upon you. Though I must ask you to be promptly back.'

'Thank you. The sunshine is so bright, just like spring. It would be a shame to miss it. I shall leave . . . just before ten . . . if that is convenient? And I shall be back by half-past, I promise. I must hasten now, or I will not be ready.'

There was plenty of time after all. When an hour before they had been racing along, now the hands of every clock in the house seemed to be held back by invisible beings. Judith put on her riding habit and boots and went through the garden to the yard to order the horses to be saddled. She had thought it out so carefully . . . and blessed God that Thomas' house was methodically run to the time of the clock. At ten o'clock precisely, the corporal came from the back door of the house, pulling on his leather gauntlets, and carrying his battered helmet under one arm, and Mistress Chadwicke dismissed the groom. From behind the eight-foot wall, she heard the garden door slam, as Nick came out for his daily walk.

'This horse is lame, I think,' said Judith. 'Perhaps you could trot her for me, corporal, so that I may see better? I will hold your horse for you.'

The corporal touched his forelock to the colonel's wife, set his helmet on his head, leaving the strap loose under his chin, and took the bridle of the mare.

Nick flexed his arm in its sling and wondered whether it would stand up to the punishment it was about to receive. He walked briskly to banish the cold, past the south-facing body of the house, with its gnarled vine against the wall. A few steps behind him young Trooper Killigrew whistled under his breath, his musket sloped on his shoulder. The crisp voice of Captain Atkins hailed Killigrew from the other side of the green holly, and the whistling ceased. Killigrew hesitated, glanced once round the garden, and retreated at speed to answer the call.

Nick took to his heels, sprinting for the gate with all the strength that his unsteady legs could muster, praying that they had not forgotten to leave it unlocked. The latch clicked up smoothly, and the gate opened wide with a soft clunk as it flew back against the yard wall. There was Judith, a few short steps away, holding the cavalry horse ready saddled, and the corporal galumphing ungainly on the other side of the yard with her own strawberry roan. Nick swung into the saddle. It was much easier than he had expected. He winked at Judith. 'I love you,' he said. 'Don't worry. I will be back.' He kicked at the horse, and it was out of the yard almost before anyone realised what was happening.

One of the sentries at the gate went sprawling face down in the straw and dung as he made to grab at the bridle, while the other fumbled with cold fingers to fire the musket in his hand. The corporal stopped in his tracks, his helmet clattering to the flagstones as he stood, his eyes bulging.

'Good God!' he said. 'I don't believe it. The devil's away! Parker, fetch the colonel, quick. The rest of you, to horse! How the hell did that happen?' He shook his head, and his eyes opened yet wider, for his mind had answered his own question. 'Mistress Chadwicke? Oh, my God!'

By the time the soldiers were rushing out of the yard in pursuit, Nick was out of sight on the track past the house, towards the Winchester road which would lead him back to Hopton's army.

'They'll not catch him now,' said Captain Atkins, happily, from the garden gate, where he stood beside the stupefied Killigrew. Judith barely heard him. She was rooted to the spot, her legs now too weak to carry her away from it. It was all done. They would not catch him now, and neither would she. . . . For a moment Judith felt the sharp sting of jealousy for a little girl she had never seen. Nick belonged to little Lucy, now, and Judith must make do with memories . . . at least, until the summer came.

Thomas came stumbling into the yard in hideous rolling haste, shouting at Captain Atkins and young Killigrew. He would have them both shot, Thomas declared. And now he came towards Judith, his face leaden grey.

'Madam,' he said coldly. 'I would speak with you. Please to go into the house this minute! I will attend you in your chamber.'

Fear gripped her. Never had she seen Thomas so angry. She drew herself up very straight and walked with slow deliberate steps through the iron-studded gate which gaped open. The heels of her boots clicked on the stones of the paved walk between the thyme which twined around them. Thomas stalked just a yard behind her and followed her up to her room. There she sat on the little stool by the desk and turned to face her husband. For what seemed an age, there was silence.

'What, in heaven's name, madam, have you been playing at?' Thomas spluttered. 'How did you come to be there with a horse ready for my prisoner to make away on? It was no coincidence!'

'No. It was no coincidence. I had it all planned,' she said.

She was drained now. There was nothing left but to accept the inevitable. 'Do not blame the captain, or Killigrew. I borrowed the key. And they did not even suspect that I would purposely leave the gate unlocked.'

'But why, Judith? If it had been Harrington, then I might have understood. Why the man Howard?' Tom's eyes looked at her with the wide pleading of a hurt child, as if he had guessed now at the truth, but wanted to be told that he was wrong.

'Can you not understand, Tom? That I . . . love him? I have loved him almost since first he came. I just could not stand by and let you . . . kill him.'

The colonel sat heavily on the chair, by the ashes of last night's fire, his lame leg stretched out straight before him, and put his head in his hands for a long minute. He raised it to stare at her.

'And . . . he?'

'Loved me. Yes, Thomas. But do not blame him for it. It was my fault. He was reluctant at first . . . but I loved him so . . . I couldn't help it. And oh, I am sorry, for I know what pain it must cause you, and how shocked you must be.'

'Shocked?' He shook his head. 'Oh, Judith, I should have known. I only knew that there was something wrong between us. You were a stranger to me . . . suddenly. I should have seen it, just as I should have seen that he was a spy. I have been very stupid, it seems.' His voice was bitter. 'I am a stupid old man, Judith. When I married you, people told me that . . . something like this would happen. You are young; so innocent. . . .'

'But I told you,' she protested. 'It was my fault! My idea!'

Thomas was not listening. 'Where our loved ones are concerned it is easy to be blind. Even my own son coveted you! Did you know that?'

Judith gasped, her hands over her ears to shut out what she did not want to hear. 'Oh, no! That is not true. It cannot be!'

'It is true. Oh, yes, my sweet wife. Young Tom wanted you for his own. That devil was in him, also. . . . So he rode away to Southampton, and then he was . . . killed, and I was glad when they told me! Not until long after did I weep for him.'

Judith cried out for the bitter pain and torment which he had borne. His kindness hurt her more than the anger she had expected. 'Thomas, please listen to me. It is with me the blame must lie. I have wronged you, and you shall punish me.'

'I love you so much, Judith. Should it be such a surprise to me that other men should do the same?' His voice was quiet, its tenderness persistent. 'I could not hurt you, because after all, you are still mine. My wife, and no one else's.'

'Not hurt me? Not even if I told you that there will be a child . . . of his . . . in the summer?'

'Judith. . . . No.'

'If you wish it, I shall leave here. The house is yours, and all in it. I have no right to stay. In a few days, I will go . . . right away.'

Chadwicke stood up suddenly. 'That will be neither necessary nor desirable,' he said briskly. 'You shall stay. I am today off to Southampton with my men to aid Dick Norton, for the order came this morning. I am to take . . . your uncle there, to see Riley. The general thinks it unsafe for us to remain here any longer, for that we are too isolated. And so it is settled.'

'You are very kind, Thomas.'

'Not kind. Selfish. You cannot leave me, Judith. Do you think that I could ever be happy in this house without you? The place would be so empty. I am an old man, Judith. Please humour me in this. Remember that I am still your husband.'

Judith wept. She did not want to stay, because for her, too, the house would be so empty. . . . 'But I have . . . my baby . . . to think of. I must go.'

Thomas frowned at her. 'Where will you go? To him? Is that why you will not stay?'

'I cannot go to him,' she sobbed. 'Simply because I do not know where. And anyway I would not wish to. He does not know about the child. I did not tell him because I thought . . . he might so be bound by his conscience.'

'Conscience?' Tom scoffed angrily. 'There's little fear of that, my dear . . . !'

She turned away from him, and he looked at her resolute chin and unwillingly admired the courage of his errant wife.

'Judith?'

'Yes?'

'It . . . doesn't matter. I am your husband. The child is mine. There is no need . . . for anyone to ever know. It is the only solution. Stay! That is all I ask.'

'For the present . . . I will stay. But I know not . . . for the future.'

'In the future we can discuss it once more. When we are both of us . . . calmer.'

'I will go and make preparations for your departure. You must be away. It is a long way to Southampton. Why did you not tell me before?'

'I thought it would keep until you returned from riding. I cannot go before my men get back.' He sighed heavily. 'There is no hurry. It'll be another fine night, and the moon bright enough.'

Judith looked out of the window at the track along the front of the house. There was not a soul in sight. They were all out, chasing a spy.

'He is in Winchester by now, my dear, no doubt. On the very wings of Lucifer.'

There was the merest ghost of a smile on Thomas' face as he spoke. 'Oh, Nicholas Howard, I owe you much! And one day I will settle,' he added grimly, and his great hands tightened into fists. Judith looked at the savagery in his eyes and shuddered.

24

A HAIR'S BREADTH FROM VICTORY

A mile or so along the track, Nick turned from the Winchester road. Though Winchester was safety, he had other plans. Northwards towards Basing he rode. He would not leave Nat so: he would beg, borrow or steal a couple of troops of horse from Lord Winchester and see what could be done to fetch Nat out of Broadoak. At Broadoak, Tom Chadwicke would be in a fury. Nick breathed a prayer for Judith's safety, and shivered in the cold, though he did not draw rein until he was clattering over the bridge to the main gate of Basing, and the great iron doors welcomed him to sanctuary behind stout walls.

Lord Winchester was walking the bounds of his property to inspect the defences, reinforced by Sir Henry Bard's now-departed mole-legion with as sturdy a set of earth ramparts as even the City of London itself would have been proud to boast. The marquis stood upon the cold walls looking down at the ice-covered greyness of the lake, a cloak of rich, red velvet covering the gold-threaded embroidery and the lace of his coat and collar. He stretched out a hand to welcome the arrival, a hand clad in the finest of musk-perfumed dog-skin gloves, and a look of polite surprise illuminated his face.

'I heard that you were sorely wounded, Major Howard: and a prisoner. I thought that you were certainly dead ere this.'

'I am not dead, my Lord, I do assure you.'

'Evidently. And I rejoice to see it.'

'But Nat Harrington will be dead if I do not do something. I must get him out of Broadoak without delay!'

'You must?' said the marquis, with heavy emphasis on the first word, as his blue eyes surveyed the shivering, white-faced figure before him. 'Now let us not be over-ambitious, Major Howard.'

'Over-ambitious?' said Nick, stupidly. He was beginning to feel very strange.

Lord Winchester smiled cynically. 'My dear fellow, I would have ventured to submit that you have come close enough, this bout. You are in no condition to go haring off to anybody's rescue.'

'All I need,' said Nick, annoyed, 'is a cloak in this damnable cold wind. I am perfectly all right.'

'So I perceive,' smiled the marquis, eyeing Nick's tumbled figure, fainting at his feet. 'Willie? Take good care of him. John, would you be so good as to send Major Cufand to me? And find Edward and Joshua Jeffery. I have a task for them.'

Not until the fever abated several days later did Nick learn that the expedition had been a failure. Cufand and his men had arrived at Broadoak only to find that Nat and his grim escort were hours on their way to Southampton and the tender ministrations of Norton and Riley. Willie Robinson brought the dire news along with a cupful of foul-smelling physick, and Nick found both items difficult to swallow. Only young Josh had refused to be beaten. He had gone on alone in the wake of Chadwicke's party to see what might yet be done to save Captain Nat.

The news hit Nick like a poll-axe. He lay staring blankly at Willie's blotched, fat face and pleaded for his own release from this new captivity of his sick-bed. Willie bleated with laughter like a downland ewe calling after its straying lamb. 'You may get up if you can,' he gasped. 'I'd not stop you, Major Howard. There's your coat and breeches on the chair yonder. You may try for them if you will!'

Nick tried and then tried again, and found that even sitting up was beyond him in his weakness, and he had no choice but to give up. The bitter-tasting physick was making him drowsy, and he looked at the lofty ceiling with its plump pink-painted cherubs swimming before his sleep-befuddled eyes, and was past caring for anything except his own miserable wretchedness.

Ned Jeffery came to cheer Nick, but even Ned was dispirited, though he was trying manfully not to show it. 'Never fear, sir,' Ned said, his chin squared with determination and an effort at a smile. 'Josh will do it, and if he cannot, then you may be sure that no one could. Not even the devil himself.' He sounded unconvinced.

'I fear I am no devil,' said Nick sadly, and turned his head away. Ned shrugged unhappily, and went back to his duty with a hard face and a slow footfall that reminded Nick of a death-march.

Everything was dead. Even the land wore a shroud of snow again, and the alders at the lake-edge poked their stiff, stark, branch-fingers through it, pointing accusingly at Nick, who took to pacing nervously around the ramparts, and watched the impassable road longingly, telling himself over and over again that the lack of tidings from Southampton was due to the weather and nothing worse.

The thaw came at the end of January, when Nick had been at Basing for more than two weeks, but it did not bring redemption. The hibernating River Loddon awoke and began to chatter and stutter its protest at having to carry such an unaccustomed load of melt-water and debris, spewing as much as it could into the water-meadows. Over the Loddon bridge came a messenger from Oxford, to summon Major Howard to the King's headquarter to see his commander. Nick set out on the second day of February with a soldier's obedience, but a very heavy heart, to see the spy-master general.

A fire of sea-coal burned cheerfully in the hearth and gave forth a heartening warmth, and my Lord the spy-master was dressed in black and silver, but otherwise nothing had changed since Nick was last there. The room was still a chaotic mess of jumbled papers, maps and books, and the spy-master himself stood staring from the window with his back to the door, as if he had not moved since July. Nick found that notion funny and allowed himself the liberty of a private smile, but the desire to laugh passed quickly as the door shut out the old man, and the straight-backed aristocrat turned to face him. The spy-master's face showed nothing: not displeasure, nor anger, nor yet welcome; just cold disinterest.

'Well, Howard,' he purred. 'I see you are once more on your feet?'

'Yes, my Lord.' Nick met the hard cat's eyes and looked down. His feet were cold.

'You have been industrious since last we met? I have heard much of your doings.'

' 'Tis a long time since I was here, my Lord.'

There was a long, awkward silence. The general stared across the room, quite unperturbed, but Nick could bear it no longer. The quicker the shouting was over, then the better it would be.

'I am sorry,' he blurted. 'I am sorry I was not . . . adequate to the task you set for me. I can only say I did my best.' He was hot and, he knew, painfully pink, and he frowned and waited for the explosion, but it did not come. He should have known better than to expect one, he reflected. This man was like Nat, only more so: so impassive that one could never tell what he was thinking, not until judgement day, when all would stand revealed. . . .

'I am sure,' said the elegant voice. The spy-master's hand, dripping with rubies, gave a wide expressive gesture, its pale fingers spread. 'Tell me then,' he continued, 'how you, er, failed, Howard. I should like to hear the story from your own lips. I have had all my news at second or third hand.'

'Where shall I start? You mean all from August, or shall I just tell about . . . Alton?' Nick licked his lips. He found the very name of the place such a painful reminder that it was difficult even to utter it.

'Tell me about Alton. It was a great grief to His Majesty.'

Nick groaned inwardly, and gritted his teeth to begin. It

was a sorry enough tale: a tale of Mottham's treachery, of Humphrey Bennet's defeat, and of his own dismal lack of perception, and how John Bolle died because of it, and it was all the more difficult to repeat since several times Nick found himself uncomfortably near to tears. 'And I've left Harrington,' he concluded. 'They took him to Southampton the same day and will have hanged him by now. Lord Winchester's men would have saved him, but they came too late, you see. I know now I should have stayed. I'm sorry.' The words died.

The cold ice-blue eyes showed not a flicker of emotion. The spy-master pursed his lips, and turned towards the window once more. 'Hmmm,' he said. 'On the contrary, Howard. In my opinion only a fool would have stayed. And one of my men dead is more than enough.' He turned back, one eyebrow raised. 'You seem to have grown an over-energetic conscience of late? Such makes for a poor spy. Forget your conscience, and there could be none to match you, I think. . . .' He sighed and came round the table to stand but two feet away. 'I am left with a considerable problem.'

'My Lord?'

'What am I to do with you?' He thrust his sharply bearded chin forward aggressively, and Nick shook his head miserably, for he neither knew nor cared, though he suspected that punishment of some kind was about to be inflicted.

'Lord Forth is to attend the Army of the West to assist Lord Hopton,' the spy-master pronounced. 'They are presently still in Hampshire, but will, I think, be making for Wiltshire ere long. Since you know both counties so well I have half promised Hopton that he shall have you for his staff. And yet I think that I could use you myself to more purpose.'

Nick said nothing.

My Lord deliberated silently for a full half-minute. 'Well, you shall go to Hopton for the time being. But I suggest you take a respite first. There will be naught of consequence in the next fortnight or so, and I should hate to lose you through mine own carelessness in over-working you. You look, sick, boy.'

Nick nodded speechlessly. He was sick, but not in body.

'Your home is in Marlborough, is it not?' the spy-master

continued cheerfully. 'You shall take a few words to Wilmot for me, and thus spare me a messenger. Be seated, I pray you, while I write.'

Nick sat by the fire, tired, steaming, and half asleep, his mind confused, and somewhat relieved. He had thought to find anger, but had found instead understanding, and maybe even sympathy. . . . My Lord finished the epistle, signed his name with a flourish, and folded the rustling paper neatly. Nick watched the hot wax dropping on the packet in bright reluctant blobs, like blood. . . .

'I should be grateful if you could deliver this for me,' the spy-master said, as he scrawled the address in illegible enthusiasm across the sealed packet. 'Now. His Majesty owes you a sizeable fortune in back pay, does he not? I doubt we are in a position to pay all our debts, but we can at least give you a few guineas on account. You look as if you are fallen upon exceeding hard times.' He unlocked the heavy chest, chuckling at his own wit, and Nick breathed a prayer of thanks. He had almost forgotten money . . . but of course he would need money if he and his horse were to eat and sleep that night. 'And His Majesty also asked me to convey this to you, Lieutenant-Colonel Howard.' The beringed hand flourished the lieutenant-colonel's commission in front of Nick's nose, and Nick stared at it in unbelief. The spy-master was smiling all over his sharp weasel face.

'Let me now take the liberty of advising you, my boy. You have done well. Do not lose heart now. All of us have our personal griefs in this conflict, and for that reason we must seek a speedy end to it. We must search for a way of honour to settle the matter once and for all. Now we are but a hair's breadth from victory. . . .'

Nick would much have liked to dispute those words, but he knew that he must hold his tongue. He listened obediently to the inspiring lecture, and knew in his heart that there was no question of giving up. He would go on fighting simply because, having once started any task, he hated to leave it unfinished, however distasteful it might be. . . .

25

SHE LOVES ME NOT

Wilmot received the letter personally, with elaborate courtesy and an ear-to-ear smile. For several hours Nick was regaled with interminable reminiscences of the fight at Roundway, and plied with too many glasses of sherry-wine. Having extricated himself, with difficulty, from Wilmot's ever-willing hospitality, he dragged himself dizzily across the square and out to the town's end, where Aunt Nan's house stood tall and shimmering in the misty twilight.

The housemaid did not recognise the dark, unshaven villain before her, commended him to the devil, and told him roundly to be gone. Nick leaned weakly against the door-post with his dilapidated boot through the door so that she could not shut it in his face, and racked his brains to remember the girl's name.

'Betty?' he said, praying that he had the name right, as she peered dubiously at him and heaved with all her considerable strength to shut the door on him. 'Such a welcome? I hope my Aunt Nan is better disposed towards me!'

'Oh, mercy!' cried Betty, and let the door go with a rush so that it yawned wide open with a bang on the wall, and Nick nearly fell in. She was curtsying, scarlet and apologetic. 'Oh, sir, I did not know you! I'm 'shamed indeed. Oh, but you gave me such a fright!'

'Do not be so worried, child,' he said, grinning at her with drunken benignity in the half light. 'To be sure, I hardly know myself just now.'

Nan Carteret swept down the stairs to investigate the commotion. Her pale, mittened hands shook as she held them out to him, and the tears poured down her face. 'Thank God,' she said simply. 'Oh, I thank God for this return, Nicholas! I thought that you were surely dead.' Her tears upset him. She clung to him like a small child needing comfort, and he put his arms round her, finding it oddly distressing to think how many times she had comforted him in the past. 'Oh, I do not know what you must think of me. Such a poor welcome you have had!'

'Not poor at all, Aunt Nan. But indeed my heart rejoices to see you smile again.'

'Have you ridden far today? Oh, my Nicholas, such a strange fellow you look! And I have worried so much over you! But I must be patient to hear how you have fared, for you must mend those villainous looks or the women will all be scared to death that a devil has come amongst us!'

By the time he came back to the great room down the stairs, Aunt Nan was more composed. She stood white-faced at the head of the table, her hair drawn back under a cap of white and silver lace, and her black dress as neat as if it had never been ruffled. She was so neat that she reminded him immediately of Judith, and a vision of Judith's fair hair drawn back from her face, and of Judith's wide-apart eyes haunted him for a minute, while Aunt Nan clucked over the evil-fitting of the dark blue velvet he wore and fussed over his thinness. He wanted desperately to tell Aunt Nan about Judith, but he had an uncomfortable suspicion that Aunt Nan might be far from pleased with him if he told her about what he had done. . . .

'Oh, Nicholas,' she said. 'You look so pale.'

'Never fear, Aunt Nan. I am indestructible.' He rubbed his aching shoulder and smiled sadly. He felt out of place here.

'What happened, Nicholas?' Aunt Nan asked, softly. 'My dear boy.'

'I was wounded,' he said, 'and captured by the rebels.'

'Dame Rebecca told me so . . . and since then there is no news. How, then, are you here?'

'I escaped. There was nothing more to it,' he said, sharp and unwilling, avoiding the small, mittened hand which would have touched his arm, and leaped for the bottle of wine on the table.

'Is there not? Then I must be content, if you do not wish to speak of it. It is enough that you are safe.' She smiled the old motherly smile, and he wanted to cry.

'Oh . . . Aunt Nan, it is hard. . . . I know not what you have already been told.'

'Nothing. Nothing more than I have said. How did you come to be hurt?'

'I tried . . . to warn John Bolle at Alton that they were to be attacked. I . . . failed. . . . The rebels stopped me, and so . . . John died. You knew that.' Nick's voice tailed off into silence.

'Oh, Nicholas, what you must have suffered.'

'Is nothing compared with others! I am a base villain, Aunt Nan. For there was a dear friend of mine . . . and of Rebecca's, who put his life in danger to save mine. He deliberately walked into their hands, and I escaped alone. He is left to die in my place. To be tortured to death, because I deserted him. Though I did try to get help, they came too late, so the rebels have him still.'

'And you are blaming yourself! Oh, child, when will you learn not to blame yourself alone for everything that happens? Will you take the sins of the world on your shoulders? Even the Lord Jesus Christ found that difficult!' Aunt Nan laughed and cried at the same time. 'You must forget all of it. Leave it all behind you.'

'Forget? Oh, God, I wish I could. I've too many scars to remind me, Aunt Nan!'

'Is your wound not healed?'

'Not that. . . . Most of the scars are on my heart and are not so easy mended. It would have been better if they had hanged me after all. Better for everyone!'

'Never say that, Nicholas! Never say it!' Aunt Nan stamped her tiny foot in fury, just like little Lucy had been wont to do, he remembered, and then felt another stab of guilt because he had almost forgotten the child until now.

'Now I am sure that you have not eaten all day. . . .' The old lady was calm again, as if she had not lost her temper at all. 'And tomorrow you shall see your little lady daughter. You will find her much changed since last you saw her.'

Nick slept well into the next morning, a heavy dreamless sleep of sheer exhaustion, and it was nearly noon when he stood in Aunt Nan's own little sitting-room with a bad headache, waiting for his lady daughter to arrive. The change in her looks was so great that it took his breath away. The nursemaid pushed the little girl into the room and closed the door, and Lucy stood tall and slim and straight-backed in front of it. The baby plumpness was all gone. She was dressed in black velvet, and the brown curls bobbing on her shoulders were tidily crowned with a lace cap.

'Sweeting?' he said. 'Come to see papa.' He was hurt to see that she was afraid of him: then, he watched determination master fear. She took four deliberate steps forward, to curtsy gravely.

'Good day, papa,' she said, as she had been taught. Only then did she throw her dignity to the winds and take shelter with Aunt Nan. He smiled at her, and, at first, she hid her freckled face from him, but then she began to play at peeping and giggled at him. Her giggle reminded him of Judith, and his heart ached with missing her. He held out his hand to Lucy, and she crept up as if she sensed his loneliness, and held on to it.

'I missed you, little one,' he said. 'Aunt Nan has been telling me that you are a gentlewoman now. I'm sorry I was so long away.'

'I'm three,' Lucy said. 'Where have you been? Did you kill lots of Roundheads?'

'Lucy!' Aunt Nan's voice was full of embarrassment, and she watched Nick's face for the shadows of yesterday, but he laughed at her.

'Yes, lots.' He smiled into Lucy's innocent eyes and wished that his conscience would allow him to be so glad about it.

'Is the King pleased with you?' Lucy demanded.

'I hope so. I think so. . . . He made me a lieutenant-colonel.'

'What's that?' enquired Nick's daughter, her fear quite forgotten in her all-conquering curiosity. When the nursemaid came to collect her, Lucy withdrew with dignity.

'Shall I see you again tomorrow?' she pleaded, with childish insistence, tempered with all Aunt Nan's gentility.

'I will wait upon you, my sweet,' he replied, bowing and grinning, and Lucy went away up the stairs chattering like a nestful of fledgling sparrows, and Nick sighed.

'You were fortunate to see her in a good mood, Nicholas. I fear we shall never really tame that one; there is too much of her father about her. You are still not happy?'

'Oh, yes, Aunt Nan. It is good to be home.'

'Well, where your heart is, there shall your home be. But I think, Nicholas, that your heart is maybe still . . . somewhere else.' Aunt Nan pronounced, with that severity she used to reserve for the least attractive misdemeanours of his childhood. He looked at her under the flopping hair curling on his forehead, and wondered how much Rebecca had told about Judith. There were times when Aunt Nan needed no telling, for she knew him too well. He stared at the grey February rain splashing down outside and sighed again.

'My dear Nicholas, I entreat you. Come away from that place and leave it all behind you. I do not want to know anything you do not wish to tell me. Yet I want you to know that I am still here to listen if you wish to talk. I have not changed.'

'No, Aunt Nan. Only I have . . . changed,' he said, turning to her and setting a hand on each of her shoulders. He kissed her cheek gently, but she stiffened, staring past him to the window.

'That, if I mistake not, is the postboy. I will go and see.'

Aunt Nan knocked at the open door of his room. 'The letter is for you.' She held out a rain-spotted missive and looked hard into his eyes. Nick's hand trembled only slightly as he took it, even though the handwriting was not Rebecca's, as he had expected. . . . 'I will leave you to read in peace,' Nan Carteret said diplomatically and withdrew.

He did not even see her go, his trembling hands were too

busy tearing at the seal to open it, desperately anxious now for the news it must contain.

Dear Nicholas, I trust that you are in good health, and that this will find you soon. I entreat you to forgive my presumption in writing to you, but there are matters of importance. Firstly Uncle Nat is safe and well. I know that you will be rejoiced in this. Joshua Jeffery and Rebecca won him clear of Southampton gaol by some means I know not, and they will not divulge it to me. No doubt Uncle Nat will tell you himself if he has the opportunity. I have given into his care the chestnut stallion of yours that was at Broadoak, and so you may collect it when you will.

I hope your family is in health. I am well, and I believe that Thomas is also, though I have not seen him since the day you left. I have told him all the truth of what passed between us, and he received it with charity. You said that you would come back. Perhaps you have already changed your mind in this, I know not. But I must say that I think it best that you should come no more to Broadoak, and that the two of us should neither meet nor communicate again. I hasten to say that this is my wish entirely, and that Thomas had no part in it. I have considered, and the reason is mine. I trust that you will respect my desire in this matter. I should like to bid you farewell, to thank you for your many kindnesses to me, and to say that I pray for you always. Your obedient servant, Judith Chadwicke.

Nick finished the string of polite words and could not believe his eyes. He read through the second paragraph again, to make certain that he had understood its meaning. But the carefully phrased words left him in no doubt: there was scarcely room for misunderstanding. Judith no longer loved him. She would willingly deny his existence and wipe the memory from her mind, as if the love between them had been nothing at all.

'Oh, no,' he whispered. 'Oh, please God, no.' She made it all sound so easy, he thought, bitterly. Here today and gone tomorrow, with none of the heart-tearing reality of parting. Nick stood blankly by the window with his burning forehead against the cool glass and looked out, but saw nothing through the grey, blurred mist of his tears. 'The reason is mine,' she said. What reason could there be for this? Why would she reject him so, turning him away without even a chance to discuss it? Had she made a promise to Thomas? She had said it was no fault of Thomas', but a decision of her own entirely. . . . If she had a reason, then he could not guess at it. The grief gave way to anger: if Judith wished it so, then so she should have it.

He threw on his cloak and stormed across the landing, down the stairs, and out into the cold, damp afternoon. He passed Aunt Nan in the hallway without even seeing her, and she stared after him in horror, for the look in his eyes was nothing short of bloody murder. She prayed that today there would be no one to stand in his way, or it would go badly with them. . . .

He walked, increasingly damp and chilled, to the riverside and back again, the words of Judith's letter running ceaselessly through his mind. By the time the sky had begun to darken, the anger had seeped away in the same way as the grief, and there was nothing in their place save a sick void. So Nick called in at The Swan, to fill the emptiness, and came back to Aunt Nan's tipsy and late for dinner. She said nothing to reproach him, but he felt guilty all the same, and so he was in the mood to argue.

'What a pity you cannot eat your goose pie,' said Aunt Nan. 'I ordered it especially for you.'

'Not hungry,' he protested, pushing the plate away, but he finished the glass of claret beside it and reached for the bottle to refill it.

'I should have thought that you had drunk enough by now to quench any thirst,' Aunt Nan observed grimly.

'Not yet. Very thirsty,' he said, aggressively.

For a moment they sat in silence and looked at each other across the polished table, and Nick emptied the full glass.

'Nicholas, what was in that letter? Was it bad news?'

'On the . . . contrary,' Nick said, stumbling very slightly over the words. 'My friend has escaped, and that is very . . . good news.' He glowered at her defiantly.

'You are insufferable!' she said. 'I will not have you coming back here in that state and behaving in this ridiculous manner. I will not tolerate it, do you hear me?'

'Then you must . . . throw me out, Aunt Nan. If that is what you . . . want?' Nick frowned ferociously.

'If I had any sense at all, then that is undoubtedly what I would do! It is you who do not know what you want, and that is most of your trouble!'

'Nay, there you are wrong, Aunt Nan! I know very well what I want: and also that I cannot have it. But I am . . . sorry. Forgive me.'

'Could I do otherwise? I am glad your friend escaped. Yet there is more, of which you have not spoken, that I also know. You cannot conceal that from me. Is it a woman, Nicholas? Is it . . . Rebecca?'

' 'Becca?' Nick hiccupped. 'Lord, no!' He laughed bitterly. 'But you are right. I suppose I must confess all. 'Tis a sad tale, will have you weeping over your platter!'

'Who is she?' she asked. 'This woman you love so deeply.'

'Aye. But she loves me not . . . it seems. Though I had thought . . .'

'You would marry her? But she refused you, is that it?'

'There was . . . no question of marriage,' Nick said limply, watching the old lady's face for the disapproval he knew would follow. 'For the lady has . . . already a husband.' He took another sip of wine while Aunt Nan digested this unpalatable revelation, and then went on. 'Her husband is a rebel colonel. So now you know.'

Nan Carteret sat bolt upright like a white statue in her high-backed chair. 'A rebel colonel? Oh, my dear Nicholas, you never do anything by halves! I might have known it! And there was more than just words between you and this lady?'

'Oh, a lot more, yes. . . . I am not a saint, Aunt Nan.'

'So you seduced a Roundhead's wife. . . . No wonder they half killed you, you foolish boy.' She was smiling in spite of herself. He was no saint, but such an endearing demon. . . .

'It was not for that reason he hated me. He did not know about that until afterwards. But also I killed his son, you see. It was for that. . . .'

'Murder, too? Oh, my gentle Nicholas.'

'Gentle? I am not that, either. Oh, Aunt Nan, I was so

sure that she loved me. She was all I wanted . . . on any terms, any terms at all. Why did she change her mind?'

'This husband of hers. . . .'

'Had nothing to do with it. She would not bother to say it unless it was true.'

'Then perhaps it was for your own sake? Or had that not occurred to you? If she loved you. . . .'

'Then she has an odd way of showing it! No matter. . . . Either way I've lost all.' He glowered again into the glass which he had again filled, almost without thinking about it.

Aunt Nan felt the time had come to be firm with her errant nephew. 'All lost? Now come, Nicholas. You have blessings if you will count them. Have you forgotten your own child? Or does little Lucy mean nothing to you now?'

'No, you are right, of course, Aunt Nan. I would rather not mention the subject again. I shall never understand women. But I'm damned if I shall go into a decline for any one of them.' He stared at the glass. It was still full, and he knew that if he drank it, he would be very sick.

26

A VERY GOOD REASON

When he came to Hopton's headquarter, the first person he saw was Sir Henry Bard, erstwhile deliverer of Basing, who came leaping out of a nearby tavern with a whoop and greeted his friend sawbones with a slap on the back as if he were a long-lost brother. Nick was ready to throw himself into any task, so that he might forget Judith Chadwicke: but there was no work, only bickering, and even patient Hopton was nearing the end of his tether, waiting only for the arrival of the gouty, bibulous Lord Forth, to take command out of his hands altogether.

'Why does Hopton not defy them?' Nick asked Henry Bard, woefully.

'Because, my friend, he is a courteous, gentle soul of the old way, and is loth to offend,' Bard explained patiently, cocking his head wisely to one side like a child that pretends to understand something which is beyond it.

'And by that reluctance to offend, succeeds in offending all instead of just a few.' Nick shook his head sadly. Henry Bard sighed and shrugged his shoulders in sympathy.

'He gets endless streams of complaints every day,' Nick continued. 'Letters from officers complaining about imagined slights from others, or explaining that they cannot obey my Lord's orders for one petty private reason or another, and that they are sure that my Lord, being a man of honour, will make an allowance for their circumstances. . . . It's unbelievable.'

Bard sniffed. 'It is entirely believable, unfortunately. It is the one drawback of having an army full of gentlemen.'

Now he spent hours in the confines of the echoing ante-room in Hopton's lodgings in the Winchester Eastgate, counting the knot-holes in the ceiling, and squinting at the view from the inadequate window, listening on and off to the angry voices at the council-table. Lord Forth's deep, aggressive voice drowned all else, because he was so deaf that he did not hear it himself: then there was Wilmot's well-bred whine, and Lord John Stuart making pathetic attempts to keep the peace. Only Hopton said scarcely a word.

It was difficult now even to feed the army. Hampshire had been stripped, Wiltshire very nearly; they must send foraging parties into the very teeth of the enemy. Waller had it so much easier, of course, for the rest of the south-eastern counties lay almost untouched. Lord John Stuart was eager to fight. Nick could hear the firm voice of the King's young cousin saying so in no uncertain terms, and he praised God that here, at least, was someone with a little sense.

'Oh, Christ,' said Henry Bard, poking his head round the door. 'Are they still at it hammer and tongs?'

'I fear so,' Nick agreed, spinning a crown-piece on the windowsill and absent-mindedly watching it twinkle as it gyrated in the thin shaft of sunlight that came through the lattices. 'I can stand it no longer,' he said, pocketing the coin. 'I would rather fight Norton and Waller single-handed than listen to their eternal wrangling. I shall ask the lords-general to give me some raw men, so that I can make them into soldiers. Hopton will give me leave, I know.'

'And he'd say you are welcome. That is a task and a half I promise you. Would need a miracle to make anything approaching soldiers out of most of those straw-chewing yokels.'

'I was always good at miracles,' Nick said. 'I will ask them now. Just as soon as they finish their argument. . . .'

Two days later Nick found himself leading a troop of yokels on a forlorn hope towards Odiham, in order to find out the strength of the rebels there. By dawn they had investigated as far as prudence would allow, and it was a weary party which began the return journey, the unseasoned men half asleep in their saddles. Nick was enjoying the ride and the dew-soaked freshness of the morning, and he was just beginning to congratulate himself on the successful completion of their work when trouble arrived in the shape of a Roundhead patrol five-score strong.

The parties became painfully aware of each other at much the same moment, but fortunately Nick had a quicker turn of mind than the enemy commander. They had no advantage of ground either way, he calculated. The rebels would have the same speed, but their strength was nearly double. It was a hard choice between charging and fleeing. The only course to avoid complete rout was to strike before they were struck, so Nick drew his sword and shouted encouraging words which he hoped would inspire, and the straggling crowd took off after him with enthusiasm and breakneck speed towards the rebels, who were still in four-files on the open down while their captain tried to recall the instructions in his military manual. The irregular line of Royalists hit them head on, and they defended themselves stoically despite their surprise that the King's men were not playing to the rules. For several minutes Nick was afraid that the Roundheads would stand firm and master them: then suddenly it was over and there was nothing but thin air left to fight with.

He wiped the hair from his sweating forehead with the back of his hand and found that the hand still held his sword, and the sword was dripping with blood. It occurred to him that his weak arm had stood up miraculously to the beating he had given it. There was one uncertainty off his mind.

'By heaven, sir,' said his captain, beaming and flushed with victory. 'That was a good ride!'

'It was well done, Gardiner,' said Nick. 'And you may tell them so. But do not crow too soon. Wait until you have a real enemy to fight. Now go see if we are any missing.'

The captain withdrew, bustling with self-importance, to his duties. He was an earl's son, and his father's pride and joy: willing, but not a brain in his head, Nick thought balefully, with a shrewd eye to the wake of the retreating enemy.

'One or two flesh wounds, sir,' Gardiner volunteered, 'but naught to speak of.'

'Then I think we shall make good our escape before there is anything worse.'

'Flee, sir? We won, did we not?' The young man gaped, his fair hair flopping over his puzzled eyes, giving him the air of a disappointed hound.

'Won?' I suppose so, after a fashion. But before long, unless I am very much mistaken, the garrison at Odiham, and that at Farnham, maybe, will know that we are here. If you want to fight them all, you may stay alone!' Nick laughed at the crestfallen face, and watched the light dawn in the hound's lugubrious eyes.

'Oh,' said Gardiner, smiling. 'I see.'

'Let us press on, before we are followed.'

By noon they were past Alton, keeping to the downs and the woods. Nick thought he could see a hint of coming spring if he used a little imagination. Freedom always made him cheerful. If they pushed on, they would be back to Winchester before dusk. It was well that he knew the way.

'Colonel Howard? By your leave, sir?' Gardiner, who had been bringing up the rear, was puffing beside him. Nick looked at the sweating bedraggled figure with the earnest, dirt-smudged face, and felt a rush of sympathy.

'Yes?' He noticed that the captain's hand was swathed in strips of linen torn from someone's shirt, and that it was bloody. The men behind him were weary and grey-faced. Nick called a halt.

'I hope you will forgive, sir. But, well, the men are very tired, sir, and the horses, too. I fear that some of them will just drop soon, if we do not take a respite.'

'Oh,' said Nick. He was tired himself, but they were nearly at Stoke Sutton, and he did not want to stop yet: not here, of all places. One of the injured men fell out of the saddle like a stone with no sound except the thud as he hit the ground. Nick was to have no choice in the matter, it appeared.

'Pick him up,' he sighed, reluctantly. 'We shall stop at the next village, Stoke Sutton. It's only a mile distant.'

In a slow procession they rode into the village, and he drew them up on the green and looked about him. Everything was just the same as it had been when he had left, just as if it was only yesterday, and not last December. . . . Chickens still searched the green for tit-bits, caring nothing for politics; and there was Matthew Jeffery's seven-year-old son dabbling in the pond, up to his knees in icy water, prodding studiously at the reedy mud with a stout pole. He let out a deafening halloo to see Nick, and sped away across the green, shouting at the top of his voice.

'I'll have no one wandering off,' Nick said. 'We shall stay here until sunset, and not a moment longer. There is a smith here . . . and a surgeon. I suggest you make yourselves the parson's guests, and if he is inhospitable, then you may remind him in my name that charity is his calling. Do not trouble the people, I am known here and I want no unpleasantness. If there is any thievery or damage I shall hang those responsible, you have my word on it. There are enough trees in the churchyard for one apiece. Carry on, Gardiner, I leave them to you.'

'Ain't he pretty?' whispered Jenny Weston, adoring and wistful, patting her curly hair into a more fetching arrangement, and fluttering her eyelashes. 'Is a real man . . . and were all mine, once.' She cuffed the pot-boy round the ear, rolled up her sleeves, and went back into The Lovell Arms to await the onslaught.

Nick looked at the exhausted faces of his men. With any luck, he thought, most of them would want nothing more than to lie down and sleep, though he hoped that the captain would have the sense to keep some of them on guard. . . .

Nat was disturbed by the chattering scoldings of a blackbird outside the window, and looked out at the soldiers on the green. Another frustrated foraging party was returning home to Winchester empty-handed, like all the others lately. He returned to the parlour table and the letter he was writing, and cursed the distraction. The pen spattered blotches of ink far and wide, and Nat took up his pen-knife and began to shave thin slivers from another quill. A hand tapped at the window, and Nat's lean face lit up with the widest of smiles.

'Nicholas! By all that's wonderful! Do not stand out there. . . . You've not been away long enough to forget where the door is, surely?'

'I've brought you some work, Nat.'

'Come in and sit down, man. Bless my soul, but I am cheered to see your battered face again, you young reprobate! I'd almost given you up for lost!'

'You are . . . well, Nat?' Nick asked, awkwardly, taking off his hat to brush the hair out of his eyes. Nothing had changed. Questions tied his tongue into knots, and he did not know where to begin.

'Never felt better! We've a horse of yours in the stable. You've been to Broadoak?' Nat enquired, innocently, pouring out a cascade of golden madeira into a glass and thrusting it at Nick.

'Of course I have not been to Broadoak! How should I go there when things are . . . as they are?' he flushed angrily. If Nat was playing the fool, then they were going to fall out after all.

'As they are? Hmmm. Do not like to see your own handiwork, eh?'

'My handiwork?' Nick exploded with fury and Nat's canary spilled wildly over the brim of the sparkling venice goblet. 'How can I go to Broadoak when . . . Mistress Chadwicke would be so offended? Did she not write and forbid me?'

'She did what?' Nat was clearly so surprised that Nick regretted his outburst. So even Harrington had not been a party to her decision. 'Now let me have it clear,' Nat said, calmly. 'What exactly – did you say she forbade you?'

'She wrote a letter. Telling me of your release.'

'Yes, I know that.'

'And also informing me that she wished neither to see nor hear from me again.'

'Why?'

'That was what I was about to ask you. I was hoping you might be able to give me an idea of her reason. I would be . . . more content if I knew.'

'I could not be sure, of course,' said Nat. 'But I think she has a very good reason . . . in her own mind. And I am sure if you were to see her, then you would know what it was. She is a headstrong child. . . .'

'Can you tell me, then?'

'No, not really. I may well be altogether wrong.'

'Then let us forget it. How is 'Becca?'

'My wife,' said Nat, with a pause for effect, and a smile of smug self-satisfaction, 'is out walking. But I have no doubt that the presence of your ruffians will bring her hasting back!' He smiled again until Nick thought that his face would crack in two.

'Nat Harrington! I thought you would never get round to it! My congratulations, friend!'

'It was the very least I could do.' Nat's face was serious now. 'Master Preston is unaccustomed to so many visitors,' he observed tartly.

The dark house across the churchyard was buzzing with life, and the parson in his Geneva bands stood outside, his hands raised to heaven, supplicating for the mercy of preservation for himself and his goods, and no doubt wishing Nicholas Howard to perdition.

'He needs a lesson in hospitality, it would appear,' Nick said, briskly. 'I heard that 'Becca and Josh got you out of gaol. How did they do it? Did you have a hard time? If you did, I am sorry. . . .'

'Nay, it was easy enough to keep Riley talking about nothing, and to let him believe that he would have all anon. You would have laughed.' He sat down on the settle and stretched his endless legs luxuriously. ' 'Becca had a high old time! Would you believe . . . she seduced the turnkey and won his trust? Then one night visited him while he was on duty, and Josh . . . did severe damage to him, while his mind was on . . . other things. So I stayed not for leave-taking.'

'I'm glad, Nat. . . . Oh, God, I was glad to hear that you were free! Poor old Norton!'

'Poor old nothing! And Tom Chadwicke prays thrice daily that you will be delivered to him so that he may wreak his vengeance. I tell you, friend, it would be a painful finish for you if you cross his path again.'

The back door closed, and the sound of 'Becca's laugh echoed through the house. Nat sprang up as if he had been stung. 'Stay here a moment, Nicholas, I'll be with you. 'Becca, my love, may I have your ear?'

Nat disappeared into the hall, his voice receding into the echoing distance of the kitchen. Nick listened hard.

'There were soldiers,' said Rebecca, 'so we thought it better to come back.'

'Very wise,' Nat replied. 'Judith, sweeting, you go in the parlour now, and sit down. I am sure you must be tired after rushing back here.'

Nick would have fled, and yet he could not. If he left by the door, then he would meet Judith in the hallway: and to leave by the window was too undignified even to contemplate. He was afraid to look towards the door.

Judith was in the room, open-mouthed and gasping, and the shocked surprise on her face was mirrored, he knew, in his own. Her hands were clasped to the breast of her high-waisted gown, and though the folds of it were carefully arranged, they could not conceal. Nat had been right, it was a very good reason. Nick held out his arms to her without realising what he was doing. She crossed the room with a rustle of drapery and nestled close to him, sobbing helplessly, and Nick smiled. Judith belonged in his arms: she belonged, and nothing and nobody could alter it.

'Oh, love,' he said. 'I rejoice to see you . . . blooming so.'

She looked at him, half laughing through her tears, and there was the same love in her grey eyes as there had ever been. Nothing had changed.

'Tell me now,' he said. 'What did you mean by . . . dismissing me? Have you no smile nor kind word left for me?'

She began to cry once more. 'I thought I should . . . never see you again,' she sobbed. 'It was awful at Broadoak, without you . . . empty. Just love me, Nicholas. I want nothing else. Just hold me and do not let go.'

'You have not answered my question. I love you. I always shall. No one can alter that, not even you.'

Judith sat down and cried harder, remembering the emptiness of the house and the silence. Not even the raucous bustling of the garrison had remained to keep her company. The little butterfly stirrings of the child had frightened her at first, but now it was getting stronger it had become a strange companion in her loneliness. She could scarcely catch her breath, for the little one was as restless as its father.

'For God's sake, Judith. . . . It's all right. I am here. But if you had not seen me again, it would have been no one's fault but your own! What possessed you? I was afraid that you did not love me any more.'

'I did not want you to know. If you had come you would have seen. I did not want you to feel bound. . . .' she gulped.

'I am bound to you by that which cannot be broken. Nor would I want it to be otherwise. When will you believe me?'

Judith looked up from the window-seat. He frowned. 'Does Thomas know?'

'All the truth. I told him about the child, and everything.'

'And what happened?'

'He assumed that it was no fault of mine, but all yours, to have led me astray. He would not listen to me! He made me promise that I would stay at Broadoak until he came back to discuss it. But I have not seen him since. I promised to stay, so I suppose I must, but it . . . cannot be for long. I cannot. I know that he wants me still, and he said we could pretend the child was his. . . . Uncle Nat and 'Becca said that I could come here, but it is too near home, and so I think I must go to Basing, and plead mercy of my Lord marquis, if Uncle Nat will help.'

'You must go to Marlborough . . . to my aunt. She will take you in. Or to my sister-in-law at Sherfield Priors. . . .'

'It's too far,' she said. 'Already it is difficult for me to go far, though it's only five months.'

At sunset, the men were all drawn up on the green, and it was their colonel who was late. . . .

'I shall come to Broadoak to see you, madam,' he said to Judith. 'Whether you like it or no. . . . You must stay there for the present, Thomas or no Thomas. I have no desire to shed his blood, though he seems exceedingly anxious to shed mine. As long as you love me, then I am content with my lot, though it be a Roundhead's wife. I would not be willing to make her a widow, for already I have sins enough at my door. . . .'

27

'WALLER IS COMING!'

Lord Forth was indulging in a sharp attack of gout which made him even more irritable than usual, and so he had taken to his bed and left all the army to Hopton. From Hopton's lodging at Eastgate House issued a torrent of orders, until the adjutant-general's eyes were bloodshot with reading impossible handwriting, and his temper frayed with the confusion in his mind. It was Nick who bore the brunt of everyone's ill-humour, for he spent his days trotting to and fro between them all, informing the deaf, gouty earl of their progress, or lack of it, taking messages decently clothed in flowery speeches from Hopton and bringing back polite but naked replies from Forth. To Nick it seemed that one half of the army was busy fetching and carrying, while the other half was on picket-duty trying to stop them.

Even the dying winter had chosen once more to turn evil-tempered, reluctant to let its power go. The weather became grey and dismal, and there were cold showers of sleet that chilled Nick to the bone and made his arm ache so that he wanted to scream. Lord Winchester came to add his genteel tones to the arguments in the council. Sir John Paulet found his recruits ungovernable, and lamented it loudly and frequently, but there were so many other complaints from all directions that his voice was scarcely heard. There were reinforcements from Oxford, but they were neither as many nor so well trained as Hopton had been promised, and so he complained to the King about that: and Nick complained of the foolishness of the marquis leaving Basing House under the command of Lord Edward Paulet, and the marquis laughed in that mirthless way of his and bade him mind his own business, and even Hopton told him not to be so fanciful.

It was almost with relief that Nick received the news that the Roundhead General Grenville had deserted to Oxford, taking with him every detail of a carefully laid plot to betray Basing into the hands of the enemy. Edward Paulet was responsible for it and was up for court-martial in Oxford.

The marquis must have keenly felt such a blow, and yet he gave no sign. His neatly trimmed pointed beard gave not a twitch as he rode off to the King's headquarter to save his brother from the gallows.

'He views it all with distaste, you may imagine,' Sir John Paulet said to Nick. 'He will not see the maggot hang, he told me so.'

'So he will likely go free?'

'For the honour of the family Edward cannot hang. But my cousin has in mind a punishment which he considers more fitting. He intends to request that Edward is to be made hangman at Basing . . . and no doubt his first duty will be to execute justice on his fellow-conspirators.'

'My God!' Nick was aghast at the cold marquis' ghoulish twist of mind. 'Heaven forbid that I should ever fall foul of my Lord Winchester.'

Sir John shrugged and smiled and turned back to his *Complete Manual of the Art Military*, and Nick trudged heavy-booted down the stairs and went in search of his horse.

When he pushed his way out of the yard past the lounging guards, they were basking optimistically in a sudden burst of sunshine which softened the hard grey outlines of the stone walls but brought little warmth.

He shivered his way back to the Eastgate, and there almost collided with a cavalry trooper and a lathered horse who threw themselves into the yard of Eastgate House just in front of him.

'Waller is on the march!' the man gasped. 'Waller is coming! The captain sent me to tell my Lord Forth.'

'Forth's abed. Tell it to Hopton,' said Nick firmly, and propelled the man through the dark doorway and up two flights of creaking stairs to Hopton's office. The general sat between the adjutant and the quartermaster, and looked up with a quick frown and a quirked eyebrow in surprise at the sudden intrusion. The wind through the open door caught at the sheaf of papers in the hand of the quartermaster and scattered them to the four corners of the room. The quartermaster cursed vehemently, but he made no attempt to retrieve them, and the cowed trooper looked helplessly from one face to the next and back again.

'Well,' Hopton said politely. 'What news?'

'My Lord general?' The man cleared his throat nervously and pulled himself up straight.

'Go on, I'm listening.'

'Sir William Waller's army is at . . .' here his face wrinkled for a moment in puzzlement, and then his brow cleared, 'Westmaine. All of it.'

'Westmaine?' repeated Hopton. 'I know not this Westmaine. Where is it?' He turned to Nick.

'I think you mean West Meon, do you not?' Nick said to the trooper. The reply was an enthusiastic nod. 'That's it, sir. Thousands of them! They were seemingly preparing to make camp. Captain Clatworthy sent me to tell my Lord Forth.'

'My thanks to Captain – er – Clatworthy. Go now with Lieutenant-Colonel Howard, here. Howard, find him a fresh horse and take him to Colonel Neville. My compliments to Colonel Neville, and will he be drawing out two troops of horse to go with this man to the place. Ask Neville to find out their exact situation, and to send me word directly. Then you may go to my Lord Forth and advise him that I will attend him shortly. You others, fetch Stawell, and Smyth, and the Lords Winchester, Stuart and Crawford. Tell them I will have a full council of war at my Lord's lodging as soon as possible.'

Nick led the bemused messenger down the stairs, and Hopton was on the landing above, shouting after them to remind Colonel Howard to be sure to give my Lord Forth his most humble apologies for disturbing him, but that it was a matter of great urgency. Nick sighed at the echoing voice of the mild-mannered general, and wondered if Hopton had ever in his life lost his temper. But then Lord Winchester was equally mild-mannered. Yet nowhere could there be a man of such ruthlessness and singleness of purpose. So Edward Paulet would be a hangman. . . .

Sir William Ogle, civilian governor of Winchester, gibbered with fury as he watched the supply wagons loading: two per regiment, and all the supplies were his own, laid by prudently for the defence of Winchester in the event of a siege. He watched his precious peas and beans and oats trundled away, and turned on Nick with another howl of protest. Nick shrugged wearily and denied any responsibility for the robbery.

'The Lord Hopton is drawing out the whole army between the city and the rebels. With his help it should never come to an attack here. If we are destroyed, sir, then I think that all the provisions in the world will not save you.'

Neither could all the explanations in the world save Nick from the rough end of William Ogle's tongue, so he made more apologies and left the last few wagons still loading to return to the tall house in Eastgate, and from there he watched the King's draggle-tailed army marching out.

Henry Bard trotted past on his grey mare, grinning from ear to ear like a schoolboy with a half holiday. He caught sight of Nick at the open window and waved. 'At last!' he shouted. 'Get the teeth of my dogs here into Sir William's throat!'

The marching grey-coats behind him set up a cheer to hear his words. Nick acknowledged Henry's greeting half-heartedly, drained the last of his ale abruptly and went down to find his horse. He rode out with his ears filled with the deafening music of the rumbling of the artillery train over the cobblestones, as the heavy horses dragged the cumbersome artillery-wagons and the great guns in the wake of the marching men, up Magdalen Hill and out on to the open down between William Waller and the city of Winchester.

At four in the afternoon of the next day Nick was in the main street of Alresford. Forth had been prevailed upon to take up residence in the inn, though the bulk of the army was encamped out on Tichborne Down.

From the inn Nick could hear the musical voice of Henry Bard telling the world what he was intending to do to William Waller. However deaf the lord-general was, he must surely hear Harry's fearsome threats from the furthest corner of the house. Nick walked away. He was not thirsty enough to be patient with Henry's foolish babbling.

Nick made his way to the town fishpond and found a seat on a tree-trunk at the brim of the dark water, wrapping his heavy cloak about him against the fresh wind which whipped thousands of tiny waves on the pond surface. A startled water rat slunk into the water and swam along the far margin with the waves lapping round its whiskered chin, its small, dirty feet treading water. It swam for several yards and then dived, leaving nothing but a momentary bubble or two to show where it had been, and the surface of the water was just the same as before. Just as the world would be the same, Nick thought, when all the disturbance and hubbub of war was over, and all the people who had fought so bitterly were themselves gone to oblivion and crumbled to dust. Not even their names would be remembered. There had been other civil wars. . . . It was a chastening thought, and one to restore a man's sense of proportion, if nothing else.

'Good evening to you, Lieutenant-Colonel Howard,' came a voice behind his back. It was a conventional enough greeting, but Nick would have known that cool, cynical voice anywhere, and he spun round with surprise and pleasure.

'Nat? And you, too, Josh! What are you doing here?'

'The same as you are, I should imagine. There will be a battle tomorrow or the next day.'

'So you have come to extend the hand of mercy. There will certainly be work for you.'

'That was not really what I had in mind, I must confess. I've extended enough mercy. This time I wish to do execution.' Nat rubbed his long hands together, and his lean face was murderous.

Nick's smile was baleful, and he shuddered. 'How did you find me, in the midst of all this host?'

'It was not difficult, since most seem to know you by reputation, if naught else. Yet I cannot say I took to your loud-mouthed friend yonder.' Nat pointed towards the inn, but there was no need, for Nick knew that there was only one person who fitted Nat's description.

'You mean Henry Bard? There's no harm in Henry, he's just enthusiastic, that is all.'

'Hmmm,' said Nat, glaring into the depths of the pool without further comment.

'I knew I'd met him before,' said Josh, beaming. 'He came to Basing, sir? Is it the same Sir Henry?'

'Yes, Josh, the very same Sir Henry,' Nick laughed. 'So we've you two as gentlemen volunteers, yes?'

'Yes, sir. We wanted to see you first,' Nat said, 'I've a letter from Judith.'

Nick looked up sharply into the surgeon's face, his heart lurching wildly.

'Fear not, she is very well,' Nat smiled his one-sided smile. 'But half out of her mind for your safety. Read.' The brown hand held out a small packet.

'My safety? Good Lord, no need for her to worry on that score.' Nick laughed uneasily at the odd expression on Nat's face, and Nat shrugged and exchanged a long look with Josh.

'You have a short memory, it seems. You should today be blessing the Lord that you have not a regiment of your own.'

'How so?'

'The man's mazed! Simply because it would make you too easy to find, my friend. If you have a short memory, there are those who have not, and at least two of them want to get even with you, to my knowledge. Waller has with him men from the Southampton garrison. The Hambledon boys . . . and Chadwicke's dragoons.'

'And they'll be wanting to settle more personal things than politics,' Josh interposed emphatically.

'Do you need me to say more?' Nat said lugubriously.

'So you have come to preserve me, is that it?'

'Do not be ridiculous! Nothing of the sort!'

'They could not find me. It would be like trying to pluck a single particular cherry from a pudding. A cherry is a cherry.'

Josh laughed, his broad young nose wrinkling with delight. 'That's good, sir! And all cherries look alike!'

'A cherry is indeed a cherry,' Nathaniel sniffed, obviously unimpressed. 'And it was a pretty speech, right enough, but a man is a man, and mortal.'

'Anyway, I am not convinced that it will even come to a battle. It would not surprise me to see Waller draw back.' Nick's tone was defiant now, because the worm of fear was beginning to devour his stomach.

'I can think of one very good reason why he will not,' Nat argued firmly. 'The London bands will be wanting soon to return home. Also a little bird told me that Lord Essex will shortly be wanting Balfour's horse back. He only loaned them to Waller for a while. Waller will never be this strong again.'

'So it is now or never.' Josh's lips issued a low whistle.

'At any rate, we must think of finding Lord Hopton before dark. . . .' Nat looked at the darkening sky. 'God keep you, Nicholas. Be careful, for her sake.'

'Can you credit it, Josh? Leaves a new wife for a battle which is none of his. Risks his neck needlessly, when he would be well out of it, and then he preaches to me! God be with you both, I shall no doubt see you anon. Hopton's men are out on picket duty in the valley.'

Nick watched the two gentlemen volunteers riding off down the road and then made haste to read Judith's letter while there was yet enough light. That day's date was inscribed clearly at the head of the page, in the round, black letters he knew so well. 'At Broadoak, this 27th day of March 1644,' he read, and smiled. A number of small ink blots clustered on the page. This had been written in a hurry, for Nat must have called in on his way here. Six or seven miles away, he knew, Judith would be sitting in the parlour, in the window-seat, and very likely she was still trying obstinately to sew, despite the failing light.

My dearest Nicholas, Uncle Nat tells me there will soon be fighting, and that not far from here. I shall pray for your preservation, and I beseech you to take care, for I am very much in fear for you, if Thomas in his wrath should be looking for you. For myself, I am well, and we have not here suffered unduly from the passage of the soldiers. Rebecca is staying in the house with me, and we shall wait anxiously for news of you both. I can write no more, because Uncle Nat would be away. I implore you to take care, and to remember that whatever happens, my love will be yours, always, Judith.

Nick folded the letter and bestowed it safely inside his buff-coat. It was twilight now, and he could see the pools of light cast on the road through the unshuttered windows of the inn, and the street was filled with the moving shadows of many soldiers, and the jack o' lantern glows from their tobacco-pipes. Above all the murmuring voices, that of Henry Bard still sounded like a trumpet calling in an empty church. It was high time that Harry was looking to the quartering of his regiment. Nick sighed and went into the taproom to remind him gently of it, and they rode together past the barricades and out along the Tichborne road, with Henry still calling down a deluge of poxes on the whole Roundhead army.

28

JOURNEY'S END

'All I've had,' Nat lamented bitterly, 'is a mere glimpse of the Parliament-men from the top of the ridge there. Just a-sitting on their backsides in the meadow.'

'Waiting for midsummer,' Josh agreed, sitting on the grass, picking at his fingernails with a small but murderous-looking dagger.

'Or for the hand of providence,' Nick added, more hopeful than he had been yesterday that Waller would not fight. 'Some of the outguards have tangled several times with Waller's patrols.'

'But we have not,' Nat complained plaintively. 'My God, this mist is in my bones.'

'Norton's definitely there,' Josh said half to himself, and then raised his earnest face to Nick and squinted enquiringly: 'We saw his men and Chadwicke's together. Didn't see either of the colonels, though. Pity. We were well within musket-shot.'

'You would have picked one off and had the rest about your ears. Just as well you did not have the chance! Tonight will see Waller draw off, I'm convinced.'

Nathaniel sniffed as if he had not heard. 'Why does Hopton not put men in that little wood up yonder? Would be a cosy quarter for an advance-guard: the hedge is stout.'

'George Lisle is taking musketeers up to it presently, on the Lord Hopton's order. Though I would have said it was too exposed to that battery on the ridge by Cheriton, if this mist clears.'

'Mist off Hinton marshes,' Josh observed. 'Be thicker yet.'

'So. . . .' Nat rubbed his stiff shoulder grimly. 'It seems unlikely to be a night attack, at least.'

'Nat why do you not go home? There will be no battle, I tell you!'

'Does the Lord Hopton think so? Then why are we all stood to arms?' Nat hissed angrily. Abruptly he turned his back on them and stalked off into the steaming night.

'What ails him?' Nick asked Josh, with an odd sickness in the pit of his stomach. 'I would have thought you would know, sir. As far as Captain Nat is concerned, Waller may ride away and take all his army with him, save only the one man. . . .'

'Chadwicke? Oh, no. . . . He has not come for that?' The sick feeling swelled. He had known, of course, all along, that only one purpose had brought Nat here today. 'This time I wish to do execution,' he had said. . . .

'Why else?' said Josh, quietly, picking studiously at his thumb-nail.

'Josh, we must stop him!'

Josh rose and stretched, smiling blandly. 'Not I,' he said. 'It would be a good riddance.'

'But – '

'And you, sir, will be wise if you keep out of it. There will be no stopping him, surely you can see it. He has good enough reasons.'

'Aye. Though he swore to me that they did not torture him. . . .'

'Not for that. For Mistress Judith, I meant. And for you.'

'Oh, dear God!' Nick, too, turned away from Josh and stumbled off after Nat, searching his mind for arguments to make Nathaniel relent, before he should get himself killed.

Nat sat amongst the musketeers under the trees, shivering in the freezing shadows between the giant glow-worms of burning slow-match. 'It's most odd,' he said, coolly. 'We are so near their outguard we can hear their voices. But it's so dark . . . and there is this mist. Not a whisker can we see. You listen.'

'No, Nat Harrington, you listen, please!'

A horse snorted. Someone in the Roundhead ranks was coughing a harsh rasping cough in the damp air. There were low, conspiratorial whispers, and then clinking noises.

'Lord,' said Nat, 'what is that?'

Nick stiffened and held his breath. There were rumbling sounds, axles creaking, and all the while the jangling of harness. Nick turned back to Nat with a slow smile of satisfaction spreading on his face. 'That is wagons being spanned. They must be drawing off.'

Nat cursed emphatically. 'Nat, it is just as well. It solves nothing to kill him.'

'On the contrary,' Nat snapped, his breath in clouds of cold vapour about his head, like that of some icy dragon. 'It solves everything. Go preach elsewhere, my mind is made up. If not this day, then there will be another time, soon.'

'I will have naught to do with it!'

'Have I ever asked you to? Now be a good staff officer and go tell the general that Waller is up to something sly.'

Waller was indeed up to something, though it was some hours before Hopton found out exactly what it was. The mist cleared to reveal that, far from drawing back, he had sent a large body of musketeers to an advance position behind a hedge a mere hundred yards away from the Royalists: and to back them up, there was a monstrous battery of guns to sweep the ridge. Hopton and Forth were forced to draw out a body of commanded men to clear the wood so that their flank would not be threatened, and that took until noon. Then peace settled once more, and the two lords-general met to confer.

'With your Lordship's permission,' said Hopton to Forth. 'If we were to take a brigade, then we might turn their flank.'

'I think not,' Forth's gruff voice replied. 'We have good enough ground here, and here we shall stay. Waller hath choice either to attack us upon disadvantage, or to retreat. Leave him now to decide. Lieutenant-Colonel Howard, pray ride to the right wing, and bid them stand their present ground.'

Nick wheeled the horse around and set off to canter along the crest of the ridge behind the line, to leave the order with every commander. The sky was blue and cloudless now, and the mist all melted. The air was still, bracing, and sharply cold, and there was not going to be a battle. Nick happily indulged in a tuneless whistle as he made his way towards Sir Henry Bard's regiment on the extreme right. Henry sat on the ground, disconsolate, at the head of his grey-coats. The regimental standard behind him drooped limply from its staff, and the ensign holding it looked miserable, and pale blue with cold.

'Compliments of my Lord Forth,' Nick said cheerfully. 'And he wishes to confirm that everyone hold their present positions.'

'Stay here?' Henry Bard exploded with fury. 'I had thought you had come to tell us to attack! That finishes me. What a damned waste of time! God's blood! You really mean we must sit here with our teeth chattering in the cold and wait for William Waller's pleasure?'

'I'm afraid so.'

'Well, a pox on my Lord Forth! I'll not bide any longer or I'll catch an ague, and you may tell him so, Master Sawbones.'

'Harry?' Nick was filled with sudden alarm, because he recognised the expression on Henry's face. Henry rose to his feet, stretching extravagantly, and before Nick could say another word, he had turned to his men.

'Come on, boys. Let us show them how the war's to be won! March on!'

'Harry, you cannot! You are disobeying orders! Are you insane?'

'No, just cold.'

'Harry, where are you going?'

'To . . . hell, I suppose. Coming? It's a great deal warmer there. . . .' Nick sat on his horse, incredulous and blank-faced, and found that he was shaking like an aspen-leaf. His voice cracked as he called after Henry, while Henry's men marched past him, steadily forward file by file, in grim, grey procession down the hill towards the enemy.

'Harry, you cannot win the war single-handed . . . !' Nick stood up in his stirrups and shouted at the top of his voice. 'Harry! I beseech you! We shall all be undone!'

It was no good. Harry could not or would not hear, and Nick knew there was no point in going after him. He kept shouting until Bard was well out of all imaginable earshot, and only then did he turn away and gallop in tearing haste back to the general's position. He knew that the whole army could see what was happening. They stared with horror-widened eyes as Henry Bard's men broke line and advanced despite the order they had been given to stand still. Behind Nick came the crackle of musketry, and he did not want to look. There was certainly no need to tell the earl what had happened, for his eyes were as sharp as any, even though his ears were of little use. He was furious, and even Hopton looked suitably appalled as Nick recounted what had passed between Henry Bard and himself.

Before the eyes of the motionless army, Arthur Hazelrigg's 'Lobsters' came sweeping down from the tidy range of Roundhead ranks, and fell upon Henry Bard's scuttling men like hawks upon a family of field-mice.

'He must move now,' Nick thought. 'Before Waller follows up such an advantage.'

Forth sat thinking, his face growing progressively more and more purple, but he said nothing for several minutes. Firing could be heard now from the left wing, also.

'Balfour seems to have attacked,' said Forth, stating the obvious, and turned to Hopton. 'Ralph, pray take horse and beat Hazelrigg off.'

Hopton took horse. They trotted neatly down the straight lane between two high spiky hedges which were covered now in a green spring mist of new leaves, and down to the open ground of the valley below. The open ground was common land, and Nick knew it to be pitted with a thousand rabbit holes and covered with short, sharp thorn bushes, and it was not good ground for cavalry. And there was only the one lane down to the common. As the King's men came pouring out of the lane's end, it was to face the whole of Waller's cavalry, who were already ranged in bodies, and ready to charge.

They charged. There was no time even to form ranks to meet them, for the Roundheads came crashing into them like a smith's hammer on a piece of delicate crystal, and shattered the frail, unfashioned line into a thousand separate slivers. Lathered horses and bewildered men floundered about in all directions, mostly backwards. Nick caught sight of Nat standing in his stirrups, flailing his sword like a dark avenging angel. Nat took off like a screaming madman towards the Roundhead battery on Cheriton Down: towards one small, brave flag which stood out in Nick's sight, too, though it fluttered amongst many others. Behind Nat rode the square-shouldered figure of Josh: and Nick followed them, because he had to. . . .

All around, men were falling victim to the slaughtering artillery. In utter confusion, with not a trace of order remaining, there was nothing anyone could do except fight for his life, or else surrender and pray for quarter. There were some, however, for whom mercy would neither be asked nor given. . . . Way behind him the King's reinforcements came rushing down the narrow lane, spilling untidily on to the common, but they could not make a stand. Lines smashed before they formed, they were being forced back on to their own infantry as the main body of Roundheads moved forward, until the whole was a milling mass of hand-to-hand combatants amid the dark swirling powder-smoke which hung like a choking pall in the still air between the two ridges.

Ahead of Nick, Nat rode, heedless of bullet or cannon shot, aiming irrevocably for the dipping, tossing standard of Colonel Thomas Chadwicke, and that standard drew ever nearer with the forward press of the enemy. Nick found himself knee to knee with two mounted dragoons of Colonel Norton's command, and was hard put to cut his way out. The bay reared and shied at the clashing swords, shuddering with wild fear at every volley from the muskets. It stumbled, its hoof caught in a rabbit hole, and crashed hideously on to its side. Nick flew rapidly over its head and hit the ground with great force, rolling over and over again on sharp dry grass, with furze and thistles tearing at his clothes, and the sword gone from his hand. The hooves of more horses thundered past him, and Nat and Josh were gone. There were only more Parliament-men, marching onwards in a blaze of orange-tawny sashes, beneath the flag that he knew so well.

Nicholas was on his knees, dazed and gaping, his leg was torn and bleeding and twisted in the fall, and it would not carry his weight, nor would it do what he told it to do.

'God help me,' he said. He tore a half-pike from a dead hand and tried to drag himself to his feet, but there was too much pain for him to stand. And where was Nat? 'Please, God, help us all!'

In front of him, a grey mare squealed in terror, and from its saddle a wounded man dropped with the ungainly helplessness of a stuffed sack. The grey was familiar, and so was the helmetless man. It was Colonel Thomas Chadwicke, with a grey, twisted face. Recognition dawned in Thomas Chadwicke's eyes, and they lit up with the great inspiration of his hatred. From malice he drew strength, and stood up again, his left hand pressed hard to his side, where a great red stain was spreading wide on his torn, mutilated buff-coat. But his right hand was steady, and in it he held a pistol.

'May God be praised!' he said. 'With this last bullet I shall settle with you, Nicholas Howard!'

Nick looked up in horror at the colonel's agonised face, and at the gaping rent in his side which poured blood between the clutching fingers. Nat had settled his account. There would be no healing that wound. Tom Chadwicke was fighting his last battle, and Nick would have been wiser, as Josh had said, to keep well out of it. Now by some supreme irony, fate would have them die together, for Nick knew that he could not flee. The leg would carry him neither far nor fast enough to escape the bullet which would come flying from that black pistol-muzzle which pointed between his eyes. For a moment he thought of trying to push the colonel over, but he knew he could not move with enough speed, and it would likely mean he would be maimed, and not quickly killed. . . .

He thought of Judith, and wondered what she would say when they told her: he thought of Judith's unborn child, and after that his mind went blank, save for a little childish prayer that he had taught Lucy, the last time that he had seen her.

'So be it,' he found himself saying, trying to be calm, although his voice was shaking with fear. 'Finish it. But for Christ's sake, shoot straight.' He took a last look at Tom Chadwicke and then closed his eyes, waiting for the bang, and the instant of torture which would bring his death. There was an ear-splitting crash, but he felt nothing. He could hear Chadwicke coughing a horrible gurgling cough, and Nick opened his eyes to find the colonel on the ground four feet away, choking and spitting blood, and Nat standing over him, sword in hand.

'Oh, God,' said Nick. 'You killed him.'

'Not dead, yet. Give him a minute or two,' said Nat, unrepentant.

Nick crawled blindly and painfully to Tom Chadwicke's side and fumbled, shaking, to wipe the blood away with his own red sash.

'The Lord's . . . infinite mercy,' Chadwicke gasped. 'It was . . . not his will.'

'Lie still, sir. You will make it bleed more.'

'Your blood . . . not on . . . my hands.' The colonel's right hand grasped at Nick's and would not let it go. 'Forgive. . . .' he said. 'I cannot help . . . hating you, still. . . .'

'I have never blamed you for hating me. Often I hate myself. I would have killed you, if you had done what I have. But I do love her, more than anything. Do you understand that? Understand . . . please, understand!'

There was a trampling of hooves, and the ensign of Chadwicke's dragoons plummeted to the ground two yards away, the flag still clutched in a half-severed hand. Chadwicke did not see him. His eyes stared blankly into Nick's face and his head rolled from side to side as each breath shook him with pain.

'Love her?' he muttered. 'Have her, now. . . . I loved her, too. . . .' He smiled an agonised smile at Nick, and then choked.

'And I'm sorry about Tom,' Nick said desperately. 'It was . . . him or me.'

'Aye.'

There was a lull now in the fighting, so that it was quieter for several minutes, and Chadwicke's breathing grew fainter. Nat cradled the colonel's head and said nothing, but all the time he was looking uneasily this way and that. The flat booming of the guns began once more to echo in the valley.

'Is that you, Tom?' the colonel said clearly, crushing Nick's hand with surprising power. 'Good boy, Tom.'

A moment later he died, his broken body shuddering in convulsion, while his hand still held that of his enemy. Nick freed himself and looked at Nat and felt anger rising within him.

'He was well on his way before I got to him, and you know it. All I did was make it quicker. What did you expect? That I would have stood by and let him kill you first? You're worth six of his kind, any day!'

'To the devil, yes!' Nick sat back on the ground and nursed his damaged leg, and wept helplessly for the man he had brought to destruction.

'I didn't kill him,' Nick whispered. 'It wasn't me.'

Nat's arm was around his shoulders. 'All right, Nicholas. Come on, it's all right. . . . Your leg is hurt?'

'Can't walk.'

'Then you must ride. Josh, get horses. Help me now to get him away. Was it you?'

'Yes, Captain Nat. Had to.'

'Better so . . . for Judith's sake. Come on, Nicholas, let me see to that leg. It's broken, I think. I shall have to bind it, so. Now give me your arm.'

'I want . . . to stay here. What . . . will they do with him?'

'Bury him, lad, and a good job, too. And you have nothing to reproach yourself for.' Nat heaved, and Nick was on his feet, leaning on the surgeon, without even noticing that his leg was neatly splinted with the broken pieces of a standard-pike.

'Oh, Nat, he thought I was young Tom.'

'For God's sweet sake, lad, come away. We've not much

time.' Nat's voice was impatient, urgently insistent.

'Not much time?' Nick repeated, without understanding.

'We are beat, lad. Cut to pieces. The cavalry is half way back to Oxford by now. Hopton says, "Retreat and save yourselves," and who are we to argue?'

They manhandled Nick to the saddle of some barrel-chested cavalry horse, and Nat tied an orange-tawny sash about him in place of his own. It seemed odd to wear an orange sash. The last time he had worn one was back last summer when it had all begun. He had unknowingly sown the seed of tragedy when he had killed Tom Chadwicke's son. Now Tom was dead, too. He wondered whether he could have made it different, if only he had foreseen. . . .

The sky was getting dark, but the horizon glowed red. Hopton in retreat towards Basing had set fire to the town of Alresford, and both ends of it were burning fiercely, the flames licking hungrily to the heavens as if to devour them, their light illuminating the clouds of grey smoke that still hung above. All Hopton's hopes were turning to ashes with the blazing town. Nick shook his head, unwilling to believe.

When he had escaped from Broadoak, he had said that he would return, not dreaming that it would be like this. They were fleeing to Broadoak, beaten men. Hampshire was lost to the King, and the mighty Army of the West was smashed for ever. The taste of great defeat was new and foul, and with dread he realised suddenly that they might even lose the war.

Inside his coat, Nick felt the comforting rustle of Judith's letter, and his mind went back to the words it contained. The words that Judith had carefully chosen. 'Whatever happens, my love is yours, always,' she said. That was all that really mattered. At Broadoak, she would be waiting for him. Nick wondered idly how Lucy would react to the sudden appearance of a step-mother in her life: and poor Aunt Nan might find it hard to come to terms with his 'rebel lady', but give her time . . . and a small baby to cosset, and she would undoubtedly relent. . . .

'Keep going, Nicholas.' Nat's voice sounded encouragement in his ear as the horse plodded on through the dark.

'There is no time to rest. I'm sorry, but we must press on back to Broadoak, out of Norton's reach. I've no desire for him to lay us all by the heels. Are you . . . well?'

'I'm all right, Nat. Just thinking, that's all.'

'Aye? Well, do not go into a decline yet. One battle is not a war. Nor one dead man, nor this many. Doubtless it will be far worse before it is better.'

'What I like about you, Nat, is that you're so cheerful!'

'Realistic, that's all. There's another day tomorrow, and more work to be done. More than ever, after today's little affair. Nearly home, friend.'

'Yes,' said Nick, smiling with sudden absolute certainty in the dark. 'Nearly home.'